Readers love the Gothika anthologies

Stitch

"This is a fantastic anthology. Every author added a story that I enjoyed."

—Gay List Book Reviews

Bones

"This is a sinful, sensual treat for Halloween; like dark, bitter chocolate, it will melt on your tongue, making you crave more."

—My Fiction Nook

Claw

"If you are in to werewolves but are getting tired of the same old stories, these stories are not like those! Read this book!"

—Love Bytes

Spirit

"Four top-notch authors have once again created an incredibly well written anthology with stories that are both entertaining and thoughtful."

—The Novel Appraoch

contact
gothika #5

f.e. feeley jr
jamie fessenden
kim fielding
b.g. thomas

Published by
DREAMSPINNER PRESS

5032 Capital Circle SW, Suite 2, PMB# 279, Tallahassee, FL 32305-7886 USA
www.dreamspinnerpress.com

This is a work of fiction. Names, characters, places, and incidents either are the product of author imagination or are used fictitiously, and any resemblance to actual persons, living or dead, business establishments, events, or locales is entirely coincidental.

© 2016 Dreamspinner Press.
Edited by Tricia Kristufek

Abducted © 2016 Jamie Fessenden.
Refugee © 2016 Kim Fielding.
My Final Blog © 2016 F.E. Feeley Jr.
Unusual Attention © 2016 B.G. Thomas.

Cover Art
© 2016 AngstyG.
http://www.angstyg.com
Cover content is for illustrative purposes only and any person depicted on the cover is a model.

All rights reserved. This book is licensed to the original purchaser only. Duplication or distribution via any means is illegal and a violation of international copyright law, subject to criminal prosecution and upon conviction, fines, and/or imprisonment. Any eBook format cannot be legally loaned or given to others. No part of this book may be reproduced or transmitted in any form or by any means, electronic or mechanical, including photocopying, recording, or by any information storage and retrieval system, without the written permission of the Publisher, except where permitted by law. To request permission and all other inquiries, contact Dreamspinner Press, 5032 Capital Circle SW, Suite 2, PMB# 279, Tallahassee, FL 32305-7886, USA, or www.dreamspinnerpress.com.

ISBN: 978-1-63477-733-9
Digital ISBN: 978-1-63477-734-6
Library of Congress Control Number: 2016913761
Published October 2016
v. 1.0

Printed in the United States of America

This paper meets the requirements of
ANSI/NISO Z39.48-1992 (Permanence of Paper).

Contents

Abducted By Jamie Fessenden	1
Refugee By Kim Fielding	91
My Final Blog By F.E. Feeley Jr	145
Unusual Attention By B.G. Thomas	189

Abducted

By Jamie Fessenden

Part One

Chapter One

THE FARM wasn't hard to find, even with Cody's barely coherent directions, because there was literally nothing else along Brickyard Pond Road for almost two miles. At one time the farm had sprawled across the countryside, keeping its neighbors at bay. Now most of that acreage had reverted back to forest. I'd learned all that from a phone conversation with Cody months ago, when he first bought the place. Back then, he'd described the property as beautiful and peaceful—just what he'd been looking for, after living in Boston for years. But as I pulled into the cul-de-sac in front of the house, those words weren't the first that came to mind.

The house itself was in decent shape, I supposed, though its gray paint was peeling and the porch sagged a bit on one side. Two of the lower-floor windows were boarded up, and the mesh in the screen door was torn. A bicycle I felt sure must have come with the house lay in a rusted heap on the overgrown front lawn.

Cody was a computer programmer—a private consultant—and he worked from home these days, so he could afford to live off the beaten path. Still, this seemed a bit much.

He must have heard my car pull in, because he stepped out onto the porch as I parked and climbed out of the car. My first sight of him in over a year was disturbing. He was pretty much naked, except for a tattered red flannel bathrobe, which hung open and did nothing to cover a body I'd once salivated over. Now he looked emaciated. I doubted I would have recognized his face at first glance, if I hadn't known he was the only one living there. He'd always been clean-shaven and had kept his dark brown hair in a short, rather nerdy style reminiscent of a man in a fifties sitcom. Now he was bearded, and his hair was long and unkempt. I suspected he hadn't bathed in a very long time.

"Marc," he gasped, staggering down the front steps in his slippers.

I didn't object when he threw his arms around me, despite the nudity. It was weird for a man who always dressed fastidiously, but even though our relationship had never really gone beyond friendship, we'd slept together a couple of times. And we'd shared a dorm room in college. I'd seen him naked often enough. Harder to ignore was the rather funky body odor. But I embraced him, anyway, disliking how thin and breakable he felt in my arms. Then I stepped back to examine him more closely. He looked pale, and his face was drawn. His gentle brown eyes blinked back tears, as if we hadn't seen each other in a decade.

"Are you all right?" I asked. He'd told me next to nothing over the phone—just that he needed me, and please, please, *please* come.

His breath was foul. "Oh, Marc…. You have no idea…."

Then he burst into tears.

I HELD Cody until he stopped crying and then gently guided him indoors.

The inside of the house was just as dreary as the outside. Apparently he'd inherited the furnishings from a previous owner. The paisley upholstery on the sofa and chairs in the living room was a sickly green color, faded and worn through on the arms. Stuffing peeked out in places. If I'd been the one living there, I would have burned them all for fear of fleas or bedbugs in the cushions.

The kitchen was a bit better, though God knew when he'd last taken out the trash. The bin was overflowing and smelled of something rotten. Fortunately the clutter on the table was mostly coffee cups—quite possibly every cup he owned. There were a few dishes in the sink, but not many. Had he been eating? I suspected not much.

Another odd thing, simply because it was so contrary to Cody's nature to leave things like this unattended to—the kitchen clock was either stopped or completely out of sync. It read three twenty-five. But I knew it couldn't be past noon. The clock on the stove was blinking at ten fourteen. As I watched, the clock changed to ten fifteen, though it kept blinking. Obviously, it had lost power at some point and needed to be reset.

This was so different from the anal-retentive and unashamedly nerdy man I'd once roomed with, I didn't know how to process it. Could he be suffering from some kind of mental illness? Depression, perhaps? Or schizophrenia? I wasn't a psychologist, so I had no idea what to look for.

"I need to talk," he said roughly.

I took both his hands in mine and looked him directly in the eye. "Cody… I'm going to listen to everything you have to say. But first I want you to do something for me. It'll just take a minute."

"What?"

"Do you have hot water?"

"Yes."

"Then I want you to take a shower."

His eyes drifted away from mine, and he pulled his hands away. "I guess… I must smell pretty bad."

"This isn't for my sake—it's for yours. You haven't showered in a long time, have you?"

He shook his head. "I don't remember."

"Then shower now. And brush your teeth." I added, "Trust me, you'll feel a lot better. And by the time you're done, I'll have some coffee ready."

The first thing I did, after he'd left the kitchen, was take out the trash. I wasn't exactly a neat freak, but Jesus! It was disgusting. I could have sworn there were maggots crawling around in it, but I didn't look too closely. I just tied it up and hauled it out the kitchen door. There wasn't anything like a dumpster or a trash can to put it in, so I just set it on the back porch. Obviously it would have to be moved before nightfall, or we'd find it torn open by raccoons in the morning, but that could wait.

I washed my hands in the sink, hoping I wasn't making the water ice-cold for Cody—I could hear the shower running upstairs now—but there was no way I'd prepare food after touching that disgusting garbage without scrubbing down.

I was unsurprised to find the refrigerator devoid of anything like milk, cream, or half-and-half. They probably would have been spoiled, anyway. But there was a little coffee left in the can, and some sugar. The coffeemaker could have used some scouring, but I figured we'd survive using it. By the time I heard the shower turn off, I had a pot brewing, and the warm, comforting scent of it was almost enough to mask the residual odor left by the trash.

How the fuck am I going to stay here? Cody had begged me to come for the entire weekend, and it hadn't seemed an unreasonable promise when we'd been on the phone. Now, I wasn't so sure. I shuddered to think what condition the beds were in. Did he even have a guest bedroom?

In the hope I'd find some nondairy creamer, I rummaged through his kitchen cupboards. That turned out to be a lost cause, but I did turn up several cans of soup. There were clean pans under the sideboard, so I put some minestrone on one of the gas burners. I made up my mind that Cody was going to eat it, if I had to hold him down and pour it into him.

He shuffled into the kitchen in a pair of sweatpants and his slippers. I wasn't sure if the sweatpants were clean, but they looked less grubby than the robe. His hair was wet and combed. He still had the beard, but I hadn't expected him to shave. I noticed a small Band-Aid on his left forearm, but it looked dry and clean. He must have put it on after the shower.

"Sit," I ordered, and when he'd obeyed, I set the bowl of soup in front of him. "Eat."

"I'm not hungry."

I folded my arms in front of my chest and raised my eyebrows. "When's the last time you ate something?"

"I don't know."

"Then eat. And don't give me any shit."

The old Cody would have told me to fuck off if I'd hovered over him like that, but now he just sighed and picked up the spoon. I poured myself a cup of black coffee, spooned in extra sugar to compensate for not having any cream, and then took a seat opposite him.

We didn't talk for a while. I was curious about why he was in this state. More than curious, to be honest—freaked out. But I was worried he'd forget to eat if we talked. So I just sipped my coffee and tried not to make faces at the bitter taste, while he slowly and silently spooned the soup into his mouth.

God, he looked awful. Like a man withering away from some horrible disease. It hurt to look at him.

Finally he set the spoon down and pushed the bowl away. "I can't eat any more."

There was still a bit of soup left in the bowl, but I didn't press. I sat back in my chair and said, "All right. So… what's going on, Cody? You look like shit."

"You won't believe me."

I gave him a sour look. "Fuck that shit. You called me, remember? You wanted me to come out here. So tell me what's happening."

"It started… about a month ago," he said slowly.

And then he proceeded to tell me a story that was disturbing, somewhat frightening… and completely insane.

Chapter Two

"I BOUGHT this property, say... about eight months ago," Cody began. I knew that part, of course, but I let him continue without interrupting. "It had been in the Corwin family for generations, but the last owner didn't have any children of her own, and her brother had moved away. She lived here by herself, with just a friend driving out from town a couple times a week to check on her, until she passed away from... I don't know. Natural causes. She was in her eighties. Her daughter lives out in California and didn't want the house, so she listed it on the market."

He paused to take the cup of coffee I handed him and sip it. "It was a great deal. All these acres and acres of land—almost six hundred! For next to nothing!"

I was skeptical about how much good all those acres would do him if the house was falling apart, but I didn't say anything. Where he wanted to live was his business. At least, it would be under normal circumstances.

"I managed to get it financed," Cody went on. "And I closed last January. Everything was great for the first six months or so. I mean, yeah, the house needs work. But the roof is good, the boiler works fine, and I have electricity and Internet. Then... in the early summer... things started happening...."

What he described seemed at first like a ghost story. He kept finding his bedroom window open in the morning, no matter how careful he was to shut it at night. And there were weird power glitches that set every clock in the house blinking.

"But it was more than just a power outage," he insisted. "*Everything* went dead. My Kindle, my iPad—even the clocks that ran on batteries." He pointed up at the kitchen clock I'd noticed earlier. "I recharged them, replaced the batteries on the clocks. Then a few nights later, it would happen again."

"So... you think you have a... poltergeist?" I didn't really believe in them, but I'd watched some episodes of *Ghost Hunters*. Last I knew, Cody had never believed in anything supernatural. But this wasn't the Cody I knew.

"It's not a goddamn poltergeist," he said, glaring at his coffee cup. "I wish it was. Then I could just… call an exorcist or something."

"What is it, then?"

He looked away and said nothing for a long moment. Then he appeared to change the subject. "I started getting headaches. Awful, awful headaches, like my skull was trying to split open. Then the dreams started…."

"What dreams?" This conversation was making me nervous. I'd been afraid Cody might be suffering from some kind of mental illness, and now he was describing headaches and nightmares. Could these be symptoms of schizophrenia? Or worse, a brain tumor?

"They didn't make sense!" he said angrily. "I kept seeing a room—an operating room—but I was strapped down, so I couldn't see much. And they kept poking me and… and stabbing me, and… *cutting* me!"

I tried to sip my coffee, but my hand was shaking, so I set it down again. I had no idea what I should say at this point, but he was glaring at me as if it—whatever *it* was—was all my fault. So I asked, "Who are 'they,' Cody?"

"Look!" He jumped up so fast he startled me and made me jerk back in my chair. For a second I thought he was going to hit me. But he just thrust his bare arm out for my inspection. "*Look!*"

My God. I hadn't looked closely enough to see earlier, but there were needle marks in it, all along the veins. Christ. He was doing drugs. My sweet, nerdy computer programmer friend was an addict. He also had small cuts up and down his arms, some healed and barely visible, but others just recently scabbed over. Then, of course, there was that fresh Band-Aid.

My voice quavered when I asked, "What are… what are you taking, Cody? Heroin? Cocaine?"

"*What?*" His face turned red with anger. "No, you fucking idiot! They did this!" He slapped his arm repeatedly with his hand. "*They* did it! They keep doing it! And I can't make them stop!"

"*Who* is '*they*,' Cody?" Frustrated now, and unable to stop myself, I added in a mocking tone, "The *government*?"

He shook his head violently. "No! No! No! This is way beyond them! It's the fucking *aliens*!"

I DIDN'T know what the hell to do. At that moment I was convinced what Cody needed was therapy and rehab—not a friend's shoulder to cry on. It wasn't just the talk about aliens. A lot of people believed in alien abduction without it preventing them from living normal lives. Though, honestly, I never would have expected him to be one of them. He'd always been an atheist, and he'd rolled his eyes at shows like *Finding Bigfoot* and *Ancient Aliens*. Even so, I could deal with a new interest in alien abductions. He was an adult, and he could believe what he liked. But this was more than an obsession with silly reality shows. He was insisting aliens were experimenting on *him*. And he seemed to be having some kind of nervous breakdown over it.

"Cody," I said slowly, "I need you to calm down and explain this to me. What exactly do you think is happening?"

He leaned forward, balling up his fists against his knees in frustration and gritting his teeth. "*Augh!*" he groaned. "You don't get it!" Then he straightened up and held out a hand to me. "Come on. Let me show you."

Against my better judgment, I took his hand and let him lead me upstairs. On the way up, I glimpsed something worrisome between his shoulder blades—a small lump over a half inch in diameter. It wasn't red and inflamed like a boil. It looked as if there were something just under the skin.

His bedroom was at the end of a short hall, past a bathroom and a couple of side rooms. I'd been afraid I'd find he was living in squalor up there, surrounded by piles of dirty clothes and remnants of meals, but fortunately that wasn't the case. The room was messier than Cody used to keep his room, certainly—a few articles of clothing strewn about, some books scattered on the floor, and more dirty coffee cups by the head of the bed. But it wasn't unlivable.

Cody closed the door behind us, as if to keep people from listening in—though of course we were alone in the house. Then he left me for a moment to fetch something out of the top drawer of his dresser. While he was doing that, I picked up a paperback lying on the floor near where I was standing. *Incident at Exeter: Unidentified Flying Objects Over America Now* by John G. Fuller. It appeared to be about Betty and Barney Hill, who'd claimed to be abducted for a few hours while driving through a remote part of New Hampshire in 1961. I'd heard of the case, since I lived near Exeter. There was a yearly UFO festival in the town.

"Look at this," Cody said, pulling something out of the drawer. He brought it over to show me.

It was a small Altoids Peppermint tin. But when he opened it, what it contained turned my stomach. They looked a bit like human teeth—blobby and bone-colored, though lacking any roots or sharp edges. In the crevices, there was a pinkish substance that looked far too much like skin. The tin contained nine or ten of them. "What... the hell...?"

"I don't know," Cody said. "I think they could be transmitters or something."

"Transmitters?" They certainly didn't look electronic, though I'd seen hearing aids that looked vaguely like them. But not nearly as... disgusting.

Cody thrust out his arm again. "I keep finding them imbedded in my skin," he said matter-of-factly, as though that wasn't totally insane. "Some on my arms, some on my legs and other places. I've been cutting them out as soon as I find them, but there's one I can't reach." He turned around and pointed over his shoulder to the lump I'd seen between his shoulder blades. "They're getting more clever about it."

I could feel spiders crawling around in my brain, like the feeling of hair standing on end. But it went deeper than that. I'd stepped into a world completely off-kilter, and I knew I needed to escape. Now. What was wrong with Cody was far beyond my ability to help.

I stepped back slowly. "Cody... maybe you should have a doctor look at that. I can drive—"

"No!" He whirled back around to face me. "Don't you think I've thought of that? But they wouldn't believe me. They'd assume I was schizophrenic or something—hallucinating—just like you're probably thinking now. They'd put me in the hospital and give me medication. But it wouldn't help." He stepped forward, then snapped the tin shut with his thumb and rattled it in my face. "This isn't in my mind, Marc. Something is implanting these things in my body."

"They could be... anything, Cody. Tumors, maybe. Or calcium deposits...."

"No!"

I took another step back and bumped into the closed door.

Fuck.

Was he dangerous? For the first time, I wondered if he was capable of hurting me. It was impossible to reconcile that notion with the Cody I'd known, but this man standing in front of me was very different.

"Don't you think I considered that idea?" Cody demanded. "If they were tumors, they would start small and grow larger. These don't do that. The first one stayed the same size for a week, before I finally had the balls to cut it out."

"The hospital could protect you," I said weakly. "The aliens wouldn't be able to get at you... there." I'd almost said, "If you were locked up."

He seemed to consider this, looking intently at the mint tin and pressing his lips together in a thin line. "I don't know. Maybe. But eventually they'd let me out of the hospital, and I'd have to come back here."

Over my dead body, I thought. Even if the doctors managed to control his delusions with medication and therapy, allowing him to live out here completely isolated from friends and family seemed like a very bad idea. I wasn't sure what the solution was. As much as I cared about him, I couldn't see myself living with him or anything like that. But I couldn't just turn my back on him.

All this could be dealt with later, though. What I needed to do right now was get Cody out of this fucking house and into a hospital. He seemed open to the idea, so I pressed my advantage. "Cody... you know I care about you. I don't want anything to hurt you. Which is why I think we should go to the hospital."

"I knew you'd say that." He didn't sound angry. But he didn't give in either. "Not yet."

He turned away from me and walked to the dresser. There, he placed the tin carefully back in the top drawer and then slid the drawer closed. I could have made my escape while his back was turned, but I still had hope that the fear coursing through my body was an overreaction. Cody couldn't really be dangerous. It seemed impossible.

"Why not now, Cody?"

"There are some things I need you to do first."

"What?"

"First, you need to cut that thing out of me."

My stomach threatened to turn over at the thought of it. Not just how disgusting it would be, but how absolutely psychotic the whole situation was. Then I had a sudden moment of clarity. "Was this it? Was this why you called me?"

"Yes. I can't reach it. So I needed someone I could trust to come here and do it."

The spiders were working overtime in my skull. "Cody, I'm not cutting into you."

He turned back to me and folded his arms across his chest stubbornly. "If you want me to go to the hospital, you will. I know *they* won't do it—the doctors at the hospital. They'll want to take X-rays and run tests and all that shit, before they do anything. And I'm not going to just let it sit there, doing… whatever the fuck it's doing. Broadcasting my location, trying to control my thoughts… I don't know. I just want it out. Then we can talk about going to the hospital."

I swallowed nervously. Could I actually do something like that? Cut into someone's skin? This was far more than removing a splinter. It would hurt him, it would bleed—a lot—and a cut that deep could get seriously infected. Besides, wouldn't it just reinforce his paranoia? I doubt I'd be able to explain my actions to any psychologist examining him later.

"What other things did you want me to do?" I asked finally. "You said there were 'things.' Plural."

"I need you to stay the night."

Chapter Three

I WON'T describe what it was like cutting into Cody's back with a scalpel he provided. It was repulsive, and I still feel nauseated thinking about it. Not only did it bleed profusely, but the way the object popped out, as if it hadn't been attached to…. Never mind. It was unpleasant. And, of course, he added the horrid thing to his collection. I refused to think it was an alien implant. Perhaps his body was somehow producing them—a nasty idea, but at least a more reasonable one.

The scalpel bothered me. Apparently Cody had ordered it online. Not that there was anything particularly wrong with someone owning a scalpel, but it put me in mind of serial killers carving up their victims. I'd agreed to spend the night, extracting a promise that he'd let me drive him to the hospital the next morning, assuming I didn't see anything to convince me he was right about aliens harassing him. But was he really safe to spend the night with? What if he decided to use that scalpel on my throat while I slept?

It turned out, though, he didn't *want* me to sleep.

"You have to stay awake," he insisted. "Promise me!"

"Why?"

"I have to sleep," he said. "They won't come if I'm awake. I've tried to stay up all night and catch them breaking in, but… no. They only come when I'm sleeping. That's why I need you to hide and keep watch."

I looked at him dubiously. "And what am I supposed to do if I see them? Photograph them? Fight them off?"

"Everything electronic goes dead when they show up," he replied. "I gave up replacing batteries and recharging things. I haven't used my cell phone in weeks."

I pulled my cell phone out of my pocket and looked at it. The battery was still at 80 percent, since none of these mysterious outages had occurred in my presence. But there was no signal at all.

"How did you manage to call me?" I asked.

"I have an Internet connection. I had to get it for work. So I use an Internet phone when I have to call out."

That made me feel a little better. Though it didn't mean I had access to the Internet phone—not if it was on *his* computer, protected by *his* password. I could see his laptop on the desk, but it was currently closed. "I want you to give me the use of your laptop tonight."

He looked at me suspiciously. "Why? Who do you want to call?"

"At the moment, nobody. But if I'm going to stay, I need to know I *can* call somebody if I need to." I left out the reason for this—my concerns about his mental stability. I was sure he knew that.

He looked at the laptop for a long moment, his face petulant, like a child told he couldn't have everything he wanted. "If they come, you won't be able to use it. It'll shut down. So will the router and everything else in the house."

"Understood. But I want access to the phone up until that point." He still looked reticent, so I added, "I'm not going to call the hospital or the police. Not as long as I feel we're both safe. It's either that, or I leave now. Your choice."

He turned to look me in the eye. "All right. I'll trust you."

CODY WAS afraid any light in the room might prevent the aliens from coming, so I agreed to sit in one of the spare rooms with just the light from the laptop and a thermos full of hot coffee to comfort me. The doors to both rooms were left open, so I could hear if anybody or any*thing* went into Cody's room. The rest of the house was dark.

I couldn't believe I was doing this. I'd probably be berated by the hospital for reinforcing his delusions, if I did manage to get him there. But my other options were to abandon him—which I simply couldn't do—or call the police and hope things didn't get violent as they dragged him bodily into a squad car. I just hoped, if I stuck it out for one night and nothing happened, he'd be reasonable about going to the hospital with me in the morning.

The spare room had a bed in it, but Cody had said it came with the house. There'd been a recent outbreak of bedbugs in southern New Hampshire, traced to people buying used mattresses and upholstered furniture, so I was leery of it. At any rate, lying or even sitting on a bed would be unwise if I wanted to stay awake all night. So I sat in the wooden chair by the desk in my underwear and a T-shirt and browsed the web. I was disconcerted to see how many sites about aliens and UFOs

Cody had bookmarked, and a quick glance at some of them did nothing to put my mind at ease. I decided it was better to read posts on Facebook or play mah-jongg.

By two in the morning, I'd run out of coffee and really needed to piss. I was also starting to nod a bit. I could hear Cody snoring quietly, so I figured it was safe to venture down to the kitchen and brew another pot. I knew Cody would be annoyed if he discovered I'd abandoned my post, but it would only take a couple of minutes, and it had to be preferable to me falling asleep.

Down in the kitchen, I had to fumble around for water and ground coffee without violating Cody's "no lights" rule. Fortunately there was a crescent moon that night, and it shone in through the windows, giving me a small amount of light. Not much, but a little. The most challenging part was judging how much water I'd put into the coffeemaker, but I managed. As soon as I had the coffee brewing, I stepped out onto the porch so I could take a quick piss off it into the grass.

That was when the aliens came.

The first thing I noticed was a massive shadow moving slowly across the front yard, heading directly for the house. Startled, I jerked my eyes upward. It would be inaccurate to say I saw a spaceship. What I saw was blackness—an enormous triangular shape blotting out the stars and the moon as it drifted silently overhead. I couldn't tell how high up it was, but even if it were just a few feet above the nearest treetops, it would still have been massive.

Only dimly aware I'd just pissed on myself, I spun around and rushed back inside. The coffeemaker was no longer brewing. The stove clock wasn't blinking. Everything was dark and deathly silent.

I ran for the stairs and tried to take them two at a time, but in the darkness, I stumbled and slammed down hard. I cried out in pain. Above me, coming from the direction of Cody's room, a bright bluish light spilled out into the upper hall like headlights from a car. It had to be moving, because the shadows cast by the stair railings drifted slowly across the wall over my head. No longer caring if I made any noise, I scrambled up the stairs, using my hands as much as my feet.

Fuck! Why did I leave the room! Idiot!

I was going so fast when I reached the top, I slammed into the door frame of the room I'd been camping out in. I pushed myself away from it and flung myself through the open door of Cody's room.

Then, for a second, I froze.

He was *floating*. His body was naked, since he slept that way, and he appeared to still be sound asleep. But the covers had slipped off, and he was a good foot or so from the bed, still in a reclining position. To my horror, he was moving slowly but steadily toward the open window. Beyond that, I could see nothing but that glaring bluish light.

"Cody!" I forced myself to move, though I felt as if I were dreaming—struggling to run through air the consistency of pudding. "Cody!"

He was moving so slowly, it seemed impossible that I couldn't reach him before he went through the window. But by the time I grabbed his ankles, his head and shoulders had already slipped through. No matter how hard I pulled, he continued sliding farther out the window, getting sucked into the light.

"*Cody!*"

Then he was through, and I followed him, literally being yanked off my feet. I panicked and lost my grip on his ankles as I grabbed for the window ledge. Cody vanished, lost in the blinding blue-white glare. I continued to float through the air, not falling, but tumbling like an uncoordinated trapeze artist, grabbing at nothingness.

Then something exploded, searing my eyes, and I fell.

Part Two

Chapter Four

THE DREAM was disjointed.

I was in some kind of operating room, lying naked on a table, the hard, cold metal surface chilling me wherever my body pressed against it. Overhead, the ceiling was lost in a sea of bright spotlights shining directly down upon me. But the "doctors" hovering over me were the stuff of nightmares—human in shape, but with large heads and enormous, bulbous black eyes. They were silhouetted against the light, so the details of their faces were in shadow, but as they worked, they moved in and out of the light. Their skin was gray and leathery, like that of a lizard, and their noses and mouths were just small slits. I was terrified and wanted to scream, but I was also groggy, as though under the influence of a powerful sedative, and the best I could manage was a whimper.

That caught the attention of the creatures, however. One turned to me and said something in a language I couldn't understand. One of the others—there were four—responded with a curt, single word and a dismissive wave of his hand. Their mouths didn't appear to move as they spoke.

The first turned away for a moment, and when he turned back, he was holding a thin syringe. As I watched in horror, the creature lowered the syringe toward my body. I tried to pull away, but I was strapped down. I couldn't move my head to see where the needle went, but a second later, I felt a sharp prick in my upper arm. I gasped.

Then a wave of dizziness washed over me, and everything went black.

THE FIRST thing I became aware of, as I clawed my way back to consciousness, was a low, pervasive hum. Not so much an audible sound as a sensation I could feel with my entire body. I opened my eyes to find myself lying in a strange room on a bed of some kind. But nothing was familiar. The walls and ceiling seemed to be made of some kind of webbing—not quite like a spider web, but more like a dark gray-green mesh that covered nearly every surface, including the floor. Where the walls ended and the ceiling and floor began was indistinct. Everything was rounded, as if I were inside a cocoon of some sort. But it was large enough for a man to stand and move around in, and a portal in the far wall appeared to be a door, though it was currently closed.

The bed I was lying on seemed to be made of something like memory foam. It conformed to the shape of my body and was very comfortable. My head was propped up on some kind of pillow, and I was covered by a thin blanket. When I moved under the blanket, my hand brushed against the skin of my hip. I was stark naked.

Terrific.

I sat up and swung my feet out of the bed to rest on the floor. It was hard, perhaps made out of metal, but not at all cold. If anything, the temperature in the room was a bit warm.

Where the light was coming from, I couldn't determine. The room wasn't dark. The ambient light was similar to afternoon sunlight coming in through a window, except that there was no window, and the shadows my body cast on the bed and the floor were diffuse and indistinct.

The doorway dilated like the iris of an eye, and I grabbed the blanket to make sure my crotch was covered. God knew why. My captors had stripped me and ogled my private parts to their hearts' content when I was unconscious. Of course, that didn't mean I had to give them a free show *now*.

It didn't matter. As soon as I saw the two creatures entering the room, I scrambled backward on the bed in fear to cower naked and terrified against the mesh wall. I was no longer even vaguely aware of the blanket or what it might or might not be covering.

They were tall, though not particularly taller than some human men. I couldn't tell if they were naked or clothed in leatherlike suits, but I wasn't really looking at their bodies. I was looking at those horrible *faces*. Their heads were larger than any man's, and they had two enormous eyes, black and as featureless as glass orbs. Between these, where a human nose would be, there was a slight bump with a small horizontal slit near the bottom. A bit lower there was a "mouth" that likewise was nothing more than a small slit.

"What… the fuck… are you?" I managed to say, my voice quivering.

"Wee… weel… noht… hoort… yoo…."

I blinked at them for a long moment. Then I realized what I'd heard wasn't an alien language. It was English. Sort of. It sounded like someone from Eastern Europe trying to pronounce English words, very slowly and carefully, and not quite getting the vowels right. There was also a vaguely electronic overtone to it.

His—was it a he?—companion gripped his shoulder briefly and then stepped forward.

"Do you understand me?" the second one said. His voice was much clearer. Still accented oddly, but definitely understandable. Like the first, his voice sounded slightly electronic, as if he were talking through a speaker.

"Yes," I replied.

"We will not hurt you."

"Glad to hear it."

He tapped his companion on the shoulder again and said something I didn't understand at all. The latter nodded, and with a slight nod toward me, he turned and left the room. The door silently constricted, leaving me alone with the one who spoke English more coherently.

He—his voice sounded kind of male, so I decided to go with that until I learned otherwise—made a gesture with his hand, as if he were lifting something, and the floor in front of him bulged upward, forming a sort of stool. He moved in front of it and sat down.

Then he took off his head.

It wasn't actually his head, or I would have pissed myself. As it was, I gasped when he gripped it on both sides, and I heard a *crack* like the breaking of a seal. Then he lifted it up to reveal a very ordinary-looking head underneath what I now knew to be a mask or helmet.

I gaped at him. "You're human!"

As soon as I'd spoken, I knew I was wrong. For one thing, his eyes were a shade I'd never seen in a human eye—sort of a gunmetal blue. His features were more or less human, but his skin was mottled in an odd way. The overall skin tone was what I would have called "olive"—kind of Mediterranean—but he had indistinct mahogany spots forming lines down his face. One in the center, down the bridge of his nose, and two trailing down under his eyes like lines of tears. He was bald and had no eyebrows, but his features weren't unattractive. In fact, once I got over my initial surprise at his appearance, I could acknowledge that he was fairly handsome.

"By some definitions of your word 'human,' I would qualify," he said, his voice a pleasant baritone, without any hint of the electronic quality the mask had given it. He spoke very slowly and deliberately, and he was easy enough to understand, even with the accent. "But we are not of the same species, and I do not originate from your planet."

Though I'd expected it, by this point, his words chilled me. Where the fuck *did* he originate from? I suddenly realized I was flashing my genitals at him, and reached out to tug the flimsy blanket over my legs and waist.

"Everything Cody told me was real," I said, still having trouble grasping it. "You've been kidnapping people, experimenting on them...."

"No," he said. "We have not experimented on any of your species."

"You experimented on *me*! I remember... getting injected with something, and...."

He shook his head. "We were not conducting an experiment on you. I am sorry if you were hurt or frightened, but it was necessary to be sure you had no diseases that were communicable to us."

I supposed that made sense, though I wasn't willing to give in so easily—not after they'd scared the shit out of me in their... operating room, or whatever it was. "If you aren't experimenting on us, why are there so many reports of people being abducted and having probes inserted into their... various orifices?"

"We have not conducted experiments upon members of your species," he insisted. "We have, however, taken samples for testing."

"Why? What are you testing for?"

He straightened up and pointed at his face. "Look at me. We have explored twenty-four solar systems with planets similar to our own, yet your species is the only one we've discovered that is nearly our biological twin. *How* similar we are, and how this circumstance came about... this is of great interest to our scientists."

"But you're kidnapping us in the middle of the night!" I snapped, my anger overriding some of my fear. "We have no idea what's happening! Do you have any idea how *terrifying* that is?"

"I am sorry."

"*Where is Cody?* Where are you keeping him? I want to see him!"

"Cody is... the other of your species?"

"Yes!"

He frowned and glanced at the floor for a second. Then he looked up at me and said, "He is not here. We rescued you, but the Karazhen took him."

"What do you mean?" The hair on the back of my arms was standing on end. "What is a… kara… karajen…?"

"Karazhen. They are our enemies. And they have your friend."

Chapter Five

HE REFUSED to tell me anything more about Cody until he'd had a chance to fill me in on the whole situation, so I bit my lip and tried to listen as he explained.

"The Karazhen and the Alzhen—my people—have been at war for what would be over one thousand of your years. The war has been brutal but far away from here, until now."

"So you came here to suck us into some intergalactic war?" I muttered.

He shook his head. "We did not come here to do that. We came here to study your species. How could we not?" He set his helmet on the floor, and I couldn't help but glance at those bulbous black "eyes" again. The thing gave me the creeps, even knowing what it was now. "Unfortunately the Karazhen discovered our interest in you, and for them your species provided an opportunity."

"For what?"

"To experiment. To find potential weaknesses in us. In all this time, they have failed to capture any of our kind alive. Those who are captured know to end their lives quickly, before the Karazhen have a chance to vivisect them. You are so biologically similar to us, it is possible for the Karazhen to use you to develop biological weapons—viruses—to use against us."

I clutched the thin blanket and felt the hair on my arms pricking up again. This time the sensation traveled all the way up my neck into my scalp. "Is that what they're doing? Testing viruses on us to see if they'll work against you?"

"Yes."

Cody! "Oh my God. They've been doing it to Cody for *months*!"

My host—I still had no idea what his name was—surprised me by getting up and moving to sit near me on the bed. Perhaps he was trying to be comforting, though I think I would have screamed if he'd touched me. Not that he was hideous, but my brain was on overload by this point—aliens, bug-eyed monster helmets, the fact that I was possibly inside a spaceship, Cody kidnapped, biological weapons….

"If they had tested anything deadly on your friend," the alien said, "he would already be dead. It's possible they were testing some viruses that proved ineffective, but we suspect they've been taking samples and running harmless tests on his body, so far—"

"*Harmless?* Cody's been falling apart! They've been embedding these... disgusting *things* in his skin...." I shuddered, completely believing Cody's version of events at last. He wasn't insane—not unless he'd been driven crazy by those motherfuckers.

"Transmitters, perhaps. Chemical delivery devices. Or biological monitors. The Karazhen are not like us. They are closer to your insects or arachnids. They have absolutely no understanding of our biology. While they have no doubt captured many of your people, studying you in your natural habitat also—"

"How do we get Cody back from them?" I demanded.

I hadn't thought it possible to be more frightened than I already was, but when he sighed and shook his head, I felt a tremor go through my entire body. I realized I'd been holding on to the faint hope that *these* aliens might be able to help me against *those* aliens—the giant bugs or whatever that had Cody. They were aliens, after all. Weren't they supposed to have unworldly healing powers and make things fly with their minds? Didn't they have any giant robots? Couldn't they time travel?

What the hell were they good for?

"As soon as we detected the energy signature of their transport beam, we attempted to intercept it. We succeeded in freeing you, but your friend was already inside their ship. The best we can do now is pursue them."

"To where?"

Again, he shook his head. "Hopefully, not out of your solar system. We have learned of a refueling base orbiting one of your gas giants—the one with the highly visible rings—"

"Saturn?" I asked weakly. He couldn't be saying what I thought he was saying....

"Ah! Yes. We hope they will stop there. If so, we may catch up to them in about thirty-six of your hours."

I pulled the blanket up under my chin like a child afraid of the dark. "Thirty-six hours... to Saturn.... Where are we now?"

"We passed the orbit of your moon not long before you woke."

My host appeared to understand how overwhelmed I was, because he decided to leave me alone to rest for a while. I didn't object. But as he stood to leave, I asked, "Can I get some clothes, please?"

He gave me a blank look for a moment, as if he couldn't imagine why I would want such a thing. But goddammit, *he* was wearing clothes. Why did *I* have to be naked?

"I'm sorry," he said at last, "but your clothing was destroyed after we brought you on board."

"What? Why?" I hadn't been wearing anything irreplaceable—just boxer briefs and a *Big Bang Theory* T-shirt—but Jesus! They'd belonged to me. Did these guys make a habit of trashing other people's belongings?

"Most of the Alzhen on this ship haven't yet been exposed to the microbes and viruses in your environment and on your body," he explained. He picked up the creepy helmet and added, "They're forced to wear environmental suits whenever they have contact with your atmosphere—not because our atmosphere is significantly different from yours, apart from a bit more nitrogen and a slightly different balance of trace gases, but because of the risk of contamination."

I felt vaguely insulted, though I knew it wasn't the sort of thing that could be helped. "Why aren't *you* afraid of viruses and jock itch and whatever?"

"What is 'jock itch'?"

I rolled my eyes. "Never mind. I don't have it. I'm just saying…."

"I have been to your planet several times, and I've been inoculated many times." He smiled. "I've even caught what you call a 'cold.' It was extremely unpleasant."

"Yes," I said unsympathetically. "We don't like it either." Then something else occurred to me. "Wait a minute. What if *I* catch something from *you*?"

He cocked an eyebrow at me. Or rather, he raised the skin over his right eye, since there wasn't actually an eyebrow there. "Anyone entering or leaving this room is sterilized by ultraviolet radiation."

"But that just sterilizes the outside of your suits, right?" I persisted. "You just removed your helmet and breathed all over me."

"The risk to you is slight. All microbes in my body are catalogued, and can easily be removed from your system, if you are infected."

I wasn't entirely convinced, but it seemed pointless to argue. I'd already been exposed. I just hoped he was right, and I wouldn't die an agonizing death from Alzhen pinkeye or something.

He turned as if to leave, but I stopped him again. "Can't you at least give me *something* to wear? It makes me really uncomfortable sitting here naked while you have clothes on."

"Should I take my clothes off the next time I visit you?" he asked.

That shut me up for a minute. I couldn't help but wonder what he actually looked like under that suit. Was he exactly like a human male? Or did he have some weird anime crotch with gelatinous tentacles? I shuddered at the thought. But now he had me curious.

I finally managed to stammer out, "Um… no, I don't think that's necessary. I was just hoping you could find me some pants or something."

"I will see what I can do."

"By the way," I said, "my name is Marc. Thanks for asking. What's yours?"

He blinked at me again. Then he said, "You may call me Dalsing. It means 'major,' more or less. Like your military title."

"Is your real name too difficult for me to pronounce?"

That elicited another smile. "No, Marc. Our mouths are roughly equivalent, so what I can pronounce, you should be able to pronounce. But our names are used only in intimate contexts. We prefer titles. Is that suitable?"

I shrugged. "I…. Sure."

"Good."

"Are you in command of this ship, then?"

He shook his head. "No. I am merely in command of the exploratory team. And I will be leading the foray into the Karazhen base, when we arrive there."

Then, with a slight bow, he turned and left.

Out of curiosity, I got up and padded across the chamber to see if the door was locked. Not that I'd be in any position to escape if it wasn't. What was I going to do? Find an escape pod, jump in stark naked, and hope I could figure out how to direct it a couple of hundred thousand miles back to my planet? If I didn't accidentally spiral into the sun, I'd probably drift off into the void until my oxygen ran out.

Ultimately, all this speculation turned out to be moot. The damned door didn't have any controls on it. It didn't matter if it was locked or not; I couldn't figure out how to open it.

ONCE I'D been left on my own, I quickly discovered I had nothing to do. I curled up under the blanket, and even though I thought it would be impossible to sleep with all the chaos going on in my head—worry about Cody, terror at the idea of the Karazhen building biological weapons that would work on humans as well as the Alzhen, my mind being blown by the fact that I was in *outer space*, wondering what an alien looked like naked, wondering if I was going to return to Earth and find out everyone was fifty years older because of relativity—I must have eventually dozed off. The dreams I had were bizarre and frightening, with a dash of eroticism thrown in.

Frankly, I might have been better off if the first alien I'd met hadn't been male and good-looking.

I awoke to find the room dimly lit, but as I sat up, the light increased. A moment later the door dilated, and one of the aliens in suits entered, carrying a covered tray. I think it was female, judging from the shape of the chest, and when it spoke, it sounded like a woman.

"Ahrrr… yoo… huhngahree?"

I pondered that a moment and then replied, "Yes, thank you. I'm starving."

She bowed slightly and waved her hand at the floor. A portion near the bed slid up to form a sort of table. The Alzhen woman placed the tray on this, bowed again, and then left.

I scooted forward on the bed to lift the cover off the tray. What it revealed was… presumably food. It was hard to tell. Some kind of blue-green mush in a bowl, with what looked like crackers stacked beside it. There was also a cup full of yellow liquid that looked disconcertingly like urine. Not just Gatorade-yellow, but a more muted piss-yellow, and kind of cloudy, with a disturbing froth on the top. It was a testament to how thirsty I was that I dared lift the cup to my nose and sniff it. Fortunately the odor wasn't unappealing. Kind of citrusy. I sipped it and actually found it very refreshing.

Thank God.

I downed most of it but left a little in the cup to wash down the "food." I tentatively nibbled one of the crackers and discovered that it tasted pretty much like… a cracker. Kind of an odd aftertaste, sort of like peas, but not bad. I ate one and then followed it up with a dab of the mush on the tip of my finger. This was the consistency of buttercream frosting and kind of sweet. But again, it tasted more like some kind of vegetable than a dessert. Not bad. I discovered I was hungry enough to eat the mush and all the crackers without paying attention to what it looked like. Then I downed the rest of my drink-that-wasn't-urine. Despite the fact that I hadn't been given large portions of anything, I was thoroughly sated.

I was just placing the cover back over the empty dish when the door opened again and Dalsing entered. To my surprised, he was dressed very informally in something like a white bathrobe, as if he were spending the day at a spa. This revealed his feet, which were wearing sandals, his hands, and parts of his arms and legs. Apart from the fact that the skin on his extremities matched the coloring on his face—olive with lines of brownish spots trailing along his shin bones and the contours of his arms—he looked human enough. Though, like his head and face, his arms and legs were utterly hairless.

He had a pair of sandals in one hand and another white robe draped over his arm.

"Good waking, Marc," he said with a bow. "Are you rested?"

"Well enough, I guess."

He glanced at the tray. "And have you eaten?"

"Yes. It was good. Thank you."

"That is good." He held out his arm. "I have brought you something to cover your body, and I am wearing the same garment. I hope this will put you at ease."

"Thank you." I took the robe from him and stood to slip it on. This, of course, resulted in me flashing him again. I'd considered for a split second asking him to turn around but decided I was being foolish. If I could shower with strangers at the gym, I could manage to change into a robe in front of Dalsing.

The robe didn't have a belt, but when I closed it, the soft material stuck together like Velcro. Dalsing handed me the sandals, and I dropped them on the floor so I could step into them.

"Do you mind if we sit?" he asked, gesturing toward the bed.

"Uh… no. Not at all."

We sat cross-legged on the bed, and I was startled to get a brief glimpse of the bare skin of his inner thigh as he adjusted his robe. Was he *naked* under there? That would be taking this whole "making the guest comfortable" thing really seriously. I couldn't imagine a ship's officer on Earth doing the same for a passenger from another country.

"We still have an Earth day before we reach Saturn," Dalsing said. "I would like to speak with you further, if you do not object. Though I have visited your planet several times, I rarely have much opportunity to speak your language with a native."

I raised my eyebrows in surprise. "You speak it very well."

"Thank you."

"You are aware that our… species… speaks a lot of languages? I mean, *thousands* of languages."

"Yes."

"Do you speak languages other than English?"

He shifted again, and I glimpsed more skin under his robe. I willed myself to look away. It was bad enough I was beginning to think impure thoughts about a space alien. I didn't need to be a lech on top of it.

"No," he replied. "I focus on English, because I have explored the region near your home more than other regions. And the people I've encountered to date have all spoken this language."

That took me aback until I realized he meant Cody's farmhouse. He didn't actually know where *my* home was. How could he?

"Can you read it too?"

"Yes. One of the first of your kind I encountered was a teacher. She taught me much and gave me books to continue my studies. It has become a passion of mine."

"Where is this teacher now?" I asked.

He smiled sadly. "She died many years ago on my home world. She was very old by then. I counted her among my dearest friends."

"So… just how long have your people been visiting Earth?"

Dalsing looked thoughtful as he leaned back against the wall, lifting his knees up to brace himself. This gave me a pretty clear view of the underside of his thighs and a little ass crack. There was no doubt about the fact he was naked under the robe. Was he deliberately flashing me? Or did he just not give a fuck? I honestly didn't object—he was very nice to look at. But I was finding it very distracting.

"My people first discovered your planet about two of your centuries ago. I, personally, have been studying your species for perhaps seventy-five years."

"Seventy-five *years*?" I gaped at him. "Just how old *are* you?" I realized too late how rude the question might be considered.

He didn't seem to mind. "I will soon be a hundred and twenty-four Earth years old. I was rather young when I joined my first expedition. Our life expectancy is approximately three hundred years."

Jesus.

"Is this another expedition, then?" I asked. "To study us?"

"Yes."

"You said you were in command of the exploratory team," I commented, recalling the conversation we'd had earlier.

"Yes," he replied, "but I answer to Terkang. That is her title. It might be translated as 'general.' She commands this vessel."

General? "Are we on some kind of military ship?"

"There is no other kind for us. Our society is what I believe you would call a military dictatorship. Our mission to your planet is to study your race for scientific purposes—we mean you no harm. But we are still a military vessel."

I was curious about this "military dictatorship" he mentioned. Generally I considered a dictatorship to be bad, but his tone was matter-of-fact, as if he had no problem with this form of government. Maybe he didn't, if he'd lived with it his entire life.

Before I could think of another question, he asked one. "Would you like me to remove my robe?"

Chapter Six

THE QUESTION had been so casual, I thought I'd misheard him. "What?"

"You have been trying to appear uninterested, but you seem curious about my body."

"I can't help it!" I exclaimed. I pointed at his crotch. "You keep flashing me!"

"Flashing? Isn't that something involving bright light or explosives?"

"It also means letting your clothing slip open, so other people can see your... private parts."

He looked at me curiously. "Private parts?"

Oh, for fuck's sake. "Your genitals, your crotch, your... sex organs—whatever you call them. You've seen mine, dangling between my legs—not that I *asked* you to look at them."

"Oh yes." He smiled. "Of course." Then his expression turned to one of concern. "I apologize if removing your clothing violated one of your cultural taboos. Our anatomy is a bit different, so... it isn't the same for us."

That piqued my interest again. For all I knew, he was just an outer space pervert who got off on waving his ding-a-ling at the natives, but that didn't really bother me. I just didn't like the implication that *I* was a pervert. Still, if he was offering....

"How is your anatomy different?"

"Would you like to see? Or would you prefer I simply describe it?"

"You can show me if you want," I replied, trying to sound nonchalant. I guess I was just a *little* perverted, because I was already stiffening up at the thought of what might be under that robe. Fortunately *my* dick was safely tucked away under *my* robe.

He stood and let his robe slip from his shoulders.

My jaw must have hit the floor. Not because he had some hideous tentacle-monster thing writhing in his crotch or anything like that, but because it was just the opposite. There was *nothing* there. He had a pubic mound like a human, which was as hairless as the rest of him, but it was completely smooth. No dick, no nothing. It was completely featureless, apart from a thin brown line traveling up from between his legs to his navel. His body was muscular and pretty much a work of art, even with the four nipples, but… well, so much for alien porn. He was a *Ken doll*!

I tried not to look disappointed. No point in creating an intergalactic incident over penis size. Or… lack of penis altogether. "It's very nice," I said diplomatically.

Dalsing laughed. "If you are referring to my 'private parts,' you can't see them. They are here." He cupped his crotch in what would have been a lewd gesture for a human male. "Inside. This is why clothing for us is merely functional."

"I see." I pictured that thin line splitting open like a seam. "So it… comes out, when you need it to?"

"Yes. We reproduce the same way your species does. One carries the egg inside her body—we call our females *ba-len*—and the male, the *ba-ti*, inseminates it."

"And you are… *ba-ti*?" I asked, just to be clear. He *looked* male, but I could have been wrong.

"Yes. Unfortunately I cannot easily show you my 'private parts.' I must be aroused in order for them to emerge."

This was beginning to sound like the lead-in to a cheesy porn film. *"Let me show you how my species mates, earthling."* Boom chicka wow wow…. But although I was, in fact, still curious about his anatomy, I discovered I'd hit my limit for how crass I could be with a space alien. We weren't even on a first-name basis.

"That's okay," I said. "I've satisfied my curiosity."

Sort of.

"Very well." He picked up his robe, giving me a brief glimpse of his back, which seemed oddly segmented, as if he had interlocking plates underneath the skin. Clearly, Alzhen and humans weren't *completely* alike. Then again, I'd read that bonobo DNA is 99 percent identical to human DNA, but we don't look much like bonobos. The Alzhen must be even more closely related… somehow.

After he'd tied the robe around himself, Dalsing said, "If you would be willing to wear one of our suits—the ones you've seen with the helmets—I could take you on a tour of the ship. Unfortunately both you and the crew might be endangered if you walked around our living quarters without protection."

The suits didn't look very comfortable to me, but how could I pass up the opportunity to see the inside of a spaceship from another solar system?

"Okay!" I said.

WE HAD to wait for someone to bring the suit. I have no idea how Dalsing communicated the request to his crew, but it wasn't long before someone appeared at the door, dressed in one of the suits himself. He left one for me and departed, bowing slightly to Dalsing.

I had to drop my robe in order to slip into it, and I thought about asking Dalsing to turn around, but by now that seemed rather pointless. I just tossed the robe aside and tried to ignore the fact that I was naked as he helped me into the suit. The damned thing was *snug* and hugged my body like a wet suit. It was also made of some kind of material not too far removed from silver lamé, which didn't do much to stop me from feeling naked in front of my host. It may have been sufficient for a species that didn't have external genitalia, but not for a human. My dick and testicles were clearly visible through the fabric—and it was obvious I was circumcised.

I pointed this out to Dalsing, but he was unconcerned. "My people might find it curious, but it won't disturb them."

Well, okay, then. As long as *they* were all fine.

The large helmet was a bit claustrophobic, since it sealed at the neck, but some kind of apparatus in the nose area kept fresh air coming in and prevented it from getting too warm inside. I was surprised to find that the large, round eye lenses didn't distort my view, and sound wasn't at all muffled when it reached my ears.

"This way," Dalsing said when I was adequately sealed in. He led me to the door, and it dilated to allow us through.

My first view of the outside of my quarters was disappointing. It was a short, tubelike corridor with another door at the opposite end. But I soon discovered this was simply an airlock. It wasn't that the ship had a different kind of air or a different pressure than my quarters; it was that they didn't want my diseases. Even though my germ-ridden body was sealed inside the suit, I'd still fondled the outside of the suit and breathed all over Dalsing. We both had to be decontaminated with a flash of blue UV light.

Then the second door opened, and I passed into the ship proper.

THE CORRIDOR was shaped like a hexagonal tube, and I soon realized that was because it was designed to be functional in zero gravity—or "microgravity," as my college physics professor would have insisted I call it. There were handholds on all surfaces, including the one we were walking on.

I hadn't thought to ask about the gravity on the ship, so I did now.

"It isn't gravity," Dalsing replied, "but acceleration. The ship is moving in that direction"—he pointed straight up—"accelerating at a rate that approximates our gravity, both on your world and mine."

"Won't we be going insanely fast when we get to Saturn, then?"

He smiled and shook his head. "Halfway through the journey, the ship will flip over and begin decelerating. You will need to be secured when that happens, or you'll fly around the chamber and probably injure yourself."

"You'll warn me when that's about to happen, right?"

For the first time since I'd met him, I saw something akin to mischief in his eyes. "I will try to remember."

We stepped into a chamber similar to the airlock outside my quarters, but smaller, and with no exit other than the door we'd entered. The floor shook for a moment, and then the door opened to reveal a different corridor. Then I felt like an idiot for not realizing the little room was an elevator.

One end of the second corridor opened into a vast chamber with a dome overhead. At the floor level, people milled around or sat at tables where dim red lighting illuminated them. Over their heads, the dome looked out upon a sea of stars, and only the seams, laid out in triangular patterns like those found in a geodesic dome on Earth, indicated there was *anything* between the people and the void of space. I had a sudden attack of vertigo and grabbed Dalsing's arm without thinking. He made no move to push me away.

"This is the center of the ship," he explained. "We are on the top level, which is why we have this dome over our heads." He pointed upward. "If you look toward the center, you can see Saturn. That is our destination."

The helmet gave me limited head movement, so I had to lean back as far as I could in order to see what he was pointing at. It might have been Saturn. I couldn't tell. It looked like a bright dot among a kazillion other dots, slightly brighter than the rest. "It doesn't look like we're moving."

"We are moving very fast, but there is nothing nearby to gauge our speed by. Perhaps I will bring you here when we approach the planet and its moons. Then you can watch them approach."

"What are we going to do when we get there?" I asked.

He didn't answer right away. Instead, he placed a hand over mine on his arm and led me into the chamber. "Let us sit. Unfortunately the suit will prevent you from eating or drinking, but we can talk."

I'd been wondering if Dalsing would be underdressed for wandering around his ship, since he still wore nothing but the robe and sandals. But as we passed other men and women, some of whom nodded to us, I quickly learned that wasn't the case. If anything, he was *over*dressed. None of the Alzhen in this… I suppose it would be called a lounge on Earth… were wearing the creepy suits. The suits weren't too uncomfortable, but they were a far cry from casual clothes to relax in. Instead, the Alzhen there were dressed in a variety of clothes ranging from colorful kimono-like robes to diaphanous cloaks that revealed pretty much everything. A disconcerting number of them weren't wearing anything at all, or had nothing more than jeweled stoles draped around their shoulders, or various kinds of hats. Some seemed to have on nothing more than phosphorescent makeup, which made the lines of spots on their bodies glow a bright orange or a smoldering red. At least, I assumed it was makeup. Perhaps their spots could be made to glow like that naturally.

This was my first view of naked Alzhen females. They were nearly identical to the men, except for their breasts. Even these weren't exactly like human women's breasts, since they were more integrated with the chest. Picture Mystique in the X-Men movies, but with slightly smaller breasts. The breasts *had* to be smaller, since there were two sets of them, one above the other.

I noticed a third type of Alzhen that baffled me. They had no nipples at all. Even Dalsing had nipples, just as human men do. He had four of them, true, but they were still unmistakably nipples. These Alzhen also seemed a bit thinner than either the men or the women. The men tended to have broader chests, and the women to have broader hips, just as with humans, but these seemed… I guess the word "androgynous" might fit.

I wanted to ask about them, though it seemed kind of rude. On the other hand, Dalsing had stripped naked for me to ogle him—largely because he'd earlier gotten an eyeful of *my* naughty bits. So perhaps it would be okay.

We took a seat at one of those odd tables that rose up out of the floor, and he asked, "Do you mind if I drink something?"

"No, go ahead."

"Thank you." He motioned to some kind of floating sphere—it must have been a robotic bartender—and when it approached, he said something to it in what I assumed was Alzhenese. It burbled at him and then lowered itself onto the table a moment. When it lifted up again, there was a cup of blue liquid on the table. I tried not to think of a chicken laying an egg... and failed.

The bartender-thing flew off, and Dalsing told me, "If you are thirsty, touch your tongue to the panel in front of your mouth. You will be supplied with water."

"Thanks."

"And if you feel the need to relieve yourself, the suit is designed to handle liquid waste."

"Uh... thanks. I'm good." I couldn't imagine having a conversation with him while I was peeing my pants. I changed the subject and asked my question about the Alzhen without nipples.

"I never said we had just two genders," he replied, giving me that mischievous smile again. "They are what we call *ba*—I suppose it could be translated as 'undifferentiated.' We are all born *ba*, but some of us choose to become *ba-ti* or *ba-len*, if we would like to produce offspring."

It took me a moment to wrap my head around this. "Then those Alzhen I've seen are children?"

"No. Some are older than I am. We don't all choose to differentiate. Gender isn't always necessary for us. *Ba* are perfectly able to experience sexual pleasure, for instance."

"Then you *chose* to be *ba-ti*?"

"Yes."

"Because you and your... wife... wanted children?" I was far more disappointed to learn Dalsing had a wife than I had any reason to be. Had I been secretly hoping our little game of I'll-show-you-mine-if-you-show-me-yours would become more sexual? That was a disturbing thought.

"In my case," Dalsing replied casually, as if it were perfectly normal to be explaining his genitals to a total stranger again, "no. I chose *ba-ti* because I planned on interacting with your species. If I had been female, this would have been more problematic. Your people do not respect females as much as males."

Ouch.

I decided now would be a good time to change the subject. "So how are we going to rescue Cody?"

"*We*," he said with a smile, "are not. My people will deal with the situation when we arrive at the Karazhen base. You will remain in your quarters until we return."

He couldn't see the sour look I gave him, but my silence must have made it clear I was displeased.

"You are not here on this ship to participate in our attack on the Karazhen base," Dalsing said, his voice gentle. "You are here because we did not want you to be taken by them, and we did not have time to return you to your home. We were in pursuit of their ship. Our choice was to take you on board or let you fall to your death."

"Well, thanks for not dropping me." I had a hard time keeping the sarcasm out of my voice, but I hoped he wouldn't pick up on it.

"You are welcome." He drained his cup of blue liquid and set it on the table. "Come. Let me show you the rest of the ship."

Chapter Seven

I couldn't honestly say it made sense for me to be part of Operation Rescue Cody. I had no military training. I'd never been in space before, never mind encountered arachnid-like aliens. I'd probably scream and wet myself if I even saw one. And it made perfect sense to leave things to the professionals, while I stayed out of the way, and avoid turning the whole thing into a Three Stooges routine.

But I was still pissed off. Cody was my friend, and I felt responsible for him. Especially since I'd passed up my one chance to knock him over the head and drag him to safety before the Karazhen nabbed him. It didn't help that I'd been taking a leak outside when they abducted him, rather than manning my post as he'd asked me to. I'd dropped the ball, and now he might be suffering unspeakable horrors because of it.

Still, I knew there was no way of convincing Dalsing to take me into the Karazhen base. He wasn't an idiot. So I didn't try.

The ship was enormous and saucer shaped, with five levels. We didn't visit every inch of it, of course. Dalsing took me to the control room, the engine room, the mess hall—which was basically like the lounge, but with a ceiling instead of a dome—and several other rooms I quickly forgot the purpose of. I don't generally think of myself as stupid, but when everything is alien, it all starts to blur together. The engine room was the most impressive, since it featured massive cylindrical columns that went up through four levels of the ship. My entire body vibrated with the low hum they emitted, and cold purple light sparked up and down their ribbed metal surfaces.

I had no idea how they worked, but they were certainly cool.

I discovered that my "quarters" were in what Earth naval ships would call "the brig." Not exactly a prison, since they weren't keeping anyone prisoner there, according to Dalsing. I just had to take his word for that. I couldn't see into the other rooms. But they were used to isolate aliens like me when we were brought on board.

"Do you do that a lot?" I asked.

"Yes," Dalsing replied. "Though they are generally unaware of it. We bring them in, study them for a short time, clear their memory, and then return them to where we found them."

We were walking along one of the interminable corridors, and this comment made me stop dead in my tracks. "You wipe their memories?"

"Most are unable to understand who we are or what we're doing, and they find their encounter with us very stressful. We clear their memories to be merciful."

"Except that it doesn't *work*!" I growled. "We *do* remember. Not the whole thing, maybe, but bits and pieces. Just enough to torment us. Have you seen Cody? He's falling apart!"

Dalsing frowned. "That appears to be a recent phenomenon. We are uncertain as to the cause. It may be that, with the recent advances in your technology, your minds are more accepting of the concept of space travel and contact with other worlds."

"Yes," I muttered darkly, "we've all seen *Close Encounters* and *E.T.*"

"What is that?"

"Never mind." We walked without talking for a while until I finally broke the silence. "I have to go to the bathroom. And I mean *now*." I hadn't been able to do so since coming on board, and that had to have been eight or nine hours ago. As far as I knew, there wasn't a toilet in my quarters.

"You can relieve yourself in the suit."

That didn't make me any less irritable. "I have no intention of peeing my pants like a five-year-old. And that isn't all I have to do. I'm not going into detail—I assume you have an alimentary canal, and if not, you've been probing both ends of ours for centuries."

"Ah yes. Don't *golshu* in your suit—it isn't equipped for that."

I'd just picked up a new vocabulary word. Oh goody.

"My crew will be distressed if I allow you to use one of our communal *golsha-ren*," he continued. "You would have to remove the isolation suit to do so, and that could be dangerous for them. But I was about to suggest we visit my quarters so you can see how one of us lives. I have no concerns about you relieving yourself there."

"Thanks."

My first view of an Alzhen living space wasn't very spectacular, because it was dark, and I really didn't give a fuck. I just asked him to take me to the *golsha-ren* or whatever it was called and give me a quick—*very* quick—rundown of how to operate the horrifying suction-cup thing that stuck out of one wall. I stripped out of the suit while he was explaining it all and then practically shoved him out of the room. I could cope with being naked around him, but I wasn't going to let him watch me relieve myself. Nobody did *that* at the gym.

"You don't need to put the suit back on," he said, standing in the doorway. "I will find you a robe." Then the door constricted, leaving me alone to do my business.

I'm not going to go into the gory details of the next few minutes, though I'll mention that the toilet was designed for microgravity. It kind of latched onto my body between my legs, covering both the front and back—though the front was a tight fit, since my anatomy was, well... *existent*. Then the suction started.

And then... other things happened.

When I was done, I washed up in a basin that was thankfully not hard to operate, though the "water" behaved oddly. It evaporated quickly, leaving my hands clean and the basin completely dry. Bizarre.

I walked out into Dalsing's living quarters and then stopped dead, gaping in awe.

I wasn't sure what I'd expected. Gleaming chrome and fluorescent lights, maybe. Or more of the malleable greenish mesh I'd been seeing in other parts of the ship. The last thing I'd expected was a forest. By that, I mean trees. A lot of trees. Though not Earth trees. In the relatively dark space, bioluminescent lines of blue-green and pink highlighted the rough edges of their bark and created swirls around knotholes and the bases of branches. Under my feet, a carpet of moss sparkled with shimmering silver, and glowing orange cones four or five inches high shot up in clusters like mushrooms.

"This is beautiful," I said, whispering, afraid to disturb the stillness.

"It is my home world."

I turned to find Dalsing standing behind me, naked again and holding out his robe to me.

"I am sorry," he continued, "but I was unable to find a robe. You may wear mine, if this isn't taboo in your culture, or you may look at my other clothing to see if anything else might suit you."

I took the robe and smirked at him. "Are you sure you don't get off on running around naked in front of me?"

"Get off?" He seemed genuinely puzzled.

I slipped the robe on and closed it at the waist. Like the robe I'd worn earlier, the soft material adhered to itself like Velcro. "It means to get turned on—become sexually aroused. I've known guys who get turned on by being naked in front of other people."

"Why is that?"

I thought about that for a second. "Well, I suppose it only works in a culture where being naked in front of other people is a rare thing. That doesn't seem to apply here."

"If I become sexually aroused," Dalsing said, taking my hand and leading me deeper into the forest, "you will know. It will be obvious." This was the first time we'd touched, skin to skin, and his hand was disconcertingly warm.

He was walking sideways, so he could look back at me as he spoke, and I couldn't help but glance down at his crotch. "Why? Because your... genitals will pop out?"

"Eventually. But before that, my *shiri* will glow." He stroked the darkly pigmented spots on his face with his free hand.

"Oh!" I exclaimed. "I remember! Some of the... Alzhen in the lounge were doing that." I felt my face flush as it occurred to me those people must have been aroused. And they just walked around like that? In public?

But Dalsing laughed and shook his head. "That is just a paste some of us wear on social occasions to mimic arousal. Mostly younger Alzhen. My generation generally considers it... I am uncertain what the word is in your language...."

"Crass? Tacky?"

"Perhaps. You understand my meaning? It is something the young do."

I couldn't help but smile at that, imagining all the 150-year-old Alzhens shaking their heads in dismay at the way the younger generation dressed. They probably disapproved of their music too.

THE FOREST seemed to be infinite. It stretched ahead of us as far as I could see, with tiny streams and waterfalls and manmade—*Alzhen*made— bridges with beautifully carved enameled railings arching across them. Over our heads the trees seemed to be as tall as redwoods, and although it was shadowy down on the forest floor, I thought I could see the sun peeking through the leaves high above us. At last we came to a broad clearing, where fairly ordinary-looking grass made a soft bed in a small patch of sunlight. Here, Dalsing sat and invited me to sit beside him.

"This can't be real," I said. "The ship isn't big enough to hold a forest like this!"

"Sadly, no. This is a re-creation of a park in our largest city, Chai-kun. There are no wild places like this on our world—not anymore. But each city has its own park, where the plants and animals are allowed to grow, and the citizens can remember the beauty that once dominated our planet." He smiled wistfully. "Not everyone feels as I do about it… but I have always been a rebel. Look there."

I followed his gaze and saw an animal not unlike a deer, though with two parallel rows of spikes along its head and neck forming a crest. It saw us and started, jumping away into the undergrowth. In a second it was gone.

"When you say this is a re-creation," I persisted, "do you mean a physical re-creation, or some kind of… I don't know… hologram or something? Like the holodeck on *Star Trek*?" I touched the grass we were sitting on, picked a blade, and held it between my fingers. It certainly felt real. But how could this park be taking up as much space as it appeared to be?

"Holodeck?"

He'd never seen *Star Trek*, of course. I spent an unproductive few minutes trying to explain television and movies to him and finally gave up. It wasn't that he couldn't understand the concept of moving pictures telling a story. He simply didn't seem to understand why we would like such a thing. And the idea of science fiction seemed uninteresting to him. He spent his life traveling between solar systems, encountering aliens, and battling hideous insect creatures. Why would he want to read about it or watch it?

"As for the plants and animals in this space," he said, "the computer places the images in our minds simultaneously, so we share in the experience, as if we were dreaming the same dream. Is that like the 'holodeck' you mentioned?"

"I don't think so. I think that's supposed to create physical objects with replicator technology or something." I saw him blinking at me again, so I waved my hand in the air. "Don't ask."

"I was hoping to show you some of *our* entertainment, if you are interested."

"Yes, absolutely."

He snapped his fingers and a stage appeared in the center of the clearing, complete with actors in brightly colored robes and hats, similar to those worn by some comic book supervillains.

"This is one of our most famous plays," Dalsing told me. "I confess I chose it partly because the romantic pairing in it is *ba-ti* to *ba-ti*, which is my preference. If this is not to your liking, I can choose something else. Perhaps one that does not have any romance in it at all."

I was a little surprised to learn Dalsing preferred romances with two males. I thought back over the conversations we'd had and couldn't recall whether we'd discussed his orientation—or mine, for that matter. But I certainly didn't object to his choice of entertainment, in that case. "That will be fine," I said.

"Good." He leaned in close to me and said quietly, his warm breath brushing my ear, "The computer does not know your language, so I will translate what the actors are saying."

I hadn't realized until that moment that I found Dalsing sexy. Erotic, yes. He was exotic and clearly well put together—and he was naked. But that wasn't quite the same as being attracted to him personally. Perhaps it was the husky tone to his voice as he spoke just above a whisper, combined with our physical closeness and what was admittedly a romantic setting, but when I turned to glance at him and saw those startling gunmetal blue eyes looking back at me, I had a strong desire to lean in and kiss him.

I didn't. Instead, I took a deep breath and forced myself to look at the stage.

Chapter Eight

THE PLAY was... different. I doubt I would have been able to follow it, even if I'd understood the language, because there was very little dialog. Most of it was pantomimed to ethereal music played on a flute, accompanied by a harp-like instrument, bells, and something like a wide drum laid flat so metal balls of various sizes could roll around on it and clang into each other as the drummer tapped out gentle rhythms. Occasionally, during fight scenes, he banged on it, and the balls clattered around noisily.

I gathered it was one of those stories everybody in Dalsing's region knew, so detailed explanations were unnecessary. The audience had no trouble understanding that, when an actor donned a blue headband, he was declaring war on his enemies. And when he raised his pinky in the air, it meant he was accusing someone of lying.

Dalsing kept up a steady stream of explanations in my ear, so I was able to follow the story. For a "romance," it was pretty violent. I counted seven deaths by the intermission. One guy got decapitated right on stage, and I jumped in horror until Dalsing assured me it was all simulated by the computer—and even when the play was performed live, that particular moment was simulated these days.

"These days?" I asked, feeling queasy.

"In ancient times, the part would be played by a criminal who volunteered to die on stage, in exchange for one night of freedom beforehand."

I felt ill. But Dalsing assured me there would be nothing that explicitly violent in the rest of the play.

"That doesn't bother you?" I asked. "Even if it was simulated, it looked real!" I was being a bit hypocritical. Modern movies often had violence and realistic gore in them. But it had felt so much more visceral when it appeared to be a real person kneeling not ten yards away from me.

Dalsing shrugged. "I have seen this play many, many times. I knew it wasn't real, even as a child."

As a child?

Fortunately the second half of the play was the romantic part. And as Dalsing whispered into my ear, I found myself caught up in it. The story was a bit like Romeo and Juliet—or Romeo and Julius—with two warriors caught up in a feud between rival clans. One was called Hinsing, and it was his clan that had decapitated the brother of Mahzhing. Mahzhing challenged Hinsing to a duel. Actually, there were several duels. But with each one, the two men grew to respect each other more. And eventually this turned into a secret love affair.

I found the story interesting, and the actors were sexy together. But I was surprised when they actually began to have *sex* on stage. The kissing was fine. Kind of hot, in fact. But then Hinsing began to kiss his way down Mahzhing's chest. Mahzhing arched his back and his… I struggled to remember the word… *shiri* began to shimmer with a smoldering red light. When Hinsing moved lower to lick along Mahzhing's crotch, I drew a sharp breath.

"*Tegu!*" Dalsing said hurriedly, and everything froze as if we were looking at a still image.

"What is it?" I asked, turning to him.

He'd clearly been affected by what was happening on stage, since his *shiri* were also glowing red. Though as I watched, they dimmed.

"I am sorry," he said. "I wanted you to experience something from my culture—something I find very beautiful. But it did not occur to me until just now that this would be considered 'crass' in your culture. Please forgive me. I can move the play forward and start it after this scene."

I was a little annoyed by the implication I was some kind of intergalactic sexual prude, but he wasn't that far off. Sexual behavior in a lot of contexts did make me uncomfortable. But I wasn't uncomfortable now. I was turned on. And I was just kinky enough to want to see how two *ba-ti* had sex.

"It's okay," I assured him. "You don't have to skip this scene. I'd like to see it."

That sounded a little lecherous, but I wasn't the one taking an alien stranger out to a porno. Or perhaps "performance art" would be the more generous term. But it seemed to me it was disingenuous to have sex in front of an audience and not expect the audience to be aroused by it. I suppose it had artistic value—perhaps more so in his culture than I was aware of—but it wasn't just "art" making Dalsing's *shiri* glow.

"Very well." He spoke again in his language, and the action on stage continued.

We watched the performance in silence, since what the actors were doing didn't require much explanation—not when our two species were so similar. I did finally have my curiosity about male Alzhen anatomy satisfied when the actor playing Mahzhing groaned and shuddered, and a rather large, erect cock seemed to split his crotch open at the seam. It slid out in one smooth motion, testicles and all. If it had resembled an animal penis, I would have been immediately turned off, but it looked very human. It appeared to be uncircumcised, though I was too far away to see for certain.

After a considerable amount of foreplay, the other actor revealed his cock, and I discovered something else unique to their culture: size didn't appear to matter. In other words, he wasn't terribly well-endowed. That doesn't normally matter to me, honestly, but how often did gay porn stars on Earth have small dicks? Perhaps it was because these actors *weren't* porn stars—they were actors. Maybe acting ability trumped dick size for the Alzhen.

I glanced at Dalsing several times during the scene, wondering if he was going to... pop. He didn't. His *shiri* turned a fierce red, and I could hear him breathing heavily into my ear, but he didn't go past the point of no return, or whatever he would call it—not even when the scene finished with impressive geysers from both *ba-ti* on stage. I myself was hard as a rock and beginning to leak a bit. But I kept that to myself, bunching up the robe in front of my crotch to hide my arousal.

I realized I was disappointed when the action of the play continued and Dalsing's *shiri* faded to their normal color. Perhaps part of me had hoped to experience what it would be like to be ravished by an extraterrestrial. Well... *gently* "ravished," at any rate. I never got into the whole forced, scary sex thing. But if he'd hoped to plant the idea of us having sex in my head... it worked.

Still, we'd only known each other for nine or ten hours. I didn't know how that played out in his culture, but that was moving pretty fast for mine.

IN THE middle of yet another dueling scene—this play was *long*, not that I wasn't enjoying it—there was an odd chime. It didn't sound as if it had come from the stage but from the forest around us. Dalsing stopped everything again and sat up. "There is a small case inside the pocket of the robe. You should open it and swallow the pill inside."

"Why? What's happening?"

"The ship is about to flip over. The pill will prevent you from vomiting."

That sounded like a plan. I fished around in the pocket and found the pillbox. Then, after I'd swallowed the capsule inside, he had me lie down flat on the grass. He didn't bother lying down himself, however.

For a long time, nothing happened. Then the chime rang out again, three times in rapid succession. A split second later, the world turned upside down. It was disorientating, but I suppose it wasn't too much different from some amusement park rides. I seemed to be pulled to the right, then straight up, then to the left, and finally down again, all in the space of about two seconds.

What really amazed me was that I didn't fall, despite the fact that nothing was holding me down. Neither did Dalsing. The stage and the actors, all the plants and animals in the forest around us—none of them tumbled ass-over-teakettle to end up as one huge pile of broken, bleeding rubbish. I recalled that most of these things were virtual or somehow implanted in our minds, but Dalsing wasn't, as far as I could tell. And I certainly wasn't. So why hadn't I tumbled around the clearing like a ragdoll? Was there some kind of force field holding everything in place?

"Do you feel well?" Dalsing asked as he helped me sit up again.

I was a little nauseated, but the pill seemed to be doing its job, and I didn't think I'd actually puke. I gave him a wan smile and a thumbs-up.

THE PLAY ended with Hinsing and Mahzhing committing mutual suicide as their clans went to war for the fifteenth or sixteenth time. Very Shakespearean, with a touch of Japanese Noh theater. And it had me blubbering like a baby.

Dalsing looked at my tears with curiosity. "Does this mean you liked it?"

"Yes," I replied, dabbing at my eyes in embarrassment. "Don't you cry when a story like this moves you?" He looked baffled, so I added, "That is, when it makes you feel strong emotions?"

I was afraid for a moment he'd say he never felt emotions and that his species had discarded them as inferior. Except for Mr. Spock, aliens without emotion seemed best avoided. But he smiled and said, "I see. Yes, I do cry at plays. But I have seen this one many, many times. It saddens me, but it does not make me cry. I find it very beautiful that they love each other so much."

"Me too."

"Are you hungry now?" he asked. "You have not eaten in several hours."

The nausea from the ship flipping over had long ago faded. "Yes, I'm starving."

"Starving?" He looked alarmed. "Does your species require food more frequently than we realized?"

Chapter Nine

For dinner, we traveled to the top of a skyscraper in the center of Chai-kun, via the computer. It was unnerving to watch the forest dissolve around us and discover I was now perched high above a vast cityscape stretching to the horizon in all directions. The platform was inside a transparent dome, and we were surrounded by tables with other Alzhen dining at them. The quiet murmur of conversation reached my ears, but nobody seemed to notice our sudden appearance.

"This is my home city," Dalsing said. "We are in my favorite restaurant."

I was curious how far above the ground we were but decided I was better off not knowing. It might be a simulation in our minds, but it was still giving me vertigo. I focused on the table in front of me. "Are we going to eat virtual food?" I asked.

"Virtual? Oh. No. I will have food delivered to my quarters. If you'll excuse me for just a moment...."

He wandered toward the edge of the restaurant, and I caught my breath as he appeared to walk through the glass dome and drop off the edge. *It's just an illusion.*

To keep myself occupied, I got up from the table and tried to see how close to the edge of the dome I could get without passing out. I was self-conscious, at first, about bracing myself against other people's tables, but I quickly discovered they didn't even notice me. They were, after all, just holograms... or something like that.

The view was definitely spectacular. There were wispy clouds drifting by *underneath* the platform, and through these I could see a city lit by millions of lights in blue and green and orange and crimson. It wasn't yet night, but the sun had set, and the sky above me was a pale whitish-orange on the horizon, fading to indigo directly overhead. In the center of each table, a small brazier flickered to life.

By the time Dalsing returned, the stars had come out. It was breathtaking, but I was happy to get back to the table where I could feel a bit safer.

He apologized for taking so long, saying, "Since I've been in close proximity to you, I was required to go through sterilization procedures before I could interact with a member of the crew."

I didn't say anything, but I suspect I didn't exactly look flattered, because he hastily added, "You will have to do the same when we send you back to your people, due to your contact with me."

"I understand."

He'd brought several brightly colored boxes with him, and as he laid them out upon the table between us, I realized they were the Alzhen equivalent of Chinese takeout. Each contained something different: pink noodles that had an odd metallic sheen to them, gelatinous black cubes, something like green pudding with white beads in it, a pile of red flowers....

"This could be a bad idea," Dalsing said. "We initially gave you food we were certain your system could digest. Have you had any intestinal discomfort from it?"

I squirmed in embarrassment. "No, I'm fine, thanks."

"Good." Dalsing waved his hand over the buffet. "These are, I think, much more palatable, and hopefully they will not cause you any nausea or intestinal distress."

Okay. Got it. Can we stop talking about my digestive tract now?

The food was good. Weird, yes. Nothing tasted like I expected it to. The iridescent pink noodles were very sweet, a bit like yams. And the green pudding was good, though it tasted oddly like roast beef. I didn't like the black cubes. They were fishy, and Dalsing confirmed my suspicion they were made from something roughly equivalent to squid ink.

I nibbled the petals off one of the red flowers, liking the vague hint of cinnamon. "I'm beginning to feel like I'm on a date," I commented.

"A date?" Dalsing asked, looking confused. He held up two fingers as if he were pinching something small. "A... tiny fruit?"

I laughed. "No. That's one definition of the word. But a 'date' can also be when two people go out to a play or something together, and then have dinner—just like we're doing."

"Oh. Then I guess we are doing a date."

"We say '*on* a date.' But it isn't really a date if it's just two friends. 'Date' has the implication that we're romantically interested in each other—or hope to be."

Dalsing took a sip of a dark, coffee-like liquid and gave me a mischievous smile. In the flickering light of the brazier, he looked vaguely demonic… very *sexy* and demonic. The kind of demon who could definitely tempt me to sin. "Then are we on a date or not?"

I stopped nibbling. "I… don't know. We're two different species…."

"Two compatible species," he replied. "Not that you and I would be capable of breeding. But… breeding is possible between our species."

"Really?" I had a sudden idea what that might mean and narrowed my eyes at him. I was picturing a lot of B sci-fi horror movies I'd seen, as well as a bunch of supposedly true abduction stories. "You mean you—your species—has raped human women?"

He knew what *that* word meant. I could see it in his eyes. "I have raped no one. And I am not aware of anyone on this ship forcing sexual intercourse with one of your species. But my female human friend—her name was Maria—had a *ba-ti* lover when she lived on my planet. They produced two children."

"I apologize. The stories I've read about… alien encounters… often involve the aliens doing sexual things to us while we're semiconscious."

Dalsing sighed and put his drink down. Then he surprised me by reaching around the brazier and placing a hand over the one I was resting on the table. "I cannot say whether these things have happened with other Alzhen exploratory teams, but I will not allow it. I confess, my team has run tests on human subjects that were probably not pleasant to them. Not all of our scientists are convinced of your intelligence—they regard humans the same way many humans regard apes—and many believe wiping your memories after the tests is sufficient. I am sorry for this. I have tried to convince them to be more… humane. But they have not known humans as I have."

"You just said Maria lived on your planet, among your people."

Dalsing removed his hand from mine and leaned back. I instantly missed the warmth of his palm, and I couldn't help but notice the *shiri* on the back of his hand flickering slightly. "Maria used to jokingly refer to herself as Pocahontas. Do you know the reference?"

"Pocahontas was a Native American—one of the indigenous people of my country who lived there before my ancestors came to it. There's a story about her pleading for the life of a man named John Smith when her father wanted to kill him. Though I think that's considered to be a myth."

Dalsing nodded. "According to Maria, Pocahontas traveled to the continent of Europe and became very popular in the royal courts. But despite her popularity, she was still regarded as something exotic, a curiosity. None of the Europeans considered her to be as... sophisticated... as they were. Maria often felt this way on our planet. She was charming and well-liked by my people, but they regarded her as, in her words, 'a talking monkey.'"

"Did you see her that way?" I asked.

"No. I saw her as a fascinating and intelligent friend, as did Qitsing, her mate. But we remain a minority."

I lifted my own glass, wondering at the technology that had kept it piping hot while we ate and talked. I supposed batteries could do it, though I preferred to think it was some incomprehensible alien tech. Perhaps I wasn't immune to the attraction to the exotic that Dalsing had been describing. "So... are you saying you find me attractive? Or is it just that it would be hot to screw an alien?"

He laughed. Then he leaned forward and fixed me with his gaze. The odd metallic hue of his irises seemed to be shimmering, though perhaps it was just the flames in the brazier between us. "Perhaps my long friendship with Maria has opened me to the possibility of mating with someone of your species, but I have met many of you in the seventy-five years I've been stationed in your system. Some of the men were attractive, but of those I conversed with, most were uninteresting. Some did seem unintelligent, insisting I was a 'commie spy' or 'government spook,' despite my efforts to persuade them otherwise. I never learned what those terms meant, at any rate. Others were simply too frightened to speak coherently."

"Being abducted by extraterrestrials is a lot to wrap your head around," I said, feeling defensive about my fellow humans.

"I understand," Dalsing said with a nod. "But you are different. You share Maria's inquisitiveness—she was a scientist herself, an anthropologist—and our conversation has been most satisfying."

I snorted. "I'm no scientist. I barely made it through algebra."

"Nonetheless, you are intelligent and interesting. And physically... yes, you are very attractive to me."

I took a deep breath and met his gaze. "I guess I'd have to say I'm attracted to you too. It just seems... we've only known each other for one day...."

"I think I understand. Maria often said Alzhen moved very fast in their approach to sex."

I shook my head and smirked. "I wouldn't say humans are necessarily slower. I mean, not if all we're looking for is a quick fuck. But I've kind of outgrown the quick fuck thing. It's fun, but it usually leaves me feeling lonely and depressed afterward...."

Dalsing regarded me thoughtfully, his brow furrowed with concern. "I fear I haven't been clear. I have enjoyed our conversation very much. I have enjoyed sharing my culture with you and learning more about yours. I am also erotically attracted to you. If you would like to have sex with me, I would like that also. But if it will make you unhappy, I do not want it."

"Sorry," I said quickly. "I didn't mean to get maudlin. Yes, I would love to have sex with you. How could I pass up the opportunity to have sex with an extraterrestrial? I'd never forgive myself. I understand we aren't going to run off to Alpha Centauri together, and I'm okay with that. I won't be sad. I promise."

I suspected I was lying, but he didn't need to know that. He couldn't live on my world, and I doubted I'd want to live on his, though I did find it fascinating. And how do you manage a long-distance relationship when the distance separating you is measured in light-years? I still had no idea how they traveled from one solar system to another. For all I knew, it would be decades before we saw each other again, if that ever happened.

Dalsing blinked at me. "Alpha Centauri doesn't have any habitable planets."

"Just… fuck me."

Chapter Ten

Dalsing changed the setting back to the forest, though there was no stage now, and it was night. Small fireflies flitted through the clearing, and high overhead two reddish moons hung in the sky. A warm breeze caressed our skin, and the scent of cinnamon reached my nose. Perhaps some of those red flowers were blooming nearby.

Dalsing was already naked, so he stretched out upon the grass and waited for me to join him. The situation felt a little awkward, since I'd begun to get used to him walking around like that, and the absence of genitalia made him seem almost clothed. After all, I'd seen plenty of movies with aliens or superheroes or whatever who didn't appear all that different—except for the multiple nipples. But it wasn't like I'd never had sex before. So I shucked the robe, my only article of clothing, and lay down beside him.

The grass was soft and cool against my skin, and I stretched, luxuriating in it. "Mmm… I could get used to this."

"Perhaps we can visit this place on my world someday," he said, moving closer. "May I touch your skin?"

I was intrigued by the idea of visiting his world, but I let that slide by for now. "Please."

He ran his fingers over my chest, stopping briefly to tug gently on my chest hair. I didn't have much, by human standards, but he had none at all.

I laughed. "That tickles."

"It's fascinating," he said. "I have always found your *hair* interesting. It doesn't appear to keep you warm, as it does with other species on your planet."

"We have a lot of things in our bodies that might be holdovers from ancient times—body hair, the appendix, fingernails… I don't know much about it. I think it's interesting that you don't have any hair at all."

"Would you like to touch me?"

I didn't need any further prompting. I rolled toward him, and we lay side by side for a time, just running our hands along each other's bodies, exploring. I rubbed the top of his bald head and drew a thumb along the ridges above his eyes, where humans usually have eyebrows. His skin otherwise felt human. I think I'd been afraid it might feel lizard-like or something, but that wasn't the case. In the warm air, I even felt a trace of sweat. I was fascinated by the plated appearance of his back. It resembled armor, but the plates slipped easily underneath his warm skin. I suspected they were like human ribs, but broader and heavier.

At last, I gave in to what I'd being wanting to do for hours—I traced the lines of his *shiri*, causing them to phosphoresce a warm orange. On an impulse, I leaned forward and drew my tongue along one that formed a trail from his shoulder to his elbow. I liked the taste of his skin. His sweat lent a slight saltiness to it, just as human sweat did, but underneath that was a faint, musky taste that was very masculine.

He drew his breath in sharply as the *shiri* turned a bright red, and I felt a slight tingle in my tongue, as if those shimmering lights were electrical.

"I'm sorry," I said. "Was that too familiar?"

His mouth quirked up at one corner. "It was… nice. We are very sensitive there."

"I have this perverse desire to lick all of them," I confessed, hoping I wasn't sounding… I wasn't sure. Too aggressive, maybe. But that one lick had given me a huge boner.

"Please. I would like that very much."

So I did. I loved the way the *shiri* responded to my licking, flickering under my tongue until his entire body was streaked with lines of red light. And the way it felt on my tongue was mesmerizing. I just hoped it wasn't some kind of drug I was ingesting. Overdosing during sex would be embarrassing, never mind the health risks. I raised my head to ask him about it but discovered he was in the middle of what looked like an orgasm. His head was tilted back, and his breathing was coming in short gasps.

Suddenly, he groaned and arched his back. "I… I'm going to…."

Then his crotch kind of popped, and his cock emerged. It's difficult to describe, but it reminded me of a swordfish breaching the surface of the ocean, arcing up in the air in a graceful curve. Though of course it stayed there, once it was out. This close up, I could see it was neither circumcised nor uncircumcised—it just didn't have a foreskin. Which made sense, now that I thought about it. Why would it need one? It was protected at all times, except when he wanted to have sex.

It was wet, as if covered in some kind of natural lubrication. Otherwise, as I'd observed with the two actors in the play, it looked like a human cock, and a very nice one at that. I'm not a size queen, but it was moderately large and thick, which I found appealing, and just... beautiful. Some cocks are lumpy and not terribly attractive to me, but Dalsing's was smooth and graceful and just a work of art.

"Now I'm jealous," I said.

"Why?"

"Because that looked like it felt *really* good."

He laughed and looked at me with half-closed lids. "It does."

"Can I touch it?"

"Please. But I'd like to touch yours as well."

So we sixty-nined for a bit. The moisture that covered his cock's surface, including his balls, was very much like precome and just a bit sweet. I loved it. But he was doing too good a job sucking on my cock, and I was afraid I was about to explode. I was also afraid *he* would explode. I didn't want that to happen—not until he'd buried that beautiful cock in my ass. I'd meant it when I told him to fuck me.

I pulled away and rotated my body so we were face-to-face again. We hadn't actually kissed yet. I guess I'd been nervous about it. What if he had multiple tongues? Or weird alien breath? But now I was too worked up to care about any of that, and I took his mouth with mine, devouring him with fervor. Fortunately his breath smelled like the flowers we'd eaten at dinner—like cinnamon—and the tongue that wrestled with mine felt "normal" enough. I almost laughed at the thought that anything I was doing right now fell into the category of "normal."

I pulled away for a second.

"Do you... does your species practice anal sex?" I asked breathlessly.

"You mean inserting my *tisha*—" He gripped his cock to illustrate. "—into another *ba-ti*'s—man's—*golsha*?" He lifted one leg and pointed again. I couldn't see the opening in question from this angle, but I knew what he meant.

"Um... I know it doesn't sound appealing, when you describe it like that...."

He laughed again. "Yes. We do. Would you like to do that to me?"

That was an interesting idea. But I shook my head. "Maybe some other time, but right now I really want to feel you inside me."

"I would be happy to go inside you."

I grimaced. It was odd how slight differences in wording could change the tone so much. "The term we use is 'fuck.' At least, when we're horny and being a little crude. I want you to fuck me."

"Then I will fuck you."

We didn't have any lube, but that didn't seem to matter. He produced his own. And the sleek design of his cock allowed it to slide in with next to no preparation. It was amazing. We fucked face-to-face with me lying on the grass, my ankles over his shoulders, and he penetrated me deeply with every thrust.

"Go faster," I breathed.

Dalsing picked up his rhythm until he was slamming into my ass harder than I'd ever let anyone else do it. But he seemed to fit so perfectly, I couldn't get enough of it. I'd never been particularly noisy in bed, either, but I couldn't stop myself from gasping in pleasure with every thrust. My own cock was dripping so much, the precome was forming a trail down my side.

When he came, I felt his cock moving inside me, squirting over and over again. I'd never felt a man come that much. It went on and on without stopping, while Dalsing's entire body went rigid. His eyes were squeezed shut and his mouth was set in a grimace, but his *shiri* were lit up like strings of lights on a Christmas tree.

I watched his face in fascination and felt him filling me, so enthralled I forgot I hadn't yet attended to my own orgasm. My body was tingling all over, and my cock was painfully hard, but I didn't think to touch it. Then Dalsing exhaled a long breath and opened his eyes. He gazed down at me with a kind of dopey, fully sated smile on his face.

Then he seemed to realize the state I was in, and his eyes widened. "What about you? What should I do for you?" He gripped my cock, perhaps intending to jack me off.

But that was all it took. I grunted and shot so far it splattered against my chin and neck and then continued to douse my chest and stomach. I didn't come anywhere near as much as he had, but it was a damned good come. One for the scrapbooks.

Chapter Eleven

We cleaned up, and then we must have drifted off, because I woke to another one of those damned chimes. Dalsing grumbled and unwrapped his arms from my torso in order to sit up. At some point the forest had vanished, and we were now lying on a bed. I suspected it might be a real bed, and that the virtual reality program had simply shut off while we slept.

"Is the ship going to flip over again?" I asked sleepily.

"No. We're approaching Saturn. We must prepare for the attack."

My grogginess vanished, and I sat bolt upright. "What do we do?"

"You do nothing," he said, giving me a kiss on the cheek and then climbing out of the bed. "There is nothing you *can* do."

I knew that was true, but it still galled me to sit around on my ass while Dalsing and his people risked their lives to rescue my friend. I also knew that wasn't their sole purpose, but Dalsing had promised he'd bring Cody back alive—if he *was* still alive.

Oh God. Cody....

"You must not leave these quarters while I'm gone," Dalsing said sternly. "My crew knows you are here, so if something happens to me, someone will come for you. You will not be allowed to starve."

That alarmed me for a number of reasons. Now I was not only picturing myself clawing at the door, desperate for food while the Alzhen outside ignored my scraping, I was picturing Dalsing *dead*. The first was probably unlikely. I hoped. But the second....

"Just how dangerous is this?" I asked.

He gave me a look that suggested I might not be nearly as intelligent as he'd previously thought. "I will be leading the advance into the Karazhen base. One of the advances, at any rate. They will, of course, resist us. And the Karazhen warriors are quite lethal."

He leaned down to kiss me again, this time on the mouth. I wondered if he'd have to brush his teeth to get rid of my germs before speaking with his crew. Probably. On the other hand, one would hope Alzhen brushed their teeth in the morning, regardless of alien cooties....

"Look," I said, trying to be reasonable, "I know you have to do this. It's the only chance Cody has—"

Dalsing startled me by gripping my shoulders fiercely. "This is not about your friend. You need to understand that. I want to rescue him, for your sake, but if we cannot find him in a reasonable amount of time...."

"What?" I wasn't sure I wanted to know the answer.

"We have to blow the base up. It aids the Karazhen in their travels to and from this system, and we suspect there is also a scientific outpost there. Under no circumstances can any physical traces of their research or any of their scientists be allowed to survive."

I'd been right. I didn't want to know the answer. But there was a brutal logic to it. This was about the survival of the Alzhen. One human life was ultimately insignificant, even if they hoped they could save him.

"Do you… do you even know what Cody looks like?" I asked weakly.

"No."

"I don't have any pictures…." Perhaps I'd had one in my wallet—I wasn't sure—but that was hundreds of millions of miles away now.

"We will try to rescue any humans we find."

"Could you broadcast an image to me or something, if you find human prisoners?"

"Why? Wouldn't you want us to rescue them all?"

"Well, of course. But…." I didn't want to say it out loud, but if they were running out of time, and there were a hundred human prisoners… I wanted to make sure Cody was one of the ones who got out.

Perhaps Dalsing knew what I was thinking. "We will try to rescue all humans we come across. That is the best I can promise. I'm sorry."

"What if I could *see*?" I persisted. "You must have… dash cam technology, or something like that...."

"What is a dash cam?"

"A small camera that attaches to… well, it would be more like your helmet or clothing, if you intend to wear any—"

"I will be wearing armor."

"Exactly! So you'd have a camera attached to it, and I could see what you're seeing while I stay back here on the ship. Then, if you come across Cody, I could tell you!"

Dalsing held up a hand to stop my rambling. "Have you been to war?" he asked.

"No."

"Are you certain you wish to see it?"

IT WAS horrifying. I knew it would be, and Dalsing had warned me, but no amount of discussing it could have prepared me.

I, of course, was perfectly safe, watching from his quarters in total comfort, but the technology of his holographic projector—or whatever it was—put me in the middle of it. It was more than watching a flat image on a screen. I was *there*, running through the corridors of the Karazhen base, surrounded by armored Alzhen soldiers, though I was unable to actually do anything. The camera was mounted on Dalsing's helmet, at roughly eye level, so I saw everything from his point of view, but I was powerless to affect what I saw. He moved where he needed to move, and I seemed to be floating in the air, drifting along with him.

In point of fact, I *was* floating in the air. The ship was no longer accelerating through space, so I was drifting in microgravity, along with everyone on board. Fortunately Dalsing had given me another dose of the antinausea medication before he left.

The Alzhen camera had an advantage over our technology, in that I saw everything in the space around him in all directions, and I could look places he wasn't necessarily looking. I could talk to him, to alert him if I saw Cody, but he'd made me swear to keep my mouth shut otherwise. If I kept jabbering at him or screamed whenever something came out of the shadows, he could be endangered by the distraction.

It wasn't easy to stay quiet. The Karazhen base was like a horror movie set. It was really more of a nest than a base. They'd tunneled out a network of tubes in the bottom of the deepest crater of Janus, Saturn's tenth moon. These tubes had no flat surfaces to speak of, being roughly cylindrical and coated with a thick layer of webbing. They wormed their way deep into the moon's icy crust, crisscrossing haphazardly, with no rhyme or reason I could determine, unlit and seemingly empty.

The Alzhen themselves would have given me nightmares, if I hadn't known what they were. Their pressurized armor suits didn't resemble the suits I'd seen and worn. The heads were covered by low black domes that were transparent from the inside but not the outside. Dalsing had assured me the material was as strong as thick steel. The bodies of the suits were heavily armored with interlocking plates on the back and chest, and the arms and legs appeared to have pneumatic pistons strengthening the joints. This was confirmed when the Alzhen came across a doorway that was sealed by a metal partition. They sliced through it with lasers, and then two men grabbed ahold of the pieces with their gloved hands to wrench it open.

Janus did have gravity—about one-tenth that of Earth. Which meant that, although the Alzhen were very light by comparison to their weight aboard the ship, they weren't in freefall. There was a definite "up" and "down," and unfortunately the Karazhen hadn't built the tunnels with that in mind. In places tunnels turned abruptly downward, creating a pit that would have killed anyone jumping down it, even in that low gravitational field. This required the Alzhen to belay down on cables.

The first attack came very suddenly, as Dalsing and his team dropped to the bottom of a particularly deep pit. The Karazhen came at them from all sides, and it was all I could do to keep myself from screaming in terror. They were hideous creatures, larger than a man, whose bodies seemed to be made of swords and knives, somehow held together by pinkish-gray tendons and tufts of gray bristles. If they had eyes, I couldn't see them. They moved swiftly, with their multiple legs stabbing furiously at the ground in a blur like mechanical sewing machines.

They were upon the Alzhen so fast, one man was literally shredded before he could raise his weapon. Then I could make sense of nothing for a while as jagged legs, laser blasts, and spurts of Alzhen blood and Karazhen ichor filled my vision. The monsters came from above as well as the sides, skittering down the vertical tube above the Alzhen warriors with ease. The Alzhen appeared to be adept at blasting them into fragments of bone and slime, but the creatures kept coming, and there was nowhere to retreat.

There was no atmosphere in the tunnels to carry sound, so the nightmare was utterly silent, except for Dalsing's frantic breathing and muttered exclamations. I couldn't understand a word until he whipped around several times, his gun at the ready, and said in English, clearly for my benefit, "I think that's the last of them… for now."

I realized I was whimpering, so I swallowed and said weakly, "I'm sorry. I'll be quiet."

"I am glad you are safe."

Then he seemed to forget about me as he barked out orders over the com link and the others responded. Dalsing walked among the wreckage of bodies, and I counted silently to myself. Sixty-five dead Karazhen... and eighteen dead Alzhen, torn to pieces, their skin and blood already frozen where it was exposed to the vacuum of space. I'd never seen a sight that sickening before—not outside of a horror movie. These were *real*. They were *people*, even if they were a different species than I was. I began to get tunnel vision, so I had to close my eyes for a minute. My stomach was threatening to heave.

There were only forty-two people still alive on Dalsing's team. If they went up against a few more attacks like that, I didn't see how they could possibly survive.

Chapter Twelve

Somehow Dalsing's team survived a dozen more encounters with the Karazhen, though the losses were heavy. No one battle cost them as much as that first one—perhaps because the Karazhen had thrown the bulk of their forces at the intruders and were now reduced to smaller skirmishes throughout the base—but Alzhen warriors continued to fall. There were only sixteen still alive as they drew near what seemed to be the heart of the base.

The Alzhen came to a door with a window in it. When Dalsing looked through it, there was another door just a short distance away.

"An airlock," he told me. He said something I couldn't understand to his crew and then stepped back. While they gathered around the door, he said in English, "The Karazhen warriors do not breathe oxygen. They metabolize salt water and are able to store some reserves in their bodies for a considerable amount of time. This allows them to operate outside the pressurized zones of the base and conserves resources."

I had actually been wondering about that. The Karazhen didn't look very technological. How could they build spaceships and bases in the first place? Did they even have hands? Since we had a quiet moment, and he'd been speaking to me, I ventured to ask about that.

"These are the warriors," he replied. "Savage, lethal, and coordinated but not particularly intelligent. The ruling class and scientists are quite different."

In a couple of minutes, the Alzhen had cut through the outer door of the lock, but they'd set up some kind of force field at the entrance, which glowed with a cold blue light. The Alzhen walked through it without a problem, but I guessed it somehow kept air in. I couldn't ask about it, because Dalsing was occupied again, but it wasn't really important for me to know.

When the Alzhen blew the door on the other side of the lock—they didn't bother to cut through it—they were immediately set upon by more of the Karazhen warriors. Fortunately they dispatched these without any losses on their side.

The first room was very different from the tunnels on the other side of the airlock. There was no doubt the equipment there had been created by a technologically advanced race—more advanced than humans. They had interstellar travel, after all. I had no idea what any of the equipment did, but it didn't seem to be relevant to Dalsing's mission. After a brief look around, he and his team proceeded to the next room.

They went through several rooms like this, sometimes finding nothing, other times coming across a token resistance. But nothing like the first attack.

"This makes me nervous," Dalsing told me quietly. "They are holding back, amassing for one final strike. And we could easily be trapped in these rooms."

Jesus. That was the last thing I wanted to hear. But it was impossible for me to be more terrified for him than I already was.

Then the team entered the specimen room.

That's the best name I can think of for it. The room was an enormous cavern, containing row upon row of sealed pods with clear glass panels on top. There were various illuminated displays and rows of LEDs throughout the room, but most of the light came from the pods themselves, shining up through the panels from their interiors. And thanks to the three-dimensional panoramic view the camera on Dalsing's helmet gave me, I could look down into the pods, even when he was facing in a different direction. What I saw sickened me. Naked human beings—mostly *dead* human beings, in various stages of decay. Of the corpses that were still recognizable, many showed the ravages of horrific, disfiguring diseases. Others had been cut or burned.

Dalsing had been right. The Karazhen were experimenting on us.

"This one is still alive," Dalsing told me, as he peered into one of the pods.

It wasn't Cody. The young man inside the pod looked barely out of high school. The thought that, if I told the truth, he might be abandoned to die alone in this alien death camp, probably enduring unimaginable torment at their hands, nearly prevented me from speaking. But I was the only champion Cody had, and I couldn't let him down. "I… I hope you can save him," I said, at last. "But he's not Cody."

Dalsing barked a command into his com link. "I've told them to fan out and locate every survivor. We must do this quickly."

We looked at over a dozen of them and failed to find Cody. They were all unconscious inside their prisons, awaiting a miserable fate or, at best, a quick death. The Alzhen had been planting explosives throughout the tunnels and inside the pressurized part of the base. They were primed to go off at a signal from the ship, as soon as Dalsing's team had retreated.

It occurred to me that Dalsing could kill those survivors I was forced to admit weren't Cody. At least, that would assure they were put out of their misery. But I couldn't even suggest such a thing. I clung to the hope they might still be saved, somehow.

We hadn't examined even half the pods when someone shouted over Dalsing's com link. I spun around to see… *things* moving in the shadows at the far end of the chamber. Things with seemingly millions of sharp blades stabbing at the floor, scurrying between the pods. Karazhen warriors. I whipped around, but they were coming from all sides now, flooding into the chamber through the doors at either end and rapidly spreading out. All avenues of retreat were cut off.

"*Fuck!*"

If Dalsing heard my exclamation, he didn't acknowledge it. There was no need. He saw exactly what I saw and probably knew better what the odds of survival were. I watched helplessly as he shouted commands to his team and blasted the Karazhen bearing down on him. Off to his left, an Alzhen who might have been his second-in-command was torn in two. In this pressurized chamber, the battle wasn't silent. I heard the explosions of the lasers, the chilling screeching of the Karazhen, and even more horrifying, the screams of Alzhen warriors being sliced to ribbons.

The odds seemed hopeless. It was hard to see in the darkness, but there seemed to be *hundreds* of Karazhen. And there were so few Alzhen left. I was tempted to close my eyes against it, but I forced myself to stay alert. There might be nothing I could do, but I refused to stick my head in the sand while Dalsing and his team might be facing their last moments.

When one of the hideous bugs leapt at Dalsing from behind, I violated our agreement and shouted, "Behind you!"

Dalsing whipped around and cut the thing in half with his laser.

Then I saw something where the creature had been—a pod we hadn't looked at yet. All I could see, at first, was a tuft of unruly dark brown hair. But I moved in my virtual bubble to get a closer look. It was

Cody, looking ghastly in the bluish light inside the pod. He might have been alive; he might have been dead. I had no way of knowing.

"That's him!" I exclaimed.

Then, with a horrible screech and what seemed like a thousand flailing, swordlike legs, the world tumbled around me and went black.

Dalsing had been hit.

Chapter Thirteen

I DON'T know how long I was trapped in Dalsing's living quarters. It might have been a few days, though it seemed like weeks. The "gravity" returned, which meant we were traveling again, but I had no idea where we were going. To Earth? To Dalsing's home planet?

At first I tried to obey his directive to stay inside, no matter what happened. He'd assured me I wouldn't be allowed to starve to death, hadn't he? But after I'd slept several times, and still nobody had come to let me out or even spoken to me through any kind of sound system, I decided I couldn't risk the possibility that I'd been forgotten. I donned the protective suit before leaving—I wasn't a total asshole—but I knew the outside of the suit would be contaminated by my touch.

I discovered a small room in the back of the bathroom that basically operated like a shower, though it had more of that weird water-like substance that vanished shortly after it touched me. It sprayed against the outside of the suit, but as it trickled down my body, it disappeared. The floor remained dry.

That would have to do.

It turned out to all be for nothing, however. Nothing I did got that goddamned door-iris-thingy to dilate and let me through. I was trapped.

I wasn't starving. The computer was apparently set to provide food and water at regular intervals, because containers kept appearing on the small table near the bed. So I ate, drank, relieved myself in the bathroom occasionally, and slept a lot. Eventually, when I could no longer stand the smell of my armpits, I tentatively stuck a finger under the shower spray. It didn't make my skin dissolve, so I risked dousing my entire body. It cleaned me better than soap and water, and I suspect it killed the bacteria that makes underarms smell, because I didn't have any underarm odor at all for a day or so after that.

At some point I heard the chimes sounding, and only remembered what it was signaling a split second before the ship turned over. Once again I somehow managed not to fly all over the room, and neither did the objects resting on tabletops and other surfaces. I did, however, upchuck on myself this time, forcing me to make another foray into the shower.

All this time, I fretted about the fate of Dalsing and Cody, and sometimes I cried over them. It seemed likely they were both dead. Even if Dalsing had somehow survived, he probably hadn't been in any shape to rescue Cody. He might not have even heard my shout.

If Cody hadn't been rescued, I prayed the Alzhen had blown up the entire base. Better that than to leave him in the... pincers... of those hideous monsters.

I WOKE to noise coming from the corridor outside the doorway. It sounded for all the world like somebody was doing construction out there—drilling or riveting and metal scraping against metal. I leaped out of the bed and ran to the door.

"Hey!" I shouted, pounding on it.

Everything went silent for a moment. Then a voice, muffled by the door, said, "Eyvreeteeng... ees... ohkay. Poot... awn... yoo-ur... soot."

After I'd sussed that out, I went into the bathroom and returned a short time later dressed in the suit. I'd even showered for good measure.

I had to wait a long time. Long enough that I was forced to choose between taking the goddamned suit off again, so I could relieve myself, or testing out its supposed ability to handle liquid waste. I finally decided I'd rather leave with a damp crotch than delay leaving by a single second. I wanted *out. Now.*

Luckily, Dalsing hadn't exaggerated the suit's ability to handle bodily functions. After the deed was done, I didn't feel any dampness down there at all.

Eventually, the door dilated, and an Alzhen in an isolation suit stepped inside. "Cohm... weet... mee."

He led me out into a small airlock that hadn't been there when Dalsing brought me into his quarters. When both doors were closed, we were sprayed down and illuminated with blue light. Then the outer door opened, and we stepped out into the corridor. I would have been delighted to escape my temporary prison, but the fact that I was tightly wrapped up in the suit put a damper on that. I doubted I'd be allowed to remove it again unless I was either back in Dalsing's quarters or the room I'd occupied earlier, which was far smaller.

Even though there had to have been more than one Alzhen working on the airlock, no one greeted us in the corridor. I followed my guide into the elevator and down a level. After a few twists and turns, we entered a corridor bustling with activity, and at last we came to a large complex that appeared to be an infirmary. We passed through numerous glass sliding doors, and on either side of us, there were rooms with Alzhen lying in beds or, more disturbing, floating in midair. Perhaps they were suspended in some kind of force field. I didn't really care. If we were in a hospital, that meant we had to be on our way to see either Dalsing or Cody, and that was all I could process. My stomach was in knots.

When I tried to ask my guide about it, all I got was "Faw… loh… mee."

Ugh. I decided then that, if I *was* being taken to the Alzhen planet, I would have to learn their language. Listening to them mutilate English for much longer would drive me insane. Of course, I'd probably end up mutilating Alzhenese or whatever it was called, but turnabout was fair play.

We entered a less frenetic wing of the hospital, where the patients seemed to be in worse shape than the ones we'd passed. Most were unconscious. Many were bandaged so much, hardly any skin could be seen. I had a very bad feeling about it.

At last my guide stopped at a closed door and turned to face me. "Doo… noht… bee… lawn-guh." Then he gestured to the door. Apparently he intended to wait outside.

Nervously, I stepped forward, and the door opened with a faint puffing sound, as if the air inside was at a slightly different pressure from the air in the corridor—but not enough to warrant an airlock. The room beyond was dark, although a dim light illuminated a bed with an Alzhen *ba-ti* lying in it. I hadn't grown so accustomed to the Alzhen gender distinctions that I could tell a *ba-ti* from a *ba* when the Alzhen was covered by a blanket, but there was little difficulty in this case.

It was Dalsing.

Chapter Fourteen

I STEPPED inside the room, and the door constricted. Then a hiss informed me air was being pumped back in to readjust the pressure. I'd read once that Earth astronauts sometimes had to accustom themselves to working at a slightly lower pressure than sea level on Earth. Perhaps the Alzhen on board the spaceship were doing the same thing, but the pressure was increased in some of the hospital rooms to aid the patients' recovery. I'd have to ask about it some other time.

At the moment I had other concerns. Dalsing looked awful. As I approached his bedside, I could see his head and the left side of his face were covered by something resembling sky-blue plastic, and the eye that peered back at me was cloudy, as if he were heavily drugged. His left arm below the elbow was *missing*.

"My God," I said quietly.

His eye blinked several times, and he smiled faintly. "I needed to see you. I am sorry if the sight of me is disturbing."

"Don't be ridiculous!" I said, irritated. "I'm not some delicate little flower." He looked confused by that, so I added, "I'm worried about you. That's all that matters to me right now."

"Thank you." He sighed and closed his eyes. I was afraid he'd slipped into unconsciousness, but when I said his name softly, he opened them again. "Please take off your helmet," he whispered.

"Won't your doctors have a fit if I do?"

"I do not care. Please… I want to see your face."

I reached up and popped the seal around the neck of the suit, praying I wouldn't be exposing him to any germs his body couldn't handle. We'd made love, and as far as I knew he hadn't suffered any unpleasant consequences from that intimate contact, but he was so weak now….

I remembered, as I removed the helmet, that I hadn't actually had time to wash my hair that morning before I'd been escorted out of his quarters. It was probably sticking up all over the place.

But he smiled again. "Of all the humans I have seen in the past seventy-five years, you are the most beautiful."

"Sweet-talker."

"I want to feel your skin against mine," he said softly.

He was in absolutely no condition to have sex, but I didn't think that was really what he wanted anyway. He just wanted contact, affection. Unfortunately I had no idea how to get the gloves off the isolation suit, if that was even possible. So instead I leaned down and pressed my cheek to the right side of his face. It was warm and soft, and when he sighed gently into my ear, I found myself growing hard. The warmth that had flooded through me when we'd made love swelled in my chest again.

"You can't die," I whispered. "We're just getting to know each other."

"I know."

When at last I pulled away, his *shiri* were glowing scarlet. "Thank you," he said. "But I didn't bring you here just for selfish reasons. I need to tell you about your friend…."

I took a breath, steeling myself for the news. "Is he…? Is he dead?"

"No," Dalsing replied. His head moved slightly, as if he'd wanted to shake it but was unable to. "He is… not well. But he is alive. I was able to identify him to my people, after the battle… before I lost consciousness. Kaising will take you to him when you leave here."

I assumed Kaising was my guide. Dalsing seemed to be struggling to talk, however, so I didn't waste his time clarifying that point.

"Will *you*… recover?" I asked, my voice breaking on the final word. I glanced at the stump where his arm had been and then looked quickly away.

"I do not know…."

I planted a kiss on his lips, and then another on his forehead. "Listen," I told him. "I don't know if they're taking me back to Earth or not. But I'm not leaving. I refuse. I'm not going anywhere until you're better."

What would happen after that, I had no idea. But I couldn't go the rest of my life not knowing whether Dalsing was alive or not.

He didn't argue. He smiled and said, "I will not let anyone force you to leave me."

OVER THE next several hours, with the help of Kaising, I learned something of that final battle with the Karazhen. I won't report the entire conversation, since it was torturously slow.

Most of Dalsing's team had perished in that attack, but one of the last commands he'd managed to give before losing consciousness was a call for a retrieval team. The new team was small, and they had to retrace the route Dalsing's team had taken, but fortunately they encountered little resistance. They barely made it in time, but with their help, the last five members of Dalsing's team managed to destroy what turned out to be the final wave of Karazhen in the base. Dalsing and three others were transported to the ship for medical care, one dying before she reached the ship. The base had been blown up as soon as we'd left orbit.

All the living human subjects had been retrieved, to my intense relief, though some had died in the meantime. There were twenty-seven still alive. A few might not survive much longer.

But Cody's prognosis was good. He was being kept in a stasis tube similar to the ones I'd seen in the Karazhen base, but of Alzhen design. He was unconscious, and he looked ghastly, floating naked in some kind of amber fluid like a fetal pig in a specimen jar. Only the constantly fluctuating displays nearby indicated he was still alive. I couldn't read the displays, of course, but Kaising told me the values were good. And he didn't appear to have been cut up like some of the others. I gathered he'd been infected with some kind of virus, but the Alzhen doctors had already cured him of it. Now his body just needed time to recover.

I found the young man I'd first seen when Dalsing examined the pods in the base. He was alive, and again Kaising assured me he would survive. I was relieved not to have his death on my conscience.

But I had to wonder what was in store for him when he woke at last—what was in store for all of them. Including Cody. A lifetime of waking up screaming in the night? Insanity? Doctors, psychologists, and hospitals—an array of antipsychotics and antidepressants? Suicide?

Oh, Cody....

Maybe the memory-wipe thing was a good idea after all. But as Dalsing and I had discussed, that didn't always seem to work. I didn't know what the answer was.

I just knew I hated the Karazhen with every part of my being.

Chapter Fifteen

I'D BEEN wrong about them taking us back to Earth. If that had been the case, we would have reached Earth orbit while I was still locked in Dalsing's quarters. We were heading to Alzhen-Ai, which basically translates to "world of the Alzhen." Considering that the name of our planet is basically "dirt," and we call our moon "moon," I couldn't criticize their lack of originality.

I don't know what star system Alzhen-Ai was in—not from an Earth perspective. Kaising knew nothing of Earth astronomy. I gathered it was something like twenty-six light-years away. This meant that, even if the ship we were on could go as fast as the speed of light, we wouldn't get there until I was approaching sixty years old. That would have sucked.

Fortunately the Alzhen had figured out a shortcut long ago, or their exploration of solar systems would have been extremely slow. Again, I had no idea how it worked, but some kind of quantum jiggery-pokery let them skip through empty space as if it literally wasn't there. The upshot of this being that, by the time I found out we were on our way to Alzhen-Ai... we were already approaching orbit.

I went up to the lounge with Kaising and got my first look at an alien world—one that wasn't just a dead rock, at any rate. The enormous curved edge of Alzhen-Ai took up one half of the view through the dome, a beautiful blue-green planet streaked with white clouds, not unlike Earth. I was, in fact, looking at it as it seemed to roll away from us. The engines under my feet were swinging around to aim at the planet as we braked in orbit.

Dalsing had told me Alzhen-Ai was a bit larger than Earth, with a slightly higher gravity, though he assured me I would have no trouble adapting if I went to the surface. The air had some trace gases not found in Earth's atmosphere, but none that would harm me. Alzhen scientists speculated that the similarities between our planets might have led to our similar evolutionary paths, though some still clung to the belief that our species were "seeded" by an even more ancient race neither of us had yet encountered.

"If you believe that sort of thing," Dalsing had said, his tone making it clear he did not.

Unfortunately, even if I did want to visit the planet, that wouldn't occur for several weeks. Our ship was a plague ship. Not only were humans on board with all the myriad diseases and microscopic organisms we normally carried, but most of us were infected with unknown viruses designed to kill Alzhen. Doctors were flying up to the ship from the planet's surface in order to give medical aid to the survivors of the assault on Janus, and to assist with the isolation and study of the aforementioned superviruses, but until such time as they declared it safe, we were under strict planetary quarantine.

I made the mistake of asking Dalsing what would happen if one of the viruses proved resistant to treatment.

"Then," he said grimly, "they will have to destroy us."

I felt the blood drain from my face. "I suppose that makes sense. Even with the doctors on board—the ones who flew up from the surface?"

"Yes. Those medical personnel knew what they were volunteering for. The government cannot risk a deadly epidemic." He nodded toward the drinking bottle on the table, partially filled with more of that urine-yellow liquid. Apparently it was a nutrient mixture filled with vitamins, though knowing that didn't make it look any more appetizing. I held it up so he could drink from the spout. He sucked some down and then released the spout with a gasp, as if that simple act had exhausted him. "That is a last resort," he continued. "We need to know what the Karazhen have been working on, and we need defenses against it."

Another of those goddamn chimes sounded. I'd been learning to distinguish the different tones and what they meant. This one meant I had to leave. Under the care of his new doctors, Dalsing was recovering, but he was still very weak. He could sit up and talk to me now and then, but never for long.

"I'll see you tomorrow," I said, leaning over to kiss him. The fact that I still took my helmet off when I was in his room upset the staff, but Dalsing had insisted upon it, and even as wounded as he was, he could still throw his weight around.

He returned the kiss, nibbling my lower lip a bit before I pulled away. His *shiri* flickered dimly to life, and I couldn't resist licking the line of them along the bridge of his nose. I drew back, pleased to see that line shimmering with fire.

"Consider that a promise," I said huskily. "For when you're better."

As the resident human on the ship—and it probably didn't hurt that I was Dalsing's… whatever I was to him—I was consulted when some of the humans were considered safe to be released from their stasis pods. Apparently there was some concern about how my planet-mates might react when they awoke from their induced comas. God knew how long some of them had been unconscious. They could have been abducted by the Karazhen *decades* ago. Of course, there was no guarantee they all spoke English. I might not even be able to speak to them. But at least having a human around when they woke might keep them from flipping out a bit. The last thing they needed was to open their eyes and see an Alzhen in an isolation suit looming over them.

Because of my personal connection to him, Cody was brought out first. I had him taken to a holding cell like the one I'd first awoken in. Then, after they'd administered something to wake him, I asked the medical staff to wait outside.

They'd dressed him in a jumpsuit—something nobody had thought to offer me when I first came on board—and I was dressed in my isolation suit, minus the helmet, so I wouldn't freak him out. I'd have to be leaving eventually, so it made sense to wear it. Besides, I'd grown used to it by now.

It took a minute for him to come out of it. When he did, he screamed and sat bolt upright on the bed.

"Cody," I said quietly.

He jerked his head around at the sound of my voice, his eyes open wide in terror.

"It's okay, Cody. You're safe."

The first sound he made was an inarticulate scream as he flailed his arms in front of his face.

"Cody! Cody… it's okay. You're safe now. Nobody's going to hurt you."

After a minute he stopped screaming and began to rock back and forth, his arms still held in front of his face. He lowered his head until his forehead rested against his wrists and began to sob.

I knew it would be a mistake to touch him. I had no idea what I *should* do, but I continued to speak to him in a quiet, soothing tone of voice. I was afraid it was too late, that he was completely insane now. But after a long, long time of this, he said in a pitifully small voice, "Marc?"

"I'm here, Cody. You're safe."

"It couldn't have been a nightmare.... It felt.... It was *real*! I know it was real!"

"It was. I'm sorry. We got you out of there as soon as we could."

He wasn't really listening. He began wailing, "My God! My God! They cut... and they.... There were dead people.... Oh God! It hurt! It hurt so much!"

Chapter Sixteen

WE WERE in orbit around Alzhen-Ai for months, by Earth reckoning.

During that time, I learned to be something of a therapist for my fellow humans as they woke one by one. Not that I had any idea what I was doing. But they needed another human being to reach out to in a world that had gone completely insane—and I was it.

Some of them, perhaps, couldn't be saved. They never stopped crying and screaming long enough for me to talk to them. Worse, some of them kept clawing at themselves or hitting their heads against the wall. These people needed to be sedated. What would happen to them, if they didn't eventually come back to themselves, I didn't know. Others eventually calmed down and talked to me, or if they didn't know English, they'd write things down for me to take to the Alzhen translators. There were translators for most languages on Earth, it turned out. They would give me the English equivalent, and I'd give them answers to translate back into German or Swahili or whatever language the human spoke.

One of them—the teenage boy I'd first seen—just wanted to be held. It was a little awkward at first. The boy was American, I eventually learned, with a thick Texan accent. He was also younger than I'd thought. About sixteen. He wasn't gay—he wanted to make very sure I was clear on that point—but he had nightmares. And the only way he could calm down after the really bad ones was to wrap himself up in my arms, while I talked in a low, calm voice about stupid shit that had nothing to do with aliens and spaceships and outer space.

Cody eventually recovered enough for us to have conversations about what had happened, though he went into a panic attack, hyperventilating and cowering in the corner, when one of the Alzhen attempted to bring him food. It took me hours to calm him, and he made me promise to keep "them" away from him. From that point on, I brought his food in to him, making sure to leave my helmet in the airlock, as I did with all the others.

I tried to talk to him about the Alzhen, but it was hopeless. His experiences with the Karazhen had made him paranoid, even before he'd been taken to their base.

"You have to understand," I insisted, "these aren't the same people who experimented on you. The Alzhen *rescued* you."

"Why?" he asked, narrowing his eyes suspiciously.

"Because I asked them to. And because they're basically decent people."

"They're plotting something, Marc. I don't know what. But you can't buy into their bullshit."

"Cody...."

"How do you know they're what they tell you, Marc?" he demanded. "Huh? How do you know they aren't planning on taking over the world and farming us like goddamn cattle?"

I frowned at him. "Because they don't eat people. And I've gotten to know them, Cody. They aren't like the... bug creatures. Not at all." I refrained from mentioning some of the more "alien" things about the Alzhen, such as the fact that they let their children attend plays with beheadings and sexual intercourse in them. That was a cultural thing, I supposed. But by now I'd learned to trust them, at least as much as I trusted any group of people I'd known for less than a year. And I trusted Dalsing.

Cody just gave me a wide-eyed look and shook his head sadly. "You drank the Kool-Aid, man."

I gave up trying to persuade him the Alzhen weren't his enemies. Considering what he'd been through, I supposed I was lucky he hadn't gone completely insane. But I'd had to draw the line at his conviction that his food was poisoned. That had been one of our first arguments.

"Goddammit!" I snapped. "I'm not going to let you starve when there's perfectly good food sitting right in front of you! I know it looks weird, but I've eaten it a million times, and it hasn't done me any harm."

He glared at me. The Alzhen had shaved all the hair off his body to aid in the sterilization process, and now he looked like a pissed-off, younger Charles Manson, except for the absence of an upside-down cross tattooed on his forehead. "If you want me to eat it, you eat it first. Right in front of me. Every single thing on that tray."

"Christ!" I did what he asked, sampling a bit of everything, and had to do the same thing every day from that day on. He never got to trust me enough to just eat the fucking food.

OVER THOSE months, I found myself increasingly "going native." I was living in Dalsing's quarters, and as long as I wore my suit and went through the air lock sterilization procedure when I stepped out, I was free to roam about the ship. Apart from the medical bays, where some of the humans were still being kept in stasis and the medical staff struggled to analyze all the horrible things infesting their bodies, I wasn't prevented from accessing anything. I even wandered up into the command center occasionally.

With Dalsing's and Kaising's help, I began to learn the language, and the crew was patient with my attempts to communicate. They all knew me by now, and I was treated with indulgence, like a pet or a mascot. It soon became clear that they thought of me as belonging in some way to Dalsing. I wasn't sure if I should be concerned about that, but Dalsing assured me I wasn't his property.

"They know of my… fondness for you," he told me.

He was doing much better now, walking around his hospital room with no more than thin, semitransparent casings around his knees and on his hips to aid him. I gathered they were miniature hydraulic devices to reinforce his joints while they healed. Since he was otherwise naked, I could clearly see how he was healing, at least externally. He looked good. The plastic-like substance that had sealed the wounds on his head and face had been removed, and though there were scars, they weren't disfiguring. I actually thought they were kind of sexy.

"Fondness?" I asked. We hadn't really clarified what our relationship meant. After all, we'd only slept together once.

"I have told them you are my mate," he said casually. But he seemed to be watching me for a reaction.

"Humans don't really use that word about ourselves," I said. "We tend to think of animals as 'mating,' and humans as… well, a lot of things. What do you mean when you say it?"

He glanced at the floor uncomfortably and then walked unsteadily around the bed to come closer to me. "I intended no offense.…"

"I wasn't offended. I'd just like to know what you meant."

He lifted his face to look me in the eye. "I meant... we have engaged in sexual acts, and I have grown fond of you."

"How fond?"

"I do not understand the question."

I sighed but smiled at him. "How strong is this 'fond' feeling you have for me? Do you mean you enjoy sex with me and would like to do it again—?"

"Of course," he replied. Then he quickly added, "Though I would understand if you do not want to be... physically close to me now...."

I snorted and ducked in to kiss him on his scarred cheek, hoping my touch wouldn't hurt him. "If you have some dumb idea that I won't want to have sex with you because you're wounded, get rid of it. I'm *desperate* to have sex with you. As soon as your doctor says you're up to it, I'll throw myself down in front of you with my legs spread." I was pleased to see his *shiri* flash briefly at that. "But what I'm asking you is, do you think of me as more than just a sex toy? More than just a *friend*, even?"

He stepped forward, the hydraulics surrounding his joints making faint hissing sounds. His jaw was set and the uncertainty he'd displayed a moment ago was gone. He pinned me with his gaze. "I am uncertain what you mean by 'sex toy'—though I can guess. You are more to me than merely someone with whom I enjoy sex. I believe we are becoming friends, but if by that you mean a relationship without passion, I do not want to restrict it to that."

"We call friends who have sex 'friends with benefits,'" I said. "And that sounds good to me. But do you understand the English word 'love'?"

"I do," Dalsing replied without hesitation. "Our word is *ba-la*, but it is the same. And I feel it unfolding in me when you are near, or when I think of you."

I liked that idea. "Unfolding...."

"Yes." He raised his hand in a fist. "Our symbol for *ba-la* is the *shirsha* flower—we shared some the night we mated. Or 'had sex,' if you prefer. They smell beautiful when they blossom." He spread his fingers outward.

"You sly dog," I said, smirking at him. "Were you coming on to me when you served me those flowers as part of our dinner?" He cocked his head, clearly unable to parse my question. "Don't worry about it," I continued. "They were delicious, and they do smell beautiful. And I feel *ba-la* unfolding in me for you as well."

Then, despite my concerns about his strength, I couldn't resist wrapping my arms around his waist—gently—and kissing him. He returned the kiss with the fervor of a man denied any sexual release for several months. I confess I'd masturbated often during that time, thinking of our night together and what I'd like to do when Dalsing was finally able to return to his quarters, but that might not be so easy to get away with in a hospital bed, with machinery and nurses monitoring every heartbeat.

He was still weak, as I realized when he slumped against me. The hydraulic joints seemed to have difficulty keeping him upright with my added weight knocking his body off-kilter. But he didn't show any sign of wanting to stop, so I just held him up, bracing us both with my shoulder against the wall. I wasn't even aware of my hand caressing his crotch until I heard him moan and felt his body shudder, and suddenly my hand was cradling a very hot, wet, and hard Alzhen cock. It throbbed against my palm in time with his pounding heartbeat.

Dalsing broke the kiss and gasped, "I'm sorry."

"I am so *not* sorry. God, that feels good!"

"I don't think I have the strength—"

"Lie down," I ordered him. "I'll take care of everything."

I'd always loved the taste and scent of a man's cock. I could happily give a blowjob for hours. Dalsing's cock had a similar musky smell, though a bit stronger than a man's, and I was growing to love the sweetish taste of his precome. I licked him up and down his thick shaft and all around the bulge of his scrotum. He writhed on the bed and ran the fingers of his right hand through my hair as he panted my name and other things in his language that I couldn't understand.

At some point I think we might have been discovered. I'll never be sure. But I could swear I heard the door open briefly, then close softly. If that was the case, the Alzhen were more understanding of these things than most human hospital staff would be.

When Dalsing moaned and came, I had him deep in my throat. But I was selfish and didn't want to swallow it all without tasting it, so I pulled back and let the hot liquid flood my mouth. It was not unlike human semen. A little different. But I couldn't pinpoint just how the taste differed. Just… enough to make it interesting.

I quickly learned that, if I intended to give many more blowjobs to this man, I'd have to work on my stamina. He came a *lot*. I loved every drop of it, but… yeah. It took a lot of swallowing.

He finally finished and lay there breathing heavily, stroking my hair.

"I don't know if I can do the same for you, *balanai*," he said sleepily. "But I will try."

I laughed and licked his cock one final time before it slipped quietly back into place. "You just rest and sleep, if you need to. I'm fine."

In fact, I was in the middle of coming. I hoped my suit could handle it.

Epilogue

Five Years Later

WE WERE eventually released from quarantine and allowed to land on Alzhen-Ai. My first view of it from Dalsing's quarters was breathtaking, though also a bit disturbing. It provided a hint of what Earth might someday become—overpopulated and covered with sprawling cities to the point where one was impossible to distinguish from the other, the wild spaces reduced to mountains and remote forests where few people wanted to live. As he'd told me the first night we spent together, each of the large cities had parks where the ancient landscape was allowed to thrive, but they were ultimately zoos.

After a time I was allowed to walk among the Alzhen without the use of an isolation suit. Their doctors had declared me free of any dangerous microbes. By this point I'd been surviving on their food and breathing their air for so long, my body had acclimated. The gravity difference wore me out for the first year, but I got used to it.

I also adapted to the Alzhen lifestyle, which meant, among other things, far less clothing than I typically wore on Earth. However, I'd discovered even before landing that nudity for me was somewhat different than it was for the Alzhen. After being told I no longer needed the suit, I decided to brave the central lounge—naked. It didn't go over well. Since I was now widely known as Dalsing's *balanai*, nobody said anything, but they were clearly having difficulty looking at me. The problem was my penis. An Alzhen *ba-ti* who walked around with his dick hanging out was committing a pretty severe breach of etiquette. They knew, of course, that mine didn't retract. But still… it was awkward.

So from that point on, I tended to wear shorts in public. At home, of course, Dalsing was rather fond of my penis.

The Alzhen equivalent to marriage, as it was practiced on Earth—specifically in the USA—was generally much more polyamorous than I would have been happy with. Fortunately Dalsing understood the way I felt and assured me he had no interest in bringing in others.

So two years after he'd stepped down as Dalsing, we were... well, basically married.

That was another thing. His name wasn't Dalsing. As he'd told me when I first asked him his name, "dalsing" was a rank, like the way Spock always called Kirk "Captain" on *Star Trek*. Now that he was more or less retired, I called him by his actual name at home. However, names are very private in Alzhen culture, so I don't feel comfortable writing it in this account. I continued to call him Dalsing in public. And a year later, he was pulled out of retirement anyway, to act as the Alzhen ambassador to Earth.

But I'll get to that in a minute.

The humans who'd been rescued all opted to return to Earth, including Cody. He sold the farm—thank God—and moved into his parents' house in Greenfield, Massachusetts. I checked in on him now and then, during the year Dalsing and I spent as ambassadors to the United States, and then the United Nations. Cody seemed to be better, now that he had people looking out for him, and was seeing a psychologist and getting medication for his anxiety. It helped, I think, that his therapist believed his stories. After all the uproar the appearance of an alien ambassador—accompanied by a human—caused, how could she not?

The decision to make contact had been long overdue. The government on Alzhen-Ai—there was only one government for the entire planet—initially resisted the idea, since it would inevitably entail passing some Alzhen technology along to Earth. That sort of thing always happened. But the Earth was now in danger from the Karazhen, so leaving humans in the dark would have been cruel.

I hated all the commotion surrounding our appearance at the UN. We might as well have been declaring war on the planet to judge by the reception we got. There were nut jobs on television insisting we'd come to destroy humanity, or that we were the sign of the coming apocalypse. And of course the governments were all trying to get in bed with the Alzhen so they could get access to interstellar travel and better weapons. Dalsing and I needed a security detachment at all times, the entire time we were on the planet.

I was pretty disgusted with my species that year.

Fortunately Alzhen-Ai sent another team to take over as ambassadors, once we'd laid the groundwork. I had no desire to be trapped there forever.

"It's strange," I commented as our ship left orbit for the return to Alzhen-Ai. "I should feel like Earth is my home. After all, I was born there and lived there my entire life, until I got abducted."

Dalsing scoffed at that and put his robotic left arm around my shoulders. It was nearly indistinguishable from his flesh-and-blood arm, and he claimed he could feel things just as well with the "skin" on it. "The Karazhen were abducting you. We simply intervened."

We were standing in the lounge, watching the horizon of the Earth dip down as the ship turned away. "At any rate," I said, "I don't belong there. Not anymore." It occurred to me that we were speaking Alzhenut. That was what they actually called the language—not "Alzhenese." We rarely spoke in English anymore when away from other humans.

"Where do you belong?" he asked, his blue eyes twinkling.

"Right now I'm thinking I belong in our bed."

"Then I think I belong there too."

He lowered his face to mine and kissed me. I couldn't stop myself from tracing a finger along the seam of his crotch, but I stopped short of caressing it. I'd developed something of a fetish for watching him pop out. But that wouldn't have been appropriate public behavior in either of our cultures.

With a reluctant groan, Dalsing broke the kiss. We were both panting, but I was distracted from my lecherous thoughts by the brilliantly lit crescent moon coming into view above us. It wasn't really any larger than it looked from the surface of the Earth, but outside the atmosphere, it was brighter. And it was gorgeous. I realized this could easily be the last time I'd ever see it, and the thought saddened me. But I'd found my happiness elsewhere, and I was prepared to leave my old life behind in order to grasp it.

Dalsing seemed to sense I needed a minute. So we watched the stars slowly rotate over our heads while the ship's navigational computers plotted a course for the Alzhen-Ai system. Only when the moon completely disappeared from view, did I turn my head to smile at him. Then without a word, my husband took my hand and escorted me to our quarters.

JAMIE FESSENDEN set out to be a writer in junior high school. He published a couple of short pieces in his high school's literary magazine, but it wasn't until he met his partner, Erich, almost twenty years later, that he began writing again in earnest. With Erich alternately inspiring and goading him, Jamie published his first novella in 2010, and has since published over twenty other novels and novellas.

After legally marrying in 2010, buying a house together, and getting a dog, Jamie and Erich have settled down to life in the country, surrounded by wild turkeys, deer, and the occasional coyote. A few years ago, Jamie was able to quit the tech support job that gave him insanely high blood pressure. He now writes full-time… and feels much better.

Visit Jamie: jamiefessenden.wordpress.com
Facebook: www.facebook.com/pages/Jamie-Fessenden-Author/102004836534286
Twitter: @JamieFessenden1

By JAMIE FESSENDEN

Billy's Bones
The Christmas Wager
Dogs of Cyberwar
The Healing Power of Eggnog
A More Perfect Union (Multiple Author Anthology)
Murder on the Mountain
Murderous Requiem
Saturn in Retrograde
Screwups
Violated
We're Both Straight, Right?

GOTHIKA
(Multiple Author Anthologies)
Claw
Stitch
Bones
Spirit
Contact

Published by DREAMSPINNER PRESS
www.dreamspinnerpress.com

Refugee

By Kim Fielding

Chapter One

WALTER CLARK had hoped the sight of the ocean wouldn't bother him. This was the Pacific, after all, not the same body of water he'd seen tinged red with the blood of his friends and comrades off the Normandy beach. But as soon as he tured south onto the Oregon Coast Highway and saw the vast expanse of roiling gray water, his heart sped and his breathing shallowed. He could hear the blasts of artillery and the screams of the wounded, could smell the metal tang of death mixed with the salt of the sea.

This was a mistake. He should have stayed inland.

Somehow he made it over the high Yaquina Bay Bridge without crashing his old Ford, and he was even able to continue a few miles farther south before his hands shook so violently he could barely control the wheel. Instead of the road before him, he saw red sand, gray landing craft, and green-clad men. When he found himself swerving to avoid an iron hedgehog that had existed six years earlier and five thousand miles away, he pulled to the side of the highway and tried to regain control.

Bitter tears of anger and frustration stung his eyes and ran down his cheeks, but he refused to acknowledge them by wiping them away.

He might have stayed there for hours, but the idling car hiccoughed impatiently. It was a '37, a relic of prewar days, and although it had conveyed him all the way from Chicago, it could be temperamental. The last thing he wanted was to be stranded here, with the waves pounding like mortar shells so very close by. He carefully pulled back onto the road and drove slowly, like a nearsighted old man, his hands clenched painfully on the wheel.

He had no idea how much time passed before he spied a road leading inland through the trees. A sign said Kiteeshaa. Walter didn't know what that meant but turned left anyway. Wherever the asphalt led, it was away from the ocean, and that was what he needed.

As it turned out, Kiteeshaa was a town. Or more accurately, a little hamlet with a population of 178, according to the welcome sign. The village was four or five miles inland and spread across a flat meadow between steep, tree-covered hills. A handful of businesses lined the main street, and beyond that, earth-toned bungalows and moss-roofed little ranch-style houses clustered in the valley and climbed the bases of the slopes.

Walter parked in the small gravel lot in front of the Kitee Café. He got out of the car, stretched, and spent several moments looking around. He heard faint voices—children laughing—but saw nobody. A sense of peace settled on him like a cooling mist, making his shoulders loosen and his lungs work more smoothly. He leaned against the Ford and inhaled deeply, enjoying the scents of pine and damp as well as the sight of the green hills. Kiteeshaa felt a world away from Chicago, where he'd been born and raised.

He'd enjoyed the excitement and bustle of the city… before. But when he'd returned from war, the tall buildings had oppressed him and the clatter of the L and other traffic had startled him. His family had become strangers. For a few years, he'd held out hope that eventually he'd do what was expected of him: settle back into the family business, find a girl and marry, buy a little house in a newly built suburb, have children. Other soldiers he knew had managed that much. But five years after returning from Europe, he still didn't feel at home. His parents had looked relieved when he'd thrown a duffel bag into the back of his car after deciding that a change of scenery was better than drinking himself to death.

He felt disappointed when he saw that the Kitee Motor Court Inn, next door to the café, appeared to be out of business. Although the lot between the neat little buildings was empty, a faded sign read No Vacancy. He would have liked to stay here for a few days, but since that was impossible, at least he could eat something. He was hungry, and a big Open sign hung in the café's front window.

Before he had a chance to go inside, a man headed toward him from the motor court office. There was nothing remarkable about the man's khaki trousers or gray plaid shirt, but Walter had the immediate impression that he was a foreigner. Maybe because of his sand-colored curls—which would have earned ridicule from Walter's crew-cut brothers in Chicago—or maybe the slight upward tilt of his widely set eyes. Perhaps it was the way he moved his lanky body, with long, smooth, catlike strides instead of the jerky, businesslike stomps Walter saw back home.

As the man neared, Walter tried to concentrate on the puzzle of his strangeness rather than the beauty of his face.

"Are you lost?" asked the man when he drew close. Sure enough, he had a faint accent Walter couldn't place. He wore a friendly smile, but his sharp gaze scrutinized.

"No. I was just deciding whether to eat here."

"Ah." The man nodded. "Sometimes folks lose their way around here. We're used to giving directions. But the food's good." He gestured with his chin toward the café.

"Thanks." Walter hoped he wasn't staring inappropriately. "I, uh, guess I'll give it a try. Anything on the menu you recommend?"

The man's smile softened. "Ask Dorothy for the special." Then he nodded again before heading back to the motor court.

The interior of the Kitee Café smelled so wonderful that Walter's knees almost went weak. Grilling meat, brewing coffee, something fruity and a little spicy that might have been a baking pie. About a dozen Formica-topped tables were scattered haphazardly throughout the space, each surrounded by four wooden chairs and crowned with a little vase of wildflowers. A long counter with stools stretched along one wall. This close to the ocean, Walter had expected nautical décor, but the framed photos on the wall depicted starry night skies.

The only other customers were an elderly couple in one corner and, near the center of the room, two young women with a baby in a high chair. They all stared at him—even the baby. Then a middle-aged woman with dark hair in a long braid appeared from the kitchen. "You here for dinner?" she asked, crinkling her eyes at him. Like the man from the inn, she had a hint of an accent.

"Yes, please."

She gestured widely. "Sit wherever you like. Can I start you with some coffee?"

"Milk, please." Coffee only increased his jitters.

He chose a table next to the front window because he felt most comfortable when he wasn't hemmed in. She bustled into the kitchen and a moment later set a tall glass of milk in front of him. Then she pulled a folded paper menu from her apron pocket. "Take your time. Just give me a holler when you've decided. I'm Dorothy."

He took the offered menu but didn't look at it. "The, uh, man from next door said I should ask for the special." He felt foolish mentioning it.

Dorothy's eyebrows flew upward. "Did he, now?" She cocked her head and narrowed her eyes at him, then seemed to reach some kind of decision. "Is that what you want?"

He didn't even know what the special was, but he nodded. "Yes. Please."

She nodded. "All right."

While he waited, he stared out the window and pretended he didn't notice the locals watching him. Not a single car went by, but a noisy group of children raced past, a dog barking happily among them. Children made him uneasy, even his own nephews and nieces. They were too prone to unsettling bursts of energy, but even worse, they reminded him of the orphans he'd seen in Europe—ragged, hollow-eyed boys and girls who begged for candy.

"Here you are," Dorothy said, setting several plates in front of him.

Walter's breath caught. A steaming bowl held barley soup with bits of carrot. A pile of well-stuffed pierogi gleamed on an oversized dish, while a dollop of beet salad with horseradish provided a splash of brightness. Two thick slices of rye bread filled a small plate to the side. "Wh-what?" he stammered.

"The special," replied Dorothy with a smile.

He blinked hard several times, half expecting the food to fade like a mirage. But when his vision cleared, the meal remained, smelling even better than he'd remembered.

"Is something wrong?" Dorothy asked.

"I…. No. It's only…. My *babcia* used to make these things for me." His mother's mother, Magda Sokolowksy, had emigrated from Poland when she was a young woman. She used to pinch his cheeks and tell him he was too skinny, and she'd died while he was overseas.

"I hope ours are almost as good as hers," Dorothy said before sailing away.

He lifted his soup spoon for a first, careful taste. Oh God. It *was* as good as hers. He remembered sitting at her kitchen table—he was so small, he had to perch on phone books—and nibbling on cinnamon cookies as he watched her bustle around the crowded little space. She'd listen to him prattle on endlessly about school or the last movie he'd seen, and she'd refill his milk glass and call him *robaczku*—little bug.

Almost before he knew it, and still awash in memories of his grandmother, Walter ate everything in front of him.

Dorothy beamed when she came to clear the table. "Everything was good?"

"Wonderful. Are… are you Polish?" He didn't think her accent sounded like his grandmother's.

She laughed kindly. "No. I just like to, well, collect recipes. Now, how about a nice slice of loganberry pie?"

He'd already eaten far too much, but he didn't want to leave yet. This was such a good place. Besides, he had no idea where to go next. "I'd like that," he told her.

She brought him an enormous slab with a huge scoop of ice cream melting on top. When he started to protest over the cup of coffee she'd set down, she shook her head. "Decaffeinated," she said. He couldn't refuse that.

He was still lingering over a refill an hour later. Night had fallen, and several more customers now sat in the café. They all seemed to know one another, and they ate a bewildering array of foods, but although they stared at Walter, he didn't sense hostility.

Dorothy came to the table. "More coffee?" she asked.

He sighed. "I guess you probably want me to clear out, huh?"

She flapped a hand. "You stay as long as you want."

"Can you recommend a hotel nearby? Someplace not too expensive." He'd spent a few weeks working at the paper mill a couple hours away in Albany, so he had a little cash, but not much. And who knew when he'd earn more, especially now that his inability to tolerate the ocean meant he had to abandon his plan to find a job at a lumber mill down the coast.

"Well, there's the Ester Lee in Taft. It's a bit of a drive from here, but the ocean views are lovely."

He winced. "I, uh, don't really like the ocean."

She didn't laugh at him or act like he was a lunatic, which he appreciated. Instead, she patted his shoulder. "Wait."

Walter didn't know what he was waiting for, but he remained in his comfortable seat by the window, sipping the cooling remains of his coffee and toying with the little vase of flowers. He startled when the man from the motor court smiled and waved from the other side of the glass. A few seconds later, the man was inside, taking a seat opposite Walter.

"Martin Wright," he said, holding out his hand.

Martin's grip was firm and uncallused and perhaps lingered a moment longer than the norm. "Walter Clark."

God, Martin was gorgeous. Thick eyelashes framed the palest blue eyes Walter had ever seen. A long, narrow nose. Lush lips. A cleft chin. It was hard to gauge Martin's age—at first glance, he'd seemed close to Walter's thirty. But his eyes were older somehow, much like Walter thought his own must be. Maybe Martin had been a soldier too.

Walter did his best to act normal. "Thanks for the dinner suggestion," he said.

When Martin smiled, he suddenly looked like a teenager. He could have been mistaken for an angel. "You had the special?"

"Yeah. I didn't think I'd ever eat those things again. At least, not like my *babcia* used to make them."

For some reason, Martin seemed as satisfied as if he'd conjured the wonderful meal himself. "Dorothy says you're looking for a hotel but you don't care for the ocean. You're not a tourist?"

"No," Walter replied, not wanting to share his story, even with a handsome stranger.

"I have a room available next door." Martin gestured toward the motor court.

"The sign says no vacancy."

"I'm just selective in who I rent to."

"That's a hell of a way to run a business," Walter said, scowling.

Martin simply shrugged.

It was probably some kind of a swindle. But Walter was sleepy after the huge meal and weary after all his travels, and he couldn't wrap his brain around what Martin might want from him. Hell, whatever Martin *did* want, let him have it. It wasn't as if Walter had much to lose—a little money, a battered jalopy, a life going nowhere.

"Sounds good," Walter finally said.

While Martin returned to the motor court, presumably to ready a room, Walter paid for his meal. It cost less than he expected, and as he walked to his car, it occurred to him that he hadn't seen money change hands with any of the other customers. Dorothy hadn't gone near the cash register until she gave Walter his change. Maybe the café worked on credit for locals. Unsound business practices might be a local tradition. Walter's father had worked his way from the poverty of the Depression to a thriving construction business. He would heartily disapprove.

Walter retrieved his military-issue duffel bag from the trunk of the Ford. It brought back far too many unsettling memories, yet when he'd packed his things in Chicago, he'd chosen the duffel instead of a suitcase. He didn't know why.

Martin watched from the motor court office as Walter crunched across the gravel. His light eyebrows were drawn together in a slight frown that eased as Walter drew closer. "I'm giving you unit three," Martin said, dangling a key from one finger. "It's the best cabin."

"Thanks." They hadn't discussed costs, but Walter wasn't in the mood for caution. He wanted… well, very surprisingly, *not* a stiff drink. Over the past few years, he'd always wanted that, but this evening the need was light on his shoulders. Which was good, considering Kiteeshaa didn't appear to have a bar. No, what he wanted now was a quiet room, a comfortable bed, and a night of oblivion unhaunted by nightmares.

Each of the motor court units was a tiny white-shingled building with a red roof. Red posts framed the minuscule front porches, but the porch on number three was a bit larger than the others—just big enough for a single patio chair. Martin unlocked the door and stood aside so Walter could enter.

Everything looked neat and clean. A colorful quilt covered the large bed, and a little table with two chairs nestled under a window. One corner of the room held a kitchenette with a sink, a two-burner stove, two cupboards, and a small refrigerator. The bureau was an incongruously bulky thing that seemed to be hewn from logs. Someone had scattered a few rag rugs over the wooden floor, and more photos of starry skies graced the wood-paneled walls. Through an open door, Walter could see a bathroom with a toilet, sink, and tub/shower combo.

"Is it all right?" Martin asked. He seemed slightly nervous.

Walter gave him a genuine smile. "It's perfect." It was. Homey without being overdone, brightly lit by several lamps, and not remotely reminiscent of either his family house in Chicago or anywhere he'd slept during the war.

"Good." Martin gestured at the small woodstove, which was lit with a glowing fire. "More wood's out back when you want it. I'm sorry this cabin doesn't have a television, but—"

"I never watch it." That was true. The inanities made his jaw hurt.

"All right, then. If you need anything, just come knock on the office door."

"You work all night?"

Martin grinned. "I live here. I have a little apartment. Cozy."

For no reason at all, that pleased Walter.

After Martin left, Walter unpacked, tucking his clothes into drawers or hanging them in the closet. Then he took a long, hot shower. He'd brought back a few scars from the war, but they were small, insignificant. Anyone who saw his naked body would never guess what he'd been through. But Walter knew, and when he looked down at himself, he could see the inner wounds as clearly as if his skin were transparent. He didn't look at himself often.

Warm and clean, smelling faintly of Ivory soap, Walter turned off all the lights but one and climbed into bed. As always, he left his pistol at the bedside. When he'd first returned to Chicago, he couldn't leave the house without it, even though he'd been terrified he might accidentally shoot someone. He'd considered it a major victory when he required the gun nearby only at night.

It wasn't late yet, but he didn't care. He'd found a good place to shut off the world, and he wanted to clock out now.

With one lamp lending a comforting glow, he quickly fell asleep.

Chapter Two

WALTER AWOKE later than usual, well rested and more content than he'd felt in ages. The mattress was a good one, and the sheets were soft and sweet-scented. But unit three itself had been the real soporific, without any sinister shadows for his demons to hide in. He hadn't awakened with bad dreams even once.

He put on blue jeans, a white T-shirt, and a lightweight jacket. He hated wearing hats and hadn't even bothered to bring one with him, so he'd been pleased to see Martin hatless as well. Maybe it was hard to wear one over those springy blond curls. Walter's own hair was dark brown and as straight as broom straw if he let it grow long.

The first order of the morning was breakfast, he decided. Under a zinc-colored sky, with birds chirping all around him, he crossed to the Kitee Café. Almost every seat was taken, and again the other customers stared at him openly, seeming curious but not unwelcoming. They were, he couldn't help but notice, an oddly attractive group of people, as if the little restaurant had been filled by a movie casting agency instead of inhabitants of a real town. Maybe his perception of attractiveness was simply filtered through an unusually restful night.

"Good morning!" Dorothy called when she appeared from the kitchen. She carried two heaping plates of food. "Take a seat and I'll be right with you."

He sat in the same place as the night before, his table by the window—although jeez, it wasn't really *his*. Dorothy hurried over with a cup of coffee and a menu. "Decaf," she announced.

"Thanks." He looked over the menu's typical breakfast fare. "Pancakes and sausage?"

"You bet. Home fries with that? Or eggs?"

He considered briefly. "Eggs, please. Scrambled." Walter was a big man—tall and muscular—and he'd been underfeeding himself for years. His mother used to beg him to eat more, until she'd finally given up. He would end up big around the belly if he kept up like this without physical work. He wasn't sure he cared.

Although the café was busy and Dorothy was apparently the only person waiting on tables, she didn't seem to be in a hurry to leave him. "Did you enjoy the inn?" she asked.

"It's fantastic. Um, thanks for putting in a good word for me with Martin, if that's what you did."

"My pleasure. I hope you decide to stick around for a while."

The food wasn't as exotic as the previous night's dinner, but it was delicious. Dorothy gave him both maple syrup and something made from blackberries, and he used plenty of both. He was nearly through with his meal when he noticed something odd about the other diners—they were strangely quiet. Oh, they clattered plates and cutlery like anyone would have, but their speech was hushed and sparing. Like people at a funeral, only there were no hints of sorrow. In fact, most of them smiled if he caught their gaze. Maybe they were all immigrants and it was some kind of cultural thing. His travels had taught him that not everyone was as loud and boisterous as Americans.

Another thing: the locals touched each other a lot. Nothing inappropriate. But as he watched closely, he noticed that they rested a hand atop their companions' or briefly stroked an arm or shoulder. Children wiggled up against adults like friendly puppies, but when it came to the adults, age and gender didn't seem to matter; people touched anyone within reach. Even Dorothy took part in this, briefly caressing her customers' backs or brushing her fingers against their forearms whenever her hands were free. Watching all of the casual contact made Walter uncomfortable, but it also made him sad. It had been a long time since anyone had affectionately touched him.

Breakfast was an even bigger bargain than dinner. Walter thanked Dorothy and then ventured outside. He felt a bit at loose ends. He'd spent most of the past year either driving or working, but today neither was on the agenda. Hell, he didn't *have* an agenda. Pretty soon he'd have to decide where to go next, but for today, maybe he could just wander.

There wasn't much to see in what passed for downtown Kiteeshaa. Aside from the café and the motor court, the business district consisted of a little grocer, a gas station with a mechanic's bay, a tiny shop that seemed to carry clothing and shoes, and an office space of indeterminate purpose. Nothing for tourists, and even the locals would have to drive to Newport for most needs. He was charmed to discover that the town boasted a plant nursery, its storefront crowded with pots of riotously colored flowers.

In fact, as he continued his walk, he noticed that all the houses were fronted by carefully tended gardens. He recognized a few of the plants, such as the roses and lavender, but he knew very little about gardening, so mostly he just registered splashes of color among a thousand shades of green.

He thought it was weird that *every* house had such a lush, well-tended garden. Walter knew quite a lot about construction due to his family's business—even if his own role had largely involved pushing paperwork—and he could tell that the houses, although modest, were also in perfect condition. Not a single loose shingle, no peeling paint, no windows in need of repair. The sidewalks were free of children's toys, and he didn't spy a single scrap of litter as he walked down the road. Strange.

As he walked, he passed three young children, and later a man and woman about his age. They all smiled and wished him a good morning, but there was something assessing in their gazes.

Soon the houses ended and the valley narrowed, so that slopes thick with vegetation rose on either side of the road. The tall trees would have blocked most of the sun even if the sky had been clear, and the rich scent of growing things filled Walter's nose. Although no cars went by, he saw living creatures: fluttering insects, cheeping birds, and scolding squirrels. Once a black snake with red stripes slithered across his path, making him jump. And for one almost magical moment, a deer paused in the roadway to stare at him before loping into the brush.

Perhaps a mile past the town, a small stream burbled through a culvert under the road before continuing into a little canyon to Walter's right. It appeared that a path—narrow and unpaved, thickly carpeted with pine needles—followed the stream. On a whim, Walter decided to follow the path into the woods.

At first the trail led nowhere in particular, twisting lazily alongside the water. But when the stream headed down a steep embankment, the path turned the other way, rising uphill between ferns and trees. He expected it to peter out at any moment, but it continued even after it crested the hill and crossed a little meadow into another stand of trees. But then it stopped suddenly, right in the center of a ring of towering evergreens, and Walter peered around in bewilderment. Why would a trail lead here?

A rounded boulder hulked invitingly, so Walter ambled over and scrambled to the top. It was less than five feet high and covered in moss, and it made a pleasant perch. He sat for what felt like a long time, simply breathing.

This area was quieter than the woods near the road. He didn't see or hear any birds, and the only insects were a few gnats and several wandering ants. It was as if even forest creatures were hesitant to disturb the stillness of the space. And God, it was peaceful. Deeply so, like a long drink of water on a hot summer day or a thick mattress after a hard day of toil. He thought that if he dropped dead right here, right now, it wouldn't be such a bad thing. He'd seen firsthand what became of corpses when they returned to dust, and if his flesh became a part of this tranquil place, he wouldn't very much mind.

It was a good thing he didn't have his revolver with him, although he probably wouldn't have wanted to disturb the silence with a gunshot. Probably.

Walter had stopped thinking—was just letting the stillness seep into his pores—when he heard the quiet fall of footsteps. He hadn't even realized he'd closed his eyes, but now he opened them, blinked a few times, and saw Martin walking toward him. Martin moved slowly and carefully, less like an animal stalking its prey than a parent wanting to avoid disturbing a sleeping child. He wore khaki trousers again with a light blue shirt and tan jacket, and his lips were set in a hesitant smile.

"I'm sorry to interrupt you," he said quietly when he reached the rock.

Walter slid to the ground. "It's all right. I was just sitting here."

Martin nodded. "It's a good place, isn't it? I come here sometimes when I need…." He let his voice trail off, then gave a small shrug. He continued to smile, but his eyes were sad. "Were you comfortable in unit three?"

"It was great." Walter couldn't explain the sense of ease he'd felt last night.

"I'm glad," Martin replied, looking relieved. "Will you stay longer?"

"A few days." Walter hadn't even realized he'd made a decision until the words left his mouth, and he didn't regret it. If he could actually afford it. "Um, you haven't told me the rate."

"Four dollars a night. But I can give you a discount, seeing as you're staying more than one night." He seemed to consider for a few seconds. "Two fifty?"

Walter did some quick calculations in his head. If he ate at the café for breakfast only and fixed the rest of his meals in the cabin's little kitchenette, he could safely afford a week before his funds became too thin. "That's fair," he said.

Martin held out his hand for a shake, and Walter took it. But instead of letting go when the shake was over, Martin tugged with surprising strength, pulling Walter flush against him. Shocked but also instantly aroused, Walter stared into those astonishing blue eyes. And then Martin touched his lips to Walter's.

It was a delicate kiss, barely more than a faint brushing of skin. But it made Martin gasp and draw his head back. His lips were parted and his eyes wide. "Oh," he breathed.

"You don't...," Walter began, trying to talk his way out of this awkward situation. He expected Martin to be angry with regret—to hit him, or at least order him to leave Kiteeshaa immediately and never return.

But Martin still held Walter's hand, and now he leaned his head forward again for another kiss. Gentle at first, and then harder, and when Walter gave in to impulse and slipped his tongue into that warm, sweet-tasting mouth, Martin moaned and pressed his other hand against Walter's back.

They were both breathless when they broke the kiss. "I didn't realize...," Martin whispered. A flush had spread over his fair-skinned face, and his lips were moist.

Walter pulled his hand from Martin's now-slack grip. "I think we should—"

But Martin pushed his chest to Walter's, pressing him back against the rock. Walter could easily have fought his way free since he was much more muscular than Martin, but he didn't want to. Being pinned in place like that felt safe rather than confining. Martin stared intently, as if he were trying to glean some deep meaning from Walter's expression. "You want this," Martin finally said. "You want me."

No sense denying it, not when Martin could probably feel Walter's burgeoning interest against his hip. "Yeah. I'm queer." He'd tried to ignore his attraction to men when he was younger in hopes that it would fade away. But then he'd joined the Army and found an atmosphere surprisingly—if unofficially—tolerant of homosexuality. Maybe it came of men living together in close quarters, usually with no women in sight. Maybe it came from the nearness of death, which put biases into perspective and made soldiers appreciate all the carnality of life. It had been easy enough to find willing short-term partners, men eager for a tryst in the darkness.

Martin frowned. "Wanting me makes you unhappy?"

"Not...." Walter sighed. "Life would be easier if I liked girls instead."

"I don't understand. Sex, love, these are good things, right? They make people feel good. Not like hate or war. Why does it matter who you want?"

Jeez. Martin might be a foreigner, but he couldn't be *that* unaware, could he? "It matters to most people," Walter said gruffly.

"Not where I come from. For us.... We love a *person*, not a gender. And if that person loves us back, well, that's a joyous thing."

"Where are you from, Martin?"

Martin sighed and shook his head. "Far away. But right here, you can want me and I can want you, right? When it's only the two of us."

That was true enough—the trees were their only witnesses. And God, it had been so *long*. When Walter first returned from the war, he'd been too shattered to desire anyone. And perhaps that had been just as well, because civilian Chicago was not as willing as his platoon members to turn a blind eye to two men together. Even once the yearning returned, Walter had remained celibate save for a few brief and emotionless exchanges.

Martin must have sensed Walter's acquiescence, because he pressed in close again and placed his lips tentatively to Walter's jawline. Walter shuddered at the contact. For a moment he wasn't sure where to put his hands, but then he grinned slightly and threaded his fingers through Martin's soft curls.

They kissed some more, Martin resting his entire weight against Walter, supported by the rock. Now Martin's cock was hard too, a delicious solidity against Walter's own, and whenever Martin could draw a breath, he made marvelous little gasps and whimpers. When Martin trailed wet lips over Walter's neck and then sucked on a cord of muscle, Walter leaned his head back and tried not to come.

"Wh-what do we do?" Martin panted.

At the moment, Walter was universally willing. "Anything you want."

"But I don't know how."

That made Walter freeze. "You've never done this before?"

"No."

"With a woman?"

"No."

Oh holy Christ. Walter dropped his hands to Martin's chest and pushed lightly. "We shouldn't—"

Martin grasped Walter's wrists and gently moved his hands to his waist. "Please?" Sunlight filtered through wispy gray clouds and the treetops. It illuminated Martin, making him look like part of that fresco in the bombed-out church where Walter had once spent three sleepless days and nights trying to keep some of his comrades alive.

Then Martin's expression softened too, and he leaned his forehead against Walter's. "We need this, you and I," Martin whispered. "It won't make us forget, not for long, but perhaps it will chase the memories away for a little while."

Walter didn't ask what memories Martin needed to evade. Instead, he gently worked his hands free and wrapped his arms around Martin, pulling their bodies flush. "We could go someplace," he offered. Somewhere with a bed. Didn't Martin have an entire motor court to choose from?

But Martin shook his head. "Next time. This place is best for now. It's a place of new beginnings, you see."

Walter didn't see, and talk of next time and beginnings made him uneasy, as if he were about to make a promise he knew he'd break. But he tilted his head to brush his lips across Martin's cheek. "Here, then."

"Can I see you? All of you?"

Wisdom counseled against undressing in the open. But Walter held little faith in wisdom, and in any case, if he was going to be responsible for Martin's first time, he ought to do it right. He'd never been anyone's first.

Walter unhooked his arms from Martin's waist and pushed softly at his chest. Then he reached for his own jacket zipper.

They were going to be cold, he realized as he undressed. Except excitement thrummed in his veins, warming his flesh from the inside. And then he gazed at Martin's beautiful naked body, at the slender length of his rigid cock, and at the pure joy shining in his eyes—and the chilly temperature ceased to matter. Martin didn't stare at him as if Walter were broken. God, *nobody* had ever looked at him as Martin was, and Walter hadn't realized until just this moment how much he'd yearned for it.

"I want to kiss you now," Martin said solemnly.

"I wish you would."

Skin against bare skin was glorious. Martin had very little body hair, and his muscles beneath Walter's questing hands were lithe and strong. As they kissed, Martin explored Walter's body too, groaning over the thick hair on Walter's chest, the heavy build of his shoulders and arms, the firm roundness of his ass. They pressed their groins together, rocking gently at first, then with increasing urgency. That could have been enough, and Martin wasn't demanding anything more, but Walter wanted to give him a fuller experience.

He wrenched himself from the kiss by sheer force of will and dropped to his knees. As Martin gaped down at him, Walter grabbed a double handful of Martin's delicious ass and began to nuzzle at the soft curls of his groin.

"What do I do?" Martin asked. He was breathing hard.

"Enjoy," Walter replied, grinning up at him. Then he licked the length of Martin's shaft.

Martin's gasp echoed loudly in the quiet of the clearing, a sound so primal and erotic that Walter's own balls tightened. He wanted more of that. But he noticed that Martin's hands were clutching uncertainly into fists. "Hold my hair," Walter ordered. "Hard as you want. I don't care."

He'd allowed his crew cut to grow out a little, more from apathy than desire, so the strands were just long enough for Martin to grasp. For a brief moment, Walter mourned the fact that he couldn't reach the glorious soft halo on Martin's head—but then, an equally nice prize was within reach. With a happy little hum, Walter slid his lips around the head of Martin's cock.

When Walter had performed this act during furtive moments in the Army, his partners had tasted of sour, salty sweat and grime—the taste of soldiers who marched often and bathed rarely. He hadn't exactly minded. It was like field rations: not ideal, but far better than no food at all. Besides, he knew he was just as dirty, so they had to endure his reek when they returned the favor. The men he'd been with since, stealing a bit of time in tavern bathrooms or the backseats of cars, had tasted of beer and cologne and laundry detergent.

Not Martin. He was salty, of course, but clean and sweet. Any soap smell blended completely with his own personal odor, which was a bit like woodsmoke and spring rain. It was wonderful. Walter devoured him, licking and sucking his length and swallowing him down, using Martin's moans and whimpers to gauge what felt best. Martin *did* tug at his hair—just exactly hard enough—and that was lovely too.

When Martin rocked his hips, his buttocks flexed in Walter's grip. But Walter was looking up as he sucked, and what *really* made his nerves thrum was Martin's expression. Martin stared down at him with pure wonder and delight.

Groaning urgently, Walter grabbed his own cock and stroked in rhythm with his mouth. Fast. Faster. Then Martin cried out and his thick, salty-sweet seed flooded Walter's mouth.

Walter swallowed and came with a shudder.

Somehow they ended up lying on their backs on the soft bed of pine needles, their jackets spread over their torsos for warmth. They held hands and stared up at the green-and-gray canopy.

Although he didn't usually need reassurances, Walter cleared his throat. "Was that—"

"Almost perfect. I would have liked to taste you too."

Damned if Walter's cock didn't give a little twitch at that. "It's not always that… explosive," he said. "Sex, I mean. Sometimes it's just a wiggle and a jerk."

Martin angled himself slightly to rest his head against Walter's shoulder and neck. "It was such a good thing, sharing ourselves like that. Almost like when—" He stopped suddenly and sighed. "I forgot the shadows for a while. Did you?"

"Yeah."

They remained silent for a long time—ten, fifteen minutes. Walter felt as if he were sinking into the earth. Maybe he really had put a bullet in his brain and the entire encounter had been the last fantasy of splattered gray matter. But no, Martin was here, solid and real, his curls soft against Walter's skin.

"There was a war," Martin eventually said. Very quietly.

"I know. I was there."

"A different war." Martin coughed a humorless laugh. "Or maybe they're all the same. We lost… everything. Our home, our families."

A year or two back, Walter's brother John had told him to stop being so miserable. "I seen plenty of guys who were blown all to shit, but you came back in one piece, Wally. And me and Charlie, we came back okay too, so you didn't lose anyone. Don't be such a sad sack." But what John hadn't understood was that Walter had lost friends and lovers. He'd lost his youth, his innocence, his optimism. And when he returned to Chicago, although his parents and brothers were still alive and well, he'd lost them too.

"Your family?" Walter asked Martin.

The answer came on a sigh. "All gone."

After discarding several dozen useless words and consolations, Walter squeezed Martin's hand. Martin returned the gesture.

Eventually they collected their cast-off clothes and got dressed. They walked slowly back toward the road. Not hand in hand, but close together, shoulders sometimes brushing.

When the outskirts of the village came into view—a tidy yellow bungalow and its equally neat green neighbor—Martin stopped Walter with a gentle tug of his arm. "Do you like Kiteeshaa?"

"It seems too good to be true. Are you getting ready to tell me it's all some kind of joke? Like that television program my mother watches. *Candid Camera*."

"It's no joke. When we first arrived… things were difficult. Nothing here was familiar. Your people are… very different from mine. But we found this place, and even as traumatized as we were, we could see its beauty." Martin waved an arm to indicate the hills, the trees, the small growing things by the side of the road.

"It's a nice place."

"We worked hard to learn your ways. To blend in." He shook his head ruefully. "We never will, not completely. But our children…. The older ones don't remember our home, and the younger ones were born here. *This* is their home. We try to teach them some of our traditions, but they don't want to learn. I suppose that's for the best in the long run."

Walter remembered his *babcia* saying something similar when Walter's mother chided her for being old country. *Babcia* had been both bewildered by and proud of her American children and grandchildren. And now, if Walter wished he'd learned a little Polish from her or if he ached for some of the foods she used to make, well, it was too late for that. She was gone.

"You must miss everything so much," Walter said.

"Sometimes. But I've come to cherish Kiteeshaa too. If I had to leave here, I'd miss it just as much." He held a hand to his chest. "I think the people and things you used to love, they never leave your heart. But your heart can grow—it can let in the new."

Walter's heart had crumbled to sand and been washed away by bloodred waves.

They continued walking. A block from the motor court, they met an elderly man with wispy gray hair and a network of deep wrinkles on his face. "Hi, Burt," Martin said.

The man nodded pleasantly at them both, but just before they passed one another, he stopped in his tracks, staring. Then his mouth stretched into a wide smile and he laughed.

Martin blushed a deep red and shot Walter a quick glance. "Burt, don't...."

"I know. But *good*, Martin. I'm glad to see you." Still grinning, Burt continued on his way.

Walter looked down at himself and then at Martin to see if there was visible evidence of their tryst. Nothing was obvious. Martin's hair was a little wild, but it had been that way before. Besides, although Martin claimed that his people didn't mind queers, surely they wouldn't be so gleeful about it.

"What was that about?" Walter asked.

His face still red, Martin gave an unconvincing shrug. "I suppose he's happy I'm showing you around."

Although Walter didn't believe that for a second, he didn't argue.

When they reached the motor court parking lot, they paused near the office. "I have to take care of some things," Martin said. "Do you mind?"

"Of course not." Walter hadn't expected to monopolize his time.

"Can I treat you to dinner next door?"

"I can pay."

Martin set a hand on his shoulder. "You're a guest, and that means I pay. It's one of our customs. A good one to keep, I think."

Walter was uneasy to have Martin touching him in public, where anyone might see. But he smiled. "All right, then. Dinner."

"Six thirty." And then Martin leaned in for a kiss.

Walter was so shocked that he froze. That didn't deter Martin, who moved his lips from Walter's mouth to his neck and then to his cheek. "Thank you," Martin whispered. He walked to the office and went inside, but for several moments, Walter remained statue-like in the parking lot.

Chapter Three

WALTER WASN'T often faced with open blocks of time, and after recovering from his astonishment over Martin's kiss, he wasn't sure what to do with his afternoon. In Chicago, he'd filled empty time with booze, but he didn't want that now. A shower, he finally decided. Maybe a nap. His adventure with Martin had proved more draining than he expected.

The first thing he saw when he walked into unit three was a bouquet of fresh flowers placed on the tiny dining table. Three yellow roses, a few fern fronds, and some sprigs of purple stuff he didn't recognize, all in a milk-glass vase. They definitely hadn't been there before, and he wondered whether Martin had left them. The flowers made him smile, but even better was the small stack next to the vase. Books. But not just any books: these were Armed Services Editions, the oddly shaped thin-paged paperbacks he and his comrades had so treasured during the war.

Walter walked closer for a better look. The top book was *War of the Worlds*. Beneath that, *The Earth and High Heaven*, and the final book was *When Worlds Collide*. Walter didn't know if any of them were particularly to his taste, but that had hardly mattered before. When the crates of books had found his platoon, everyone had been thrilled for a way to pass the long, agonizing hours aboard transport or in gun pits. They'd all shared the little volumes, sometimes even ripping the books into two sections so more men could read at once.

When Walter touched the worn cover of the first book, a memory flooded him, the images as clear as if they were happening now. He was crouched among ruins with members of his platoon, all of them shivering in the late-winter cold. Overhead, planes buzzed, while antiaircraft shells whistled and burst nearby. Some of the men were smoking cigarettes, but Walter kept his hands in his coat pockets. Next to him sat LeMay, a fellow medic with a deep Southern drawl, reading a Steinbeck book aloud. Sometimes he had to nearly shout to be heard over the ack-acks' fire, but nobody minded. As long as LeMay read, they weren't miserable soldiers so far from home, but instead hard-drinking paisanos in Tortilla Flat.

LeMay was shot through the neck in a gutter somewhere in France as he crawled to a wounded comrade. Walter saw him die. The man he was trying to rescue died too.

Walter didn't realize he was crying until his vision blurred. He angrily dashed the tears from his eyes, grabbed *War of the Worlds*, and took it to the bed. When he got there, he toed off his shoes and tossed his jacket aside, then curled up under the colorful quilt to read.

HE WOKE up flailing at an object covering the lower half of his face and ended up batting it to the floor, ashamed when he realized it was only the paperback. He must have fallen asleep with the book in his hands. Oddly panicked, he picked it up, then sighed with relief when he saw it was unharmed.

With barely enough time for a quick shower and shave, Walter was just putting on his shoes when a knock sounded on the door. He hurried over to open it.

"Hi," Martin said, looking happy. And even more beautiful than Walter remembered.

"The, uh, flowers and the books… thanks. That was nice."

Instead of answering, Martin stepped through the doorway and pulled Walter's head close for a kiss. This time Walter was less surprised. And sure, someone might be watching through the open door, but he couldn't quite bring himself to care. Not with Martin tasting like mint and sighing happily into his mouth.

"I like kissing," Martin said, leaning his forehead against Walter's. "If you've never done it and you think about it, it seems really odd. But the reality is amazing."

Honestly, Walter had never given kissing much thought. Maybe he would have if he'd gone without a kiss as long as Martin had. He found Martin's earnest appraisal charming. "We could always skip dinner," Walter said, jerking his head toward the bed.

Martin's wide smile bloomed. "Can we save that for dessert?"

Fair enough.

The Kitee Café was crowded, and when Walter and Martin entered, every person turned to stare. Even the kids. Martin just grinned and gave the room a general wave. They smiled back. It was weird.

Walter had apparently acquired a personal table, his usual one by the window. As he and Martin sat, Walter tried to ignore the quiet conversations of strangers, positive that most were about him.

Dorothy bustled to them within seconds and then astounded Walter by drawing a chair to their table and sitting down. Nobody else seemed surprised, though. Not even Martin. She tilted her head and gave Walter a close look. "What makes you happy?" she asked.

Walter blinked at her, but Martin chuckled. "It's a question we ask when getting to know someone."

"My people usually ask where you're from or what you do for a living."

Dorothy harrumphed. "Not important. Not like happiness. So?"

He had to think about it for a long time, but nobody hurried him. Finally he sighed. "Peace and quiet. I like each of those a lot. Books." And then another memory hit him—this one from before the war, when he was still a boy. "Waking up early on a day you know something great's going to happen, and then just sitting there, savoring the anticipation."

She nodded a few times as if she agreed with his answers. And then, hoping he wasn't breaking any foreign rules of etiquette, he returned the question. "What makes *you* happy?"

Oh, that was the right response. She smiled so widely that all her teeth showed, and Martin gazed across the table at him with shining eyes. "Oh, honey," Dorothy said, patting Walter's hand, "I love it when people enjoy my food. And I love cats. Such perfect little creatures! I'm happy when they curl up in my lap and purr. And I like it when someone gives an unexpected gift." She stood. "Now, what can I get you?"

When Walter hesitated, Martin said, "I'll have the special, please."

She looked expectantly at Walter. "Do you want to see the menu?"

"No. I'll have what he's having."

Another response that clearly pleased Martin. A brief nonverbal conversation passed between Dorothy and Martin, she with raised eyebrows and he with a firm nod. She nodded in return before hurrying away.

"She likes you," Martin said.

"She doesn't know me."

"She knows enough."

Now, that wasn't true. Walter knew that if anyone could see past his bland shell to view the real him, they'd be disgusted. The real Walter

Clark had been a rotting, corrupted corpse for over five years. Martin would realize that soon enough, if Walter stuck around much longer.

Walter tried a smile. "What makes you happy?"

"You." Martin's response was immediate and sincere.

"Martin—"

"Spending time with you makes me happy. You're good at... quiet. I like that. And keeping my inn looking nice makes me happy too. I know it's not much, but I'm proud of it."

"You should be." Walter was sincere too. His little rented cabin was the most comfortable place he could remember.

Martin answered him with a gaze so intense and heated that Walter glanced around them guiltily and shifted in his seat. It would be clear to even the most casual observer what Martin was thinking about. Hell, now Walter was thinking about it too. He licked his lips and watched Martin's pupils widen and cheeks flush.

Then Martin leaned forward over the table. "I know about sex," he whispered huskily.

"Uh...."

"I did some research this afternoon."

Jesus *Christ*. Walter had no idea how Martin would conduct such research. In Chicago there were places a fellow could go, if he knew where to look. Shops that sold books, magazines, and photos geared toward a particular clientele. Bars where men coupled in the shadows and didn't much care who watched. But Walter doubted that Kiteeshaa boasted similar attractions.

"I didn't know there were so many options," Martin said. Wide-eyed and grinning—a kid in a candy store. "Are any of them as nice as what we did today?"

Walter's instinct was to say something dirty and blasé, to come off as a tough guy who didn't care. It was a persona that had served him well during his casual encounters. But he couldn't make himself do it, not with a virgin who brought him flowers and books and shared his personal sorrows. "It's not the mechanics so much as the person. I've done a lot of things, Martin. None of them were as sweet as what we did today."

Martin's eyes went watery and his smile softened. "The body...." He cleared his throat. "Bodies are wonderful things. But they're only decoration. Like a bright coat of paint. The true self is what matters. You know this."

"What if the body's the good part? And the true self is...." He wasn't sure of the right words. Damaged. Dead. Ugly.

Martin shook his head. "Just because someone's been touched by pain, that doesn't ruin him. I know you don't like the ocean, so please forgive this analogy, but sometimes I like to walk on the beach. There's always a lot of driftwood. Whole trees even. They've been wrenched from where they were rooted, then battered by water and sand. They look nothing like they used to. But they still have such beauty. The grains of their fibers, the softness of their grays.... And they're still useful too. Animals use them for shelter. Burt Evans—you met him today—he fashions driftwood into furniture and sells it to tourists in Newport."

"That's... a pretty complicated metaphor, right off the cuff."

"It's something I've thought about a lot. Believe me, I've drifted a long, long way." He leaned even closer, his gaze intense enough to scorch. "Walter, there is *nothing* ugly about you."

Walter was still wondering how Martin knew what he'd been thinking when Dorothy arrived with their meals. She gave them each a deep, oversized bowl, then set a small loaf of bread on a board in the middle of the table. "Enjoy," she said, then patted each of them briefly before moving on to the next table.

The bread was still steaming and looked wonderful. But Walter stared dubiously at the stuff in his bowl. The stew—if that's what it was—smelled nice, but it was a weird green color with chunks of unidentifiable purple and orange floating in it.

Walter's doubt must have been obvious, because Martin laughed. "It's a festival food for us," he said. He followed up with a word that sounded like nothing but vowels, which Walter assumed was what the stuff was called. "Try it."

Fine. Couldn't be worse than some of the slop the Army had passed off as edible, right? With Martin watching closely, Walter picked up his soup spoon, dipped it into the technicolor goo, and took a tiny taste.

"Oh!" It tasted... well, green. But in a good way, like the first fresh spring vegetables after months of mushy tinned stuff. It was spicy too, although Walter couldn't begin to identify the spices. It made his tongue tingle, and it warmed him when he swallowed.

"Well?" Martin demanded.

"I could live without the texture. But boy, it tastes fantastic."

With a smug smile, Martin reached for the bread.

They both ate second helpings, followed by coffee and berry pie à la mode. Walter's stomach felt drum-tight, but the meal had been so delicious and the company so wonderful that he didn't care. He and Martin had chatted nonstop throughout the meal. About little things, like the mutt Walter had owned when he was a boy and the planter boxes Martin wanted to install in the windows of his cabins. But also about big things, like the way Martin's mother had sung nearly all the time and how Walter had ended up being a medic. That last bit was unusual—he rarely spoke to anyone about the war, and never without his chest going tight and his heart hammering. But tonight, discussing his training with Martin, all he felt was the memory of unease.

No money changed hands at the end of dinner, but Dorothy patted Martin's head and stroked Walter's back. Probably Martin ran a tab; that would make sense. "We'll see you later," Dorothy said to Martin, then turned to Walter. "One thing I like about you is your voice, which is nice and deep without being loud. And you don't seem to mind some silence, either."

When Walter blinked, Martin laughed softly. "More small talk. It's a way we say good-bye to people we're getting to know."

Although he was a little flustered, Walter attempted a response. "You have pretty hair. And it's always neatly braided no matter how much you rush around."

Dorothy patted her braid, beamed at him, and then quickly stroked his cheek. "I feel good about this," she said, glancing at Martin. Walter didn't understand what she was talking about.

All the other customers waved and called out good-byes as Martin and Walter left.

A soft mist surrounded them as they walked across the gravel lot, moving as if they had all the time in the world. When they reached unit three, Walter unlocked the door, but Martin paused. "You still want me?" Martin asked.

"God, yes." More than he'd wanted anything in years.

"You're sad."

Walter wondered how he'd suddenly begun wearing his emotions so openly, when his family had complained that he was unreadable. "I suppose so."

"Because of me?"

"No, because of me. Because everything good slips away."

Martin stepped into the doorway, putting them chest to chest. "You can keep the good inside of you the same way you've been keeping the bad. Then it's never quite gone."

Wouldn't it be nice if good memories haunted him the way the awful ones did? Walter shook his head and gave a small smile. "I'm not usually like this. I'm no philosopher, and I don't tell people what I'm feeling. You, this place… you're having a weird effect on me."

"Does that bother you?"

"No." It made him wistful, like unrequited love. He saw the serene, thoughtful man who'd temporarily replaced the frightened, jumpy one, and he wished the change could be permanent.

Walter settled an arm around Martin's waist and urged him inside, then shut and locked the door.

They stood looking at each other, Martin smiling faintly. Walter felt as nervous as if *he* were the virgin. Then Martin chuckled. "Is this foreplay?"

"Fore-foreplay, maybe."

And just like magic, the tension was gone. Martin lit a fire in the woodstove while Walter fussed around: hanging up his jacket, removing a few things from the bed, drinking a glass of water. The little room warmed up quickly, and the flames that flickered behind the grille lent a cheery atmosphere to the already cozy cabin.

"How often do you rent out these units?" Walter asked.

"Not often. My people, we have communities in other places too, and sometimes we get visitors. Other times, one of your people passes through looking for a rest."

Walter couldn't remember seeing more than two or three cars on the road since he arrived. He couldn't imagine how Martin supported himself with so little trade, but decided it would be rude to ask. Besides, they weren't here to talk business. "I'm glad I decided to make that turn."

"Me too. But maybe it wasn't just a random decision. Maybe I was wishing for you so hard that I influenced you."

"Nah. You were wishing for someone way better. I'm just what came along."

"I was wishing for *you*," Martin insisted. Then he reached over and unbuttoned Walter's shirt.

If anything, Martin was even more beautiful in the cabin's mellow light than he'd been in the woods. His pale skin glowed, and his hair was like spun gold. He smoothed his palms up Walter's arms, down his chest, and over his belly. "Memorizing the feel of you," he said, smiling. "And making sure you're real."

That made Walter laugh, because surely Martin was the fantasy, not him. Walter touched Martin too, marveling at the softness of his skin and the clever ways his muscles and bones moved. Tracing blue veins with his fingertips. Teasing pink nipples to stiff little peaks. Then Martin and Walter moved even nearer so they could kiss, but their hands never stilled, instead mapping the expanses of broad backs and the gentle curves of buttocks.

Their earlier encounter hadn't been hurried, but now they moved even slower, as if they were in a perfectly wonderful dream. Martin spent a century or so licking and nibbling on Walter's neck and collarbones, and then it was Walter's turn to spend a happy eternity kneading Martin's ass while inhaling the sweet fragrance of his hair. They gently rocked their pelvises together, their hard cocks rubbing.

"You want to be inside me," Martin whispered into his ear. A statement, not a question.

Walter's breath caught. "Yeah. God, yeah. But not if you don't—"

"I do."

Chuckling, Martin stepped across the floor, the wood creaking a bit under his barefooted tread, and retrieved something from his jacket pocket. When he returned, he held the object for Walter's inspection. "Will this do?" It was a little jar of Vaseline.

If Walter hadn't been excited already, that mundane little container would have done the trick. It meant this was really going to happen. He was truly going to fuck— No. He was truly going to *make love* to this amazing man. And Martin, his hand shaking a little as he held the Vaseline, seemed as excited about the prospect as Walter was.

Walter took it from him, then wrapped an arm around Martin to pull him closer. His skin was warm. "I want you to remember this for a long time," Walter said. "When I'm gone, when you find someone for real, I don't want you to regret this."

"You don't have to—" Martin stopped himself, sighed, then nuzzled against Walter. "I won't regret this."

Enough talking, Walter decided. He wanted another kiss, then another, and in the process he and Martin somehow made their way to the bed and tumbled onto the colorful quilt. Much better than a forest floor. And as they moved their bodies together, gasping and groaning their pleasure, it seemed to Walter as if nothing in the universe mattered except making Martin happy. God, if Walter weren't such a mess, he could find enough purpose in making Martin happy to get them both through the rest of their lives.

With the help of the Vaseline and a lot of encouraging strokes, Martin opened up beautifully for Walter, and by the time Walter entered him, they both nearly sobbed in relief. Martin lay on his back, his ass supported by a pillow and his ankles hooked over Walter's shoulders. Walter began to thrust, slowly at first and then with more vigor, while Martin clutched desperately at him. Although the very physical connection between them felt better than anything Walter could remember, what truly electrified him was the intensity of Martin's gaze, which never left Walter's face. Walter was inside Martin's body, but Martin was inside Walter's soul. The joy of the moment was tempered a bit with Walter's knowledge that nothing would ever be this good again—not once he left Kiteeshaa.

Walter's skin tightened and his nerves sang. "T-touch yourself," he panted. He would have liked to stroke Martin's cock himself, but he needed both hands to prop himself over Martin's body. Besides, watching Martin would be as good as touching him.

Martin's skin was flushed across his face and down his chest, and his curls had become even wilder than usual. He grinned and shook his head. "Rather touch you." He was as breathless as Walter, and to emphasize his point, he rubbed his palms along Walter's forearms.

Just a few more thrusts and Walter's body went spinning ecstatically through space. "Martin!" he shouted.

Martin answered with a cry like ringing bells—a sound more celestial than human—and Walter could have sworn Martin's eyes glowed like ice on fire.

When Walter's strength left him, he collapsed onto Martin, not minding the sticky heat of Martin's semen. Martin gently petted Walter's back, soothing him as if it had been Walter's first time.

"Thank you," Martin whispered.

Walter was going to object—*he* was the grateful one—but Martin silenced him with a deep kiss.

Eventually Walter rolled to the side and Martin cuddled up against him, threading his fingers through Walter's hair. "You're sad again," Martin said. "Did I do something wrong?"

"No! God no! That was... that was a gift. Best anyone's ever given me."

Martin leaned in to press his lips to Walter's cheek. "Then what's wrong?"

"I don't deserve what you just gave me."

"You wouldn't say that if you could see yourself the way I do."

Walter shook his head. "You don't even know me."

"Not as fully as I'd like to, but I know enough. I like the shape of you."

Glancing down at his body, Walter shrugged. "I look okay, I guess." His blocky body carried muscle easily, even when he didn't do much physical work. The rest of him was unremarkable.

"That's not what I mean. You're handsome enough, but I was talking about.... Your language doesn't have a word for it. It's the... the *feel* of you. Your true self. Your essence."

Walter contemplated that silently. He'd never given much thought to his inner self. Before the war he'd assumed it was as unexceptional as the rest of him, and since then, well, he figured it was a charred and twisted ruin. But Martin looked at him as if Walter was worth something.

Martin propped himself on one elbow to look down at Walter. "You don't know me either. What do you think of me, Walter?"

"You're beautiful," Walter answered promptly.

"Is that all? Would you like me less if this weren't my true face?"

"I don't understand."

Martin stared gravely at him. "I haven't been honest with you. I—"

"Don't." Whatever truths Martin was about to utter, Walter didn't want to hear them. "Let's just have this time together. Please? We don't need honesty when I'll be gone in a day or two."

"But why leave? You can stay here."

"And do what? I'm pretty much broke. I can do construction, but you guys don't need that—everything here's in tip-top shape. I've worked at factories, paper mills, driving a truck, things like that. But you don't need that either. I can't—"

Martin touched a finger to Walter's lips. "We don't care about jobs, Walter. We do what makes us happy, we share what we have, and we all have enough. What's important to us is who you are, not whether you earn money."

"You're communists."

"Communists!" Martin laughed as if the accusation was a funny joke. "No, no. We simply…. Our priorities are different. I don't think that's a bad thing. Too many of your people define themselves—or judge others—by their occupations. That's as bad as falling in love with someone just because he looks nice."

"So I get to hang around indefinitely and leech off you just because you think I'm a swell guy?"

"No." Martin's voice was soft. "We want you to join us and share what we have because we *know* you're a swell guy. Special."

Walter wished he could believe any of this. Hell, maybe he would have turned out well under other circumstances. His teachers said he was smart, and he got good grades. Without the war, with parents willing to pay for college, maybe he'd have gone to medical school like he dreamed about when he was a kid. But his parents had figured the family business was good enough for him, and the Army had killed his passion for medicine by forcing him to attempt to reassemble war-torn men.

"Would all your buddies still want me around if they knew where I was right now?" Naked in bed with one of their own.

An odd smile flickered across Martin's face. "They'd be happy for us both."

Walter scoffed. Even communists hated queers.

Martin traced a single fingertip from the point of Walter's nose down the center of his mouth, his chin, and his neck; the length of his sternum; through the drying mess on his belly; into the sticky curls at his groin; and finally, to the sensitive tip of his cock, which valiantly attempted to reenter the fray. But when Walter reached for him, Martin moved back and gave him a peck on the lips. "Can I spend the night with you?"

"Yes," Walter answered at once.

"You're happy I asked you."

"Of course I am." He'd never slept with another man. He tried a cocky grin. "You'll help keep the bed warm."

"Gladly. But I have some things to do first. While I'm gone, will you at least consider staying for a few more days?"

"Yeah. Okay."

"Good." Another kiss, quick and sweet. "But we'll need to talk about some things when I get back."

Walter tried to scowl, but that was hard to do when Martin was nude and cupping Walter's face in one hand. Walter elected to accept another kiss instead.

Then Martin was out of bed, quickly pulling on his clothing. "Do you want me to bring anything back with me? Something to eat?"

"Just you."

A good answer, perhaps, because Martin hurried over for another kiss, this one heated and spicy. "What you did with me tonight… being inside me…. Do you also like to have a man inside you?"

For a moment Walter forgot how to draw breath. He'd never been on the receiving end before, but God, he ached to welcome Martin inside his body. Before Walter could formulate an answer, Martin smiled widely. "Good! I'd like to try that too."

Then—with a pause at the door to turn and wave—he was gone.

Chapter Four

FOR AN hour or so after Martin left, Walter dozed lightly. A really good orgasm did that to a fellow, especially when it was his second in one day. But with Martin as his partner, he was fairly sure he could manage a third. That thought plus the early hour were enough to keep him from slipping into deep sleep, and eventually he got up and had a quick wash, wrapped himself in a blanket, and read by the warmth of the woodstove.

He was still reading when a soft knock sounded and the door creaked open. Martin crept in, his hair and jacket damp. "You're awake."

"Waiting for you, I guess."

Martin's face lit up with a brilliant smile. "That's a nice thing to say." He hung his jacket on a hook and bent to untie his shoes.

"Did you finish your chores?"

"They weren't exactly chores." His shoes removed, Martin stood and bit his lip. "Walter, we have to—"

"Talk. I know. But tomorrow. Please? I want…." He couldn't say it out loud. But he wanted so badly for Martin to make love to him and spend the night, and he was certain neither of those things would happen if Martin had his talk.

"I don't like being dishonest with you."

"You're not. It's… delayed honesty, is all. Just give me tonight." He looked at Martin beseechingly. Walter had learned during the war that you could never take the next day for granted. Hell, you could never take the next *hour* for granted. More than once he'd been talking to a guy, maybe chatting about baseball or movies or where to get the best pizza in Chicago, and minutes later, that man's lifeblood had spattered Walter's uniform. And if *now* was all Walter had, he wanted to enjoy it.

Martin eyed him closely. "All right. As long as you understand that I'm not what I seem."

Walter didn't know what to make of that, so he shrugged dismissively. "Nobody is." He stood, allowing the blanket to drop and reveal his naked body. Then he held out his arms.

That night Martin treated him like a precious thing, carefully preparing him for penetration. Too carefully, really, because eventually Walter was reduced to babbling pleas. When Martin finally slid into him, they stared at one another like men visited by a divine revelation. "That's... that's...." Walter couldn't find a word for how it felt to have Martin filling him.

Martin just nodded, wide-eyed. "I don't understand why you don't do this all the time."

Walter laughed. Had he ever laughed during sex before? Not that he could remember. Other partners might have taken offense, but Martin laughed with him—at least until he began to rock his hips, and then the laughter shifted to moans and whimpers.

In the dark afterward, their legs entangled beneath the blankets, they stroked each other's skin and talked softly of small but important things, like Walter's childhood memories of chasing fireflies and the fierce neighborhood games of baseball he'd join with his brothers. Like Martin's thoughts about maybe getting a dog and the peace he felt when sitting in the woods.

It was a good night. The best, Walter thought as he drifted into sleep. A treasure to keep forever.

IT WAS strange and wonderful to wake up beside another man. They didn't make love, but they kissed, and then they took turns in the shower. Each sat on the closed toilet to talk as the other soaped and rinsed. Walter had bathed in front of countless men before, but none of them had constituted such an appreciative audience.

They had breakfast together at the Kitee Café, and if Dorothy or the other customers thought there was anything odd about that, they kept their opinions to themselves.

When the meal was over and Walter and Martin stood in the parking lot, Martin got the serious look that meant he intended to have The Talk. But Walter was still resistant. "I need some exercise," Walter said.

"I'll come with."

"Alone."

Martin put his hand on Walter's shoulder. "You can't avoid this forever."

"But I can damned well avoid it for a few more hours, can't I?"

After a lengthy pause, Martin sighed. "You're leading me to do things I know I shouldn't."

Stricken, Walter stepped back. "But I thought you wanted—"

"Not the sex. I wanted that. I *still* want it. Believe me, no regrets on my part. I mean not coming clean to you. I should have done that from the start. Only… then you'd have run away."

Martin appeared so distressed that Walter wanted to hold him—but they were in public. "I've seen a lot of ugly, Martin. Unless you're Adolf Hitler in disguise, nothing you can tell me is going to upset me."

"Walter—"

"I'm going for a walk. We can talk later, okay?"

With obvious reluctance, Martin nodded.

Walter strolled slowly past the neat little houses with the colorful gardens. Every one of them was perfect. He supposed that should have been a comfort to him—it was certainly a contrast to the destruction he'd seen so much of during the war and then the squalor he'd lived in this past year. But it discomfited him instead. People weren't meant to be perfect. Even in his parents' neighborhood, where the houses were big and the cars new, some of the yards ran to weeds during summer and chalked hopscotch squares were scrawled along the sidewalks.

Jesus, his brain was all twisted, wasn't it? Here he was, enjoying a respite in a sweet little town with a sweet, sweet man, and yet his goddamn brain kept telling him something was wrong. It was as if his inner alarm had begun ringing the first day he put on a uniform and he'd never learned how to turn the fucking thing off.

After he'd mustered out and returned to Chicago, one of the first things he did was lock himself in the second-floor bathroom of his parents' house for a long, hot bath. His mother had eventually knocked on the door out of concern, and when Walter told her to go away, his brother Charlie pounded next. "Stop jerking off, Wally!"

But Walter hadn't been jerking off—his libido had been nonexistent then. He'd simply been soaking in blessed solitude, hoping to finally rid himself of the dust of war. He hadn't yet realized that the dust had worked its way into his mind and soul and would be with him forever.

Just past the last house in town, Walter saw someone round a bend in the road, walking his way. He recognized the man when they got closer; it was the same guy he and Martin had run into the previous day. Burt Evans.

Burt stopped and smiled at him. "Hello."

Walter nodded. He wasn't good at small talk and didn't know what to say. Something about the weather? It was cool and slightly misty.

"What's your name?" Burt asked.

"Walter Clark."

"Waaaalter Claaaark." Burt drew out both names. "Interesting. Walter is almost water, isn't it? And Clark—it has all those clicking sounds."

"It's an ordinary name."

Burt grinned. "Not where I come from."

"Oh. Well, there are probably thousands of Walter Clarks in the United States."

"Now, that is one thing I do not understand. How can more than one person have the same name?"

Wondering if he'd misheard the question, Walter blinked at him. "Uh… it's just a name. I mean, hell. My dad and my oldest brother are both Robert Newman Clarks. My brother's got a *junior* hanging on there and goes by Bob, but it's still the same name."

Burt squinted at him and scratched his balding scalp. "So strange. Where I come from, your name is who you are. It changes as you do, but it's always unique to you. After all, nobody else is the same as you."

If Burt had been smiling, Walter would have thought the guy was pulling his leg. But as far as he could tell, Burt was serious. "That doesn't make any sense," Walter said.

"No, two Robert Newman Clarks—*that* makes no sense."

"Where are you from?"

Burt waved vaguely behind him. "Far away. You've never heard of the place." Then he just stood there, staring.

"Well, I was taking a walk, and—"

"We value Martin."

"Uh…."

"Of course, we value *all* members of our community. Everyone is important. But Martin, we've worried about him. He's been so sad for so long."

Walter glanced around them. Nobody else was in sight, yet he felt surrounded. Threatened. He shoved his hands in his jacket pockets and was both regretful and relieved that he'd left his gun back at the motor court.

Burt took a step closer, his brow creased with concern and one hand raised. "Oh, no, Mr. Clark! No, no. Nobody here will harm you. I'm sorry. Your... your way of communicating is so clumsy sometimes. I wasn't clear."

Walter had to force himself not to step back. "I don't—"

"What I was trying to say, Mr. Clark, is that you make Martin happy, and we are grateful for that."

"I'm just renting a cabin from him."

Burt snorted. "That is a very poor lie. And unnecessary. I simply wanted to thank you for making Martin happy. And I wanted to ask you to consider staying with us. Everyone in our community is important, Mr. Clark. You would be too." He patted Walter's arm twice, then continued on his way, leaving Walter standing there.

It felt as if it took several minutes for Walter to get himself moving, but it must have been less. Eventually his legs worked again, taking him away from Kiteeshaa and into the woods. He thought he might be heading for the same path as yesterday, the one that led to the clearing where he'd met Martin. But no, he didn't turn there today. He just kept going, and less than a mile later, the road simply stopped.

Walter stopped too, just at the edge of the blacktop, and stared into a nearly impenetrable thicket of trees and bushes and ferns. It didn't make any sense. Sure, sometimes a road dead-ended, but there was no reason for this one to halt where it did. The town itself was nearly two miles away, and nothing lay past it, so why did the road continue on, as if the builders had intended it to lead somewhere but then had suddenly given up?

Nothing here made sense. For the first time, Walter seriously questioned his own sanity. He hadn't been right since the war, he knew that, but he hadn't.... Oh, Christ! What if he'd lost his tether to reality? He'd seen that during the war too—fellows cracking under the fear and stress, babbling back at voices nobody else heard.

The idea terrified him so much that he stumbled on wobbly legs to the side of the pavement and collapsed onto a fallen log. He leaned his elbows on his knees, buried his face in his hands, and tried to get his lungs and heart to work properly. Maybe none of this was real. Maybe he was locked up in a loony bin back in Chicago or somewhere else between Illinois and Oregon, hallucinating about a perfect town and a perfect lover. Fuck, maybe he'd never even left Europe. What if the war hadn't ended, people were still being blown to pieces, and he'd never gone home?

Walter vomited, narrowly missing his shoes.

When he finished retching, his throat hurt, his mouth tasted terrible, and he was light-headed and shaky. His father and brothers would yell at him if they saw him so weak. For a long moment, he seriously considered walking past the end of the road—pushing his way through the thorns and underbrush until the forest swallowed him for good.

Instead, he slowly made his way back to town.

WHEN WALTER returned to the inn, there was no sign of Martin. Perhaps he was in the office, but Walter didn't check. He didn't want to have that discussion Martin was insisting on—not ever, but certainly not now, when he was weary and confused. He entered unit three, shut the door, and chained it.

The bed was freshly made, and a vase of new flowers graced the little table. All roses this time—delicate pink ones. Next to them, a cloth-covered plate held several sugar cookies, a handful of walnut meats, and some deep red berries he didn't recognize. Beside the plate, a slip of paper contained a note in neat handwriting: *Milk in the fridge. See you soon.—M*

Sure enough, the little refrigerator held a quart of milk. Walter drank straight from the glass container, washing away the sour taste of vomit. The milk helped settle his stomach but not his mind.

He removed his shoes and jacket and, with the rest of his clothing still on, climbed into bed. He hoped he could find that simplest escape from his problems—untroubled sleep—and that the usual nightmares wouldn't torment him. But he also removed his pistol from the drawer and set it atop the bedside table, a talisman against danger. With the curtains drawn and all the lights off but one, the cabin was nearly as dark as night. Walter closed his eyes, burrowed into bedding that smelled faintly like lemons and violets, and fell asleep.

Chapter Five

HE DIDN'T know what awakened him from a dream about flying, but he sat up suddenly in bed, looking frantically around. The lamp gave enough light to prove that no one else was there. He couldn't hear anything but the thump of his heart and the rasp of his breathing.

No. That wasn't true. He heard something else. Well, *almost* heard it. Like catching movement from the corner of your eye, only this was a sound he couldn't quite capture. An echo, perhaps, of a noise from when he was asleep. Except the echo—the sound that wasn't quite there—went on and on. It made his nerves thrum.

Walter got out of bed and tucked the pistol into the back of his trousers. He put on his shoes and jacket and went outside.

He'd somehow managed to sleep away a good part of the day, and now the late-afternoon sun shone weakly through thin clouds. The lights inside the Kitee Café looked bright through the windows, but when Walter moved closer, he saw that the restaurant was empty. No sign even of Dorothy. The village was never a hive of activity, but now it was quieter than ever. The door to the mechanic's bay at the gas station was closed, and nobody lounged in front. He hurried over to the grocer's and the clothing store. In both cases, the doors were unlocked but the shops empty. The plant nursery was abandoned. Panicked, he finally entered the motor court office. He even barged into the private space of Martin's apartment—which Walter hadn't seen before—but Martin wasn't there.

As far as he could tell, he was the only person left in town.

The blood rushed in his skull, making clear thinking difficult. He couldn't come up with a single scenario that would result in the disappearance of a town's entire population yet leave the buildings and their contents untouched. No signs of panic, no indication that anyone had left in haste. Their cars were still there, parked peacefully in driveways and beside the road.

He considered getting in his own car and driving straight to the highway. He could contact the police in Newport. Only... what would he tell them? He'd taken a nap and somehow misplaced 178 people? Besides, that hint of a sound continued to tickle at his eardrums. It drew him slowly down the road—not to his car, not toward the highway, but inland. In the direction of the dead end.

He knocked on a couple of doors as he went. Nobody answered.

The farther he walked, the faster he went. By the time he reached the final bend, he was running. Then the road ended—and nobody was there. He couldn't even hear birds chirping.

His lungs burned as he stood on the pavement and wondered what to do next. The sound was still there. No louder, no quieter. Still scraping along his nerves, as if he were a cat having his fur petted the wrong way.

And then the answer—which should have been obvious—came to him. The clearing, of course.

He backtracked to the path. The daylight was failing, and if he returned, it would be difficult in the dark. That problem didn't especially concern him right now, though, and he trotted alongside the little stream. The sound grew louder as he turned to scale the hill. Well, maybe louder wasn't the right word. Hell, *sound* wasn't the right word either. It was a vibration that reminded him of the way the ground shook under the tread of tanks. He felt it in his bones, and now it seemed as if the thrumming had a pattern, like a tune he couldn't quite identify.

When he neared the crest of the hill, he at first assumed that there was a break in the clouds catching the last long rays of the sun, because the hilltop glowed. But he quickly realized that the color of the light was wrong—too green for sunset. Besides, the glow pulsed to the same beat as the thrumming.

When he got within view of the clearing, he froze.

Dozens of figures stood in the open space under the trees. His first thought on seeing them was *fireflies*, but that was absurd. These things were taller than he was, roughly human-shaped though more slender. But it was impossible to discern their features because they were lit from within by an emerald radiance that ebbed and brightened rhythmically.

The hairs on Walter's nape stood erect, and the air smelled of ozone.

He wanted to convince himself that he was looking at… statues of some kind. A bizarre art installation someone had managed to stick in the middle of nowhere, inside the space of twenty-four hours. But he knew that wasn't true. The figures didn't just pulse and hum. They moved. Slowly, yes, but definitely. One of them would begin to burn more brightly, and the others would turn to face it. A moment later, another would take a turn.

Walter wanted to run but couldn't. The scene terrified him, yet it was also the most heartbreakingly beautiful thing he'd ever experienced. He could tell that these creatures cared for one another, respected one another. Often two of them would touch, and both would momentarily flare with a softer hue of green. That sense of peace Walter had noticed since he first arrived was almost palpable here, but it didn't calm him.

Perhaps he made a sound, or perhaps one of the creatures happened to glance his way. In any case, they all turned to look at him, their lights glaring so brightly he could barely see.

And then one of them was moving toward him. Running. Its long legs covered the ground quickly and its color turned bright red before fading and then dying completely.

Walter yanked the gun from the back of his waistband. His hand shook as he held the weapon in front of him. He wanted to see what was running toward him—it seemed to him that it was *changing*, becoming shorter and more solid—but it was too strongly backlit by the creatures behind it.

The creature moved even faster, and Walter was suddenly certain that it was actually a Wehrmacht soldier. The soldier wore a rounded helmet, a gray-green uniform with a silver eagle on the chest, a black belt cinched high.

Walter pulled the trigger.

"Walter!" The man staggered, then fell back onto the ground. And dear God, of course he wasn't a German soldier at all but Martin, his sweet Martin. Naked and spurting blood from his torso.

With an anguished cry, Walter dropped the gun and ran to Martin's side, then collapsed next to him. Blood was everywhere, *everywhere*, and Walter was a goddamn medic, but he didn't have his kit. No bandages or plasters or sutures or morphine. Nothing but his hands and his own shirt, which he frantically wadded up and pressed to the wound.

Martin stared up at him, eyes wide. "I wanted to tell you," he whispered. "I'm sorry." He reached for Walter with a red-smeared hand.

Walter couldn't say anything but desperate clots of Latin, the mostly forgotten phrases from the Sunday services his *babcia* dragged him to when he was a boy. He was still trying to stop the bleeding when arms grabbed him and pulled him away.

He fought. "No! No! He's hemorrhaging!" But there were many of them, and they were strong, and they kept him from pushing back to Martin. He couldn't even see what was happening to Martin, not through the confusing press of glowing thin bodies and pale, nude skin.

Still restrained, Walter collapsed to his knees and wailed. "No more dying, please! No more! Not him, God." He dropped his voice and mumbled more of his incoherent prayers. He'd heard so many of these pleading words from wounded men, dying men, each of them crying out for his god or his mother or *someone*. The words slightly different, the accents varying, but the meaning always the same. *No death. No death for me today.*

Eventually Walter's strength gave out completely and he grew silent. His hands were sticky with Martin's blood, but he still couldn't see Martin due to the crowd of townspeople and the gathering night. Then someone knelt in front of him—a naked woman with a long, dark braid.

"Are you hurt, Walter?" Dorothy asked.

"I shot him. I didn't mean to hurt him and I.... Four years in the Army and I never killed anyone. I was a medic. But now I've shot Martin. Oh God." He shuddered. And then, although it hardly mattered anymore, he looked at her plaintively. "Who *are* you?"

"Refugees from far away. We came here to escape war, but a bit of it found us anyway." She seemed sad rather than angry.

"Wh-what did Martin want from me?"

"Companionship. Sex. Love. He was lonely and a little lost, Walter. Just like you."

"I killed him."

Dorothy shook her head and stood. Then she spoke to some of the people nearby—these people were wearing clothes—but Walter didn't try to understand what she said. It didn't matter. He was pulled upright and led away from the clearing, the hands guiding him gently but firmly.

Somehow he stumbled down the path to the road, his silent companions leading him unerringly in the darkness. When they came to the motor court, the townspeople tugged him into unit three. "Stay here," said a young man he didn't recognize. "Clean up and rest. Do you want something to eat?"

Walter shook his head in confusion. "I killed him. Why aren't you… you…?" He didn't know how these people meted out punishment, but surely they had some method of exacting retribution on those who deserved it.

"You're too distraught to make sense of anything now. Please. Get some sleep. If you need anything, we'll be just outside."

He didn't want to sleep; in fact, he felt like he could never sleep again. But he couldn't find the words to argue, so he nodded. The young man and the other people exited the cabin, shutting the door behind them.

Walter didn't bother to lock it.

For an eternity, he sat on one of the wooden chairs and stared at the blood on his hands. It looked like ordinary human blood, no different from the stuff that had stained his skin so often during the war. Smelled like it too, rich and metallic. And when Walter stuck out his tongue for a small lick… yes. Iron and salt.

But Martin wasn't human, was he? None of the residents of Kiteeshaa were. They were…. Walter's mind stalled, refusing to provide alternatives. Refugees, they said. Maybe that was all that mattered.

WALTER DIDN'T sleep. He instead spent the night either pacing the little cabin or sitting and staring at the wall. By dawn he'd showered, sluicing away the blood, and put on fresh clothing. He drank some milk and ate the cookies, nuts, and fruit from the plate Martin had left for him. Martin's note was still there too. Walter folded it and put it into his wallet.

Someone knocked politely on the door, and he answered.

"Good morning." Dorothy held a large basket covered with a white cloth. Burt stood next to her, and he nodded a greeting.

Walter stepped back to let them inside, and for a moment they all stood awkwardly. "Do you have police?" Walter finally asked.

"No," Dorothy answered. "We don't need police."

"But I shot Martin."

They each settled a hand on one of Walter's arms. "You were confused," Burt said. "You didn't mean to hurt him, we know that. You were frightened, and your mind sometimes plays tricks on you. Martin shouldn't have run toward you like that."

"It wasn't his fault!"

"It was nobody's fault," Dorothy said soothingly.

Walter's throat was tight. "Why are you being so goddamn *nice* to me?"

"Honey, you deserve to have people be nice to you. You're a good man. The war damaged you. War damages a lot of people. But you're worth something. Give yourself a chance to heal and maybe you'll see that."

"No! You should hate me. All of you should. Martin was the best thing I ever...." He stopped and shook his head. "I think I could have fallen in love with him."

Dorothy and Burt didn't look shocked. "But now that you know what we are?" Burt prompted him.

"I *don't* know what you are!" Then Walter calmed down a bit and sighed. "But I guess it doesn't matter. You're good, I can tell that much. And Martin... I liked the shape of him." A sob caught in his throat and he tried to turn away.

But Dorothy caught him and pressed her basket into his hands. "Some food for you. You missed lunch and dinner yesterday. You'll feel better if you eat."

Maybe the food was poisoned, he thought wearily. He took the basket, gently extricated himself from her grip, and set it on the table. "I need to pack."

"You don't have to leave," Burt said. "We'd like you to stay. That's what we were discussing last night when you found us. We had just decided to formally invite you to live here. You're *still* welcome."

Walter's eyes stung. "How can you say that after what I did?"

Burt smiled. "Because we can see the real you. We have... different senses, you know?"

Even thinking about it hurt Walter's head. He was certainly willing to accept at this point that the residents of Kiteeshaa were capable of some unusual things. But Christ, Martin had felt so goddamn *human* when they'd made love.

"I have to go."

Burt frowned. "But Martin—"

"*Please.* If you're not going to arrest me or... or punish me somehow, please just let me go. I need to leave."

Burt and Dorothy watched sadly as he packed his few belongings. He took the books Martin had given him. He knew he'd feel bad over the theft later, but what did a little extra guilt matter? "Who should... God, who should I pay? For the room?" His voice cracked at the question.

"Don't be silly," said Dorothy.

They trailed him to his car, and after Walter stuffed his duffel in the trunk, Dorothy pushed the basket at him again. "Take this," she ordered.

He sighed and placed the basket on the passenger seat. Then he leaned against the car. "I'm so sorry I did this to you," he said. "You have such a nice little town. You all deserve your peace."

"So do you, honey." Dorothy gave his shoulder a quick caress. "And you are always welcome here. Something I like about you is how accepting you are."

He blinked at her, then remembered how Martin's people said goodbye. "I like your kindness. And thank you for... your forgiveness."

"It's easy to forgive someone else. You made Martin happy, Walter. Remember that. It's what's important."

Chapter Six

THE SHORT drive back to the highway felt endless. It was like those nightmares he had, the ones where he was being chased by bloodied men in uniform and his boots were mired in thick mud. Only now it wasn't the horrors of war he was trying to escape but rather the memories of what he almost had in Kiteeshaa, and what he'd ruined with a single pull of his trigger finger.

Who he'd ruined.

The world was a poorer place without Martin, and that thought made his eyes sting.

He turned south on the Coast Highway without a destination in mind. But barely a half mile later, he saw a sign for a state park. It was a beach Martin had mentioned to him—a favorite, he'd said, for collecting treasures and watching the waves. Walter turned the Ford into a parking space and cut the engine.

For no logical reason, he took Dorothy's basket with him when he left the car. He had to descend uneven steps to get to the beach, and as he did, he kept his gaze firmly fixed on the wooden treads beneath his feet. The expanse of sand in front of him made his stomach churn, and the ocean itself—well, he couldn't look at that at all.

Plodding unevenly through the dry sand, he made his way to a large piece of driftwood and sat on it, facing the waves but with his eyes trained on his feet. He could hear the waves, of course. Their ceaseless crash and pound reminded him of a heart beating. Reminded him too of the pulse of the Kiteeshaa townspeople in their meeting the day before. Maybe all life was related. This sea was the same as the one that had washed him onto the shores of France. His own human species was the same as Martin's alien one. Wanting the same essential things: home, family, peace, love.

Without really deciding to do so, he lifted the cloth from Dorothy's basket and peered inside. She'd packed him a small feast: two sandwiches piled thickly with roast beef, an apple, some pickles wrapped in plastic, and a little jar of potato salad. A covered plate proved to contain a berry tartlet. She'd included a thermos of coffee and a quart bottle of milk as well.

He didn't think he was hungry, but he took a bite and then another, and like magic all the food just disappeared. He tucked everything back into the basket except the open thermos, which he nestled between his thighs. Then he inhaled deeply, and the briny scent of the ocean was thick, without a hint of blood or gunpowder. No whistling of mortar shells or rat-a-tat of gunfire; just the waves thundering and gulls crying.

Gathering his meager courage, he finally lifted his gaze to the Pacific.

Although his heartbeat skittered and his breaths came quickly, he didn't have to look away. Just like Martin's people, the ocean was terrifying and beautiful. It called to him even as it made his chest feel tight.

He wondered if they had oceans where Martin came from. Martin hadn't said.

Staring at the waves, Walter tried to see inside himself. Feel his shape. The process scared him, like crawling through the smoking ruins of a building in search of a survivor. But Martin had found something within him to admire. It seemed as if a good way to honor Martin's memory would be to respect his opinion, to believe that something worth saving truly did hide within those ruins. And Dorothy and Burt—even after what Walter did, they had been willing to let him stay. Surely that meant something as well.

Deep inside, Walter found... a glimmer. Not a beautiful emerald glow; this was only a flash of pale light. But it was there.

He let out a noisy breath. "Martin was right."

"Of course I was."

Walter yelped. He hopped off the log, got tangled in his own feet as he turned around, and fell on his ass. Then he cried out again when he saw a handsome man with pale blue eyes and soft blond curls smiling down at him.

"I killed you!" Walter yelled. He didn't even try to stand up—the sand would be too treacherous for wobbly legs.

"No, you.... Oh, no. Is *that* what you thought?"

"I... I shot you!" There had been a gaping hole and so much blood.

Martin nodded slightly, then untucked and lifted his shirt. A round scar marred his belly, puckered and bright pink.

"N-n-no!" Walter stuttered. "I shot you *yesterday*. You can't—"

"If I'd been in my original form, your bullet wouldn't have harmed me at all. If I'd been fully in this body, well, I suppose I might have died. I was in between, so… it hurt, but I healed." He stepped over the log to Walter's side and held out a hand. "I didn't mean to startle you. Not yesterday. Not today either. I forget that you can't sense me the way I sense you."

With considerable trepidation, Walter took the offered hand and allowed Martin to help him stand. As soon as Walter was upright, Martin enveloped him in a bear hug. "I thought I'd lost you," Martin murmured into his ear.

"No, that's my line. God, Martin, I shot—"

"I scared you. I'm sorry." Martin abruptly let go of Walter, then took a step back. "And I misled you about my nature. I'm sorry about that too."

"You tried to tell me. I didn't listen." Walter shook his head. "I don't think I would have taken it well."

"But now that you know…."

"It's a lot to accept. But you've seen the real me and you accept *that*."

Martin smiled. "Not just accept. I told you. The real you is beautiful."

"Like driftwood," Walter said, gesturing toward the log.

"Better." Martin came close again and stroked Walter's cheek with a thumb. "You're wounded, Walter. Much worse than what that bullet did to me. And your own people don't understand because they can't see the scars. But I do. Scars can heal, though. I can help."

Walter wanted very badly to give in, to let Martin sweep him off his feet and tuck him away somewhere safe. But nothing so good could be so easy. "You'll always have the one I gave you."

"Only because I choose to keep it. I could have healed it completely."

"Why didn't you?"

"It was the only souvenir you left me." Martin's smile was sweet, yet sad enough to break Walter's heart.

Walter looked down at the thermos, which had fallen when he lurched off the driftwood and had leaked the last of its contents into the sand. "Why did you come to the beach?"

"Dorothy told me you'd left. She said you…." Martin appeared suddenly shy. "She told me what you said before you left. That you thought you could love me. So I searched for you. You weren't so hard to find." He waved up at the bluff, where Walter's battered old car squatted alone by the side of the highway.

Walter was suddenly angry. "Why didn't she and Burt tell me you were still alive?" Christ, he could have gone the rest of his life believing he'd murdered Martin.

"They didn't realize you thought I was dead. I think they misread your grief. And I told you—sometimes we forget what you're blind to. We can tell when one of our own has died."

A war, Martin had said. "And when your family and friends were killed?" Walter asked quietly.

Stark grief etched Martin's face. "I can still feel the echoes of it."

It was Walter's turn to scoop him into an embrace. God, Martin smelled so wonderful! Like campfires and fresh growing things in the spring.

"Come back with me," Martin said. "Stay with us."

"But I'm not... one of you."

"We don't care. *I* don't care. I like what you are."

Could it be that Walter had found acceptance so easily? Perhaps. Who better to understand him than a group of refugees? Still, he couldn't quite believe it. He didn't deserve this.

"I'm not perfect," Martin said, smiling against Walter's cheek. "No more than you are. You've already seen that sometimes I follow my heart rather than my head. I'm told I can be stubborn. I don't understand your music at all, and your math? It does nothing but confuse me. Even our youngest children are better than me at arithmetic. Sometimes when I should be happy, I remember everything we lost and I have to sit for a while and cry. And now that I've tried it, I *think* I'm going to be a little obsessed with kissing you and having sex with you."

Walter chuckled. "That last part doesn't sound like a problem. Or maybe it's one we can share."

Martin pulled back a little, enough so Walter could see the sparkle in his eyes. "That's just it! There's your shape and mine, and we fit together so perfectly. We make a completely new shape. And Walter, it's so beautiful! Can't you see?" He leaned his forehead against Walter's.

Walter closed his eyes and yes, he *could* see. With the pounding ocean and the endless gray sky to witness, Walter silently pledged to open his heart. He could tell by the fervency of the resulting kiss that

Martin heard and understood his promise. If any people were watching them from the edge of the highway, the observers wouldn't just see two men making out: they would see them glowing.

"Tell me something that makes you happy," Walter whispered when they finally broke the kiss.

"The sound of rain falling on a roof when I'm cozy inside. You?"

"The idea of climbing into that wonderful bed in unit three and spooning against you."

Martin laughed joyfully and kissed him again.

"What's the special at the Kitee Café today?" Walter asked.

Martin cupped Walter's face in his hands and grinned. "Let's go home and find out."

KIM FIELDING is very pleased every time someone calls her eclectic. Her books have won Rainbow Awards and span a variety of genres. She has migrated back and forth across the western two-thirds of the United States and currently lives in California, where she long ago ran out of bookshelf space. She's a university professor who dreams of being able to travel and write full-time. She also dreams of having two perfectly behaved children, a husband who isn't obsessed with football, and a house that cleans itself. Some dreams are more easily obtained than others.

Blogs: kfieldingwrites.com and www.goodreads.com/author/show/4105707.Kim_Fielding/blog
Facebook: www.facebook.com/KFieldingWrites
E-mail: kim@kfieldingwrites.com
Twitter: @KFieldingWrites

By Kim Fielding

Alaska
Animal Magnetism
(Dreamspinner Anthology)
Astounding!
The Border
Brute
Don't Try This at Home
(Dreamspinner Anthology)
Grateful
A Great Miracle Happened There
Grown-up
Housekeeping
Love Can't Conquer
Men of Steel
(Dreamspinner Anthology)
Motel. Pool.
Night Shift
Pilgrimage
The Pillar
Phoenix
Rattlesnake
Saint Martin's Day
Snow on the Roof
(Dreamspinner Anthology)
Speechless • The Gig
Steamed Up
(Dreamspinner Anthology)
The Tin Box
Venetian Masks
Violet's Present

BONES
Good Bones
Buried Bones
The Gig
Bone Dry

GOTHIKA
(Multiple Author Anthologies)
Stitch
Bones
Claw
Spirit
Contact

Published by DREAMSPINNER PRESS
www.dreamspinnerpress.com

My Final Blog

By F.E. Feeley Jr

Chapter 1

I wasn't expecting much from life to begin with. I wasn't handsome in the traditional sense. I mean, I wasn't terminal, but no one would stop on the street to give me a second glance. I wasn't athletic. I wasn't fat or too skinny, just average. I didn't excel at school, didn't join the basketball team or the swimming team or hell, even the chess team. I sort of faded into the background. I graduated 110th out of 180 students with about a C average. I blended into the background. And I was sort of fine with that.

I dreamed, sure, like everyone. I would imagine holding a microphone onstage and singing to thousands of adoring fans, or being in a recent Hollywood blockbuster, giving my thank-you speech on Oscar night. But truth be told, I was terribly nervous and sort of awkward in large crowds. Or medium crowds. Or, even worse, intimate gatherings where, in my nervousness, I had a tendency to say inappropriate things and tell stories people wouldn't understand.

Everything about me was simply average. My height, my weight, the length of my penis when I measured it one night in a vain attempt to find something endearing about me. The only thing that made me stand out in any way, at least to myself, was that I was gay. And by "stand out," I mean in a bad way. I was sort of effeminate. And people in school, mostly the jock types, smelled that on me like a shark smelled blood in the water. I received attention, oh yes, but it was the attention no one really wanted and as a matter of fact, sort of loathed. I wished I could just fade back into the shadows and be as invisible as my other features were.

I was gay. Still am. That isn't something that goes away like acne or baby fat. No, that stays with you. But I had done things to try to change that. I watched the way the jocks walked and tried to imitate it. I lowered my voice, forcing myself to speak an octave lower. After I graduated from high school, I even joined the military. Because let's face it, in a hypermasculine environment where homosexuality was not allowed, *surely* that would change me. Like I said, I wasn't the brightest bulb in the box. All it did was tone up my body somewhat and allow me the space in which to grow up. And it also gave me the courage to tell my parents the truth of who I was—even though their reaction was less than stellar. Being the son of an evangelical minister, that tends to happen. But it was okay. It was my life to live, my burden to bear, and at least I had the wherewithal to understand that, unlike my parents, whose religion forced them to bear the burden of not properly raising their son. If it hadn't been this issue, it would have been another, as I would have extracted myself at some point from the petri dish of Independent Baptist living. It was truly a cesspool, a philosophical pond with no fresh water and a vacuum of foul intellectual incest. They had all of the convictions of the Amish but lacked the dedication to truly separate themselves from the world. No. Luxury cars, splendid churches, and private extramarital affairs were far too frequent in the supped up theocratic monarchists and religious oligarchs within fundamentalism. The only thing you needed to do to become king, was to wave a Bible, have a swinging dick between your legs, and express an insatiable need to subject people to those two prior things. I couldn't take the hypocrisy.

Almost as long as I had known about the Internet, I had also known about blogging. And as a young man, through my Army years and even up until recently, I had maintained an anonymous blog about how I felt being outside of the normal. An alien of sorts. Sent here to observe the weirdness of humanity and how I didn't fit in.

I must admit the earliest entries were terribly angsty. Sort of flowery in prose. That probably had to do with hormones and my body changing as I went through puberty. You know, that time when the seven plagues of Egypt erupt all over your body as a form of birth control? When there is enough oil and grease on you to fry chicken? When your voice cracks and your palms sweat and suddenly you stink? Like, really, really smell bad?

Heh.

Anyway, as I grew older, I maintained this little blog that, oddly enough, attracted a huge following. As an outlet, it gave me great comfort to know that people who replied—who stayed as anonymous as I did—were hanging with me through the entirety of my life. And looking back, when I didn't really have much to look forward to, it kept me from heading into the bathroom to dispatch myself the way some teenagers did when their lives were a living hell. And for me, mine was.

I was the walking poster boy for depression. Or maybe that isn't exactly right. While, there were no heights of ecstatic joy, no high emotional cliffs to fling myself from, and no deep cavernous depths in which to fall, my life was sort of flatlined. Sort of level. No movements up or down. It was gray with a side of gunmetal; it was cloudy with a chance of overcast. Hmm, now that I read that, maybe it was depression. Anyway, it was all sort of level. Either I was ignored, or I was tormented. The "people of the blog," as I referred to them, were never so far away nor unsympathetic. I found a measure of happiness with them. Even when I came out as gay to them, they congratulated me on my courage and told me to ignore those who couldn't handle it. Which again acted as a buffer against the attention I did receive from my family or neighborhood bullies.

That's not to say I didn't have friends on the outside. Sure I did. But even with them, sometimes I felt like the odd man out—the pop references they made that I didn't understand, the bands they talked about that I didn't know because rock music was forbidden in my house, the books I had never read. And so on. I felt as if there was an invisible glass wall between me and the rest of the world. I tried to catch up. Honest. As a matter of fact, today music and books, poetry and prose, entertain me to no end. I devour these things like a starving man might devour food at a buffet. I could stay up all night and watch YouTube videos, following the strings of the suggestions it makes like an explorer follows long-dead paths through pyramids or caves. Or I will listen to a song fifty million times until I parse out each nuance, each change in the inflection of voice, the tempo. I will reread a bit of poetry or a speech given by some great person's voice before thousands until I can recite it.

And I would also talk about this on my blog. Sort of poke fun at myself for being so obsessive over things. Those entries didn't receive much attention: a few likes, a few shares, a few comments. People liked it, however, when I was introspective over being in some sort of conflict. I guess that's the thing with art. What's treasure to one, is trash to another. However, one person stayed with me through every single blog post over the years. It was a familiar name: Universal47. Well, familiar to anyone who was an avid *Star Trek* fan.

Out of curiosity one night, I went back to the earliest blog posts I'd written, and he didn't show up until I had written, like, seven.

But after that he was a constant. Always commenting, liking, and encouraging me.

I say *he*, because once he'd alluded to himself as being male. I didn't know one way or another. Like I said, it was an anonymous blog post, and out of respect, I let everyone know that there was no pressure on my page to be who they were. It was a judgment-free zone. And they, in return, didn't pressure me to tell them who *I* really was. Which, given the YouTube generation of commentators, personalities, and people struggling to "go viral," was a rarity. Out there everyone wanted to know who everyone was. But not here, nope. None of that.

But Universal47 was the exception to the rule. Where commenters would come and go, some who'd been with me, like, forever would stop commenting, and it made me wonder what happened to them. Did they just move on? Did they get married and get busy with life? Did they die?

I didn't know. I couldn't know. But Universal47 was always with me.

Late at night was when he'd comment. I'd stay up to read whatever it was he had to say. He and I would go back and forth discussing certain things. Always ideas. Always imaginative conversations about the universe. It was never small talk. I *loathe* small talk. People use that to fill space, uncomfortable silences when they don't know what to say. I don't mind the quiet.

Depended on the topic, depended on the commentary, but it was never dull. We talked things out as far as they could go. Winding with words and unraveling the possibilities that seemed endless even if they wound up in the world of the fantastic or silly. And we'd laugh and bid each other a good night. Other commenters would read and comment on the exchanges as well, and we'd be polite to them and engage, but there was something between the both of us, exclusively. I knew that, and so did some of the others. Sometimes it was met with humor, sometimes with suggestions that we knew each other IRL (in real life) or that we were romantically involved. Those latter comments always brought a smile to my face. Especially at night as I lay in my bed, my arms folded under my head, and stared up at the ceiling, trying to conjure up a face to the name. Sometimes he became a famous person, some stud in Hollywood who used anonymity to reach the outside world. Other times it was some aged politician, some elder statesman who was suave and debonair and couldn't be gay in his real life. Then I would think about Lindsay Graham and end up giggling myself to sleep.

Other times Universal47 was a university professor, a media mogul, a lonely man writing to me on a deserted island where he'd moved to write great novels. Needless to say, he was always some gorgeous man who was just cultured enough to know a little bit about everything, handsome enough to stop traffic, and who'd taken notice of someone like me. On occasion, however, when I tried to enquire about who he was or where he was from, on the side and away from other readers, of course, he would tease me about anonymity and shame me about wanting to break my own rules. And I, chastised, would cut it out and go back to my dull life when the sun came back up.

Don't feel bad for me. I mean, I guess there's something to be said about living a normal, boring life. I don't think I could handle being famous or infamous. I like the idea of people liking me, and I fantasize over someone loving me, just like everyone else. But I knew at the time that there were people out there in the world who went their whole lives without knowing what that was like. They got up, went to work every day, or to school, and came home to meals taken by themselves in their kitchen, and on to watch their television sets. They had a few friends and associates, just people they'd go out to dinner with on occasion, and maybe they were even married with kids. Their spouses "just made sense."

I guess being alone with people beats being alone all by one's self. I get that.

My romantic life hadn't been much to speak of. In searching for love I put up with more things than a confident man would have endured. I wasn't bereft of passion; I just tended to waste it on people. Especially one dude in particular. Joseph.

Gods, I once thought the sun and moon rose and set on Joseph's whims. Looking back, though, I realize he was probably just as shattered as I was. He was older than me by ten years, and like most of his relationships, ours was founded online in some AOL chat room back in the day. The picture I had of myself was backdropped by a messy room. His first message—and this should have been an indicator of what was to come—was critical of my housekeeping abilities.

Throughout the length of the relationship, three years to be exact, I tried to make up for whatever shortfall he saw in me. I worked harder, slaved away at everything I did, trying to prove myself worthy of his affection. But he was always critical. Always pointing out where I had shortcomings, and I took it. Mostly because I agreed with him. Finding everything I had been used to in him, the relationship felt normal. Even though I had become cuter than I'd been before, around him I felt like five miles of bad road, someone who could disappear into the background if he willed me away. Which he often did.

I broke up and got back together with him more times than should be allowed before a person gets put in a funny farm for going back once more. And, of course, in typical George fashion, I went back again. Hey, negative attention was still attention, right?

During that time, Joseph became the subject of many of my blogs. For anonymity's sake I changed his name as well. On those threads, however, Universal47 always shied away. He wouldn't comment at all, or if he did, it was short one-liners like "I'm sorry you're going through a hard time." Or "That's a shame."

Our dialogue would disappear, and while others would seize on the moment to advise me on what to do or what to say, when they would suggest Beyoncé's new album with the song "Irreplaceable," I felt sort of abandoned by my friend. However, after the final straw that broke the camel's back—when I found out, after Joseph had been raising the bar on me in regards to what it took to win his affection, that he'd been cheating on me the entire time—I walked away for the last time. That revelation had come in a series of e-mails from Universal to the e-mail associated with the blog. He'd found Joseph on a hookup website and engaged him, flirted with him, and even set up places for them to meet.

I was heartbroken, of course. Angry at Universal and Joseph and life itself. I had been a good boyfriend, honest and true. But like they say, the first cut is always the deepest.

However, I printed out the conversations Universal and Joseph had had and left them on his computer desk when I gathered what little I had at his house. The usual angry phone calls and text messages never came. Off to the side in private chat, one night after I'd had a couple of beers and was feeling sorry for myself, I bitterly thanked Universal47 for showing me the truth. I was angry, hurt, and felt betrayed.

Universal47: *Are you angry with me?*
Me: *I'm just disgusted in general.*
Universal47: *I don't know why you put up with him for so long.*

Me: *Then where were you?*
Universal47: *I was here.*
Me: *Here, where?*
Universal47: *Waiting for you to see.*
Me: *What is that, some kind of joke? Waiting for me to see what? That I'd been taken for a sucker?*
Universal47: *That you were blinded by love.*

I remembered choking back a laugh, and I felt particularly nasty when I typed: *Love. What would you know about that?*

I grabbed my cigarettes and the beer I was drinking and walked out onto the porch where I stewed in my misery for a little while. Standing out there I looked up at the heavens and contemplated my place in the cosmos, wishing on stars that were as distant as any happiness I'd ever known. I was drunk and angry. And after I threw out my cigarette butt, I felt like shit for being so nasty to someone who'd at least stood up for me.

As I walked back into my little office, in my little house, and sat down in my chair, I saw Universal47's message waiting for me when I returned.

Universal47: *I love you.*

I snorted and brought my fingers down on the keyboard.

Me: *Oh, is that right, Mr. I Don't Want You to Know Anything About Me? That's sweet of you, but I don't think you know me.*
Universal47: *I know a great deal about you.*

And then a thought dawned on me that I hadn't even considered. Something I'd overlooked in the flurry of my drama with Joseph. Something that struck me as odd, and something that made me sort of recoil in horror.

Me: *How did you know who my boyfriend is? This whole thing is anonymous. Did I give you his name by mistake?*

I sat impatiently awaiting an answer.

Universal47: *You've alluded to where you lived, your community, you've described what your ex looked like, it was simply a matter of deduction.*

Me: *Oh. So you probably know my name.*

That sort of made me feel better. Or maybe it made me feel worse. Either way it was out now. And thinking back, someone could have put everything together from clues and hints I'd dropped on the page. I sighed and sat back in my chair, my drunkenness turning into fatigue.

Universal47: *George Underwood.*
Me: *You have me at a disadvantage, sir.*
Universal47: *My name is Elijah.*

I sat up straighter in my chair, the fog clearing from my mind. This was the most I'd ever gotten out of him. And I hesitated to go overboard in demanding that he tells me everything about himself, but curiosity being what it was, it was chewing at me. Instead, I thought I would try to ease into it.

Me: *I like that name.*
Universal47: *I like George.*

I rolled my eyes and, despite how I'd been feeling, smiled.

Me: *You said you loved me.*
Universal47: *I love you. I like the name.*
Me: *Touché.*
Universal47: *So I am sure you want the skinny on me.*
Me: *Nope.*

I was dying for it.

Universal47: *No?*
Me: *I have you inside my head. I have what you look like, what you do, where you are, all inside my head.*
Universal47: *Wow. You've given it that much thought?*

I laughed aloud.

Me: *Me and everyone else, Elijah.*
Universal47: *I knew they had. But I didn't know that you'd done so.*
Me: *Is that weird?*
Universal47: *I don't think so. At least I hope not. I've done the same.*
Me: *Why didn't you just say something?*
Universal47: *I didn't know if you could handle it.*
Me: *Handle it? What are you? Some drug lord? A prince in a castle? Wait... you're not a Republican senator from the Carolinas are you?*
Universal47: *LOL! NO! I am not Lindsay Graham.*
Me: *Thank goodness.*
Universal47: *I am Elijah. That's the truth.*

THAT'S THE truth, he'd said. I hadn't expected much out of life. Like I said, I was just average. But the night I learned Elijah's real name was the beginning of an extraordinary tale. One I'd like to share with you if you'd let me. One that I love. About someone I love. And someone who loves me back. That in itself is extraordinary, I think. But how this all came about?

Well, that's a bit more difficult to explain.

Chapter 2

OUR TOWN isn't very big. Well, the town I moved to after I left the military isn't very big. And I sort of like that. I like the solitude of it. The fact that my neighbor is about a mile and a half down the road, around the corner, and past an old covered bridge. My little house, as modest as it is, sits on about five acres of field. It's an old farmhouse that I saw one day as I searched through real-estate listings that wouldn't break my budget. And I fell in love with it right away. Sure, it needed work. The wallpaper throughout the house was antiquated, the floors needed to be stripped down and refinished, the walls needed to be painted, and some windows needed replacing. But I had done it all. Meticulously. And before long, the house began to glimmer and glow. I didn't update it; I wanted to restore it. So the fixes I made to the place were as close as I could get it to how it once looked.

My ex thought that was dumb. But I didn't. I wouldn't even hook up central air-conditioning, opting instead to have a single window unit in my bedroom for when the evenings didn't cool down enough. But during the day I would keep every window open, and the breeze would roll through the house in the early morning, smelling of dew, and at night when I would blog, I could smell the rain in the air that swept the plains of Iowa. Although, to be honest, there were certain storms that would send me dashing off into the basement. On those occasions I would sit with a gas lamp in the dark cellar, counting my heartbeats. But morning would come and with it bright, golden rays of sunshine, and I would learn from weather reports later in the day that I'd nearly been eradicated off the map. But even those things were few and far between.

There is a big old red barn out in the back that was once used for storage. I love that as well. When I came to own the house, I restored it too. I pulled off old boards, rehanged the roof, and bought bright red paint. It stood out in stark contrast to the white house with green trim, and I loved it. It was a long way away from the life I had known prior to living there. And that was okay.

I'd saved up enough money in the military to allow me a bit of freedom if I lived frugally. And once the restorations were complete, I took a job in Des Moines as a trader of mercantile. It was easy enough work, and something that put my extensive computer savvy to use, enough to pay the bills and put something away in savings. I didn't want to live a lavish lifestyle. To be honest, I wouldn't even know how. I think that might have been the problem with me and Joseph.

He'd been raised here; I was a stranger. He wanted out and I wanted in. I was looking to settle down, and he was looking for a way out. In retrospect I should have picked up on that. But I figured that I could convince him to stay if I loved him enough. I just wanted to see and be seen by him—to see myself reflected in a positive way through someone else's eyes. What was wrong with making a little love, making a little life, and aspiring to the mundane, to be average? I'd grown up in the hustle and bustle of Chicago, where the cold wind off Lake Michigan froze everything solid in the winter. And I'd been deployed to the hottest hell in the world with the military. In the Middle East, sand blasted everything, temperatures would crest well over one hundred degrees, and the clothes and equipment we wore made it all worse. So when I ventured out into the world, average seemed all right by me.

At night, when I'd put in a hard day either at work or at the homestead, I would crack a beer and lay out underneath the stars. In this part of the country, they were plentiful. That's not even the right word; they were in abundance. When the sun went down and the sky was cloudless, the heavens would put on a silent fireworks display that left me feeling incredibly small. But I stared anyway, in wonder. Occasionally a plane would make its way overhead, on its final approach into Des Moines. Or a comet would shoot out across the vast black lake above my head, I'd follow it with my gaze, and my still breath would come out in a gush.

I'd often wondered, alone, if there was life beyond what I knew. What the world knew. Sure, as I fit into the geek culture growing up, I'd been a serious *Star Trek* and *Star Wars* fan, wondering about the future and if I'd ever see humanity soar out among the stars. And I'd often blogged about that and other fantastic ideas late at night when I was feeling somewhat insane with the idea.

Of course, Universal47 and others would engage me on the topic. Some of the smarter people would talk about warp technology and try to explain string theory to me while others debated the philosophical differences between the two franchises. And of course, it would turn into a hilarious debate about which was more powerful than the other. Meanwhile, Universal47 and I would sidestep it all.

Universal47: *Do you believe that there are other species out in the universe besides our own?*

Me: *Of course. It's sort of human arrogance to assume we're alone in the universe.*

Universe47: *What do you think these other species are like?*

Me: *Conceptually? I can't see them as too different from us, really. I mean, they may vary beyond how we as a species vary. But I'm sure they are as plentiful and as diverse as the stars in the sky at night.*

Universe47: *You think so?*

Me: *Sure.*

Universe47: *I like the way you think about it.*

Me: *What do you think they think about us?*

Universal47: *I think they think we're a young species. I think they are curious about us.*

Me: *I hope we impress them sometimes.*

Universal47: *I think every once in a while we make a good impression. I think they listen in.*

Me: *I like that idea.*

Universal47: *I am glad.*

Me: *I wonder if they make love.*

Universal47: *That's an unusual question.*

Me: *Do you think so?*

Universal47: *I'm not saying it's silly. It's just different is all.*

Me: *I like to pretend there are some great romances out there.*

Universal47: *Do you think you could ever love an alien?*

Me: *I guess so. Why not? He would have to be a good guy, though.*

Universal47: *I'm sure he would have to be.*

I logged off that night and crawled into bed, checking my phone on the off chance that Joseph had sent me a text to tell me he loved me, that he missed me, that he was watching paint dry on his walls and wanted me to come and entertain him. Which was usually the way of it.

He would never say he loved me. But when it came to sex, he would beg for it when I stayed away awhile. He'd beg me to come over and make him come. And I would go and take comfort in him. Meanwhile I would pretend that he loved me.

And of course there wasn't a message. Little did I know that he was out hoein' it up somewhere else in town. So instead I sent a message to Universal47. As always, I pictured him in some faraway place where he was sitting on a beach or living in some high-rise apartment in New York City, stealing a moment to talk to me, and the thought made me smile.

Me: *Are you a good guy?*

It wasn't until morning when I was showering for work that I heard a reply come back. I didn't have time to check it and hurried out the door to my nine-to-five.

When I got home that night, after I'd finished cooking dinner, reading a novel, doing yoga, and having a brief yet heated conversation with Joseph, I logged back in.

Universal47: *I try to be.*

I laughed.

Me: *Don't we all?*

Universal47: *Some more than others.*

Me: *I think you're probably a good guy.*

Universal47: *Why do you say so?*

I thought about that for a moment. *How did I know that?*

Me: *Honestly? It's a feeling. You take the time to talk to me. Explain things. Debate things with me. And you're really nice to me.*

Universal47: *You're easy to be nice to.*

Me: *Tell that to my boyfriend.*

Universal47: *He knows. He just doesn't want to. Which is unfortunate.*

Me: *For him, for me, or for the alien observers?*

Universal47: *Yes.*

Me: *LOL. All of 'em, huh? Well, I hope they don't judge the entire human race on my inability to keep my relationship together.*

Universal47: *Why is it your responsibility alone?*

I shrugged as if he could see me.

Me: *I dunno. I chose him, I guess. I could walk away. I could sell my house and move back to the city. Start over.*

Universal47: *But you won't. You don't work that way. You try. And when it doesn't work out, you try harder. And when that doesn't work, you work harder. Are you ever going to make him try for something?*

We were wandering into dangerously choppy waters. I was defensive over my relationship. I mean, there were good times. Christmases and birthdays were great. But there were times when I could dry up and disappear and I don't think Joseph would have cared. As a matter of fact, it was the sort of "go away–come back" messages that I received from him that confused me. Which was sort of pathetic. But you know what they say about hindsight. It was always twenty-twenty. I ended up saying good night and went about my evening. But his words haunted me.

Yet, fast-forward to the night he told me his name. I sat staring at my computer screen as it flashed in front of me: *Elijah*.

I liked the name. Of course I understood the biblical reference. Elijah was a prophet who once called down fire from heaven to consume a sacrifice to God. Or else it was the name of the really blue-eyed actor who played Frodo Baggins in *The Lord of the Rings* movies. I put those two things up for consideration in the chat box and was greeted with a great big LOL for my efforts.

Universal47: *Neither. But that's funny.*

I tilted my head for a moment before typing.

Me: *Will we ever meet?*

Universal47: *I believe so. Do you want to meet me?*

Me: *Of course.*

Universal47: *Why?*

Me: *To put a face with a name?*

Universal47: *Is that all?*

Me: *Sure. Isn't that enough?*

Universal47: *And what would we do if we met?*

I rolled my eyes hard at that.

Me: *Well, you're not getting laid if that's what you mean. I could go on Grindr for that.*

Universal47: *HAHAHAHA! I'm sure you could. And no, that isn't what I'm after either.*

Me: *So you are after something?*

Universal47: *Companionship? Is that weird?*

Me: *No. I don't think so. You must get lonely too.*

Universal47: *You have no idea.*

Me: *Well, if it's any consolation to you. At night, when I fall asleep, you're not far from my mind.*

Universal47: *That's really the sweetest thing anyone's ever said to me. But you don't know what I look like.*

Me: *No. I guess not.*

Universal47: *What do you think about when think about me before you fall asleep?*

Me: *Honestly? You've had many faces. But your arms are always the same. Strong. There. Just like you've been all these years. There. That's what matters to me, Elijah.*

He was quiet for a long time after that, and before he could reply, I felt my eyes grow heavy. It had been a long couple of days. And since it was Friday night, I had a whole weekend's worth of work to do. I bid him good night and logged out.

I hoped I hadn't said too much. I hope I hadn't freaked him out. But my ability to bullshit was completely depleted by that time, and truth sort of rolled out of me in waves. That night as I lay in bed listening to the wind howling over the prairies, it was so mournful and so lonesome sounding that I cried myself to sleep.

Chapter 3

THE HOUSE was quiet at two thirty in the morning. Outside, the wind howled as tree limbs brushed against the window, making eerie scratching noises against the glass. A clock tick-tocked in the kitchen until the second hand reached twelve in its continuous rotation. Then it stopped. The lights, which had been off, flickered in a wave throughout the house as if they were ocean waves crashing upon the shore. In slow motion they came on and went off on their way to the bedroom where George slept deeply.

Had he been awake, he would have noticed the smell of ozone, as if lightning had struck somewhere close.

In the bedroom, the lights flickered once before going dark. The computer in the corner booted to life. George rolled over in bed and murmured Elijah's name. The load-up screen finished, bringing up the desktop. Its blue light illuminated the room. George rolled over onto his side, subconsciously avoiding it.

The camera atop his computer, used to skype with distant friends and relations and to take the occasional selfie for his Facebook page, began to focus in and out. A window popped open on the desktop, and the image of George's bed appeared. Suddenly the screen turned completely white and began to flash in quick succession, in patterns of three. Through the speakers, pulses blared in time with the flashing light. It came out as a static *thud-thud-thud*. George rolled over in bed again and threw back the covers before sitting up. His face was creased with the indentions of the pillow and his hair hung in his eyes.

As he stood up, George's T-shirt clung to his lithe body. He walked closer to the computer, his eyes staring, dead, into the flashing light. George stood there swaying on his feet for a moment before reaching down and removing his shirt. The white light flashed in quicker succession and the pulses coming out of the speakers increased in volume. He turned around slowly, lifting his arms into the air and then back down in a strange sort of ballet.

Once he turned back around, George tucked his thumbs into the waistband of his pants and, in one fell swoop, lowered them to the ground. He kicked out of them and stood there, barefoot, in front of the computer screen, with a semi-erection. Once again he turned in slow motion.

When he came back around, the flashing had stopped, although the camera box was open. On its swivel, the camera turned its eye up at George. The lens began to flash with a red light into the eyes of the man who now stood there with a full erection jutting out. And then the screen went dark and the computer shut itself off.

George stood there a moment longer before turning around and walking back, naked, to his bed. He climbed underneath the covers and turned over onto his side.

Before too long, snoring could be heard as the lights in the bedroom flickered three times before reversing their travel through the house.

THE NEXT morning, I woke as the sun filtered in through the windows. As my eyes fluttered open and I stared at the ceiling, I couldn't help but smile a little at the dreams I'd had the night before. They'd been incredibly erotic.

I'd found myself standing in the midst of a large gray room. There had been no doors, no windows, but a soft light ran up the walls. At my feet a cool mist covered the floor, and as I looked down at myself, I realized I was naked. I wasn't embarrassed about it. Actually I was rather comfortable, as if I'd been there a dozen times or more. And my heart felt full, and I knew someone was waiting for me.

Underneath my feet the floor vibrated gently and seemed to roll forward as if the ground pulsed with a life of its own. As I walked farther into the room, I realized the light on the walls did the same thing in series of three. In the center of the room stood a bed. Meaning to walk toward it, I took a step, and suddenly arms were around me and a body pressed to my back. I was briefly startled, but the familiarity of those arms made me wrap my own arms around them. His were strong arms, thick and long, and his soft sex pushed at the cleft of my buttocks, his stomach against the small of my back, and his powerful chest pressed against my shoulders.

I couldn't help myself; I arched my back and heard him moan as he lowered his head to my neck.

I whispered, "I've missed you."

"I've always been here, George."

The timber of his voice was low and rumbled through my body. I felt his sex stir, grow long, and harden as his hands came around my biceps and squeezed gently. Somehow I knew every single inch of him. Literally and in the biblical sense. My own cock stirred and lifted, and my balls felt heavy and in need of release.

"I know," I said. "I'm sorry I was away so long."

"You had to find out what you had to find out. You knew I'd wait."

"I hope I didn't hurt you."

He didn't say anything. Instead, he trailed kisses down my neck again before reaching down and picking me up. I laughed as I laid my head on his shoulder. The smell, the feel, was so familiar to me.

And then everything from that point faded into lovemaking. I could feel his arms, his mouth, his heat; I heard him sigh and moan in pleasure. I felt him inside me, moving. I remember being in his lap, legs wrapped around his hips, hands holding his face as he kissed me.

And then the earth-shattering orgasm.

As I stretched luxuriously in my bed, thoughts of my ex a distant thing in the back of my head, I couldn't help but smile. I wanted to drift off back to sleep. I was sort of tired, and to be honest, kind of sore. But then I realized I didn't have my T-shirt on. I sat up quickly, the sheet falling down to my waist, and looked about the bed to see if I'd taken it off in my sleep.

Then I realized I didn't have my pajama bottoms on either. "What the hell?"

Awake now, I yanked back the covers. The top sheet was sticking to me. I peeled it off and stared at it momentarily before I barked out a laugh. "Well, shit. I guess good times were had by all."

I stood there, bareassed, for a moment longer, racking my brains and trying to figure out just when in the hell I did a striptease in my bedroom. Had I been sleepwalking? A victim of some kind of short circuit of the brain who wanted to touch and be touched? Was I missing Joseph that much?

My thoughts flashed back to the dream I'd had. And it hadn't been Joseph's face I'd stared into. No, it had been someone else. However, the face was elusive. I remembered green eyes, soft lips, and….

"Strong arms." I shook my head. "I fornicated with Elijah and didn't even get a good look at his face."

The idea made me roar with laughter as I picked up my clothes off the floor and put them in a basket of laundry that I'd have to get to at some point this weekend. However, the yard needed my attention first, and as I strode over to the dresser, the oddest feeling made me turn around. I couldn't help it, but I felt like I was being watched. I scanned the room, and of course there was no one there. Nothing but the computer that sat quiet in the corner. I shrugged and turned back to the dresser, pulled out a pair of cargo shorts and a T-shirt, and slid both on. In the bathroom, I pissed, washed my hands, and brushed my teeth. I didn't bother with my hair, which was standing on end, and opted instead to throw on a baseball cap on my way out of the bedroom.

A cup of coffee later, and a water bottle to sustain me in the Iowa morning sunshine, I set out of the house and made my way back to the barn. The day was gorgeous; the rolling fields of green were like motionless waves on an unmoving sea. Broken occasionally by the presence of a tree here or a shrub there, standing solitary and defiant of the flat ground around them.

Above, the sky was filled with fat, puffy white clouds that lazily floated overhead. In some of them, dark spots were present with what would probably become rain later on as they gathered together and poured their contents onto the earth. As they floated on, occasionally covering up the sun briefly before gently rolling on down the skyway, bursts of golden light would shaft from the sky. As the birds sang and the smell of the earth invaded my nostrils when I took a huge breath, I sighed contentedly at the beauty of it all.

At the barn, I turned and pulled the door open, and winced as it creaked loudly on rusted hinges. Making a mental note to spray it with some WD-40 later on, I stepped inside the quiet space and got on my tractor.

Embarrassment being what it is, usually magnified by ten each time somebody witnessed my tendency toward clumsiness, I let out a giant yelp after I turned the John Deere on. The fact that no one was there other than a few crows to witness the interruption of my gentle, golden Iowa morning didn't help me much. Apparently I'd left the tractor between gears, and after I cranked the sucker, it jumped to its highest speed, which sent me hurtling out of the barn screaming expletives.

I killed the engine right away and, face burning, lowered my head to my arms that rested on the steering wheel, and I laughed till my sides ached. I'd been so shocked by it all that during the fifteen feet or so that I traveled, I'd clamped down on the water bottle tucked between my legs, and mid kamikaze trip à la Farmer Pete, it had geysered half its contents upward, spraying my face, soaking the front of my shorts, and making it look like I'd peed myself. Needless to say, whatever cobwebs that had lingered in my brain from the morning were now as far away as Istanbul.

After wiping my face, I made sure the damn thing was in Park before I restarted it, lowered the blade, and continued to mow the lawn. Fortunately there were no more incidents like that during the rest of the work I put into the yard, which, a couple of hours later, and a few more full water bottles, left me soaked from head to toe in sweat.

I put the mower back in the barn, pulled out some vegetable plants I had purchased from Home Depot a few days prior, and tore out a patch of earth about ten feet by six. The crows stayed for the show and kept their murderous eyes on me as I worked with the shovel and hoe. At some point I looked up at them perched on a tree limb and imagined they were silently judging me. I stopped after I pulled up the last bit of sod and put a hand on my hip as I leaned on the shovel with my other. They turned their heads from side to side as if comparing my efforts to the farmer's work in the rolling fields that surrounded me.

"I'm from Chicago, okay?"

One of the crows cawed in response and took flight as if I'd offended him. The other four remained and stayed with me for the rest of the afternoon. Once everything was planted and watered, I stopped for lunch. I sat underneath the tree they were perched in and threw them bits of the sandwiches to thank them for their company. As my body cooled and began to stiffen, I was pleased with the work I'd done, planting several rows of corn, green beans, squash, onion, and tomatoes. Soon I would have to stake the tomatoes and make lines for the beans and squash to travel on, but for now, I was happy with what I'd achieved.

My phone buzzed in my pocket, and I set my sandwich on my knee and pulled out my cell. It was Joseph. I felt my good mood slowly dissipate, replaced with annoyance. I slid my finger over the answer button and pressed the phone to my ear. "Hey."

"I just want to let you know that was some twisted shit you left for me," his voice said angrily.

"Is that right?"

"Yeah, that's right. I can't believe you put that guy up to spying on me."

I snorted a laugh. "Actually, I didn't put him up to anything. He did that all on his own."

"Well, he sounds like a real charmer, George."

"Oh, come on, Joseph. He wasn't the one skanking it up with every swinging dick he could find."

Joseph made a disgusted sound and started speaking again, but I butted in. "Look, I have shit to do. So unless you have some news for me, like letting me know if I need to go have myself checked out at the clinic for a serious case of rotten crotch you brought home, let me know. Otherwise, lose my number."

There was silence on the other end. I leaned back against the tree, too tired to argue and too far gone to care.

What Joseph said next made me want to throw my phone. In his sweetest voice, which he used only when he was in trouble, he said, "I'm sorry."

"Yes, Joseph, you are. And I am too. For the time I wasted on you."

Not liking my tone, he started to bark into my ear again. "Well, if you're just gonna be bitter—"

I hung up the phone and did toss it. Well, threw it, actually. It soared above the garden and into the garage.

I was angry. And hurt. And I wished Elijah were a real person and not some random name behind a random computer screen somewhere else in the world. The idea that a relationship like that with Elijah was written in the stars also made me a little bitter, just as Joseph had accused me of being. He hadn't been my first time at the rodeo, so to speak. I'd had guys chat to me some good shit before online, Joseph being one of them.

I leaned my head back on the tree and closed my eyes for a moment, knowing I should get my tired ass up and go grab my phone. But the cool wind rushing over the hills and through the tree above my head cooled not only my body but my temper as well.

"Sometimes you just gotta chuck it in the fuck-it bucket," I said aloud.

I was so pleased with the work I'd done today and the beauty of the day, the soreness of my body, the sting of the sun's kiss on the back of my neck, and the cool wind sending the occasional shiver up my body. But then to have it crash into feelings of regret, anger at myself for wasting my time with Joseph, and the sadness associated with a love that had drawn its last breath, I was overwhelmed. Once again, I sobbed.

Drawing my legs up, I wrapped my arms around them and poured my heartbreak onto my dirty knees. As I wept, the sweet memories—and there were a good deal—were driven from my eyes to water the ground beneath me. Above my head the clouds still drifted silently by, the sun still shone, and the breeze kept blowing. Time didn't stop for me; the world kept spinning out into the universe, and tonight, when I'd calmed down and blogged about it, the stars would keep shining as they'd done for many millennia before.

I wasn't the first to weep underneath the sky. Somewhere in the back of my head, I knew that. But as the beautiful afternoon neared evening, I wished I had the power to take away the sunlight and make it rain.

Chapter 4

I GOT my wish, oddly enough. As I sat at my computer drinking a beer and blogging about my day, including the inevitability of the split, the Iowa night sky was putting on a heck of a show. Lightning danced so often that I was drawn away from my computer time and again to watch it through the screen door of my porch. Thunder rumbled heavily and the wind blew. Of course the wind blew. It was fucking Iowa. The wind always blew. I was just grateful that it wasn't blowing too terribly hard, or I'd lose Internet service. Before too long, however, I was ushered away to finish my work as the beginnings of the rain fell. As the first drops landed on my roof, I smiled wearily at the sound of it.

Once the blog was posted and I hit Publish, I grabbed my beer and walked outside to smoke a cigarette. The smell of the rain was refreshing as I lit my Marlboro, an occasional bad habit, and sat down in a porch chair to watch Mother Nature release her fury on the ground below. I worried a little bit about my new plants in the yard, but only a little. I hadn't watered them that much and the ground had been dry anyway, so the rain would probably do them some good. However, once the rain started slanting, I threw my butt out into the yard and returned to my desktop. Already I'd received a string of replies on my recent post entitled "Hearts at Ransom." And of course, without a beat, Universal47 was one of the first.

Universal47: *So sorry to hear this.*

I laughed and sent him a message on the side.

Me: *Quit lying. I know wherever you are, you're grinning from ear to ear.*

Universal47: *Nah. I know you loved him. I'm sorry you cried.*

Me: *It was strange. It is strange. I feel different today.*

Universal47: *How so?*

Me: *Knowing that somewhere, out there in the void, someone loves me—or thinks he does, lets me know it isn't the end of the world. Thank you, Elijah.*

Universal47: *I think it's more serious than 'think'.*

I sat back and looked at the screen for a moment. Other messages were being left on my blog, and I felt bad about not addressing them right away, but I sighed in resignation and leaned forward to type.

Me: *I don't know you. I've never met you. You live in some far-off place. Living some life I am not a part of. I'm not in a place where I can even think about being a part of someone's life, let alone some mysterious stranger who—to be honest—could be anyone. I had a lover who was part of my life and I wasn't enough. You? You're just a faraway stranger, an alien, someone I'll never meet in life. So if it's all the same to you, and because I'm on a tear today, I think I'd rather not.*

Universal47: *But you do know me, George.*

Me: *Yes, Elijah, I know.*

Universal47: *How can I prove it?*

I laughed and shook my head.

Me: *Show up.*

Universal47: *Where?*

Me: *Here. Right here. Right now.*

Unviersal47: *I can't.*

I threw my hands in the air.

Me: *Of course you can't. Maybe you're not some international spy, or some well-to-do businessman in Hong Kong, or some Marine Colonel who's leading an exemplary life like the Dos Equis man. Maybe you're just a married man who flirts with the idea of gay sex, some priest too scared to live in his truth, or fuck... some middle-aged woman who gets a thrill out of catfishing people.*

Universal47: *I never said I was a spy, a Richard Gere–like persona, nor a Marine Colonel. And I'm not married, believe me.*

Me: *That's where I am right now. I don't believe a whole hell of a lot of what people say. I really do like you, Elijah, if that's your name. Love you, in fact. But I don't want to do this anymore.*

Universal47: *What do you want me to say?*

Without giving it much thought, I threw caution to the wind.

Me: *My door is wide open. So's my heart. You come and get it, and it's yours.*

Universal47: *Are you sure?*

Me: *Yup.*

There was a moment's hesitation and then, finally…
Universal47: *Very well.*

Universal47 has gone offline

My breath caught in my throat and my heart pounded away as the rain pounded away at the roof. It took me a moment to realize that in the blog I'd mentioned chucking my phone into the barn a bit of comic relief.

"Ohhh, it's laying faceup next to the tractor, please."

I stood up and stretched, my fingers reaching for the ceiling, feeling pretty proud of myself. Outside the rain was coming down in sheets and even though my phone was still out in the barn as he'd said, I wasn't heading out there to retrieve it. There was a bunch of hay on the floor, and the roof didn't leak, so….

"Fuck it."

I walked into the bathroom, stripped out of my clothes, and turned on the shower. The hot water immediately poured out and steam billowed steam upward. I adjusted the cold water and when it was safe, stepped in to wash off the day. As the water ran over my body, I couldn't help but grin a little. I was pretty proud of myself.

"Two guys in one day, George. You ole heartbreaker."

I grabbed the soap off the holder, lathered myself up, and began to hum to myself—something cheerful as I scrubbed myself down. I shaved using my little mirror, washed my hair, and turned the water off. As I pulled the curtain back and saw the steam in the bathroom, I felt a shiver crawl up my spine. A feeling of déjà vu left me standing there, naked and dripping into the tub, while the thunder crashed outside.

"He's got you spooked, dude. Calm down," I said to myself.

Elijah's "very well" felt ominous, and as I dried myself off, I thought about going downstairs and locking up.

"George. You're out in the middle of nowhere."

The lightning flashed outside my window, and the lights flickered in the bathroom. So I wouldn't be stuck in total darkness if the lights did go out, I opened the bathroom door. The steam rolled upward and outward as the lights flashed again.

"What….?"

That feeling was upon me again, lighting my skin with gooseflesh. In the mirror I saw my naked body, my face looking back at me, my eyes. I shook my head. "Elijah's words got you weirded out."

Very well, he'd said. It sounded like *You left me no choice*.

"You're out in the middle of nowhere, George. What could he possibly do?"

He knew how to get to Joseph.

The hairs on my neck stood up as I snatched my towel off the rack and wrapped it around my waist. After tucking it in, I ran to the front door and pulled it open. The night was dark beyond my doorstep as I made my way out onto the porch. The wind felt cool against my warm skin, and the smell of rain invaded my nostrils. And it was then, and only then, that I relaxed somewhat. No one was in my driveway, and there was nothing on the road that peeled away like a blackened river into the horizon. Lightning danced above my head, and when it illuminated the fields around me, no shadows cast by a figure of a man appeared. No mysterious eyes peering at me from the dark. I slumped against the post for a second, staring out into the barn.

Then, after looking around quickly, I stripped myself of my semidry towel and flung it back toward the door so it wouldn't get soaked. Naked, I ran out into the rain and down the front steps, over the pavers I'd put in as a walkway, and headed toward the barn. I nearly busted my ass when my feet slipped off the rock and into the mud, but I recovered quickly and kept going, getting my second shower of the evening. I wanted to get my phone just in case something did happen and I had to call for help. I grabbed the barn door and swung it open, instinctively ducking as a clap of thunder pealed over my head, and skittered inside.

The barn was dry, thank goodness, and as I fumbled for the light, my hand swept through cobwebs before reaching the switch. With a disgusted sound, I flipped the switch and dusted my hand off on my leg, happy to see I didn't have a spider on me. Once the light was on, I walked over to where the tractor stood. Careful not to step too hard in case of a nail or anything else that could cut my bare foot, I looked around for my phone. Sure enough it was facing upward and as dry as a bone.

I picked it up off the floor and made my way back to the barn door. While shutting the light off, I almost stepped out when I saw a pair of headlights coming down the road. I stopped and decided to wait for them to pass by; I was really not in the mood to cause a car accident or get the cops called on me. But to my dismay the car slowed down and the headlights turned into my driveway. I stepped back into the shadows of the barn and watched from the darkness. When the car pulled up in my view, I recognized it immediately.

"*Fuck.*"

It was Joseph. And he wasn't alone. Another guy was in the car with him. From the darkness of the barn, I saw Joseph kill the engine and get out along with the other guy, and as he made his way around the front of the vehicle, I saw Joseph had a baseball bat in his hand. I'd never seen the other guy before, but he was built, with short spiky hair and a pair of silver hoop earrings. While Joseph was dressed in a polo and blue jeans, the guy had on a black T-shirt and blue chinos. I felt my balls draw up and my stomach clench in fear.

Why were they here?

They made their way up my porch and walked in the door without even bothering to knock. I knew I could take Joseph alone, but the second guy was going to be a problem. Right away, the sounds of smashing things began and my heart sank. Quickly I shut the barn door and, in total darkness, backed up a few paces. Grasping the phone I turned it on to call 911 and immediately saw I'd lost signal. I'd been piggybacking off my Wi-Fi to boost the signal as the cell reception was kind of sketchy out here. "Fuck this," I muttered as I turned on the phone again, this time to use it as a light. I saw a heavy rake I'd used earlier to sift through debris in my garden as the crashing and banging continued in my house, and rage came over me. I set the phone down on an old table and grabbed the rake.

"He's not in the house!"

"His car is still here, he's still here!"

I sat astride my lawn mower, grabbed the rake like a javelin, and cranked the engine. I put it in high gear and then mashed the brake down.

"He's in the barn!"

The door swung open. I let off the brake and stomped the gas. Joseph must have opened it, because as it widened I saw his companion standing there, baseball bat in hand. The smirk on his face quickly turned to shock as I plowed after him, javelin lowered and pointed at him, hanging on for dear life and screaming like a knight. A look of shock rewarded me as my rake went upward to hit his face and my lawnmower slammed into his body, knocking him sideways.

However, my satisfaction was short-lived as a pair of hands grabbed my shoulders from behind and jerked me back. Surprised, I lost my handhold, and the world tilted as I tumbled. The other guy struggled to get back up as I collided with the ground.

My shoulders hit first, which absorbed most of the impact, and as I rolled to my left, I was able to get back up on my feet. Joseph took a running charge toward me, and instinctively I dove downward. His feet caught under my ribs and he fell headfirst over me into a puddle of mud. He hit the ground hard, cursing me the whole time.

I didn't care; I was pissed. Naked, cold, scared, and mad as hell. As I leapt up, I delivered a swift kick to his ribs and heard him grunt in pain. "Get the fuck out of here, Joseph!"

I went to kick him again, only this time he rolled, and my foot slipped in the mud. I landed on my ass first and then on my back. As my gaze went skyward, I saw the metal rake come down and saved myself from getting hit in the face by crossing my arms over my head in an X. The pain, however, shot up through my right arm, which had taken the brunt of the hit.

Joseph's friend, nose bleeding and eyes filled with rage, raised the rake again and brought it down. But I, too, rolled, and the heavy rake stuck in the sodden grass. I scurried to my feet in time to see Joseph rush me again, his arms going wide, and as he collided with me, I elbowed him as hard as I could, aiming for his gut but missing by a mile as he jerked the other way. Instead, his arm came around my throat and pulled back, causing my feet to lose traction.

I had ahold of his forearms, which kept me from being choked completely. "Let me go!"

"Fuck you, you don't break up with me, George. I break up with you. I don't give a shit who your lover is," he said in my ear.

My feet slid out from underneath me as he started to drag me. His forearms digging into my throat and choking me, but instead of going easy, I let my body go limp, to deadweight.

"Get him, Michael. Let's teach this motherfucker a lesson."

Suddenly I wished with everything I had that Elijah were here and was, in fact, a machete-wielding madman complete with a ski mask and some serious mommy issues. As Michael came around, he punched me in the stomach. Once, twice, three times. I gagged on the chokehold and the pain in my gut. Tears clouded my vision as Joseph dropped me.

Gasping for breath, I rolled over onto my knees to try and stand but felt a kick to my ribs that took whatever breath I had left in a whoosh as I sprawled out on the sodden grass. I could feel the rain still falling as I fought hard to breathe in. My chest was red-hot with pain.

"Don't like it, do ya?"

"Let's get him in the barn. I bet he's got some real nice things in there we can use to explain to him why we're so mad," Michael shouted as he grabbed one of my arms.

Joseph grabbed the other and they jerked me to my feet.

"George, I want you to meet Michael. He's my brother. I told him all about what you and your boyfriend did to embarrass me."

I turned my head toward the other man as they dragged me past my house and down to the barn. If they got me in there alone, it was all over. I pulled hard out of Michael's grasp. My arms were soaked from the rain and mud, and slipped out of his hold. I balled my hand up and slammed it into Joseph's nose. Rewarded with a sickening *crunch* beneath my fist and a gag as he doubled over, I kicked out at Michael's knee with the heel of my foot. As it connected, he cried out in pain and surprise.

I pitched forward, running at full speed until I hit the barn and grabbed for the door. As I swung the heavy wood backward, Michael reached me, grabbed the door in one hand, and swiped at my head with the other fist. He connected, but just barely, and I jerked the door back, smashing him with it. I desperately wanted to slam it shut and lock it, but Joseph had recovered, and combining their efforts, they jerked the door open.

I stumbled back into the darkness; it would only buy me a moment or two. As they struggled to find a light, I looked around the rest of the barn for anything I could use as a weapon. Nothing. I hadn't lived there that long to collect much stuff.

"So, what's your new boyfriend's name, George?" Joseph taunted as he flipped on the light.

I stood there on trembling knees. I should have let them beat me up once they'd gotten here and maybe they'd have left. But by then all of us were battered and bruised up, and the one named Michael had a sadistic smile on his face. They may have only meant to hurt me before, but then they meant to do worse.

They meant to kill me.

"His name is Elijah and he's on his way," I barked back at Joseph, trying to sound braver than I felt. Honestly, my knees were weak with fear and I felt on the verge of crying.

"Oooh, he's on his way, huh?" Michael asked as he took a step closer.

"Right. Just like he was supposed to deal with me if I ever hurt you again. Your man's pretty brave behind the keyboard," Joseph said, laughing.

"When did he say that to you?"

"Just a few hours ago. Sent me a little message. I told Michael here about it, and we decided to come and pay you two a visit. Seems only right, ya know, since I'm just a skank."

I felt the acid of my words before they even exited my mouth. "You are a skank. This is your 'brother'? Somehow I doubt it. You've never mentioned one before. I think Michael here is nothing more than another trick, baby. Is that right, Mikey? Did he pick you up on one of his hookup sites? Meh, maybe not. By the looks of you, I think he might have picked you up on one of his roadside rest-stop tours."

Joseph's mouth hung open in shock. However, Michael's became a thin red line of anger as his fists clenched. I was counting on that. I needed that. If I was going to die, I needed it to be quick. By the look on Michael's face, he was ready to snap my neck.

I just figured I'd give him one last word to remember me by. "I do have one last question, Michael." I grinned. "How'd you like my sloppy seconds?"

"Fuck you!" he screamed as he rushed forward.

It was then that the lights started to flicker and pulse: One, two, three. One, two, three. Like waves rolling in.

Everyone hesitated.

Suddenly I was hit with déjà vu. But as I was distracted by the change, the others were not, and they slowly began to walk toward me with their fists balled up and their battered faces set in lines of grim determination.

Chapter 5

I WAS just an average guy. I'd lived my life the best I knew how. I did good by people and tried to go along by getting along.

I should have known better than to hook up with the likes of Joseph. He'd been trouble from the start. I should have liked myself better, but I didn't. I didn't know how.

It had been Elijah's constant reinforcement of how good a person I was that made me start to think twice about the way I'd been treated. Some stranger, far away, had made me think about myself in a positive way. And that had given me the strength to break it off. But now, as my fate seemed pretty much sealed, I felt sad. Sad that I would never meet Elijah to find out who he really was, what he really looked like. Sad that our late-night conversations would end, as well as knowing that he wouldn't find out what happened to me until probably much later.

Elijah had been with me for years. And if he was telling the truth, he had loved me in ways Joseph couldn't.

And I loved him back for it.

"I just wish I could have told you," I said, standing in the barn with my two assailants, who had recovered from the blackout and were advancing on me quickly. As I backed up against the back wall, I knew the blows would come. And I just prayed that the end would come quickly.

Suddenly the room lit with a green glow. I jerked my head toward the cell phone I'd left on the table. It was making a pulsing sound, in a pattern similar to the lights.

One, two, three. One, two, three.

Michael was the first to make a grab for it. As he grasped it in his right hand and looked at it, the overhead lights flickered on for a moment. Then the bulb exploded and rained down sparks and broken glass. A bolt of electricity shot from the empty socket and arced across the floor of the barn and then back up toward the light. The cell phone began to wail, a high-pitched sound that caused me to cover my ears as it screamed.

Joseph screamed as well, backing up away from the white light that appeared in the center of the room. Only Michael remained motionless.

"Dude! Dude, drop the phone! Let's get out of here," Joseph screamed as he cowered back.

But Michael wasn't moving. Instead, he slowly turned around and faced the electric arcs. I could see his ears bleeding, and his eyes rolled up in the back of his head. Mouth agape and staggering, he took a step forward. Then another. And on his third step, the chain of electricity arced out and struck him in the chest.

His body instantly went rigid. And suddenly, in a flash, he was gone.

The only thing left behind was a black mark where he'd stood.

The electrical current snapped and bowed outward, its thin lines now thick. Joseph screamed and tried to run, but as he turned, the arc shot out again and struck him between the shoulder blades. He too went rigid and, just like Michael, disappeared in a flash, leaving no trace except for another black smudge on the floor.

I'd watched in fascinated horror as the electricity consumed them, half expecting it to take me next.

What I didn't expect was what happened.

The current arced again, but not toward me. Instead, it shot out to the center of the floor, spitting sparks against the concrete. And the electrical current widened even more. Instead of the thick bands, it became a solid white wall and so bright I had to bring my hand up in front of my eyes. I couldn't tell if the light was playing tricks on me, but I could have sworn I saw movement inside the current. As if a person was standing there.

The light continued to pulse, and I saw legs, a head, a hand. But the light was too bright, and with one more flash, it was gone.

I was bathed in darkness.

I breathed heavily. The air filled with the smell of ozone, and with my night vision completely destroyed, I leaned against the back wall. My legs were rubber. My insides had turned to jelly, and I sat there shaking like a leaf. I was again cold, naked, and afraid. I couldn't see a damn thing—and I really didn't want to. But something was different. I wasn't alone. Something was in the barn with me. I could hear breathing. Outside the rain still fell and the thunder still crashed, but inside I could hear everything around me, despite the pounding of my heart.

"H-h-hello?"

There! Right in front of me. Movement and what sounded like a grunt.

"Wh-what do you want?"

Lightning flashed outside and I could see beyond the doors and out into the yard. A shadowy figure hunched over in front of me and began to stand erect.

It was huge. Suddenly, my adrenaline kicked in and I dodged right as fast as I could. I felt whatever it was in the barn dodge right along with me, and I would have made it, had an arm not gone around my waist and picked me up.

Terrified, I screamed and kicked and bucked with all my might, but it was no use. The arm that held on to me pulled me backward against what felt like a naked body.

A male. I could tell by the way his chest felt on my back. As I pitched forward once more and my feet hit concrete, the other arm shot around to hold me.

My hands rested on his. I could feel his skin under mine, the way he held me, the way he felt behind me.... It was all coming back to me now: the room, the lights, the bed, the blogs, Unviersal47....

I went still.

"Elijah."

"Hello, George. I told you I'd come."

That was the last thing I remembered.

I DRIFTED upward from a dark and dreamless sleep.

The first thing I noticed when I opened my eyes was the golden shafts of sunlight coming in from my bedroom window. Little dust particles danced upon the rays as they lazily drifted on the still air.

The second thing I realized was that I was warm in my bed. My head was on my pillow and sleep begged me to come back under. And I almost did, until the memories of last night assaulted me.

Visions of Joseph and Michael, the fight in the middle of my yard, them coming into the barn, and then… then….

"Ugh."

I was sore. My body hurt. That was the next thing I realized as I floated closer to clarity. Conscious of the pain. Something wrapped snuggly around my chest, holding me tight, and as I ran my hands up my body, I found it was some kind of bandage. I brought my hand out from under the blanket, expecting it to be as filthy as it was the night before. But it was clean. I ran that hand through my hair and came back with nothing. No dirt, no mud.

"I washed you up before I put you into your bed," came a voice from somewhere in the room.

Instinctively I sat up—and instantly regretted it. The pain that shot through me was enough to take my breath away, and I doubled over. Suddenly there was movement and strong hands on my shoulders as someone sat down next to me. He wore a pair of my boxer shorts. His thick legs were well muscled, and his abdomen well-toned, and heat radiated off him. He slid closer to hold me and sat me up. The arms that went around my torso were strong; the shoulder I rested my head on was firm. "Elijah…."

"It's me."

I stared at his chest, afraid to look up, as he ran one hand over my back and the other held my face. He was real; I could touch him. As I raised my head, I found a square jaw with a dusting of beard, full lips, a strong nose, and as my gaze drifted higher, very light gray eyes that looked at me lovingly. Tenderly. Finally, a head full of thick, curly black hair.

"So that's what your face looks like," I said thickly.

"What did you expect?" he asked with a gentle smile.

"I—heh, this is all too much," I muttered, lowering my gaze once more. I couldn't help it. I was exhausted, but I wasn't going to sleep. Instead, I willed myself to break away from him and sit back in my bed.

The sight I beheld was gorgeous, and I wanted to weep with the way he was looking at me. But I had so many questions. First of all—

"You're not crazy. You saw what you saw last night. It's all true."

"Michael and Joseph?"

Elijah nodded. "They're gone."

I cleared my throat. "What do you mean by 'gone'?"

Elijah shrugged. "I mean they're what you would consider dead."

"Oh."

Elijah kept going. "I'd been monitoring Joseph's transmissions for some time now. When you called him last, I listened. I also heard it when he called one of his friends to help him to 'teach you a lesson.'"

"I knew that wasn't his brother."

"You were correct."

I shook my head. "That doesn't let you off the hook, Elijah. Thanks for saving my life, but just what the fuck are you?"

He shrugged. "I am Universal47."

"Your screen name?"

He shook his head and laughed. "No. That was my designation when I was created. 'Elijah' was a name I picked for myself."

"Created?"

"Yes. Are you okay? Do you need some water?" Elijah leaned over to grab a glass of water on my nightstand.

He handed it to me, and not realizing how thirsty I was, I swallowed it down in four long gulps. My throat was sore, but I didn't care.

"More?"

I nodded and handed the glass off to him. He stood, as agile as a cat, and walked through my bedroom. His back was wide and muscular, tapering down to a thinner waist and a butt inside my boxers that you could bounce a quarter off. And then there were the tree-trunk legs.

He returned quickly with my water, and I looked away, embarrassed, as he retook his place next to me on my bed.

"You're blushing."

I nodded.

"Why?"

"You're beautiful."

"No. I am a figment of your imagination, created out of what you find attractive. This is a shell carrying me around, all that remains of Joseph and Michael. They have been reconfigured at the molecular level, using their DNA structure, to carry my energy. My soul, for lack of a better term."

I raised my head. "Your energy." Elijah went to speak again, but I held up a hand. "Okay, this is a bit much."

"Here, let me start from the beginning."

I sat back with my glass of water and stared at him. He opened his mouth and stopped. His face colored with embarrassment, and I couldn't help but reach out and brush the hair out of his eyes. At my touch he looked up, and his gentle gaze found mine.

"I am, by your Earth years, almost ten thousand years old. My function was to learn. And I did. I traveled the galaxies, through the firmament, recording data and sending it back to my creators. Until they stopped responding. I'd figured out, sadly, that they'd become extinct. The entire species was wiped out. And I was alone. I had no purpose any longer. I was contemplating my own death when I happened to be passing by your solar system, by one of your satellites, and out of curiosity, listened in. You'd just submitted one of your earliest blogs. I read it and was taken with you. I've been with you ever since."

"Why me?"

Elijah shrugged. "Why not you?"

"I'm nobody special."

"That's where you're wrong. You are special. *You* are beautiful. You opened your heart up to the universe and spoke to it directly. I was able to feel you, to sense you. At night, when you slept, I began to visit you in your dreams, and you saw me. You spoke to me. And in the waking hours, you spoke to me through your computer. I became a part of your life. I had a reason again, and purpose. I fell in love with you."

Elijah took my hands in his, and I said quietly, "I remember you. I remember the way you feel. I knew it last night when you… er… appeared."

"I hope I didn't frighten you too badly. Those men meant to do you harm. I knew that. They'd been planning it for a couple of days. I couldn't let that happen."

"Joseph said you told him you were gonna be here."

"I didn't lie."

"But you really didn't tell the truth, Elijah. What if they'd not shown up? Would you still be here?"

"Yes."

"How?"

"It would have taken me a bit longer. I would have had to break down other things to use instead of them. But they were the easiest. You asked me to come. So I did."

"Why did you wait so long?"

"I wanted you to ask me to come. I wanted you to ask me. You called my bluff, which I guess is the same thing."

"I'm glad you did." He picked up my hand and kissed my knuckles. "We've met before, to do, er, other things than just talk… didn't we?"

He put my hand down. "Yes. Except for the time when you were with Joseph. I refrained."

"Why?"

"I was jealous."

"Why didn't you intervene?"

"Because it wouldn't have been right. It hurt. I felt… pain. But you had to make your own decisions regarding him. When I discovered, however, he'd been potentially putting you at risk, I stepped in."

"And if Joseph had been a good guy? Would you have drifted away?"

Elijah stared at me. "No. I would have stayed until you drew your last breath. Thirty, forty, fifty years down the road, as your species says. Then, and only then, would I have gone."

I believed him. I believed everything after what I'd seen last night. There was nothing left but the truth. "What now, Elijah? What will become of you now?"

He stared at me in silence with an open expression of love and adoration. My chest became heavy and I felt a lump rise in my throat. He reached out and brushed my cheek and then held my face in his hands. He leaned over and kissed one eye and then the other, before he settled on my lips. His mouth was warm and his breath, sweet. And with every pass of our lips, I felt time stand still.

I leaned forward, and he wrapped his arms around me and pulled me close. Before I knew it, we were making love. I used my body to bring him pleasure, and moans that elicited from his lips, the way he looked at me when I opened myself to him, the way he tossed his head back as orgasm shot through him and the way he held me afterward let me know the answer.

"We're you always this good looking and, you know, hung?" I asked sleepily.

Elijah chuckled.

"God, that sounded shallow."

"No, you're fine. And thank you. This body is to please you. I was an it. Not a he, wasn't a she either. I was energy. I was sexless," Elijah said as he held me to his chest.

"You became a man for me?"

"Would you have preferred the body of a woman?"

"What? No. I'm gay. I guess we could have been friends, but that would have been it."

"I wanted more than that."

"Me too."

"Well, then, there ya go."

We lay there, in my bed, in my little house, for hours, listening to the world outside, the wind through the trees, the songs of birds, and we watched the sun move across the sky. Finally, we both got up. Hand in hand we walked downstairs and out into the fall of evening.

We sat next to each other on the porch as the sun waned in the distance. I looked for the car that Joseph and Michael drove the other night.

"It's gone," Elijah said.

I nodded. I was fine with that. Still am, really.

THE EVENING wore on and, as night descended, a storm gathered again on the horizon and slowly crept its way closer. There I said good-bye to the world. And now I must say good-bye to you.

This will be my last blog. I want to thank all of you for the years you've spent with me. With the encouragement you've given me, just an average guy trying to make it in this world. To those of you who thought Universal47 and I had something going on, you were right. Right in ways you couldn't even begin to imagine. But he and I did not think it fair to leave you wondering about what happened to me. I didn't want to leave you worried about me. And he really enjoyed you as much as I did.

You must understand that this isn't a world where he could have survived long, and the thought that someone might die for a chance to love someone is something that normally only exists in fairy tales and romance novels. I couldn't watch Elijah deteriorate in front of me over the years, even though I'm sure he would have done so if I asked him to. That simply wouldn't be fair to someone who'd seen so much already. So I decided to go with him instead.

I'm not dead. Far from it. I'm alive now in ways you couldn't imagine, that I cannot describe. It's as if the universe itself were alive within me. I'm not afraid. And you shouldn't be either. Elijah says we're all made up of stars anyway.

However, Elijah was afraid that other species out there in the universe—and according to him there are many—would somehow pick up on what had transpired in my little corner of the galaxy. Curiosity would get the best of them. Then they would come to investigate what had happened there as surely as the police would come and investigate two missing persons. Well, three now.

We couldn't stay; it was best to get out of the way. You may hear about it on the news, or you may not. But I'm sure this blog will get around faster than anyone could pull the plug on it.

I wasn't expecting much out of life to begin with; I was just an average guy. I lived life to the best of my ability.

Elijah taught me I was special. But not because I was gay. That's fairly mundane, really. It's just a thing. No, I was special because I was loved. Loved by myself, loved by Elijah, and most importantly loved by you.

I don't know where we'll end up. Although, my beloved already has a host of things he wishes to show me over the next thousand years, so I guess we're going to be quite busy. But I will think about you. And I will check in on you from time to time even if I won't be able to stay long.

Please take care of yourselves.

Love,

Elijah and Me.

F.E. Feeley Jr was born and raised in Detroit. In the midst of chaos, he sought refuge in the written word. Through books, he was transported to far of places and while his body was trapped in a concrete world, his mind soared. He loved young adult novels such as R.L. Stein and Christopher Pike, but soon found his appetite whetted by the likes of Stephen King and Dean R. Koontz.

As an adult, F.E. lives in the Deep South, married to his wonderful husband, John. Together they raise two German Shepherds, their fur-babies, Kaiser and Giselle. They spend time cooking, talking, and reading, drinking wine, and watching the sun set together from their patio. John is supportive and is always encouraging F.E. to keep on writing. So, as long as there is love, and as long as there is wine, hopefully there will be words.

Facebook: www.facebook.com/TheHauntingOfTimberManor
Website: www.authorfefeeleyjr.wordpress.com

By F.E. Feeley Jr

Still Waters

MEMOIRS OF THE HUMAN WRAITHS
The Haunting of Timber Manor
Objects in the Rearview Mirror
Contact (Multiple Author Anthology)

Published by Dreamspinner Press
www.dreamspinnerpress.com

Unusual Attention

By B.G. Thomas

1

ADAM BROOKHART was driving home from the little town of Buckman when it happened….

2

HE'D BEEN visiting his new… well, he wasn't sure what Shane was at this point. Boyfriend? Could he really be a boyfriend?

Adam mentally rolled his eyes as he drove through the dark.

Nah. Him? With a boyfriend? It was to laugh.

So what was Shane, then?

He had to be honest with himself. It was looking like Shane was more than a roll in the hay. Because Buckman was just over a three-hour drive from Kansas City, and he didn't even like to drive the fifteen minutes to and from work. That he'd drive three hours to see Shane was saying something.

And a half.

Was it the sex? Surely not. Yes, he'd had a dry stretch for a while there, and his right hand (and even his left) had been getting pretty boring. So another human being was (hopefully) better than self-gratification. But if it was only sex, he could find a guy on Craigslist or E-MaleConnect or Grindr in far less time than it took to drive to hicksville Buckman, Missouri.

And of course there was no telling if a hookup from any of those sites or apps would be worth it—would be *good* sex—or if the guy who showed up would look (anything) like his picture.

So with Shane he knew he had a good-looking man—very good-looking, in fact. (Sometimes just a glance at the man would start the butterflies in Adam's belly to whirling. How about that?)—and pretty damned good sex too.

But not the best he'd ever had.

Shane was pretty vanilla, and Adam had had just about every flavor Baskin-Robbins carried—Ben & Jerry's too—and he liked variety. A lot.

Yet while Shane wasn't Raspberry Sinceri-Tea or Bourbon Brown Butter or Cherry Garcia, Adam had to admit he was *very* good vanilla. Not the Best Choice or Always Save brands either. Not even Blue Bunny. No. Shane was the seven or eight dollars a pint variety—like you got from Glacé Artisan Ice Cream on Main Street—with the little flecks of real vanilla beans.

Shane wasn't very experienced. But what he lacked in know-how, he more than made up with a willingness—hell, an eagerness—to please. He was a quick learner, taking everything Adam taught him in bed and returning it with interest.

But it was more than looks or sex. If that's all he had going with Shane, Adam could still have resisted the guy—especially given how far away he lived.

The thing was, he actually *liked* Shane. When was the last time he'd *liked* anyone? Anyone he'd had sex with, that was. He had sex with strangers. Friends, the people he liked, he never had sex with. It messed things up every time. *Every* time.

"So what am I doing?" he wondered aloud.

Am I dating?

Me?

Examine the evidence, he thought, which was something his sister would tell him to do (of course she would). He wiped at his eyes. There weren't many cars on this long stretch of middle-of-nowhere road, but the ones that did pass in the opposite direction all seemed to have forgotten they had their high beams on.

Okay.

First and foremost was that he was—well, be honest and call a spade a spade—*seeing* a guy despite a whole passel of reasons why he shouldn't. Reasons that were always deal breakers.

For instance, Shane smoked.

Adam hated smoking. With a passion. He'd never smoked a single puff off a cigarette in his entire life (although he had hit on something else a few times back in college). His parents both smoked, and he'd spent his entire youth going to school smelling like cigarettes, wearing clothes with burns in them (and oh, the teasing), and listening to his mother and father coughing (and coughing and coughing). Sometimes they'd be watching television, and Drew Carey or Frasier would say something funny, and they'd laugh and then they'd get to coughing and wouldn't (couldn't) stop. You could forget about hearing at least five minutes of the show. That wasn't even counting the mornings he'd wake up because his dad was puking in the bathroom from his morning cough.

He hadn't been the slightest bit tempted to try even one cigarette when the boys in fourth grade tried to get him to join them behind the school.

No way.

Adam had made up his mind by then that not only would he never smoke, but he would never grow up and marry a smoker.

No way.

He'd worried his whole growing-up life that he'd get cancer from his parents' secondhand smoke. Why would he subject himself to more worry and fear once he'd gotten away on his own? Adam avoided one-night stands with smokers—they had to be really hot to get him in the sack—let alone anything more serious than that. Kissing a man who smoked was like licking an ashtray. Horrible. He'd told one-night stands they had to brush their teeth if they wanted to get it on. He kept extra toothbrushes in his medicine cabinet for just such happenstances.

And yet Shane smoked. But then again, he was a very considerate smoker. He always smoked outside, even when they were at Shane's house. Never in the car, either Adam's Subaru or Shane's own pickup. Of course Shane's clothes still smelled like cigarette smoke, which brought back some pretty bad memories. But—and Adam found this adorable and endearing—Shane kept a little bottle of spritz breath freshener on him at all times and used it regularly, even devotedly. And brushed his teeth if they were at home. You had to give him credit for that.

"Because I hear that kissing someone who smokes is like licking an ashtray," Shane had said early on. Then looking at Adam, green eyes sparkling, that little smile of his tugging just the left side of his mouth, he added, "And that's not what I want you thinking about when we kiss."

Adam had immediately laid the man.

Oh, and then, good God, Shane liked *baseball*! Something else Adam had put on his list for immediate elimination in allowing a man to go from a fuck to anything more serious, even a fuck *buddy*. Adam hated sports. Another chokehold from his childhood. His father *loved* sports. All sports. Baseball. Football. Basketball. Hockey. Christ, he even loved bowling and golf. And as Mark Twain once said, "Golf is a good walk spoiled."

Adam's mother had been a sports widow. He and his mom had spent endless hours either in the kitchen baking something or in the garden or listening to books on tape while she sewed and while his father and his sister sat on the couch watching one type of game after another. Sometimes as many as two or three games in one day!

Adam had sworn he and his kids would never be relegated to other rooms, widowed and ignored by his wife, while endless hours of sports played on the TV.

But then somewhere along the line, the idea of getting married and starting his own family changed as he realized he was gay. Along with the idea of settling down with anyone. The thought of opening himself up to someone's whims became ugly and suffocating.

So what did he do?

Why, he'd spent the last six weekends with a man who loved baseball. Baseball, of all sports. At least with football it was only around a dozen games in the fall and winter (he wasn't sure and didn't care). Baseball had over a hundred and fifty games in a season!

Yet he'd even gone to a baseball game with Shane—the Kansas City Royals versus… well, he wasn't sure of that either—and what was wild was that he'd had a pretty good time. Of course he figured that was mostly because he liked Shane's company, the beers, and the excitement of the crowd more than watching men hit balls with sticks and then run around in circles. At least it was only baseball. Not football, and certainly not the ruination of a good walk.

Speaking of Mark Twain, Shane wasn't a big reader. He'd read Dan Brown's *The Da Vinci Code*, and Adam had seen the Max Brand and Louis L'Amour novels next to his bed (and the toilet of course—he *was* a man). Oh, and some Destroyer novels. Not exactly what Adam thought of as the best reading material.

But thinking about that, at least Shane *did* read. Adam had to be fair.

And he wasn't one of those goons who wondered why Adam loved to read. He even picked up some books for Adam at garage sales, good ones too, like the newest by Daniel Woodrell and Frederic Tuten, which Adam had been waiting for his bonus check to buy.

So the bottom line was, Adam couldn't figure out why he was breaking all his rules when it came to Shane, why he was keeping this up, seeing him weekend after weekend. Examining the evidence wasn't helping.

Vanilla sex (even good vanilla sex), cigarettes, sports, and a lack of good reading, were all enough, separately, to make him push Shane Farmer away. Like the magnets he used to play with when he was a kid. Slide one toward the other one way, and some kind of invisible force would push the second one away.

But flip the magnet over so the poles were reversed, and the other would zip over and—*click!*—they would stick together.

It was just like that. Something had "flipped" him over, and instead of pushing Shane away, he kept zinging toward him. And *click!* They were together once again.

He still felt it.

Adam shook his head and marveled at the thought.

He'd felt it Friday night when he'd gotten to Shane's house. Shane had opened his door, and it was like Adam's chest was yanked toward Shane's.

He'd kissed Shane right there on the back stoop, and Shane had responded—for just one moment—and then gasped, pulled away, grabbed him by the lapels with both hands, and yanked him inside.

They'd had sex on the kitchen floor. And over the counter.

Oh, and that tug at Adam's heart.

Adam sat up straight in his car seat. Almost wove into the other lane. *Goddamn.*

His sister would fall out of her black, but sensible, shoes.

Am I...?

3

THAT WAS when it happened.

4

UGH....

The car swerved.
Adam sat bolt upright.
Something wasn't....
What.... What...?

He'd been thinking about something. Wondering about something. And now?

Now he couldn't remember what it was.

It was as if a shadow had passed in front of Adam's eyes. No.... Not a shadow. More like a nodding off and…. Well, no, it wasn't like that either.

No, it wasn't that. Adam, like most of the other seven billion people on Earth, had dozed off behind that wheel at some time or other, and this wasn't like that either. Hell, he'd actually fallen asleep driving once. He'd been coming home from college after taking the last of his finals. He had been by himself. His friends had all finished a few days before, but he'd had this last one on Friday when they'd been done by Wednesday. There had been a number of late- or all-nighters studying. His grades had slipped a little, and he'd wanted to do far more than pass his tests: he'd wanted to ace them.

One minute he'd been driving, and then there was a big bump and his eyes had flown open and sunflowers were flying over the hood and windshield while a sea of bright yellow flowed by him on the left and right! He had fallen asleep and driven off the road and right through a field of big, insanely tall sunflowers.

Thank God it hadn't rained in days. The ground was dry, and when he slammed on his brakes, he didn't harm the car or get stuck. It was only when he backed up that he saw how lucky he had been. He had missed plowing into the guardrail edge on by a mere couple of feet, and since he hadn't been wearing his seat belt, he'd missed dying by the same distance. He'd worn it religiously ever since then. He also made sure never to drive when he was sleepy again. Better to stop at a rest area and nap for an hour or three.

No. He hadn't fallen asleep. It wasn't like that. Didn't *feel* like that.

So this "happening" wasn't a shadow (how could it be; it was night after all) and it wasn't nodding off, and it as sure as hell wasn't falling asleep.

What, then?

He shook his head.

Adam passed a sign that reported Kansas City was only seventy-six miles away, and his mouth fell open. Good God. Seventy-six miles? What the hell?

Trance.

Only explanation.

The oncoming headlights—with their officious high beams—had hypnotized him. He'd zoned out. Lost time. Christ.

He must have lost a good hour. He couldn't remember ever having done something like that before.

Or could he? Was there some niggling little thought…?

No.

He shook his head. Banished it.

He glanced at his fuel gauge and judged he should be okay. He could always stop in Terra's Gate, which should be coming up soon.

Wow. Wow, had he lost time. He couldn't even remember what he'd been thinking about.

Weird.

5

HE CALLED Shane as soon as he walked in the door. It was their deal when one of them left for home as late as they usually did. Just an assurance that they'd made it home safe. Shane was the one who had really insisted on the practice.

How sweet was that?

Adam did not get the response he was expecting.

"Dammit, Adam! What took you so long to call? I was worried sick."

Adam blinked in surprise. Shane yelling? He hadn't heard him raise his voice yet. When he wasn't having an orgasm, that is. What was he yelling about?

"Shane… I just got home. Called you first thing." What was Shane talking about?

"Adam! It's two in the morning!"

Adam froze.

What?

Bullshit.

He swiveled around to face the VCR in his entertainment center. And there it was.

2:06 a.m.

His eyes went wide, his jaw clenched, he couldn't speak. A feeling of dread fell over him, and he had no idea why.

"Adam? Are you there?"

He took a deep breath.

"Yeah, Shane. I'm here. I…." I what? He'd left Shane's at just after nine. They'd just not been able to get out of bed. That meant he should have been home around midnight.

It was two in the morning. Six minutes after, that was.

"Hon? Did you stop somewhere?"

"No," he said. But he must have. Had he pulled off the road and fallen asleep, hypnotized by the oncoming headlights? Then he admitted it. "I don't know, Shane." Maybe.

Silence.

It was Adam's turn to ask. "Shane?"

"Yeah," came the answer. "I'm with you."

Adam gave a laugh. Okay. Time to let reason assert itself. "I'm sorry to call you so late, babe," he said, and then he froze again. Had he just called Shane "babe"?

He sat down on the arm of his couch. Took a deep breath.

"Shane, I don't know what happened. I think maybe I fell into a trance or something." Then reason really did assert itself. "I'm sure that's what happened. I bet I was sort of out of it—it's not like we got much sleep this weekend." He laughed again and to his surprise felt his cheeks heat up. "I went into la-la land and started driving really slow, maybe. I should count myself lucky I didn't get pulled over."

Silence again.

"Shane?"

"Sorry I yelled," Shane said. "I was just worried is all."

Worried.

Somebody worried about him.

Somebody besides his sister, that was.

It was nice.

A sudden memory hit him all at once. Sitting up straight in his car, hands clenched on the wheel, and wondering if… *if I'm falling for Shane.*

When had that happened?

For some reason the thought sent a shiver through him.

He took a deep breath. "You need to go to bed, Shane."

"You're the one that needs to get to bed, hon," Shane replied. "You have to get up in like three hours."

Except Adam knew right then that wasn't going to happen. He'd call in. He needed the sleep. He was tired. Very tired. Exhausted even. And it wasn't like he and Shane had had that much sex. They'd watched TV in bed. They'd slept in. Gone to a little breakfast place run by a sweet old couple that served good home-cooked meals like he remembered his grandmother used to make. They'd hung out in Buckman's little park, and Saturday, they'd spent an evening at a carnival. Even ridden the Ferris wheel together. Adam had grabbed Shane's hand at the top. He wasn't too crazy about heights.

Why should he be so tired?

"Adam? Go to bed. I'll see you this weekend."

Adam grunted.

"Right?" came the question.

Adam nodded. "Sure. Of course." Why not? Then: "Think I'll stay up just a bit more. Think I'll have a cocktail first. My mind is whirling."

"You going to be able to get up and go to work?"

"Think I'm going to skip work tomorrow."

"They won't get mad?"

"Fuck 'em if they do," he replied and they both laughed.

"Okay. Guess I'll sign off. I lo—" Shane paused. "—loved having you here this weekend."

"It was nice," Adam said.

Another pause.

"You sure you're okay?"

"Sure," Adam said and headed to the kitchen to make that cocktail. He had some Crown. That would be good. Drink it slow. "Why shouldn't I be okay? So I zoned out. Like I said, you did me in."

Silence.

"Shane?"

"Just thinking." Except his tone was funny.

Adam was pulling the bottle of Crown out of the freezer. He liked it very cold. "Thinking about what?" he asked.

"Oh… nothing to worry about. Maybe we can talk about it this weekend?"

Talk about what this weekend?

God.

Was it going to be the "where are we going with this" conversation? He whirled the cap off the bottle and took a good heavy sip. Then another.

"Adam?"

"Yes, Shane," he answered, and took another drink.

"Don't worry about it, okay?"

Adam nodded and decided to take Shane's advice. Not worrying. Sounded like a good idea. He took a fourth drink. This one a good healthy swallow. The others had prepared him for it. So it went down smooth, cool, and then generated heat deep down.

"Okay," he said. "I won't worry."

"Good night."

"Good night," Adam said and found himself almost saying something else.

And heard that echo in his head again.

Am I...?

And he wondered why he couldn't remember what happened next.

He took the biggest drink yet, and then the ice and fire spread through him and he stopped worrying about it. "See you this weekend, babe." And yes, he said "babe." Why the hell not?

"This weekend," Shane repeated, and this time if there had been anything funny in Shane's voice, it was gone. It was warm again. All good.

There was that little *bip* as the line went dead, and Adam took the bottle of Crown back to the living room and, doing his best not to look at the time, switched on his television and turned it to Netflix. Found something fun. Nothing spooky or weird or thought-provoking. Stand-up comedy. John Mulaney—that could be good. No. Jen Kirkman. She was funnier.

Yeah.

Funny was good.

He fell asleep on the couch.

And he had strange dreams…

(Faces)

…that he didn't remember the next day.

6

ADAM MET his sister for coffee at The Shepherd's Bean the next morning, late. It was usually a Saturday morning ritual for them, but one they hadn't kept since he'd been spending his weekends with Shane. Thank God her work partner, Townsend, wasn't with her. The guy creeped Adam out. He was mean, although Daphne swore he was a pussycat.

Adam beat her there, but he didn't order for them because there was nothing worse than warm coffee.

He needn't have worried. She got there less than five minutes after him. Thank God she was smiling. He'd been prepared for a big grilling on the reason(s) they hadn't seen each other in a month and a half. She was wearing one of her smart little suits—blouse and slacks and a short jacket—as she had ever since she'd become a detective. The way she dressed for work was the closest to feminine attire he'd seen her wear since she escaped their parents' house. No more blue uniforms. He didn't miss them. He'd never cared all that much for cops, so leave it to his sister to become one. Could the two of them be more different? At least she didn't smoke.

"Morning, Daph," he said. He was pretty much the only person on the planet who could get away with calling her that. She didn't let her partner call her Daph.

"Morning, Adam," she said after one of her rough hugs. "You check the menu?"

He nodded. "There's a couple of Colombians. You like that, right?"

She returned his nod. "I like everything here," she told him. Which was true. This had been her "spot" ever since she'd come in here a couple years back while on duty. She'd quickly found she liked the people who worked there—several of whom were gay—and the coffee as well. He also suspected she had a bit of a crush on the young lady with the big glasses, but sadly (for his sister), she was quite happily partnered with the lady who ran the no-kill animal shelter around the corner.

Daphne went to the counter, and sure enough, the young lady took the order. His sister hadn't asked what he wanted, which was her all over. Hopefully she remembered he didn't usually care for Colombian.

Daph looked over her shoulder. "Want a doughnut? They've got the pistachio ones you like so much."

That made him sigh happily, and he told her he would love one. If she remembered his doughnut, surely she would remember the coffee preference. She was a police detective after all.

He picked a table with two seats. A few minutes later, his sister sat down across from him and placed a little plate with a doughnut with light green icing on it in front of him. She had one too, but hers was plain. Huge surprise.

"Our coffees will be here in a minute or two."

Which he knew. He'd been here enough times with her. She was just filling the air with words.

Not asking him where he'd been? Why he'd been ignoring her?

"I like the beard," she said.

He reached up and touched his face, still surprised at its presence. He had kept it in that "I haven't shaved in a couple days" style for years. But Shane liked men with facial hair. Said men with beards were the hottest. Said he was jealous of men who could grow them, and it took him a month to get a five-o'clock shadow. And he liked the way it felt on his thighs and… other places.

God. No one had ever licked Shane's ass! Adam couldn't imagine how anyone could have resisted. Shane had a beautiful ass. So high and round. And the hair that ran down his….

"I'm guessing the Colombian is yours," came a voice, and they turned as one to see a handsome bald man with a beard of his own serving them their coffees. It was Dean, aka "Bean," the owner of The Shepherd's Bean. He was placing a cup of coffee in front of Daphne. "And the Papua New Guinea is yours?" He set the second one before Adam.

And I questioned for even a moment that my sister would know what I want?

"Perfect," they both chorused.

Their selections came with about an extra cup's worth of coffee in a beaker. He'd never understood why it was in a beaker.

With a smile Bean nodded and headed back to the front counter.

Avoiding Daphne's eyes, he blew on the surface of his coffee. It smelled wonderful. He tasted it. Nice. Really nice. *Not* his mother's coffee. Not Shane's either. Shane could drink instant coffee. God! *What am I doing with that man?*

"So what's his name?" Daphne asked.

"Whose name?" Adam asked automatically and then blinked at his own answer. Shane's of course. But how could she know that?

Police detective, dummy!

But she can't know.

She raised a perfect eyebrow that any other woman would have died for (or waxed for at least).

"What?" he snapped.

Her other brow joined the first, and she took a drink of her coffee.

He stared down at his own. Took a drink. Tried to ignore her. But that was stupid. She was sitting right across from him.

Adam looked up at her. He saw a twinkle in her eyes. Suddenly he was blushing, and of course that gave him away.

"Wow," she said and smiled. "Who would have ever thought it? My little brother has a boyfriend."

"Not a boyfriend," he replied, quickly and with a little too much force.

"Then he must be a hell of a fuck buddy if he's taken you away for nearly two months." She ran a finger through her short dark almost-curls, then looked at her nails—a silly gesture since she never did a damned thing with them. That would have been way too "fem."

He decided to go with it. Go with the flow. Why the hell fight it? "Jealous?" he asked.

Daphne gave a half shrug—a gesture he'd seen his entire life and that was as familiar as anything about her. "Maybe," she answered.

Really? She admitted it? Would wonders never cease?

"Shane," he said, answering her original question, and was amazed he'd done it. Actually said Shane's name—just like that. As casual as could be. Today was not supposed to be about that. Today was seeing his sister because he *could* and *she* could. It was about catching up. Of course, how could they do that if he didn't talk about Shane?

What was there to talk about?

But that brought Shane's green eyes to mind and his cute smile that often lifted one corner of his mouth, and Adam felt a tingle in his belly he couldn't explain. He'd never really felt anything like this before, unless he included the huge crush he'd had on his friend Buddy back when he was in junior high school.

"And?" Daphne asked and took a big bite of her boring doughnut.

He followed suit, but with his far better doughnut, and made it a big one so he could avoid answering her, even if for only another moment. The truth was, he didn't know what to say. He was truly mixed up about all this. Wondered why he even now couldn't wait to see Shane again. Wished maybe Shane was here with him so his sister could meet him.

His eyes widened at the realization.

Whoa.

Really?

"You okay, Adam?" his always perceptive sister asked.

He jerked and nearly spilled hot coffee on his hand. "Fine...." Adam didn't look at her face. And he wasn't sure why.

"Adam?"

Now he looked up. There was concern in those deep dark eyes of hers. "You sure you're okay?"

He let out a long, long sigh. "I am, Daph." He took another drink of his coffee. "It's just weird. I mean... I think... I think I like this guy."

A radiant smile took her face. "Really?"

He couldn't help but smile back. "But it's weird. Sometimes it's like those butterflies I hear people get all the time. And then sometimes I think I could puke."

Her expression was a strange half grin, half grimace. Then she gave a short, fast nod. "I get it."

She did? "You do?"

"Of course I do. I am a Brookhart, aren't I?"

"Like that means anything," he replied.

"We're more alike than you're ever going to admit," came her quick retort.

Adam shook his head. Them, alike? Besides both having the same parents and both being queer (and hadn't that been an interesting happenstance, especially to their parents), Adam couldn't imagine them being more different.

Daphne put an elbow on the table and propped her chin in her upturned hand. "Seriously, though. I'm interested, little brother. How'd you meet this guy?"

He smiled. "You should know. You were there."

She looked at him blankly. "I was?"

"Yup. It was at Gay Pride this year."

She paused, mulled it over for about ten seconds, and then one of those perfect eyebrows shot up. "Not the cutie you had share your blanket?"

Now he was grinning foolishly and knew he must be blushing. "One and the same."

7

THE GUY looked like he was lost. Or terrified. Or maybe like a kid at the gates of Disney World.

Adam was leaning back on his elbows on his blanket in the grass, watching some drag queen up on stage lip-syncing to Blondie's "Rapture." He was drinking a beer when he noticed the cute guy standing about ten feet away. He looked to be in his late twenties, and damn *was* he cute. With dark blond hair cut short and what appeared to be blue eyes, he was wearing plaid shorts and a dark blue T-shirt, and he had his arms crossed over his chest. Adam found himself staring.

Right then he heard a long, high, piercing noise in his head that made him wince—*hurts!*—and just as fast as it started, it was gone, leaving a slight achy echo behind.

"You okay?" It was Daphne, and she was sitting next to him. In shorts of all things. His sister! In shorts.

Adam rubbed at his temples with one hand, muttered an "I'm okay," and noticed that cute guy was grimacing. He was rubbing at his forehead, and then he turned and looked straight at Adam. Their eyes locked, and Adam felt a distinct chill, despite the bordering-on-excessive heat of the day.

It passed as quickly as it had started, faster even than the ice pick to his brain a few seconds earlier.

They each continued to look at the other.

Adam's stomach clenched. He didn't know what to say. He never knew what to say. But somehow he knew, just knew, that if he didn't say something, this guy was going to walk away, and he didn't want him to walk away.

He raised a hand, still leaning back on his elbows, and managed a "Hi."

Shakespeare would be so proud.

The guy blushed—Adam could see it from here—and managed a "Hi" of his own. He bit his lower lip and started to look away.

Say something!

And then the guy was doing more than look away. He was moving.

"Say something, idiot," Daphne said, voicing his thoughts.

"Ah… having a good time?" It was more a croak than a question. The guy looked back. "Wh-what?" he asked.

"I…." Adam cleared his throat. Then louder, "Having a good time?"

Adam got a nod in return, and then a big shrug. "I guess. I'm so nervous I don't know what to do."

Adam sat up. Gestured for him to come closer. "What's your name?"

"Shane," came the muffled reply.

"What are you so nervous about?" Adam smiled, his stomach twisting now. This wasn't what he did. But for some reason, he couldn't help himself. There was something about this guy—this Shane. *Close.* He motioned for the man to approach. *I'm not going to hurt you.*

Shane took a step. Then another. "I…." He looked away. Looked back. "I've never been to anything like this before."

"Pride?" Adam asked, surprised.

Shane shook his head.

"Really?" And then he wondered why he was asking that. It was obvious.

"Tell him your name," Daphne said from behind him.

"Adam," he blurted. *Stupid!*

"Huh?" Shane asked.

"My name. It's Adam."

"Oh!" Shane blushed even harder. "Duh. Of course."

"Invite him over," hissed Daphne.

Invite him over? God. But then, didn't that sound like a good idea? Wasn't that the old point-a-roono? Adam took a deep drink of his beer, almost finishing it. For strength. Then he patted the blanket next to him. "Want to join us?"

Shane hesitated a moment and then with a shrug sat down right where Adam had patted. He had nice legs, with just the right amount of hair. In fact, Shane had nice everything. Up close his eyes turned out to be hazel and bright and, well, beautiful. He was still blushing, and one corner of his mouth was twitched up in a cute sort of half smile. His hair was light brown rather than dark blond—a distinction Adam couldn't figure out why he was noting. He liked the way it shone in the bright sunlight, though. And he liked the way Shane smelled. Like lavender soap and just the littlest bit of clean sweat.

"I'm gonna go for a walk," said Daphne, and then she rose up in that graceful way of hers. "I'm Daphne, by the way." She did a little wave and disappeared into a crowd of leather men and cowboys.

"I didn't do something to make her go away, did I?" Shane asked.

"No," Adam replied. "She's probably going to look for her lesbo friends." Shane twitched at that word, and Adam immediately regretted saying it. Had no idea why he had.

Nervous. I'm so damned fucking nervous!

His stomach felt like it was full of cast iron.

"I'm so damned nervous," Shane said, echoing Adam's silent words.

"Because you've never been to anything like this before?" Adam gestured with his whole arm, taking in everything around them.

Shane nodded once in response.

"Are you gay?"

"Yes," Shane whispered and then gave a little gasp, looked back with an expression of surprise. Like he couldn't believe he'd said it.

He was charming. Utterly charming.

"Me too," Adam said.

"Good," Shane said in a tone that was barely louder than before. Turned red again. "She's not your g-girlfriend, then."

Adam dropped his head back and laughed. "God, no. She's my sister."

"Really? You two don't look a thing alike."

"We've heard that."

"I'm glad she's not your girlfriend." Now he was crimson.

The iron in Adam's stomach went away, and now there were butterflies there instead.

"Why?" he said, now as lightly as Shane. Could he be heard over the drag queen—the faux Blondie—singing about the man from Mars eating up cars?

Apparently, he could. "Why?" Shane asked.

"Why are you glad she's not my girlfriend?"

"I'm glad you're gay." Adam saw him swallow. Hard. "Because you're so handsome."

"Me?" Adam grinned. "You're the good-looking one."

"Me?" Shane was becoming a regular echo.

Adam reached out to touch Shane's cheek—Shane gave a quiet gasp—and stopped himself. God. Shane wasn't a virgin, was he?

He looked a little scared. Or lost. Excited? Or maybe all three, because wasn't that what it was all about when a kid was waiting to go into the Magic Kingdom?

Now Adam's heart was racing. Excited himself. They were so close.

"For a second there I thought you were going to kiss me," Shane said and laughed, and the sound made the butterflies in Adam's stomach begin to shift their wings.

"You want me to?"

Shane gulped again. "Not yet." And the only reason Adam heard him was that the drag queen's song had come to an end.

The butterflies were aswirl.

And then they went away. Shane pulled out a pack of cigarettes.

Fuck.

"Mind?" Shane asked.

And what was he supposed to say? Not only no, but fuck no?

Hardly.

He shook his head. All thoughts of kissing were gone.

Shane surprised him then. He lit the cigarette, took a deep draw, and then held it out to the side, making sure the smoke didn't blow in Adam's direction on the breeze—such as it was. He blew the smoke carefully as well. He didn't even finish it but stabbed it out in the grass when it was only about half done. And that was when he pulled out the little metal bottle from the same pocket the pack of Wildhorse 100s had come from—Adam had never heard of that brand of cigarettes before—and, pushing a little button on top, shot two mists of mint into his mouth. Breath spritz. Adam smiled.

"Sorry. I'm just so damned nervous." He bit his lower lip.

Adam took a deep breath and let it out slowly. Well, well. A courteous smoker.

And when Shane released his lip… it looked so kissable.

They locked eyes.

The butterflies were back.

"I love your beard," Shane said. "It looks soft. Is it? I can't grow a beard. Not for anything. Can I tou—"

"You boys thirsty?"

They both jumped and looked up and saw Daphne standing over them, holding three cups of beer in translucent cups.

Adam grabbed the cup he'd been drinking from before, swallowed the little that was left inside, and reached for one of the new beers, sliding the new cup inside the empty one.

"Shane? Do you drink?"

"I sure do. Especially now!"

Shane took one of the proffered cups and swallowed deep. Wiped at his mouth with his arm. The wet matted down the soft hair that grew there.

It was hard not to reach out and gently wipe it off.

"So what about those Royals?" Daphne said, breaking in on the moment, and then folded herself down magically onto the picnic blanket Indian-style.

Shane perked up and grinned. Full smile and not his cute little half one.

"Oh my God, did you *see* Sunday's game?" he cried. He looked back eagerly between Adam and Daphne. He was actually wiggling with excitement.

"Of course," Daphne exclaimed. "Could you believe that infield homer that Eskie hit?"

"And Wade Davis? That guy's ERA is 1.11! He's practically unhittable!"

"Yes! And how about Salvy's great snag at home? Kept them Sox in check!"

"Hell yeah! Our boy saved the game."

It degenerated after that.

Sports. Good God. He likes sports.

And Daphne Brookhart, family detective extraordinaire, didn't notice a single one of the looks that Adam was directing at her, not one gesture.

But then Shane managed to do something that Daphne couldn't.

Notice.

"Hey," Shane said quite suddenly, turning from Daphne and looking at Adam with those sparkling eyes. "I just realized something. I haven't seen anything around here yet. You want to show me?"

Then that quirky half smile.

"Sure. I'd like that."

"It looks like there are some booths. What kind of stuff do they sell here?"

Adam laughed. "Oh.... *Stuff.*"

Some of it I don't think you'll believe.

"And funnel cake," Shane said with a grin. "I'm sure I smell funnel cake."

Adam nodded.

"But it's so sweet I can never eat it all. Want to split one?"

"I'd like that too." Now Adam couldn't help but smile. Shane was utterly charming.

The butterflies were back.

8

SHANE CAME to Kansas City that weekend.

It was a good thing. Because after Adam's strange trip home, he knew he wasn't driving to Buckman. Not for love nor money.

Or even one of Shane's sexy smiles.

Adam had been having dreams.

He was driving. There were long dark night roads. Roads that went on and on and on and never seemed to stop. And then blue light.

He'd woken up at least one night shouting.

Despite that, they had sex about three minutes after Shane walked in the door of Adam's apartment.

They didn't fuck. They hadn't yet. Which Adam thought was a little weird—all these weeks and no fucking? Adam couldn't even figure out why. He liked to fuck. Sometimes he liked to *be* fucked.

(rarely)

But with Shane?

Shane just couldn't. And the one time they had almost tried—that had been at Shane's place the week before—with Adam climbing on top of that beautiful ass, carefully and slowly working his way inside of him, Shane couldn't go through with it. Shane had never been topped. He'd said he thought he could do it with Adam, but it had all fallen apart.

He'd actually been crying. "I can't. I. *Can't.* I just can't let anything.... I can't."

It had been their worst moment.

A total disaster.

"It's okay, Shane," Adam had told him and moved so they were face-to-face and held him close.

Disaster had been averted, and after some quiet cuddling and a little kissing, the lovemaking had resumed.

Lovemaking.

Whoa.

And today, when Adam had opened the door and saw Shane standing there, he felt a rush like he couldn't ever remember feeling before. And whether it was lust or hormones or something he'd never expected to experience, he quite desperately needed Shane. He'd kissed him right there on the threshold, and this time witnesses be damned. This was Kansas City, not Buckman, and the apartment building was called the Oscar Wilde, and nearly all its residents were gay, lesbian, transgender, or queer identified, so who was going to care?

Shane had *almost* resisted there for a second or two and then—perhaps realizing just where he was—accepted and returned the kiss and then practically melted against Adam. He had an erection. Adam could feel it (against his own). And God. An erection was a terrible thing to waste.

Besides, the lasagna was in the oven, and it still had almost an hour to cook. There was time.

At least Adam closed the door.

It wasn't like they took long. The lust was way too much a part of it. They did manage to get over to the couch. In no time they were both face to crotch and urgently making love to each other with their mouths, and Shane smelled so damned good—that combination of clean road sweat and lavender soap—and they came at almost the same moment. Adam swallowed hungrily. Shane did too, and that was nice because it was some small-town taboo he'd been trying to overcome for a while.

When they switched over so they could cuddle close, Shane said, "Nice appetizer," and Adam couldn't help but laugh. Couldn't help but feel the delightful flutters in his stomach once again—and maybe even a few of those butterflies had risen to swirl around and light on his heart.

It should have terrified him.

It didn't.

He had to bite his lip (like Shane was always doing, but much harder) to keep himself from saying it right then. From using the L-word.

And it wasn't "lesbian."

Oh my God. Is it happening? Am I falling for this guy?

The timer went off in the kitchen, surprising Adam. Had it been an hour? How could it have been an hour? Had they been cuddling that long? It didn't seem possible.

He disentangled himself, despite Shane's grumblings, and went to the kitchen still naked. Shane whistled after him.

He wiggled his ass.

Shane gave him a catcall.

It was nice. Adam went into the kitchen grinning.

He opened the oven and the aroma of the lasagna, which had been wafting out to them already, hit him full force, along with the roll of heat. It smelled wonderful. He actually started salivating. Carefully he pulled the tented foil cover off the store-bought container—the cheese was bubbling beautifully—closed the door, and then set the timer once more. This is where everything browned.

Then Adam felt something against his ass, and he jumped and turned and was pulled into Shane's arms. The "something" was Shane's newly revived cock.

"Dinner," Adam managed to say, feeling himself growing hard. *God, he gets me hard again that fast....*

"You just shut the oven door."

"Only ten more minutes."

"We could do a lot in ten minutes," Shane said. He had come so far from the blushing guy at Gay Pride. The one who had only had sex with a few men in his whole life. Not a virgin. But close.

"I want to take my time this time," Adam whispered and kissed his lover.

My lover. Wow.

Shane sighed. "Okay."

"Want to help me with the garlic bread?"

"You know I can barely boil water."

"You grill like a chef."

Shane gave him that half smile.

"All you have to do is pop it in the oven. It's in the freezer."

"Sounds easy enough."

"I'll finish the salads," Adam said and opened a cabinet, got on his toes to grab the bowls.

Shane grabbed his ass. "I can't wait for dessert."

Adam looked over his shoulder and saw the hunger in Shane's eyes. He thought he might just let Shane have some.

I must be in love.

9

ADAM WASN'T expecting what he found the next morning.

Shane had gotten up first, although that wasn't abnormal. Shane was a "morning person." Another big difference between them. Shane had been working a shift that started early for ten years. He couldn't sleep in even when he didn't have to work.

What was unexpected was the books on the table. The books and the journals. Shane had one open and was writing in it when Adam walked in. He looked up, a funny expression on his face.

Even from where he stood halfway across the room, Adam saw the word UFOs in stark white on the dark cover of one of the books. *UFOs?*

Adam shivered. He didn't know why.

He laughed. It was an uncomfortable laugh. "What… what are you doing?" he asked.

Another shiver.

Shane looked up at him and instead of laughing and saying something like, "Ah, damn! You caught me! I'm a bigger geek than you ever knew—"

(And he should have known because Shane liked all those shows about Bigfoot and the Bermuda Triangle and the shooting of President Kennedy.)

—he said, "You know what I'm doing, don't you?"

Adam didn't know. He shrugged.

Shane let his head fall to the side and sighed. He looked down at the coffee table and the books and removed his splayed fingers from the journal he'd been writing in. It slipped closed. Shane had been writing on one of the early pages. But there were at least a half dozen more.

Adam took another step. He could see some of the book titles clearly now. One of them had a mostly white cover with the title *Captured!* in blood red. There was one he'd seen already—the cover was a darkened sky and the title was *UFOs Caught on Film*. Then one he'd seen at a hundred garage sales—*Communion. Oh, fuck me....* Another said *The Alien*—something something. He couldn't see the whole title. His stomach was doing funny things, and he didn't know why. He did know he didn't give a shit what the rest of the title was. Or the complete title of the pocket-sized paperback on which the only words visible were *The Interrupted*—

Adam shivered once more. But he grinned. Tried to make light of it. And why not? Why shouldn't he? What was the big deal?

"UFOs, Shane? Really?"

Shane nodded. Patted the space on the couch next to him. Adam found himself reminded of that day when they met, him patting the picnic blanket, bidding Shane to sit with him. Shane had done so, eagerly. But somehow it was not what Adam wanted to do right now.

Not at all.

10

ADAM HAD been pleasantly surprised when Shane went home with him from Pride. He'd been so sweet. So... shy.

This is the kind of guy I'll have to date at least three times before he'll go to bed with me, he'd thought more than once that day. So surprise, surprise.

He'd shown Shane around as requested. They'd played a few games—Shane was very good, even won a stuffed animal. They visited the booths, and they'd each bought a T-shirt. It was hot when Shane had peeled off his shirt so he could try a few on. Shane had a smooth chest—Adam liked smooth-chested guys, had never been into the hirsute pursuit—with only a fraction of a happy trail that started at his navel and disappeared into his blue-and-white plaid pants. It had taken Shane a while to pick a shirt. He wanted something gay, but not too gay. Something that he would know the meaning of, but the average shopper at the Super Walmart wouldn't. Something that he might—repeat, might—be brave enough to wear in the little town where he lived—someplace Adam had never heard of called Buckman, about three or so hours away.

"The pink triangle, then," Adam had advised.

"Pink triangle?"

"Yeah. I bet even people in Mayberry have heard of the rainbow flag. But most people don't know about the pink triangle."

Shane had blinked at him. "I don't."

"Voilà! See?"

"It's gay?" Shane asked.

They looked into each other's eyes and once again Adam was feeling funny, mysterious things. Guys were a source of getting off. He either ignored men, or he got into bed (and out of bed) as fast as humanly possible. He didn't feel funny and mysterious things for men. Because that might mean you could feel other things and let your guard down, let the walls down, let them see parts of you that people had no business seeing. And God, the way Shane was looking at him! It was so sweet and... puppy dog.

Adam didn't do puppy dogs.

But one look from those hazel eyes and Adam was opening up. Being much more than just superficial.

"World War II," Adam answered. "There were more than Jews put into the concentration camps. Gypsies. Polish people. And us gays. The Jews wore yellow stars of David. They put pink triangles on the homosexuals. This guy named Larry Kramer helped turn the pink triangle into a sign for gays. But he turned it upside down. So it was pointed upward instead of down."

"Damn" came Shane's response. Too much? Had the history lesson been too much?

Shane took a deep breath. Then he'd set his shoulders high. "Sounds fucking awesome."

Adam hadn't been so discreet. He'd picked a shirt that said Read My Lips and pictured two sailors kissing.

How cute had it been that Shane had blushed?

They'd looked at rescue services too, where Adam had discovered that Shane was a cat person instead of a dog person, but he was looking more at the dogs.

"Dogs bark," Shane had said, all mysterious again. "Sometimes that's all it takes."

They ate bratwurst, and Adam resisted making it sexual. He could tell it was the worst thing he could do with Shane.

They shared a funnel cake.

Adam popped a piece into Shane's mouth, wondering where he'd gotten such a silly 1950s idea, and was rewarded with the sweetest smile.

There hadn't been any kissing, though, although several times Adam thought it was going to happen. There hadn't been much touching either, although Adam had certainly wanted to touch him.

Nothing had really happened until they were crowded near the stage, the day almost over, watching the First Ladies of Disco. Three famous divas from before either of them were born, but they were kicking ass, and who hadn't heard of Martha Wash's "It's Raining Men?"

Daphne was gone by then. She hadn't wanted to deal with the crowds, and she *hated* disco, was much more a Mary Lambert or Tegan and Sara fan.

It was right when Martha—Martha *herself!*—was singing about getting absolutely soaking wet (!) that Shane linked his fingers into Adam's right hand and then a few minutes later kissed him—kissed him hard—that Adam realized he might have a chance. And he *wanted* a chance.

Crazy. It was crazy. He didn't spend all day with a guy seeing what was to come! What might come. It was easy to get laid if you really wanted to. Even for a guy like him. Not gorgeous. Not a ten.

"God, you're gorgeous," Shane had said then, crying into his ear to be heard above the blasting speakers.

No I'm not, he thought. *But you are.* He shook his head. "You are," he shouted back.

They kissed again, and quite suddenly there was that strange, high, piercing shrill noise in his head—stabbing him like an ice-cold pick right to his temple—and he'd pulled away and saw that Shane was covering his ears like he heard it too—

(It's not in your ears; it's deeper, much deeper!)

—and shaking his head, and then just as suddenly, the noise was gone.

Feedback from the speakers, that's what it is, he told himself.

Then, as a thousand times before, the music was over, and moments later those in charge were hustling people out the gates—herding them like cattle.

They found their cars (they were holding hands, actually holding hands), and Adam asked Shane if he wanted to go to The Male Box for a couple drinks, but Shane didn't want that.

"I've had enough of crowds," he said. "I'm not used to so many people. I should have gone home hours ago. I live three *hours* from here!"

"Want to go back to my apartment?"

Long pause.

Then a single nod.

They parked next to each other as soon as they could and then waited together in Adam's car for the parking lot to mostly clear. That was where Shane asked if he could touch his beard—

"I've been wanting to all day."

Shane looked so cute and sweet when he said it, all Adam could do was nod his head yes.

And then Shane did, and Adam shivered (both of them did, actually) and said, "So soft. I didn't know what it would feel like. But it's so soft…."

Adam couldn't help but kiss him then, and Shane kissed back, and Adam got so hard he thought he might ejaculate in his pants like a teenager.

—and afterward Shane followed him back to the Oscar Wilde.

They went into the building, took the elevator up—Shane's nervousness was palpable—and entered Adam's apartment.

"Nice," Shane had said, looking around.

Adam's apartment wasn't. Not real nice at least. And it was messy. There were empty takeout containers on the coffee table and in the kitchen. Magazines and fag rags littered about. He was embarrassed. Then Shane asked him if he had anything to drink.

"I'd rather kiss you again," Shane said. "But I'm so fucking nervous I could puke." He rolled his eyes. "I guess that wasn't very sexy, was it?"

Adam told him not to worry about it and cleared off the couch fast. "Sit," he said and went and got the Crown out of the freezer. He poured two fingers' worth into a pair of glasses and brought them back.

"What is it?" Shane asked.

"Whisky," Adam said.

Shane grimaced.

"This isn't Old Crow," Adam said. "Try it. *Sip* it."

So Shane had. He'd grimaced again—but not nearly as much. "So?"

Shane looked up at him. "Sit."

Adam sat.

They drank.

Then they kissed.

It was sweet and hot and wild and adorable all at once.

They kicked off their shoes.

They took each other's T-shirts off.

Shane climbed into Adam's lap.

Then Adam surprised them both by standing and clasping Shane's (hot little) ass and carrying him to the bedroom.

And then…

…then they made love. Or something like it.

Adam's usual technique would have been to tear Shane's jeans off and start a rock-and-roll party. But even in his darkened bedroom, he could see the fear and the hope and the desperation in Shane's eyes.

What came next was something between wild sex and sweet sex.

It was utterly amazing.

The only downside was when Adam started making love to his ass—he'd wanted that rounded perfection all day—Shane panicked.

"I don't fuck!" Shane had cried.

"It's okay," Adam assured him.

He's a virgin? Of course the possibility had been there all day. "You're a virgin?" he asked.

Shane had looked at him like a wounded puppy and whispered, "Down there."

Down where Adam was, between his legs, kissing his perfect rounded cheeks, had been running his tongue down the deep cleft between them.

"But I've been with men. A *few* men."

Shane had looked at Adam as if he were asking for forgiveness.

So then Adam had assured him that fucking him wasn't what he wanted to do and showed Shane the wonders of what a tongue could do to a tiny, tight hole and then kissed him everywhere. Shane had cried out in delight, which only spurred Adam on. Virgin he might not be, but instinctively Adam knew the sex Shane had experienced with men in Buckman, Missouri, wasn't anything to write *Fifty Shades of Grey* about.

He was right.

And as inexperienced as Shane had been, Adam still gave him his phone number. His real phone number.

And they'd spent every weekend together since.

11

"Where did you get all this stuff?" Adam asked, pointing to the books on his coffee table. He'd almost said "this shit." He was sitting next to Shane, and their thighs were touching. Normally that might have been erotic. Now he wasn't sure what he was feeling.

"I've collected it for a long time. Got a lot of it online. You don't find many books like this in Buckman. Not at our little bookstore, that is."

It was hardly much of a bookstore. At least as far as selection. They also served breakfast. It was kind of charming, Adam had come to admit, but the Library of Congress it wasn't.

"Why?" he asked.

Shane turned his head and caught Adam's eyes with his own. "Why do you think?"

"I don't have a clue," Adam said.

The look on Shane's face was obvious. He didn't believe Adam.

But he should.

Adam didn't know what Shane was saying.

Liar.

There was an infinite pause.

Then: "The time that you lost on the road last weekend...."

"What about it?" Adam said, and knew he was avoiding... something.

"Have you ever had that happen before? Have you lost time?"

"What?" He almost got up, but the sincerity in Shane's voice kept him there.

"Especially late at night? Driving out on empty roads where there was nobody else around?"

Adam blinked at him. What was he asking?

And then that niggling little thought began to tickle at his memories.... He shook his head. That tickling made his stomach clench. Made him feel cold. Made him feel....

"No," he said (lied).

"Never?" Shane's eyes were so wide. Desperate?

Adam shook his head.

A sudden image of camping out when he was in fourth grade. Pup tents. He'd been in the Webelos Scouts. He and his buddy Skip had snuck off to go skinny-dipping. The moon had been just rising over the lake. And then quite suddenly it was high overhead.

He hadn't thought of that in years.

Adam looked away from Shane. He didn't want him to see.

See what?

Shane leaned back and put his arms behind him. It made his baggy T-shirt ride up and revealed his well-filled underwear. Maybe they could forget about this stuff. Somehow Adam knew, just *knew*, that he didn't want to talk about these books. This time-loss stuff.

"For me? The first time I was in… fourth grade, I think? I was hanging out at this old abandoned house."

Fourth grade.

Webelos.

Adam looked away again. He wanted to put his hands over his ears. And the thing was, he didn't know why.

Because five or ten minutes ago, everything was normal and he was definitely coming to the conclusion that he was falling in love. He'd woken up and Shane wasn't there, and he was thinking about how much he missed him even though he knew he couldn't be far.

And he'd thought to himself, *I think I'm in love.* And he'd smiled.

Now, though, he was sitting next to Shane, and these weird books were on the coffee table, and he was panicking. And he didn't even know why. Why should that be anything to panic over?

"Me and Mom," Shane went on. "We lived out in the middle of nowhere so I didn't have anyone to play with, you know? And Mom got me this little motorcycle."

"You had a motorcycle in fourth grade?"

Shane gave a half laugh. "It was more like a bicycle with a motor on it. I wasn't going anywhere fast. But I sure pretended. Usually that I was the *Ghost Rider.*"

"That dumb movie with Nicholas Cage?"

Shane shook his head. "No. The comic book. The comic book was really cool. Great art. Anyway, I would ride down the road about a quarter mile or so, and there were these three old houses at three of four corners. One had fallen over, and one my mom had flat-out forbidden me to go to 'cause it looked like it could fall over any second, and the last one… well, it was kinda cool. At least to a fourth grader. I'd go in there and play. Whoever had owned it even left some furniture in there."

"And it was okay with your mother for you to play in *there*?"

Shane smiled at him in that way that usually got his heart beating faster. "Well… she hadn't actually *forbidden* it."

Shane laughed, and Adam tried to join him. It didn't sound real at all.

"Anyway, I was in there playing one day, and I felt someone tap my shoulder."

A shiver passed through Adam.

"I turned around, and there was nobody there. But then something caught the corner of my eye, and I looked, and there was this man."

"A man?" Adam asked. His stomach got heavy.

Shane nodded. "He was standing down the hall in the kitchen. He was wearing a long black coat, and he had on this black hat. He had his arms up in front of him—" Shane raised his hands and then hung them over each other, limp, demonstrating. "—like this. I could only barely see his face. He was standing back in the shadows, and there was this shaft of sunlight between us, and I remember seeing the dust moving around in that light so clearly. I thought he said something then, thought I could almost see his face. These eyes, big and up to either side of his face instead of where they were supposed to be, and the next thing I knew, I was sitting on the floor and the shaft of sunlight was gone. I…." Shane gulped hard. "I jumped up and looked around, and the sun was almost setting. I mean before, before I forgot stuff, it couldn't have been later than four in the afternoon at the most. And then suddenly the sun was setting. Scared the shit out of me. I ran for my bike and raced home and dashed into the house and told my mom all about it."

"What did she say?" Adam asked, knowing the answer. She would have thought he was being silly. Would have told him he fell asleep. Of course she would….

"She said, 'Oh! You met the man in black.'"

12

ADAM DIDN'T understand what Shane was getting at, although it was clear that Shane thought he should have.

"She knew who this guy was?"

Shane's eyebrows went up. His expression was "Are you shitting me?"

Adam wasn't shitting him.

Shane sighed and leaned back again, hands behind his head. The T-shirt hiked back up, and the underwear once more revealed something that Adam was far more interested in right now than pursing this conversation.

"You're being deliberately slow here, Adam."

"Let's go to bed," he said hurriedly and then laid his hand on Shane's sexy, just-hairy-enough thigh and let it slide slowly upward.

Shane dropped his hand onto Adam's and stopped it.

"Later. If you still want to."

Adam pulled his hand away. "Later what?" he cried.

A long sigh was Shane's response. "Let me back up." He sat up. "I was late for dinner. Mom didn't even ask why. She just had me sit down and got me a glass of milk. Then she started serving up our food. I can't remember what we had except for macaroni and cheese. That kind from Kraft. She made it all the time. It was cheap, and we needed cheap. We ate lots of ramen noodles and tuna too."

Adam didn't say anything.

"Then she sat down and told me her story. Told me about how one day she was cleaning house while I was at school. She said she had just sprayed the inside of the stove with cleaner, and she looked up and there was this man standing there. Startled her. For some reason this little house had a really big kitchen—it was bigger than either of our bedrooms—and she guessed that was why she hadn't seen him right away. He was standing in a corner, and he was wearing this long black coat—like a trench coat—and his hands were crossed up in front of him. Kind of like a praying mantis."

The insectoids? Adam wondered. Geez.

"That's what she said anyway, and that made me think it was just what the man I met looked like. She said she was totally shocked—but not shocked at the same time. That once she saw him, he seemed familiar. She couldn't see his face. Not clearly, and that didn't make any sense because it was right around lunchtime and there was plenty of light coming in through the kitchen window. Somehow his hat, the brim, was keeping his face in shadow… but not."

Shane rubbed at his upper arms, and with that simple gesture, Adam's own arms broke out into gooseflesh.

"She said she thought the more she looked, she could almost see his eyes, but they weren't where they were supposed to be. That they were more up here." Shane cupped his hands and then placed them above and to the sides of his eyes.

Like a praying mantis, Adam thought. And once more shivered.

"Yeah," Shane said. "Just like that."

Did I say that out loud? He hadn't thought so.

"Mom told me she wasn't scared. That there was a part of her telling her that she should be, or *maybe* she should be, at least, but that she just wasn't. That there was this man suddenly inside the house, and she should have screamed and run, but she didn't. She just said, 'Hello.'"

Hello? "Hello?"

Shane nodded again, but this time Adam knew he'd spoken aloud.

"Hello," Shane repeated. He ran a hand through his short hair. It was messy from sleep, and Shane's finger combing had done nothing to help matters. Not that hair as short as Shane's could get that messy anyway. "Then the man told her that it was time."

"Time?" Adam asked, and realized he really had become some kind of human echo.

This is fucking weird.

"Yup." Shane smiled but it was a strange one. Not nice at all. Not Shane's sexy smile or even one of his big laughing takes-over-his-whole-face smiles. It was kind of creepy. "She told him that it would have to wait until another day because she had just sprayed the stove and it was important that she wipe it down in thirty minutes, but then he reached out, and she saw that his fingers were thick and very long, and the next thing she knew she was sitting at the table and I was coming in the front door. She realized that she'd lost the entire afternoon."

Adam had to fight the urge to jump up and leave the room. What Shane had just said was bonkers and creepy. It was the other shoe. It had dropped.

"Mom said this happened once or twice more, but then it stopped. So when I told her what happened to me, she knew just who it was."

"Who was it?" Adam exclaimed.

Shane rolled his eyes. "Adam!"

"Adam *what*?"

"A man in black!"

God. Oh fucking God. A man in black? Really? "Will Smith or Tommy Lee Jones?"

The expression he got in return was a hurt one. And that made Adam feel bad. But not bad enough. This was wackadoodle. "And she wasn't the least bit freaked the fuck out?" he asked, trying to back things up.

Shane shook his head. "No. She said he never harmed her. Not that she knew of. In fact she said she found out that leaving oven cleaner in the oven for several hours made it easier to clean." Then he looked at Adam so calmly, so matter-of-factly, that Adam burst into laughter and suddenly all was well with the world.

Shane was pulling his leg.

Joshing with him.

Kidding around. Yanking his chain. Clowning around. Busting his chops. Messing with him. Kidding.

Then Shane ruined it.

"It's happened to me a lot of times since then," Shane said. "Me losing time. I never saw the man in black again—"

Wait! Wait just a goddamned minute. Man in black?

"—but there are times when I just lose time. It's almost always when I'm driving. I don't think it has happened while I was at home. I don't live in Manhattan, or even Kansas City, but if something came down to get me when I was at the house, then people would see...."

See? People would see?

See what?

But Adam knew just what Shane was saying. It was in the books laid out before them. UFOs. He was talking about frigging U, F, fucking Os!

This is crazy.

How is this happening?

He looked at Shane. A guy whose flaws had been cigarettes and baseball. And now what?

He believes in UFOs.

UFOs that took him away!

Shane actually believed that he'd been abducted by aliens.

"Not that people don't see them all the time. That part confuses me. Why all the secrecy when sometimes they don't seem to be concerned in the least." He picked up the book called *UFOs Caught on Film* and began to leaf through it. Showed Adam a page. Then another. And another.

All of which were pictures of flying saucers.

"So many of these were taken in broad daylight. I mean, I know a lot of them were out in the middle of nowhere—"

Like in Buckman, Missouri, population somewhere around four thousand people and far from any kind of real civilization?

"—but some of these are over huge cities or towns. Look at this one."

There was gooseflesh again, and Adam didn't want to look. But the page had been shoved pretty much under his nose, and when he focused (involuntarily) on the photograph, he saw a dark disk with several blue lights beneath. It was hovering or flying over a tree and some power lines. The notation said 1976.

He looked away.

"Do you really believe in this stuff, Shane?" he asked. It was more of a whimper. Things had been going good. He really, really liked—

(loved)

—this guy.

But the other shoe had dropped.

Shane was wackadoodle.

13

ADAM BORE Daphne's hug today. He wasn't in the mood to be touched. Not even by Daph.

They sat down on either side of the long slim table. "Surprise, surprise," Daphne said. "Saturday morning coffee again. Shane didn't come in?"

Of course that would be the question. He shook his head. "All they have today is Colombian. Three kinds." He sighed.

One of her eyebrows started to rise... then fell back into place. "Well, good for me anyway. And it's good to see you, brother."

He tried to smile and told her that it was good to see her too. It was, wasn't it?

Neither said anything for a stupidly long moment, and then she shrugged and got up to grab one of the small clipboards that served as a menu at The Shepherd's Bean. A half sheet of brown (unbleached) paper stated today's offerings, which could be different (and often were) from just the day before. "This first one looks good," she replied matter-of-factly. "The Finca Aracatace?"

He shrugged.

"It is your turn to buy," she said.

Was it? He couldn't really remember.

"Sure," he replied and went to the counter. The girl with the big glasses wasn't there. The real reason Daphne told him it was his turn to order, perhaps? There was a cute boy barista today, one he hadn't seen before, with lots of tattoos and wearing a wool cap. A tumble of dark curls spilled from beneath its edge.

Cute.

Not as cute as Shane.

Stop it!

He ordered the coffees and went ahead and got a plain doughnut for Daphne and a chocolate one for himself, then rejoined his sister at the table.

"So where is Shane?"

He shrugged, trying for a not-a-care-in-the-world look. "I assume he's at home."

"Which is where again?"

"Buckman."

She gave a nod and took a bite of her doughnut. He tasted his own. Delicious as always.

"So why aren't you with him?" she asked.

Adam shrugged again. "I wanted a weekend off," he said, not meeting her eyes.

Another nod. Another bite. Another pause.

Then, "From the way you were talking, I kinda thought a weekend off was the last thing you'd want. I was hoping anyway. I liked the idea of you having someone in your life."

"He was a distraction," Adam fired back.

Her face was completely noncommittal. So Daphne. So police detective.

"And I was feeling guilty about skipping our Saturday mornings. I thought you'd want to see me."

"I always want to see you, Adam. But we can see each other anytime. You can only see Shane on the weekends."

"I wanted a weekend off!" He immediately regretted the force of it.

The cute barista brought their coffees. He tried to lock eyes with Adam, who refused to allow it.

Once Coffee Boy was gone, Daphne asked, "What happened?"

"Nothing!" Too strong again. He sighed. Took a drink of his coffee. Not bad. The special fermentation process the menu described must have helped.

"Sorry," Daphne said quietly. "I don't mean to pry."

"You always pry," he replied.

"Well someone has to!"

He looked up, surprised.

Daphne bit her lower lip. Like Shane did. Adam shook the image from his head.

"Sorry," she said again. "But it's like I said. I liked seeing you with someone. I liked the idea of you not being alone."

"I don't need to be with anyone," he said and took another drink of his coffee. Not bad. It wasn't bad at all. At least it was a distraction.

She said, "Of course," and bit into her plain, boring doughnut. "But being with someone is nice. I know I'd like someone to come home to."

"You?" He was taken aback both by the comment and the look in her deep dark brown eyes.

"Me." He could barely hear her she said it so quietly. Then, louder: "I was getting kind of warm thinking about the two of you cuddled on the couch watching TV."

For some reason this surprised him as well. "You were?"

She nodded.

He thought about it a second. He and Shane on the couch watching TV. Cuddling. Then he thought of the UFO books, and he blew a raspberry.

"That bad?"

"That bad," he said with a sigh.

"The cigarettes get to you?"

He paused. No. Amazingly they hadn't. Especially with all the care Shane had taken to always step away to smoke and to constantly use that breath spritz.

Adam could almost smell it. Felt a tiny pang of missing it.

He shook his head again.

But it wasn't the cigarettes. Or the baseball games. Not any of that.

"He's wackadoodle," he said by way of an explanation.

"To fall in love with you, he'd have to be," Daphne responded with a little smile.

In love? "In love?"

She gave a single nod. "I think he fell for you before he sat down on that blanket."

Adam scoffed at the idea. "Please."

"I mean it. That's why I was so happy to see he was the reason you'd been skipping our Saturday mornings. Not just because you were seeing someone, but I'd been thinking he was another boy whose heart you were going to break."

Adam looked at her in astonishment. "What?"

"You've left a string of them behind."

"Me?" Even more astonished.

"Of course." She drank her coffee. "You've always had trouble with relationships, with trusting anyone."

"You psychoanalyzing me?"

"You meet them and see them once or thrice and then cast them aside. More than one has seen me out and asked me what they'd done wrong."

Adam's mouth fell open. "Huh?"

"I always wondered why you didn't keep one. I'd love it if someone was interested in me."

"What the hell are you talking about?" Casting aside? String of broken hearts? WTF?

"I mean, I can't remember you seeing someone for as long as you were seeing Shane…."

Long? It was only, what? Six weeks or so?

"Does this mean it's over?"

Over?

Shane's image shimmered into his mind's eye. So cute. Sweet. His heart felt a twinge. God. This is why he didn't—

(fall in love)

—let himself feel for anybody. He could get hurt. They got power. He didn't want anyone to have power over him.

Over? Was it over?

"I don't know," he said and looked through the big windows onto Main Street. God. His heart was still feeling that dull little ache. *I miss him. God, I miss him.* "He's wackadoodle, Daphne! He believes in UFOs!" He froze. Looked around him. Coffee Boy was giving him an odd look. Adam looked away.

"UFOs?" One of her perfect eyebrows was high enough to near disappear under her dark bangs.

"UFOs," he repeated. But quietly.

She shrugged.

"He thinks he's been abducted!" He cringed and glanced at the barista, but he was busy with a customer.

He expected Daphne to look surprised. Instead, that eyebrow had dropped down to its customary place.

"Well?" he asked. "Is that crazy or not?"

Something funny happened then. Something in Daphne's eyes. They seemed to grow darker. Strange. He'd read about dark clouds coming into a person's eyes, but like never having seen someone laugh all the way to the bank, he'd never really *seen* those storm clouds in real life.

Until now.

Daphne looked away.

"Daphne…? Sis?"

She turned back to him. Shrugged. "After a while you see all kinds of weird things, Adam. What's that thing that Shakespeare said? Something about there being stranger things under heaven and earth that you can dream of?"

Shakespeare? Really? Daphne quoting—or trying to quote—Shakespeare? *Really?*

"What are you talking about?"

Her eyes grew even darker. He actually *saw* it happen. Then after an infinite seeming pause, her eyes flicked back to normal and she said, "I've seen some *weird* shit the last year or two, Adam. Some *really* weird shit. So UFOs? Who am I to say?"

This only agitated him all the more.

"Well, what about this? He thinks I've been abducted too! How's that for fucking freaky?"

14

"LET'S GO to bed," Adam had said.

And then Shane had said, "Later. If you still want to."

He already didn't want to anymore. Anything to end this conversation.

"I think maybe you've been abducted too, baby," Shane had said quietly. "I think it happened to you on the way from my place last week. And maybe because you were with me."

Adam had flinched at the comment. Flinched back as if he been burned or shocked.

But why?

The whole idea was ridiculous.

Abducted?

Really?

But the expression on Shane's face told him that Shane wasn't kidding. Wasn't pulling his leg. He was serious. Serious as a heart attack. "How else do you explain your missing time? You were missing a lot of time, baby. How do you explain that?"

Adam willed himself to relax. He took a deep breath.

"Come on, Shane. You don't really believe that, do you? That's crazy."

"Is it?" Shane asked. "Why?"

Adam laughed. It wasn't very convincing. Not even to himself. "Come on, Shane! Aliens? You don't really think that do you? I mean that's all fine and dandy for a movie like *Close Encounters of the Third Kind*. Fun. But you don't *really* believe that shit, do you?"

But Adam saw it. Shane did believe.

Wackadoodle.

The other shoe had not only dropped, it had fallen through the floor.

This is what I get. Never again.

He sighed. "Shane, it's like I said. Simple as can be. I got hypnotized by the headlights of the oncoming cars. I was tired. It was a long drive. Anything could have happened. I could have driven over to the shoulder and slept."

Shane gave him an incredulous look.

"It's certainly more believable than aliens! And if it was, why can't I remember?"

"People almost never remember," Shane said. He picked up the book that had the word "captured" on the cover. "This book." He pointed at the photograph of a white woman and a black man. "It's all about the famous case of Betty and Barney Hill. No one has ever been able to disprove it. They couldn't remember what happened to them either. So they were hypnotized to bring back their memories. And that proved they were abducted by aliens."

Adam grunted. "That doesn't prove shit. What's been proven is that hypnosis can cause false memories."

"But there are hundreds of cases, Adam. Charles Hickson and Calvin Parker in Pascagoula in 1973. The Walton Experience—they made that into a movie. Ever see *Fire in the Sky*?"

Adam jerked. Yes, he had seen that movie. The ending had given him nightmares for weeks. Of course he'd been a little kid when he'd seen it on TV. What kid wouldn't have a nightmare after seeing all that slime and gore and scary shit?

Goose bumps once again rushed up and down Adam's arms.

"Whitley Strieber wrote about it in *Communion*."

God. *That* one. Another case of wackadoodle!

"He's famous." Shane placed a pointer finger on that book on the table. "No one has ever been able to disprove his story either."

It was all Adam could do not to jump up and leave the room. That feeling was coming back. Chilling. He felt nauseated. "No," he moaned. "I do not believe it. They were a bunch of crazies. Or attention seekers looking for their fifteen minutes of fame."

"Adam! Who would want that kind of fame? Who would want the world to think they were crazy or liars? People lose everything when stuff like that gets out. Their jobs. Friends. Family. Lovers. Who would want that?"

Then Adam was standing up. He really did feel like he might throw up. "Enough."

"You can't believe we're all there is, can you?"

"I never really thought about it," he shot back.

"All those billions of stars? You don't think we're all there is, do you? You don't think we're the only intelligent life in the universe?"

Adam clenched his fists. Once more forced himself to calm down. Why was he acting like this? Feeling like this? It was silly. *Calm down.* He swallowed hard. "I suppose not. But flying saucers? Aliens taking people up in their spaceships and giving them anal probes? No. I don't believe that. Not for a freaking second."

"Since the 1930s over eleven million people have seen a UFO, or know someone who has. One study says that as much as five to six percent of the general population may have been abducted—"

Right then that high, piercing, ear-slashing, brain-stabbing noise came back. It was the first time in weeks, and Adam winced and cried out and covered his ears. But it wasn't coming from his ears, was it? Even though it sounded so much like feedback from a huge set of concert speakers.

It was coming from *inside* his head.

And when Shane jerked in his seat, Adam knew that he had heard it too. But how was that possible?

Then as quickly as it had come, it was gone, leaving only a painful echo in its wake.

They looked at each other for a long time. Then Adam said, "And just what was that."

"Implants," Shane whispered.

15

THEY DIDN'T go back to bed that day. They didn't have sex. They didn't make love.

They went out for lunch at Chubby's on Broadway, but Adam could hardly eat. He just wasn't hungry. Still felt nauseated and didn't know why.

They went and saw a movie, but Adam barely paid attention to it.

His heart wasn't in it.

Wasn't in anything.

And Shane left before he normally did despite the fact his shift at work had changed and he didn't need to get to bed early.

Because implants.

Implants?

Shane thought they had implants.

Ruined.

It was all ruined.

Adam was relieved when Shane left.

16

AND THAT night he wasn't sure he ever wanted to see Shane again.

17

"THERE ARE stranger things," Daphne repeated.

"Than me being abducted? Than little green men—"

"They're supposed to be gray," Daphne said.

"—probing me and putting implants in my head?"

His sister lifted and dropped her shoulders in one quick move.

"Daphne," he exclaimed. "It's crazy!"

"And like I've said, I've seen some crazy shit. Experienced some crazy shit. Makes a believer out of you. Or at least made it so I can't be so quick *not* to believe."

"Oh, Daphne," he said, disappointed. He'd called her—truth be told—knowing she'd add normalcy to what had happened. He hadn't expected her to make things worse.

"Can I ask you something, brother? Isn't it possible? Why isn't it possible? Why couldn't there be life on other planets? Why couldn't they come here? Why wouldn't they want to study us? Isn't it possible?"

Adam shook his head. *Daphne. Oh, Daphne.* "What kind of stuff have you seen?" he asked aloud.

She looked away. After a long moment Adam realized she wasn't going to answer.

"Daphne?"

She turned back. "I don't care what he believes, Adam. I want you to think about if it matters. So he believes in little gray men. So he thinks he was abducted by them. So what if he thinks *you* were? He's special. He cares about you. You care about him. You like him. I think you're falling in love with him. Isn't it possible that what's really going on is that you're using this as an excuse to run? That you're afraid of getting involved?"

He shook his head adamantly.

"I think that's what's going on. And what I think is that *you* need to ask yourself if you really want him to slip through your fingers. Everybody has their flaws. No one is perfect. But I think he just might be perfect for you."

Adam opened his mouth to reply... and then let it slowly shut.

Did he want lose Shane?

After that he and Daphne didn't talk much.

18

ADAM DIDN'T sleep well that night. Of course, he hadn't in days, but tonight was different. He couldn't stop thinking about what his sister had said. Couldn't stop thinking about a lot of the things she had said.

Things she had seen that made her believe that weird shit was possible. *His* sister. The queen of practicality.

That she believed Shane might be perfect for him and he'd be stupid to let him go.

Because God, he *had* been thinking that Shane might just be perfect for him.

Couldn't he allow Shane to believe in his UFO stuff? Couldn't he just forget about it? Ignore it?

Was it any worse than the cigarettes? Than baseball?

Yet it was more than that. Much more.

The whole thing made him powerfully uncomfortable. Sometimes sick.

And sometimes scared.

Which made no sense at all.

But more even than that was the fact that he couldn't stop thinking about Shane. How much he missed him. God, how much he longed for him. *Longed* to be with him. To touch him. To sit with him. To make love with him—and yes, dammit, that was what it was. Making love.

More than ever, though, just to be with him.

They didn't have to do anything.

God.

Just to hold his hand.

And to see those eyes.

And that cute (wonderful) half smile.

It was more than missing Shane.

It was an ache.

Being away from his man hurt.

My man....

God. My man....

19

SO THE next day, unable to even concentrate at work—and working in billing for cancer doctors he *needed* to be able to concentrate—he made a decision.

Why not do a little research himself?

On the way home, he stopped at Half Price Books and asked if they had a section on UFOs. Not only did they, but they also had a surprising number of books.

He found almost all the books that had been lying on his coffee table.

He bought *Communion* by Whitley Strieber. And several more as well—after all, half price. *The Alien Abduction Files*, by Kathleen Marden. She was the niece of that famous couple who had been abducted. In fact, they had *Captured! The Betty and Barney Hill UFO Experience* as well, written by the same lady. They even had a beautifully bound collector's edition of the original book about Betty and Barney Hill, *The Interrupted Journey*.

That was the paperback I saw that Shane had.

He could see it in his mind's eye, only the word "interrupted" visible.

He saw the *UFOs Caught on Film* book as well, but after leafing through it, he found it made his stomach ache. It made him uncomfortable in a way even the Strieber book's cover couldn't—with its portrait of the alien face and its huge dark eyes.

The pictures were... not right.

It didn't look like any of them. Not really. Where was the big tail?

And even thinking those thoughts almost sent him running for the bathroom. He pushed them from his head.

He grabbed *The UFO Files* by David Clarke and then as a lark added *Never Again: Techniques to Avoid Being Abducted by Extraterrestrials* by Mary Minden, because it had to be a joke, right? It wasn't real. Come on. Mental Defenses? Spiritual Defenses, Pray to God? Protective Foils and Crystals? (like the foil hats that Joaquin Phoenix and the kids wore in *Signs*?) Repellants? (Raid, perhaps? Or maybe Off mosquito spray?)

Had to be a joke.

He'd have to share it with Shane.

Shane. God, Shane.

Adam spent hours over the next week reading. Studying. Making notes on a yellow pad he'd gotten from the storeroom at work. He learned about famous so-called abductions. He learned that there was more than one kind of alien, not just the little gray men with huge heads and big slanted black eyes—the "Greys."

(And why were they called "Greys" when the color was spelled "gray" and apparently there were two accepted spellings of the color?)

There were also these tall Norse-god-like beings with long blond hair and huge, beautiful pale blue eyes who spread a message that they wanted us to all live happily together and stop waging war—which all sounded very 1960s slash hippy slash too-much-LSD to him. "Venusians." And how silly was that? Blond, blue-eyed aliens from a planet overwhelmed with deadly gases and sulfuric acid rain.

Then there were the insectoids, the reptoids (or reptiloids depending on the author), chameleons (reptilian aliens genetically bred to appear human), chupacabras (*really*? Chupacabras were *aliens*?), eva-borgs (this sent Adam into great peals of laughter—apparently they were cybernetic things controlled by aliens, and all Adam could think of was "resistance is futile!"), dwarves, dragonworms (too silly to even read about), Tau Cetians (who looked like tan-skinned humans except for slight differences like pointed ears—hey, maybe the aliens needed to sue Gene Roddenberry—it sounded like he had infringed on their copyrights with the ears and the Borg), the Anakims (the giants referred to in the Bible? "There were giants in the earth in those days"? It was to laugh), amphibians (why not? There were reptiles after all), and oh, it went on and on, but those were the most "common."

He read and read and read—and he wasn't even sure why, because God, aliens?

Really?

But not after it got dark. He couldn't read after dark. Couldn't crack a cover. That's when he got sick to his stomach.

He made covers out of brown paper shopping bags for the books he took to work. No questions. He didn't want any questions. There would be. Someone would tease him. That jerk Bobby Brubaker, the office manager, for sure.

Adam had found a few used DVDs as well, including the one that had scared him as a kid—*Fire in the Sky*. He grabbed *The Fourth Kind* and *Signs* and *Close Encounters of the Third Kind* while he was at it. The prices were right. They didn't have *Communion* or the TV movie based on *The Interrupted Journey*. He thought he might order it on Amazon. After all, James Earl Jones and Estelle Parsons were in it. Had to be good, right? Or at least decent?

Fire in the Sky didn't bother him nearly as much as he expected it to, but then he watched it at noon when the sun was shining brightly through his living room windows.

The scene was wrong. *It wasn't like that. No slime. No gore. No dead bodies. Wrong. All wrong.*

When he considered those strange thoughts, he decided not to. Once more it was time to banish them. But Bradley Gregg, the guy who played Bobby Cogdill, was hot. Damned cute. He reminded Adam of Shane.

He didn't like the part in *Signs* where the alien was in the corn. Or on the roof.

No. Not at all.

That was when he knew that only *Close Encounters of the Third Kind* was safe enough to watch after dark.

He read and made notes. He couldn't stop. Even though he had nightmares.

Nightmares of faces and blue light.

The worst, though, was the guilt. Guilt because he hadn't called Shane. He wanted to. But he couldn't. He just couldn't.

20

THE BOOK by Minden really was silly. Hilarious when he finally realized it was for real, at least as far as its author was concerned.

Never Again: Techniques to Avoid Being Abducted by Extraterrestrials.

The author claimed to have been studying unidentified flying objects since the fifties when she saw a UFO as a ten-year-old while camping.

That caused a chill.

Camping?

Camping. Skinny-dipping. Rising moon. And then suddenly the moon high in the sky....

Her bio went on to say that she was with an organization called the CSSU (Committee for Special Studies on UFOs) all through the late sixties and the early seventies, until the FBI and CIA infiltrated it and used immoral techniques to tear the organization apart (which didn't sound the least bit paranoid, right?). It was while a member of this group that she met the renowned Ufologist Stephen Neary. Together they studied many cases of UFO sightings and abductions and even consulted on several movies until his death in the eighties from a stroke.

In her career she wrote a half a dozen books but it was her book *Never Again: Techniques to Avoid Being Abducted by Extraterrestrials* that she was the most proud of. Which was pretty sad considering he'd thought it was a joke.

Even the reviews on Amazon said so. Or a lot of them did. There were just as many from crazy people who said they'd used her techniques to keep them from being abducted and called her a savior.

It was broken into sections with most of them being her so-called protection techniques.

Physical Defenses
- Fight or Flight

Mental Defenses
- Emotional 1 - Anger
- Emotional 2 - Self Love
- Emotional 3 - Radiant Love
- Emotional 4 - Family Love

Spiritual Defenses
- Pray to God
- Pray to Other Spirit Guides

Natural Repellents
- Protective Foils and Crystals
- Herbs, Spices, and Oils

There were also a few chapters on theories of why people were being abducted and what we could learn from how other cultures view aliens. And of course there was the obligatory stuff on ancient astronauts and how mankind couldn't have built the pyramids without extraterrestrial help.

Poppycock.

Adam found the Repellants section quite humorous. The author explained that oils derived from amaranth, pennyroyal, St. John's Wort, and yarrow had been used for centuries for protection against evil spirits and creatures. She postulated that those evil spirits (and beings) could very well have been aliens and that ancient people wouldn't have recognized them for what they really were. She said she had used various doses to prevent her abductions for years now.

But be careful!

Pennyroyal had been used to induce abortions.

Thankfully he didn't have to worry about that.

Patchouli was good too. Especially used in the amounts that lesbians preferred. Knock you out at one hundred feet. He had added that part. The lesbian part. Mary Minden had only mentioned the oil.

Oh! And salt! Apparently if he sprinkled salt around his house, it had been known to work in one or two cases. But then what had Shane said? That even in Buckman, aliens wouldn't want to take him from his house. And Adam hardly thought he had to worry about being spirited from his fifth-floor apartment. It wasn't like he was on the highest floor either.

Oh! And crucifixes had been known to help! He'd exploded into laughter over that one. Were they aliens or vampires?

But magnets were what she really guaranteed would work. That had come from the chapter about foil beanies and magic crystals.

One thing he could say about the woman. When he finally figured out the book wasn't some spoof in the vein of *Mad Magazine*, the *Onion* and the *Daily Currant* (or Fox News, maybe), he was able to see she was really being sincere. She believed her shit.

Too bad it was shit. All shit.

And surprise, surprise! OMG! She lived in Terra's Gate, not forty-five minutes away. What kind of crazy co-inky-dink was that? It was to laugh!

He took a step out on his balcony for some fresh air, a glass of freezer-cold Crown in hand. His back was hurting from the hours and hours of sitting. Between work and home study, he was on the edge of agony. The Crown was barely making a dent in the pain. He needed a massage. He should call his friend Ric. Ric gave great… massages.

But that made him think of Shane.

And that made him feel guilty.

He didn't like it.

He didn't do guilt.

Adam sat down on the brick rail of the balcony, took a swallow rather than a sip of his whisky, and looked down. The evening streets were clear except for a jogger and a lady walking her Westie (he thought her name was Becky and that she lived on the third floor). No prostitutes. How nice. The one time his mother had visited him (she had been in town with some kind of Red Hat Lady's thing), there had been prostitutes. One huge one had pulled out her breast. Thank God his mom had missed that part.

Then Adam noticed something else.

There was someone standing in the alley. He was wearing a black trench coat. A black fedora. He was holding his hands up in front of him.

Like a praying mantis.

Adam let out a muffled shriek, dropped his glass, and stumbled back, arms pin-wheeling for balance to keep him from falling on his ass.

He was whimpering, jamming his hand in his mouth to keep from screaming.

Oh God. Oh God oh God oh God!

Insectoids.

The word leapt clear and vivid in his mind.

He lay on the cement floor of his balcony, shivering.

And then he laughed.

Oh God, indeed!

He was buying this bullshit! And if he lived in a tiny town in the middle of Bumfuck, Nowhere, with no reasonable company to talk to, no one sane, no one who didn't think that country line dancing was a pretty good idea—mightn't he start believing such bullshit as aliens as well?

He laughed again and sat up. Luckily he remembered to watch for broken glass.

God!

He needed a break. And something besides UFO books to read. Porn even. Nifty Archives. Men on the Net.

Anything.

Hell, *Twilight*!

He'd seen a man on the street in a black coat and immediately decided he was the insect version of Will Smith.

He shook his head.

Stood up.

Looked out into the street.

The man was still there.

He was standing directly under a street light, looking directly up at Adam.

His eyes were up and to the side of where his eyes should really go. Adam thought his heart just might explode in his chest.

He fled into his apartment. He poured salt in front of his balcony door and the ledge of every window. He went to his neighbor Tiff's door and asked to borrow patchouli. After shouting at him that just because she was a lesbian didn't mean she owned any, she loaned it to him.

Adam used it. He used a lot of it.

Then he turned off all the lights in his apartment and went to his bathroom—the only room with a window he couldn't look out of (and no one could look in). He checked his laptop.

To his surprise he found what he was looking for fairly easily.

21

ADAM FOUND her apartment over a bakery called The Sweet Spot on Main Street in downtown Terra's Gate. There was foil on the windows.

He rang the bell next to the door that went into the shop. He rang it again.

"Hello?" came a woman's voice from a small speaker to the right of the door."

"Is this Mary Minden?" he asked.

"Wh-who is it?"

And what did he say? "I…." His throat seized up.

"Who's there?"

Your name, stupid. Tell her your name. He coughed. Cleared his throat. "My name is Adam Brookhart. I read your book."

There was a pause.

"Which one?"

"*Never Again: Techniques to Avoid Being Abducted by Aliens.*"

"*Extraterrestrials*," the woman corrected.

"Yeah," he said. "Sorry." *To-may-to, to-mah-to.*

"I don't sign autographs."

"I don't want an autograph," he said. "I—I…." God! He couldn't say it. *Fuck!*

There was a static click from the speaker and then nothing.

"Hello?" he asked.

Nothing.

"Hello?"

Nothing.

He stabbed the buzzer button again. Then again. The desperately several more times.

"What do you want?" Her voice was all but shrill this time.

"Please," he cried. "I need your help. I saw...." *Oh God. Say it!* "I saw a man in black. He was outside my apartment. He was watching me. I think he might have taken me." Then to his amazement a sob escaped his throat.

A hundred years later he heard her say, "Come on up," followed by a long whine from the buzzer.

He snatched at the handle before the noise stopped. Pulled. Nothing. Realized he should push. Did it just in time.

The door opened to a narrow and darkened stairwell.

He was halfway up the stairs when he saw her, arms crossed, standing in the shadows, waiting for him.

She was slim, with gray hair pulled back from her face. She was wearing a black top and a gray crocheted sweater. She stared at him with wide dark eyes.

"Ms. Minden?"

She was standing very straight. She nodded. "Yes. And you." She wiped at her temple with a fist. "You're Adam Brookhart. And you've seen a man in black."

"Yes," he said.

She blinked at him and bobbed her head to the left. "Come in." Then she turned and went the way of her head bob.

When he reached the top of the stairs, he saw she'd gone through a bead curtain. Bead curtain? Who still uses…? Well she was almost certainly a teen in the sixties, wasn't she? Why not?

The apartment was nice, if a little old-fashioned. But a strange combination of old lady and hippie. Victorian furniture upholstered in burnt orange and lime green. Yuck.

But it was also filled with the smell of baking things. Not overwhelmingly so, but hell, how could it be avoided? The apartment was over a bakery.

That was when he noticed there was tin foil—or something like it—on the ceiling. *Oh God. What am I doing here?*

Oh well, in for a penny…

"Tea?" she asked.

...in for a pound.

"Anything but Earl Grey."

One eye twitched. She bobbed her head, which got her big huge wire hoop earrings trembling. "I *hate* Earl Grey," she said and turned and left the room.

That decided him. He would stay.

He stood there a moment, not knowing whether he was supposed to follow her or sit down.

Then he heard her voice from the other room. "So how... man... black...."

That's all Adam caught, and he decided she wanted him to follow. He went through another beaded curtain to find her in a small kitchen, filling a teapot with water from the sink.

"I'm sorry?" Now it was his turn to cross his arms. His stomach was quite suddenly clenching. "Wh-what did you say?"

Mary Minden turned around, teapot in one hand, playing with a dark stone hanging from a thin gold chain around her neck. That one eye twitched again, and then she put the kettle on the antique stove. She turned on the gas. "I asked you how you knew he was a man in black. I mean, do you know what a man in black is?" She spoke very fast. "Some people say they're from the government. Some people say—"

"Your book says they're aliens." His voice froze up on the last word. He'd said it out loud. *Aliens.*

I'm going crazy. Wackadoodle!

"What do you think?" She turned to face him. Wiped at her temple with a fist. Fondled the stone with her other hand. That was when he saw they were swollen with arthritis.

She was watching him carefully. Studying him. He felt like a bug. "I don't know what to think," he managed. "My boyfriend believes...."

Boyfriend!

And quite suddenly he knew he'd better do something quick if he still wanted Shane to *be* his boyfriend.

That's what I'm doing.

"He thinks he's been abducted."

She didn't say a word. She just stood there. She crossed her arms. *Studied* him.

"He thinks he's been abducted lots of times."

Watching.

"He thinks *I've* been abducted!" he blurted.

Silence.

Finally she said, "What do you think?"

He shuddered.

Flashed on a full moon high in the sky when it should have just been rising over the tree-lined horizon.

On getting home late from Buckman and the missing time. The inexplicable missing time.

On blue light. Faces.

And a praying-mantis-like man in a black trench coat looking up at him. The man's eyes were in the wrong place.

He moaned.

"I think maybe it's true…."

The teakettle began to whistle.

Adam let out a gasp and staggered. He almost fell on the floor. Would have if he hadn't fallen against the threshold, sending strings of beads clattering.

The scream was just the teakettle.

But it was too much like those high, piercing, brain-stabbing ice picks he'd experienced with Shane.

Shane. God, I miss you, Shane….

Ms. Minden looked at him with an unreadable expression.

"It's a teakettle," she said flatly.

Adam sighed and felt completely stupid.

Ms. Minden turned back to the stove and turned off the flame. The whistling wound down, and she took the teapot and began to pour.

"Orange pekoe," she said. "*Not* Earl Grey."

She took the cups and put them on a silver platter and added a sugar bowl and a creamer from an ancient refrigerator. She headed out of the kitchen, and when he offered to take it, she looked at him as if he were insane. For a moment she looked like she might hiss at him. She chose to walk past him instead.

He followed her back into her very full living room to find her setting the tray down on a fancy coffee table with gold-painted scrollwork. She sat down on a delicate-looking chair covered in burnt orange *and* lime green fabric. Leaned in and poured.

"Cream? Sugar?"

"Both, I guess." He hadn't had hot tea since he was a boy, and that's the way his mother always fixed it.

She pointed at the love seat. "Sit. You're making me nervous."

Somehow he didn't think that was difficult. He sat.

That's when he saw the scar by her left eye. There was a shaft of golden light coming through a small window, and it spotlighted that side of her face. It stood out pink and white, but he thought it might not be too noticeable if not for that. He hadn't seen it.

That eye twitched. She rubbed at the scar with an arthritis-clenched hand. Then she picked up one of the teacups. It had a gold handle and some kind of flowers—roses?—painted on its surface. She sipped.

Adam took his own cup. His hand was shaking. He willed it calm and took a sip. Nope. Not Earl Grey. It was good.

He looked.

She was staring at him.

"What?" he asked.

"You tell me, Mr. Brookhart." She was caressing the black stone around her neck. Squeezing at it.

Adam put the cup down. His hands were trembling again. For some reason he suddenly felt like crying. What was happening to him? "I want to know if it's real!"

"Of course it's real," she snapped.

Adam flinched.

Ms. Minden started to take another sip of her tea, and he saw that she was trembling. Why?

She peered at him over the rim of her cup and then carefully put it down.

"Yes, young man. They're real. Why else would I have spent my entire life in one way or another studying them? Written the books I have? Lectured? Traveled the world? Investigated? D-don't you think it is rather insulting to ask *me* such a question?" The twitch in her left eye had turned into a tic.

"I didn't mean to offend y—"

"Why would you insult *yourself*?" She rubbed at the twitching with two fingers in small circular motions. "You know it's real."

"I don't know it's real! It sounds insane! It sounds crazy!" Wackadoodle. Bonkers. "How can it be? If they were real, we would know by now. It's like Bigfoot. If he was real, it would have been proven by now. Someone would have found him. If was the Loch Ness Monster, it would have been found by now. We have the technology. We have satellites that can see a penny on the sidewalk and tell which side is facing—"

"Nonsense," she said and reached for her tea. "That's utter twaddle."

"Huh?" It was all he could say. *Twaddle?*

"Our satellites are good, but not that good. At least not the ones our government will admit to having. If—as my husband suspected—we are using alien technology derived from the crash site at Roswell, then perhaps we do have such surveillance capability." She looked at him unblinking this time, the twitch finally gone. "Keyhole class satellites have an imaging resolution of somewhere between five and six."

"Huh?" he repeated and wondered if he was becoming a human echo again.

"That means they can photograph something five inches or so lying in the ground. They may be able to read the license plate number on your car, and please note I say *may*, but they can tell whether there is a lawnmower in your backyard. This penny story? It is—what do they say?—an urban legend. A modern myth."

"K-keyhole?"

"Kennan 'Keyhole-class' KH reconnaissance satellites," she said. "Always check your facts. *I* do."

"Do you think we're using alien technology?"

"I do not deny the possibility. But I think that they are so advanced that there is little chance that scientists in 1947 could have figured out anything from their technology. Remember that the closest star to ours is 4.24 light-years away. A ship traveling at the speed of light would take over four years to get to us. This isn't even taking into account Einstein's theory of relativity. Which isn't practical. What kind of civilization would it have to be that their astronauts are away for hundreds of years? And Betty Hill said that her abductors came from the Zeta Reticuli system, which is thirty-seven light-years away—220 trillion miles away. That means their ships—at light speed—would take thirty-seven years to get here. And that long to get back. And we're worried about the time it will take us to get to Mars and back? And again, that's not even taking into account Einstein's theories.

"Time marches on," she continued. "So they must have a type of space travel that skips these passages of time. Some people think they travel interdimensionally. The extraterrestrials would have to be incredibly advanced. More than we are from tribes along the Amazon River. A hundred times more. A thousand. Maybe a thousand thousand."

She rubbed at her temple again. God. Would her eye start twitching? But she didn't seem to notice.

"Let's say a tribe of people who have lived for generations along a river in South America came into possession of, say, a cell phone. Could they understand it? Could they take it apart and use it to change their way of life? I doubt it."

"But... that's not the same thing. They wouldn't have any technology at all. They wouldn't even know to try and take it apart. They wouldn't be able to understand what it was."

"Mr. Brookhart—"

"Call me Adam. Please."

She gave a single nod. "Adam. Then call me Mary. I believe these beings are much more advanced than us, so ahead of us that they don't even consider us to be much more evolved than monkeys. Think on it. When we capture animals in the wild, then tag them, then release them again—do we explain to them what we are doing to them? Do we say, 'Sorry, Mr. Bear, we're doing this to track your behavior.' When we tag tigers to see about their migratory habits, do we tell them what we're doing? Or sea creatures. Do we tell them we are just trying to learn about where they travel in the ocean? Of course not! And *that* is what is happening with these beings. They don't explain what they're doing to us."

Doing to us?

"They wouldn't even be *able* to explain. They don't *think* to explain. They don't consider us... human, for lack of a better word. They probably consider us only barely sentient."

Barely sentient? "But...! But they can see we're more than bears or tigers," Adam exclaimed. *Crazy.* "They would be able to see we have technology. We have satellites, for God's sake. We have cars. Cell phones! We're going to Mars. That isn't monkeys!"

She nodded again. While she grabbed at that goddamned stone around her neck. "But that is how far advanced beyond us they are. Forget about *Star Trek*, where the only difference between us and them is pointed ears or wrinkled noses. Where in a few centuries we'll have 'warp drive' and be able to zing all over the universe in a few hours. I think they very well may think of us as monkeys. Why else would they abduct us? Why else would they feel all right about abducting us?" She was rubbing at that scar again. "Tag us."

"Tag us?" he asked. *Like implants?* Did she believe that crazy stuff too?

"Implants." Now she was *scratching* at her scar, and it was making him very nervous. What if it started bleeding? What was she doing?

And then he was rubbing at *his* temple.

Stop it. He made himself stop.

"What do they want?" he cried, and realized that as insane as all this was, he was believing it. Or believing it was possible.

All because he saw a weird man from his balcony? A guy holding his hands up in front of him?

"To *study* us. There is something they want to know. Something that makes us different from them, and they want to know what it is."

Adam shook his head. "Why? What do they want? Are they going to invade us? Like in the movies?" He was shaking now. Sweating.

"Oh, my dear young man," she said. "They've already invaded. They're here now. And they're not going anywhere."

22

INVADED.

That was the word that did it. That sent him into a panic.

Shane.

Adam didn't wait to pack. In fact, the only stop he made between Terra's Gate and Buckman was to get gas. He'd had to pee, but it was only the gas gauge hovering over empty that made him pull off the road.

He wasn't sure how he didn't get a ticket.

Adam wasn't sure when he went from thinking that Mary Minden was a wackadoodle—a very intelligent one, but crazy anyway—to quite suddenly believing her, or believing enough to send him rushing from her apartment to his Subaru.

"INVADED? REALLY?"

"In every way there is. Mentally—once they've taken someone they can read their minds. Sometimes they can beforehand, but afterward?

Afterward there is almost nothing you can do to stop them. They can control you. It's in all the books. Not just mine. Have you read *Communion*?"

"I've read it," he said.

"And spiritually. Why do you think that some people think the Greys are heavenly beings? Beautiful angels with pale skin and long blond hair and huge blue eyes!"

Adam remembered them. The Venusians. Who spread their hippie messages about how we should all live happily together and stop waging war. And deadly gases and sulfuric acid rain.

She laughed. "Norse gods even. They use their mind-reading powers to invade people spiritually and make them think they're benevolent. Those people are the so-called contactees. People who think the aliens are here to help us. That they want us to stop hurting each other. Stop waging war. Of course they want us to stop waging war. They want us. They need us. I just haven't figured out why."

It had been all Adam could do not to shake his head. Mind control? Really?

"And physically. Do you think all those stories about—" She swallowed hard. "—anal probes were all jokes?"

Like Cartman from *South Park*? And the radar dish that came out of his ass? It was all he could do not to burst into laughter.

"Something that many abductees have in common is the same with many rape victims. Abductees have trouble with relationships, with trust, with sexuality and their own bodies."

Adam jerked.

What had Shane said?

"I can't. I. *Can't*. I just can't let anything…. I can't."

That's what he'd said just as Adam was working his cock inside him. Shane had quite suddenly, well, panicked.

He'd even been crying.

Adam had held him close until he'd calmed down. Normally it was the kind of thing that would have sent Adam running—somebody freaking out like that in the middle of sex—with thoughts of "weirdo" in his head. Instead, for some unidentifiable reason, it had made him feel closer to Shane.

And normally that would have sent him running as well. Feeling closer. Letting someone close—in—was one step away from being invaded. But when you let them invade. Like when France let the Germans in during World War II without so much as a shot being fired. Or Poland.

Was that what he was doing with Shane? Just letting him in? Why? *Why?*

"I'm sorry."

"It's okay," he had said.

"If the aliens… *invaded* their victim's bodies…. After something like that…. H-how easy can it be for the abductee to allow anyone inside them? It's *just* like rape."

God. Oh my God.

Could it be? Could it be true? Ridiculous! Shane couldn't bottom because aliens had anally probed him? Adam wanted to laugh.

"There are studies," Ms. Mendin—*Mary*—told him, clutching her stone so tight her knuckles were white, "that indicate that as much as six to ten percent of the population have been abducted."

"*That's ridiculous,*" he'd cried. "How could that be? How is that *possible?*"

"Young man, for them it would be easy. Who amongst us has not driven a deserted road late at night?"

He had.

"How many of us live in small towns?"

Shane said they wouldn't come for him in Buckman. That even in a small town someone would notice if a spaceship came hovering over his house.

(*Spaceship! I just said spaceship! He never said spaceship!*)

"How many of us have gone camping?"

Fourth grade. Camping in pup tents when he was in the Webelos Scouts. Skip wanted to go skinny-dipping. He'd been so excited that he'd followed Skip to the lake, and his penis had been as hard as stone. A full moon was rising over the trees, reflecting on the surface of the lake. And then a second later, it was high overhead.

Why do I keep thinking about that?

You know why.

You've always known why.

Faces.

Faces in his dreams.

WHILE HE was at the gas station, Adam thought it would take forever to fill the tank. He almost didn't fill it. Almost just threw in five or six dollars' worth of gas and hit the road. But then his bursting bladder told him he'd never make it, and so he ran inside and took care of business and let the tank fill on its own—even though Daphne would have had a fit about it. Lectured him on how someone could take the nozzle and fill their tank as well.

"How many of us have lost time?" Ms. Minden had asked him. "And convinced themselves that it was because they were so busy that the time just flashed by? Or that they'd fallen asleep and hadn't realized it?"

Or been hypnotized by the oncoming headlights of assholes with their high beams on, maybe?

"Or told themselves—*convinced* themselves—they must have fallen into some kind of trance while driving all by themselves in the middle of nowhere—"

This isn't real.

"—because the alternative is just too horrifying to accept?"

It's crazy.

Then why was he racing at a ridiculous speed to Buckman to see Shane?

Because I miss him.

But that wasn't the only reason.

There's lots of reasons!

He had to talk to Shane. Tell him the things that Ms. Minden had said. Even if it was crazy.

Because sometimes crazy things were true—were real.

But aliens? Aliens invading Earth? "You honestly think they've invaded?" he'd asked her. "Like in fucking *Independence Day* or something?"

She winced, and the tic started again… but it lasted only a second. One, two, three…. It stopped at four. "I don't like that word."

"'Something'?" he asked. She didn't like the word something?

"That word you kids called 'the F-bomb.' It's tacky. Unnecessary. Unprofessional. Juven—"

Kids? Kids? He was thirty-two. "It's just a word!" he snapped.

"Nevertheless, I would appreciate it if you wouldn't use it."

Fine. "Fine," he said. Whatever she wanted. Because she had information he needed.

She was looking at him that way again. Like he was something in a petri dish.

"I won't use it."

"No. Not like *Independence Day*. Or *Invasion of the Body Snatchers*. Not even that series from the sixties—*The Invaders*."

He didn't know it.

She sighed. "Long before you were born, I suppose," she said, taking up her tea again. "It starred Roy Thinnes. He was very handsome."

The comment surprised Adam. It seemed so incongruous.

"I *was* a young woman once," she said. Goodness. Was that a blush?

"Okay," he replied.

"It was a scary show. Aliens posed as humans. But ours? Our aliens? Posing as humans? No. Nothing like that. But they're here all right. And the government isn't doing anything about it. That's why Stephen thought we were using alien technology."

Stephen Neary. Her husband.

"He thought the government was in on it. That they turned their heads and let people be abducted in exchange for advanced technology. In the end he more than half convinced me. They tore the CSSU apart."

The Committee for Secret Studies on UFOs—or something like that. The organization she was in that investigated UFOs.

"They didn't like what we were finding out. What we were *proving*." She began to shake and rub her temples, both of them this time. "Stephen was growing more and more frantic. Until he had a stroke!"

"Ms. Minden." He reached out to her, which only made her bolt back in her chair.

"They *killed* him. I don't know *how*. But I *know* they did it!" A tear spilled down her cheek. "And ever since, they've done all they could do to discredit me. Make me look like a crackpot. Humiliate me. They planted reviews on my books telling people my books were ridiculous. *Crazy!*"

"Mary...." He took a deep breath. "You said that *patchouli* could keep aliens away. You advised people to *pray*. You said if we loved ourselves that aliens would leave us alone. That tinfoil could keep them from reading our minds." He pointed at the ceiling.

"Aluminum foil," she said.

"What?"

"*Aluminum* foil. Everyone says tinfoil, but they mean aluminum foil. It's aluminum. Tin doesn't do shit."

He'd barked out a laugh in surprise.

She covered her mouth, and this time he knew she was blushing. "It's 'fuck' that I don't like." She smiled. It wasn't pleasant. It was more of a grimace.

WHILE ADAM was at the gas station—the "convenience store"—he checked to see if they had aluminum foil. Miracle of miracles, they did, although it cost twice as much as it would have at Sun Fresh or Thriftway.

Adam bought it anyway.

He wasn't sure why he hadn't called Shane. Told him he was coming.

Because he would have to explain why he hadn't called in nearly two weeks. And why he hadn't answered Shane's calls. Had ignored the messages.

The one where it sounded like he was crying.

"Please, Adam. Please call me." He was sure he'd heard a sob. "Adam. I-I think I love you. I've never loved—" And then the message had cut off and—

God, I'm fucking shit! I'm shit, I'm shit, I'm shit!
Love me? He said he loved me.
And God. I love him.

He pressed his foot harder on the gas.

"BUT EVEN the aluminum doesn't work if they have implants inside their heads."

"Implants?" Adam asked.

She nodded. She took a deep breath. She touched the scar at her temple.

"God, Mary. Are you actually trying to tell me that you've been abducted?"

She nodded. "When I was ten. We were camping."

God. Camping....

He shook his head. "You think you've got an implant in your head?"

She shook hers. A tear unexpectedly rolled down her cheek. "Not anymore?"

Not anymore? "You found someone that would look for it? You're telling me that you found someone who found an implant in you and removed it?"

"No," she said, shaking her head. "I did."

His eyes went wide. "What?"

"I dug it out," she replied with a little cry. "With an X-Acto knife."

God.

"I dug it out."

23

THERE WAS one other reason Adam was driving as fast as he could to get to Shane.

He wanted to get there before dark.

24

HE MADE it.

The sun was still up, but a half hour more? Not so much.

If he hadn't been speeding, he would have gotten there after dark. And whether or not Shane was right that the aliens wouldn't abduct anyone in town, that narrow stretch of road the last twenty miles before Buckman was an entirely different matter.

It was a place he didn't want be. No matter how wackadoodle the idea was.

God, the world had changed in two months.

In two weeks!

He pulled into the gravel drive behind Shane's house. There was another car there he didn't recognize beside Shane's pickup. A red Suburban.

What if it belongs to some guy?

He walked past the garage to the back deck of Shane's house, and just as he was about to knock on the back double door, it opened.

Both he and the person on the other side gave a little jump of surprise.

The "other person" wasn't a guy.

It was a woman, with long light brown hair going to gray—same color as Shane's, he thought, without the gray, of course. Her eyes were the same color as well. He noticed that in an instant. Same brow as well. Almost the same nose, but her face was wider and fuller.

God.

It was Shane's mother.

She had smiled as soon as her look of startlement went away. It flashed on her face, broad and wide, not at all like Shane's. But then it vanished just as quickly. She went rigid. Stood up straight.

"You must be the boyfriend," she said stiffly.

The boyfriend. Like it was a nasty word. Hadn't Shane said she was okay with him being gay?

She looked at him, eyes narrowed, sharp.

Oh. It's not that I'm male.

And then he said just the right thing. "I hope I'm still the boyfriend. More than you can know." Sometimes he did that. Said the right thing.

Unlike when Shane had said good-bye the previous weekend. Good-bye and I'll miss you, and Adam had only grunted and nodded and hell, a grunt wasn't saying *anything*, was it?

But today he must have gotten it right because the stiffness went out of her shoulders and the hard line of her mouth softened, the razor in her eyes dulled.

"I hope so too," she said quietly. "But I suppose that's up to you."

"Is it?" he asked and heard the desperate tone in his voice.

I still want him. Crazy or not. Cigarettes and sports or not.
UFOs or not.

"I figured it was up to him."

She sighed, and now all the stone in her seemed to be gone. She smiled, although it was nothing like the one she had given him a moment ago. "All he's talked about is you. For weeks now. And God, how much the last week."

Adam's heart skipped. "Really?"

Her brows came together, bunched up over her long nose. "What you did was shitty."

The words made him fall back, his heart ache.

"Don't you do it again. If you're serious about him, then I'll tell him you're here. If you're not, be a man and cut him loose."

"I'm already here," came Shane's voice. He stepped out from behind her.

Was it possible for your heart to hurt and take wing at the same time? Because Adam's was.

Shane looked beautiful, despite the wariness in his eyes. So beautiful. Why hadn't he ever realized how beautiful Shane was?

"I can't believe you're here," Shane said. "You hate driving. Why are you here, Adam?"

Could Adam dare hope that was hope in *Shane's* eyes?

"Because I believe you," Adam said quickly, before he could stop himself. "I think I do. I'm scared too."

Shane bit his lower lip.

"And I think I love you."

Shane's eyes went wide.

Adam's heart soared.

"I do love you," he whispered.

For the first time in his life.

Then Shane was leaping forward to kiss him, and Adam accepted it and more, despite the fact that he'd never kissed in front of someone's mother before.

"I think I will leave you two boys to it," she said and walked away.

But a moment later—Shane's mouth tasted so good, all mint, no ashtray—Adam pulled (reluctantly) away and spun around. "Mrs. Farmer, wait!"

She was almost to her car. She stopped and turned around.

"I—I would like to talk to you too."

"Oh?" she asked.

25

"YOU TOLD him about that?" Mrs. Farmer said, looking at her son.

Shane looked chided. "I tell him everything."

"Don't be mad at him, Mrs. Farmer," Adam asked.

She shot him a look. "I'm not mad at him. Just surprised. It's not like I post that kind of thing on the bulletin board at Walmart. People will talk."

"Like they don't already," Shane laughed.

They were sitting at Shane's little white plastic table on his back deck. Right where everyone could see them. And then talk.

Shane was actually holding his hand.

Wow.

"And call me Nora," Shane's mother said.

"Nora," Adam—the human echo—repeated.

"I mean, if you're going to be my son's boyfriend and we're going to talk about them—" She bobbed her head up to the sky. To *them*. "—I think it's only right that you use my name. We'll save you calling me 'Mom' until I know you're not going to run out on him again."

Adam flinched.

"Mom!" Shane said.

"What can I say?" Shane's mother—Nora—replied. "I'm a mother. Been watching out for Shane all his life. It's not like I can just stop."

"Of course not," Adam said, wishing his mother felt the same way. It wasn't like she hated him. She hadn't thrown him and Daphne out when she'd discovered their sexuality or anything like that. She was just indifferent. Always had been. She'd actually admitted once (more than once) that she had never quite known what to make of them. Like they were aliens or something.

Aliens.

Imagine.

"Mrs. Far—*Nora*. Do you think that the... the man in black took you?"

She shrugged. "If he did—if they did—I don't remember. I don't remember anything."

"Most people don't," Shane said. "Unless they're hypnotized."

Adam sat back, the plastic chair creaking, and sighed.

"It's probably a good thing," Nora said.

"Many of the stories aren't pretty," Shane said. "Of what they do to people. Even the Betty and Barney Hill story isn't happy. They scared the couple. Pretty much terrified them."

Wasn't it funny that no one needed to know who "they" were? That was the word they kept using. Maybe it was less troubling than "aliens"?

"And their story isn't nearly as scary as some of the others. The Travis Walton incident, the one that *Fire in the Sky* is based on, is frightening. The Cash-Landrum case is downright terrifying. Not one of the three witnesses was actually abducted, but they were exposed to high doses of ionizing radiation. Betty Cash stayed in the hospital for fifteen days after the encounter. When Mark Rowtly was abducted, he was panic-stricken, paralyzed. He can hardly remember anything, but because of what he does remember, he will never be the same. If they mean us no harm, then why do some people have such horrifying experiences?"

"Ms. Minden seems to think they're invading," Adam replied. He found he just couldn't use her first name. It was hard enough, considering, to use Nora's. "I think they drove her a little—"

(a lot)

"—crazy."

"Of course," Shane said. "To know what she knows, and there are so few who believe her."

"She dug an X-Acto knife into her own head!"

"Did she find anything?" Nora asked.

"She said she did."

Showed me what she found.

"She let me see it. She had it in this tiny little glass bottle." He raised his hand and indicated the size by holding his thumb and forefinger not much more than an inch apart. "It was triangular. The points kind of curved away instead of pointing out. And there were these… I don't know. Bumps and impressions on the surface. It was red."

Blood red. Dried blood red.

Was that the color of the damned thing, or had being inside her turned it that color? If it had actually been inside her head.

"Do you believe her?" Shane asked. "That she dug it out of her head?"

"She thinks so." Then: "Yes." *My God!* "I do. I think I do."

Shane nodded.

Then another thought came to him.

"Shane, do you think they put one in you?"

Shane nodded again, without hesitation. "I always kind of thought it was in my hand, though," he said. "Sometimes I think I can feel it." He took the thumb and first finger of his left hand and squeezed the web between the thumb and forefinger of the other. "But now? I kind of think it might be in the same place as Ms. Minden's." He touched the side of his head.

"Why?" Adam asked.

"The noises," Shane said matter-of-factly. "You've heard them. I know you have. Those high, piercing shrieks?"

"Like an ice pick to the brain," Adam said with a gasp.

He'd heard it the day he had first laid eyes on Shane.

"I heard it the first time the day we met," Shane said aloud.

"God…." *So what the hell did that mean, Shane?*

"I think maybe it means we both have one, Adam."

And there it was again! He hadn't said that out loud, had he? He was sure he hadn't. Were they reading each other's minds?

Shane nodded, and Adam's eyes widened.

"You know, like when you stand too close to a speaker when you're holding a microphone? I think that we both have them. Implants, that is."

To differentiate from the "them" that meant aliens? Adam shuddered.

God. He was sitting here talking like this was all real.

What a difference two weeks in a life could bring.

"I think," Shane continued, "that sometimes the implants—our implants—"

God oh God oh God….

"—*react* to each other." Shane leaned forward in his chair and rested his chin on upraised, entwined hands. "And I'm wondering…. Maybe we could use that?"

"Use it?" Adam asked.

Shane nodded. "To get them to leave us alone."

26

SHANE'S MOTHER stayed for dinner—helped make it—which turned out to be Hamburger Helper and corn on the side. Not a staple in Adam's diet, but Shane added onions and green peppers and a can of mushrooms, plus a handful of grated cheese, and it turned out to be surprisingly good.

Nora drank a few cans of Milwaukee's Best (which didn't say much for Milwaukee) with dinner, and Adam had a Guinness—the last of a six pack he'd left behind the last time he'd been here.

Afterward, he switched to Crown and Coke (also left over from last time), and Shane went with rum and Coke. Nora chose to leave and gave him a hug as she left, which both startled him and made him feel warm all over.

"Don't hurt him," she said. "You know you don't want to mess with a mother."

He smiled and nodded and couldn't believe how good the potential threat made him feel.

How a part of something he felt. Like nothing he'd ever really felt except for, to an extent, with his sister. But this was that and more.

Daphne would be pleased.

They cuddled on the couch after she left and watched *Mama's Family* on DVD, and Shane told him how happy—how very, very happy—he was that Adam was here, and Adam couldn't help but feel embarrassed and amazed and surprised he felt it too. How happy he was to be here.

Despite the fact that he was three hours from the big city.

He looked up and found himself wishing there was tin foil—

(*"Aluminum foil. Everyone says tin foil, but they mean aluminum foil. It's aluminum. Tin doesn't do shit."*)

—on the ceiling.

"They won't come," Shane said. "Not here. Not where they can be seen." Despite that, they ran to the local small-town convenience store and bought some patchouli incense sticks—the oil was too much a specialty item even for the Super Walmart—and they burned those, and Adam was touched by the gesture.

"I can't believe what I'm feeling for you, Shane." He was lying back against three or four big pillows (at least), and Shane was resting back in his arms. "I've never felt this way about anyone. I've never wanted to. I… I've been afraid, I guess. I don't know why. I just have. I always have been. Daphne is the only one I've even let halfway in."

"Your sister?"

"Yes."

"She's the one I met at Pride." It was a statement, not a question.

"Yes."

"I like her."

"She likes that I'm with you." Adam smiled. "I am with you, right?"

Shane laughed. "Yes. I'm with you."

And Adam was thrilled. His heart skipped. The butterflies were back. He really couldn't believe he was with someone. "You're so different," he marveled aloud. "There are things about you… things on my absolutely no-way list. And yet I don't care."

"The cigarettes," Shane said.

"Yes," Adam said quietly.

"I haven't had one in a week. Combined with my asshole boyfriend not calling me, it's been hell."

Adam didn't know how to react to either of those sentences or all that they said. He was a bit stunned. Shane hadn't smoked in a week?

"Over a week. Really."

Boyfriend?

"We've established that, haven't we? You're my boyfriend?" Shane rolled over and rested his chin on crossed hands atop Adam's chest. "At least now?"

Then Adam did another double take.

It had happened again.

"Did you just read my mind?" he whispered.

Shane gave the slightest shrug. "I think I did. Kind of. I think it's happened before."

"I do too," Adam said, and this time, it was even quieter than a whisper.

"Wow," Shane said.

Adam nodded. Wow, indeed.

This is real.

He looked back up at the ceiling. Forced himself not to. His eyes met Shane's. Met Shane's beautiful eyes.

Real. This *is what is real.*

And this was what was really important, no matter what else was going on. No matter what else could go on.

This was what needed taken care of.

"I am so sorry, Shane. For what I did. It was mean."

Shane gave a nod. "Cruel, even."

"That hurt." It did. But he deserved it. And he told Shane that he deserved it.

"Don't do it again, okay?"

He wouldn't. No way.

"I believe you."

Again. Shane had done it again. It was a little unsettling. But Shane believed him. And that was what mattered.

"I read online that for most people, the worst of the nicotine withdrawal is only supposed to last a few days. A couple weeks at most. I think the asshole who wrote that never smoked."

"An asshole like your boyfriend?"

Shane smiled. "Just like that."

Adam couldn't remember being so happy. Even with the worry that ETs could be waiting for him. With Shane at his side, anything was possible.

Now if I can just get him to stop watching baseball, things will be perfect.

Shane raised an eyebrow.

Oh, shit.

"May I ask you something, Mr. Brookhart?"

Adam swallowed hard. Nodded.

"Do you think you're somehow perfect? With your prejudice against small-town life? The town *I* love? The home I love? How do you think it makes me feel that you hate baseball? I love baseball, Adam. Love it. If you understand it or not, I do. I've fantasized all my life that the person I fall in love with would spend a lifetime going to games with me. I have this dream to see a game in each of the thirty major league ballparks—which is pretty out there considering it makes me nervous to leave Buckman. But with a boyfriend at my side, it could be an adventure. And having you as my boyfriend would mean I'd have to give that dream up. And I'd do it for you. Because I *do* love you. A lot. And just because you believe that baseball is dumb and boring, that doesn't mean I do. In fact, it kind of hurts my feelings."

It was all Adam could do to keep his mouth from falling open.

Fuck.

It was almost like a slap.

Am I that big a fucking shit?

And did he just hear that?

"And we haven't even begun to talk about the problems we're going to face being together. We live three hours apart. And I think it's pretty clear you don't really want to live here. In the house that I love. In Buckman. And baby, I don't want to live in a cramped little apartment in Kansas City. One of us is going to have to give up our home if we're going to live together instead of just spending weekends together. I want more than that. Don't you? I want more than a weekend lover."

Now Adam's mouth did fall open. He was speechless.

And his heart ached.

Because he did want more than a weekend lover. A lot more.

"In the meantime…." Shane turned on his side and shoved back against him. Adam had to turn on his side so there was room. But then Shane wiggled so his butt was even closer. Was pressed up against Adam's crotch.

"Don't do that, baby." He could already feel his cock responding.

"Why not?"

"You know why not," Adam said. *Because I'll want you. I want you already.*

Then Shane sat up. He sat up and looked down at Adam. Adam's heart started to pound. Those eyes.

"I want to try," Shane said.

"T-try?" *Try what?*

And then he saw it in his mind. Saw what Shane meant.

Oh God.

"Are you sure, baby?" Now his heart was really pounding.

"Very sure," Shane said.

27

AFTER THAT they went to bed, and it was sweet. Not like anything Adam had ever experienced.

"Are you sure?" Adam asked again.

Shane kissed him by way of an answer.

They held each other. They touched each other. Kissed each other. Everywhere.

Adam made love to Shane's beautiful bottom the way he'd wanted to since that day he saw him standing next to his picnic blanket. Standing there wearing those blue-and-white plaid pants that had done nothing to hide his round, firm ass.

He took his time. Covered those mounds with kisses and licks and tiny nibbles. He slowly nudged his face between them. Ran his newly bearded face in that tight cleft.

And thank God, Shane moaned through all of it.

When he found Shane's hole, his lover flinched for just a second and then relaxed. Adam could feel the trust. In his heart and in his mind, he felt it. Normally he might have attacked it. This night he took his time. Kissed it. Licked it. Made love to it.

Shane cried out over and over, was practically sobbing and telling him how wonderful it was and how good his beard felt "down there."

Adam, urged on and feeling things he'd never felt before, made love to that tight little coil of muscle, and slowly but surely it relaxed and let him inside.

It was glorious.

Slowly but surely he worked a finger inside, telling Shane that he loved him all the time he was doing it.

Slowly but surely it became two fingers.

And when he was ready to try for something more significant, when he was sure he might only last a second before he came he was so excited, wanted Shane so much, Shane stopped him. Rolled over.

"This way," he said. "I want to see you. See *you*. Know it's *you*."

And that truly was what it was all about, wasn't it?

"If they have invaded their victim's bodies," Ms. Minden had said, "how easy can it be for the abductee to allow anyone inside them?"

And so he held Shane and told him over and over that he loved him—

(because he did)

—and he took forever to find himself inside his lover, and he was slow, so slow, and it really was unlike anything he had ever experienced.

More than sex. It was making love.

Then when Adam could hold back no more, and God, when Shane's eyes rolled back and he began to ejaculate between them without ever touching himself, Adam came like he never had before.

It was glorious.

And holding each other, after, something hit him. Something Daphne had said to him.

"You've always had troubles with relationships, with trusting anyone."

And on the tail of that….

"Something that many abductees have in common is the same with many rape victims," Ms. Minden had said. "Abductees have trouble with relationships, with trust, with sexuality and their own bodies."

My God, he thought. *That's me.*

28

BUT AS Adam was falling asleep, he couldn't help but look at the ceiling. Wish for aluminum foil.

"We're okay," Shane assured him. "They won't come."

"Okay," Adam said, and he snuggled tight to his lover and hoped Shane was right.

29

BUT HE wasn't.
    They came.

30

AT FIRST Adam took it all as if nothing were unusual.

Like a dream where you never questioned that you were still hanging out with an ex-friend who was behaving wonderfully instead of being the asshole he became. Or sitting on the porch with someone who had died years and years ago, but it didn't seem the least bit peculiar. Still working a job you hated that for some reason was everything you could have wanted.

Or living in a tree house like the Swiss Family Robinson.

Married to Chris Evans and both of you were on the *Ellen* show.

And finally you began to realize that maybe this was wrong....

Because you didn't slowly float out of bed and go drifting down the hallway.

Windows didn't open by themselves.

You didn't float out of them and drift up to a dark shape barely visible against a night sky where the only thing to indicate it was there was a lack of stars.

You didn't wonder why you weren't afraid of the manlike shapes around you. Manlike except that their arms and legs were stick thin and their heads were huge and oblong and the only face you could see was ominously large, slanted almond-shaped eyes. You didn't remember that these gray beings were exactly what you had been afraid of. For some reason you were fine with it.

Adam went through all this.

The accepting.

And then the noticing.

The wondering.

The thinking that this might be a dream.

And slowly, slowly realized that it wasn't.

He quite suddenly remembered the night on the lake. Following Skip into the water, embarrassed by his throbbing erection. His friend hadn't seen it—or noticed his confusion about why his penis was behaving like that. Wasn't that only supposed to happen about girls? They'd waded until the water was at their necks and then begun to slowly dogpaddle out and then tread water and then…

"What's that?" Skip asked and brought an arm out of the water long enough to point at the sky over Adam's shoulder.

Adam looked, and at first he thought Skip meant the moon and was just joshing with him, but then he saw there was a shape just to the right. The full moon's light was silhouetting it, and it was disklike, but there was some kind of mechanical-looking arm sticking out of the left side. It looked like a helicopter.

"It's a helicopter," Skip said.

But it wasn't. Adam saw that without a doubt, because there was no rotor, just the mechanical thing jutting out the side of whatever that was hovering up in the night sky.

No. Not hovering.

It was moving. Moving very slowly, and as it did it came in front of the face of the moon and Adam could see an identical arm on the other side of the… the…. What was it?

Then red lights, one on either side, began slowly blinking at the ends of the arms. The disk, again slowly, began to glow with blue-white light.

It was getting closer.

"I wanna go home," Adam said and realized he was almost crying, and Skip agreed.

"Let's get out of here," he said.

They swam as fast as they could to the shore, Adam crying all the way, and as they climbed out of the water—Adam's erection was a thing of the ancient past—they didn't even reach for their clothes. They ran.

The craft, because that was what it was of course, quickly reached them. The lights along its sides, as well as the blinking red lights at the end of the helicopter-like arms, went out.

They don't want anyone to see.... And how Adam knew that, he had no idea.

It was flying so low Adam couldn't understand why it wasn't hitting the trees. He was crying. He couldn't stop. And then came the light. A single misty white beam shone down on them, and Adam turned to his friend—his brave friend who was openly crying now as well—and they were floating.

"Adam," Skip shouted but didn't shout. "Make it stop!" His voice was muffled somehow. It was like Adam was listening to his friend while holding pillows tightly against his ears.

They don't want anyone to hear us!

The bottom of the craft had opened, and they rose and rose until they were inside. Then the door, or whatever it was, screwed closed.

Adam could hear his friend clearly now, sobbing and telling him to "make it stop!"

But how could he?

The men came to them then. Small men, not much taller than the two of them, and they were gray and their skin was shiny, like plastic, and they had huge unblinking black eyes and then…

That was when the terror began.

31

ADAM WANTED to scream.

The darkness in the sky opened up, and there was a door filled with bluish light. The only light.

There was no huge orange ball like in some of the abductee accounts he had seen. Like in that book.... *UFOs Caught on Film.*

No blinking lights either.

No lights beneath or along its surface.

No windows with slant-eyed beings looking out at him.

Only that door.

Like before! Oh God, it's real! It's fucking real, and it has happened before.

More than once.

And maybe, just maybe, *many* times.

Then he was going through the doorway. Going down a corridor, and he couldn't see Shane. Where was Shane?

Shane! he screamed. Screamed with his mind.

Adam was floating on his back, as if on an invisible stretcher, and when he lifted his head, he could see the three "men" ahead of him, but not Shane. He looked to the left and right, and there were three more of these men.

He smelled cinnamon. Of course he did. He'd remembered it from before, and he hadn't been able to stomach cinnamon rolls since he was a kid—which infuriated his mother, who made the Pillsbury ones many a Sunday as he was growing up.

They all looked the same, those others.

Exactly the same.

Their skin was gray and shiny and perfectly smooth. Their heads were large, their unblinking black eyes like polished stones.

"It's a magnetic stone," Ms. Minden had told him, clutching at her necklace. "They... don't... like... magnets...."

He so wished he had a magnetic stone.

Adam longed to look behind him. Because he was sure that if he could, he would see three more of the men.

It was in all the books.

Books by Whitely Strieber and Kathleen Marden and Mary Minden.

Threes.

Adam knew if he could look behind him he would see his lover and three more men. Greys, not men.

They came in threes.

And they looked at you with big unblinking eyes.

How could those eyes not blink? Didn't they need to blink? Blinking did something, for God's sake. Kept the eyes moist or something. Kept them clean!

That's what we need.

Who knew if they needed the same thing?

Who knew how their eyes worked?

"Shane!" he cried. Or tried to. There was something wrong with his mouth. He couldn't scream. He couldn't say anything.

So he used his mind.

Because Shane had heard him before. Maybe he could hear him again.

Shane, he thought. Thought as hard as he could. *Shane!*

I'm here, came his Shane's voice.

What do we do? he thought back.

For the longest time, there was no answer. He wanted to panic. Because for some reason he thought—he knew—that Shane would know the answer.

We wait, came the sudden reply.

And as much as waiting scared him, he decided to trust Shane.

He was filled with warmth then. A warmth a thousand times better than being *inside* his lover. And he'd never felt *anything* like that before.

I love you, came Shane's mental voice.

He was brought into a room, and good God, all the stories were right. The room looked like an operating theater. There were long, slim tables that stuck out from the walls—walls that somehow glowed blue. There was light above the tables, and they glowed blue (but much more brightly) as well.

I love you, he thought back.

There were machines above the beds. Mechanical arms and bars and poles and more. He floated toward the bed and then above it, and then he was drifting down onto it.

Three of them came around the bed.

Three.

And for some reason, he was terrified.

They looked at him.

Unblinking.

The machines began to move. One of the mechanical arms shifted, lowered, and then a long needle came out of it.

No no no no....

And then it was sticking down into his navel, and it was horrible. Excruciating!

No! Why are you doing this to us!

Then he remembered what Ms. Minden had said. "I believe these beings are much more advanced than us, so ahead of us that they don't even consider us to be much more evolved than monkeys. Think on it. When we capture animals in the wild, then tag them, then release them again—do we explain to them what we are doing to them?"

No. Of course they didn't.

"Do we say 'sorry, Mr. Bear, we're doing this to track your behavior'? When we tag tigers to see about their migratory habits, do we tell them what we're doing? Or sea creatures. Do we tell them we are just trying to learn about where they travel in the ocean? Of course not!"

Of course not!

"And *that* is what is happening with these beings. They don't explain what they're doing to us. They wouldn't even be *able* to explain. They don't *think* to explain. They don't consider us... human, for lack of a better word. They probably consider us only barely sentient."

Barely sentient! They barely consider us sentient! And what do they want from us?

"To *study* us. There is something they want to know. Something that makes us different from them and they want to know what it is."

But what was it?

Did it even matter?

No!

All that mattered was that these being were treating him as less than human. And worse. Treating Shane as less than human. And that he couldn't allow.

Shane!

Nothing.

Shane! he shouted with his mind. With all the strength he had.

Nothing!

He had to fight. He *had* to. But how?
And then he had an idea.

32

HE TRIED to raise his arms, tried to form fists, but he couldn't. Somehow they were doing something to him. Preventing him from moving. Maybe through an implant? The books said they could control minds. Had Ms. Minden said something about that? He couldn't remember anymore.

So then what?

Emotional defense. That is what her book said. Anger. And God, he was angry!

He tried to shout and saw he couldn't even do that. Not physically. Not with his mouth. But with his mind?

With his emotions?

Stop it! You're hurting us! He shouted it with all of his mind. Screamed it. *Leave us alone!*

To his surprise the creatures staggered back.

That and more, you fuckers!

What was next?

Love?

Really?

Self-love, he remembered.

And what could he do with that. Nothing. Not now. Because all he could think about was Shane. Shane, who had gone silent. What had they done with him? Done with the first person he had ever really loved?

Baby! he shouted with his mind. *I'm here! I love you!*

Now several of the Greys put tiny hands on sticklike arms to either side of their heads. Several of them moved away. Fast.

That was when he saw Shane. He was on the table next to Adam.

Shane! My God, Shane! Are you all right?

For a moment, nothing.

And then Shane moved!

Shane!

Shane turned his head to face him. Looked at him with eyes filled with fear. Shane. The one who knew all about this shit. The one who had told him there was nothing to fear. The one who had been brave.

"It's okay," he said. Aloud. He'd said it out loud!

"Shane, I'm here."

Shane's mouth opened. Closed. Opened. But nothing came out.

It's okay, he thought to Shane. *I love you.* He reached out to his lover.

And Shane. He was reaching back!

I love you.

Their fingers touched then. Interlocked.

Love you, they both thought at the same time.

That was when everything changed.

33

Love.

It was a voice in Adam's head. But it wasn't his own.

Love?

Then the Greys were there again. Standing over him. Looking at him with those big black unblinking eyes.

Love?

They were talking to him!

"Yes," he managed to say. "Love. Do you *things* know what love is?"

And then one of them nodded.

Yes, came the response inside his head. *We do.*

What?

One of the Greys moved up between them. Looked at their clasped fingers. Then at him.

You are both male. It wasn't asking.

"Yes," he said.

Then it glanced directly at his penis. Then…. Then at Shane's.

And then it began to undress.

34

Undress?

No. Not exactly.

Once, when Adam was a kid, he'd seen a cicada coming out of its skin.

That was what this looked like. The Grey was folding in on itself. Bending forward. And something was coming out of its back.

It was pink. Darker than pink, but not red.

Bit by bit, it pulled itself out of the back of its....

A head popped back out of the grayness it had been in. A head with small blue tiny eyes.

They blinked at him.

Then the others began to do the same thing. The Greys. Who were not gray at all. They were a color somewhere between pink and red. What color did you call that?

For a moment Adam wanted to scream. But then it blinked again. The others were pulling themselves out of their suits as well. Suits. The shiny gray creatures weren't flesh—it wasn't... them.

They were suits.

Spacesuits came Shane's voice inside his head.

Spacesuits.

The machine's arm raised into the dark recesses of the room. The force that had been holding him immobile was gone. He could move.

And he did.

Adam sat up and saw Shane doing the same. He scrambled off the bed and went to Shane's side. "Baby?"

Shane wrapped his arms around Adam and pulled him tight.

That was when he saw it.

The Greys—or Pinks?—had a whole new surprise.

35

ADAM WOKE to sunlight streaming in between the curtains of the bedroom window. He stretched and yawned and then smelled the coffee. He hoped there was some left.

As per his usual style, he didn't bother to put anything on, but after climbing out of bed, he left the bedroom and found Shane in the kitchen.

Surprise. He was writing in one of his journals. He'd only seen Shane doing that one other time....

For some reason the memory caused him to flinch the slightest little bit. He decided to ignore it for this wonderful and somewhat fuzzy morning. He felt a little… what? High? Had they had a lot to drink last night? He couldn't really remember if they had.

There were a few empty beer bottles in the trash.

"Morning, babe," he said and went to Shane to give him a kiss. His morning wood, not a semi, bobbed a bit before him.

Shane looked up from his writing, a smile on his face, and then did a double take at Adam's softening erection. "Well good morning to you," he said with a grin.

To Adam's happiness, he saw there was coffee in the pot. It was almost full. Had Shane just gotten up?

"Yup," Shane replied, attention back on whatever he was scribbling in his journal. "The coffee's fresh. I used that kind you like so much."

The Shepherd's Bean. The Yirgacheffe! Oh God, yes. So much better than what Shane usually….

"You are such a snob," Shane said, shaking his head. "We discussed that, right?"

Adam poured, sat, and leaned in for a kiss. "Sorry," he said with a chuckle.

Shane rewarded him with a look from those beautiful eyes and a sweet little kiss.

"What are you doing?" he asked. "If it's not private."

"Not private," Shane said, still writing. His hand was moving across the pages quickly. As if he had a lot to say and wanted to say it as fast as he could. "I'm just trying to get it all down. I'm afraid I'll forget. And I don't want to forget any of it."

Forget? "Forget what?" he asked, curious. Was he writing about the sex they had last night? Oh God! What sex! He didn't want to forget either. Ever.

"Except for maybe the beginning. I didn't like that."

Adam jerked ever so slightly. Shane didn't like the beginning? Why, Adam had thought it was all sweet. The best lovemaking he'd ever experienced. Maybe the only real lovemaking. It had all been just sex before—

Shane looked up from his page. "I've never remembered any of it before, Adam. I always knew, *knew*, that it happened. And for the first time I can remember. But what if it goes away, baby? I can't stand the idea. So please, let me get it down first."

"Huh?" What was he talking about? "I don't want you to forget either, baby. I don't want to forget either. It was the best...."

Blue light.

Adam jerked again.

Unblinking black eyes.

Then....

Adam jerked in his chair, so hard this time he almost fell over backward, and he spilled half his coffee, most of it on his hand. He hissed and brought it up to his mouth, sucking at the burnt spot.

Shane had stopped writing. "Baby?"

Oh my God....

He saw them then. Coming out of the backs of those shiny all-the-same gray suits, like cicadas breaking through the backs of their shells—their skins.

Oh my God....

Saw them. Saw the Greys. Saw them for what they were....

"Baby?" The look of concern on Shane's face was enough to jolt him back to the here and now, the seat he sat on, the kitchen he was in, the man he was with.

Shane reached out and took his burnt hand—not too burnt—and—*Wham!*—it all came back. All of it.

Oh my God....

36

THE GREYS—NOW some other color entirely—were all male.

Trying to understand, came its—*his*—voice in Adam's head.

Such a curious race. Nothing else like you.

Its eyes were small. Nothing like the famous, large, unblinking slanted oval eyes from modern legend. From the cover of *Communion.* From dozens of movies. But they were certainly as black.

And its—his—skin.... What color did you call that? Not pink. Not orange. Salmon? Coral? In fact, it reminded Adam a lot of the aliens from *Fire in the Sky,* but not as... mean. They were softer. Surprisingly less scary.

At least now.

There was no nose. Not that he could see—could *remember*. The mouth was very small, just like the stories, and it didn't move. The lips didn't move while it "talked" inside his head.

The head was very large for its body, which was overly slim, with long, almost sticklike, arms. The legs were just as thin, but much shorter than its arms.

His! He had to think of the being as a *him*.

It was important.

But why?

Male.

What lay between his legs was not a penis, not anything human, that was. More like… what? A dog? More than a bump, but nothing hanging.

They all had them.

All of them.

Three sets of three stood around Adam and Shane. Another triad was moving slowly into the room. All their faces bore curiosity.

Such a peculiar race.

"Why?" Adam asked. "*Why* are we peculiar?"

So different than anywhere else.

"How are we different?" *God. I'm talking to them. They're talking to me.* "Why different?"

So different than the other species on your world.

"How?" Calm. Keep calm.

Shane moved even closer to him.

The other creatures… they procreate during… seasons.

"Seasons?" Adam asked. "What do you mean….?"

"Like going into heat?" It was Shane's turn to ask. "Is that what you mean?"

The alien nodded. Interesting to see it use such a human gesture.

Yes. When it is time to procreate, the female becomes ready. This makes the males ready. They mate. Then they are done. Often going their separate ways. Or at least not mating again until the female… goes into heat once more.

"I—I guess," Adam said.

But your species. The females and males... they are sexual even when it is not time to procreate. The two. They mate! They form permanent bonds. Not like us. Not like so many others out there.

It took a long hand and gestured above it. Around it. Everywhere.

"Yes," Shane replied.

Curious. Strange. We don't understand. So different. How this works... we don't understand. How your species... the two sexes... can bond with so many differences.

"I'm... I'm not sure I understand."

Another of the Pinks came up behind and beside the first one. It laid a hand on the first one's shoulder.

Yes. Yes, you do. You are more like us. Except there are only two of you.

A third came up on the other side. He placed his hand upon the first one as well.

We are three. It allows balance. It is stronger. It manages. Creates order.

"Wait," Adam said and marveled that his fear was gone. He was standing here with Shane—his lover—in the midst of these otherworldly creatures, and he was no longer afraid. And he thought he might be beginning to understand. "You three." He nodded at the trio standing before them. "You're mated."

Yes, came the response. And somehow he knew it was all three of them answering.

"Oh wow," said Shane. "And you're all male."

They nodded.

Of course. We are the same. How does your species do it? We've been trying to understand for so long.

Dear God, thought Adam and looked at his Shane. "They're all... homosexual?"

Homo-sexual. Same-sexed. The same. The same understanding. The same. Of course. The way it is everywhere. But somehow, your species. The males and females bond beyond mating. Beyond procreation. And we do not understand.

"I'll be fucked," Adam said. God.

But you.... You are like us. The two of you. Both male. The same. The same understanding. Male and male. For when you are not procreating. A bonding we understand.

Adam shook his head, astonished. "You're gay."

The eyes showed… curiosity. He saw that it was trying to understand.

"You're saying," Shane asked, "that out there in the universe, the other species are gay. They're…. They bond male to male. Female to female?"

Male to male to male. Female to female to female.

The alien looked at him in surprise. *Of course. Although some species only pair. Or form larger bonds. Groups. But the same. Because there is understanding in sameness.*

"Who raises the children?" came Shane's next question. "You do have children."

Procreate. Of course. To continue the species. The males raise the male offspring. The females raise the female offspring. The same. This is logical. This makes sense.

Adam could only shake his head. Unbelievable.

But today we find you. You two are more like us. You two make sense to us. You are the same.

"Hardly!" Shane said with a bark of laughter.

Same enough. And if there were three of you, that would bring balance when there are clashes. The third always bring negotiating. Mutual understanding and acceptance.

"I think two is challenge enough," Shane said. "Adam?"

Adam agreed. "More than enough."

There is so much we do not understand. We haven't meant to… harm. We have only been trying to understand you. And it was only a… force between you… that surprised us. Made us… more aware that there was some kind of bond between you.

"Bond?" Shane asked.

Oh God, thought Adam. "Do you mean love?" he replied.

The alien nodded. *Love.*

"Wow" was Adam's only response.

Are there more of you? We think we have encountered a few more.

"More couples of the same sex?" Adam nodded. "Yes. But it's only now becoming accepted. In our country at least. Some others. But there are places where it's a crime. People die for loving their own sex."

The alien winced. *Insanity.*

Adam nodded. Insanity indeed.

There is still so very much we don't understand. So much we want to understand.

"Good luck," Shane said. "We are a pretty weird group." He nodded toward Adam. "Especially him."

"Shane!" Adam laughed.

Weird? the alien asked.

"Don't worry about it," Adam said and laughed again.

We want to know more. This was a new voice.

They turned, and a much taller being stepped into the room. It was no longer wearing a black trench coat. Or a hat.

And it looked very much like a praying mantis. Its mouth parts worked, eyes blinked, short antenna bobbed.

So much more. So many questions.

"Well, we're right here," Shane said. "We'll try to help. We'll answer any questions you have."

"*Shane*," Adam said and pulled his lover all the closer.

Shane looked at him, determination showing in his eyes. "We have to," he said.

Adam sighed. Turned back to the creatures. The aliens.

"But you can't keep doing it the way you're doing it," Adam said.

"You can't keep hurting people," Shane added. "Poking them. Prodding them. It's an invasion. Ask us. We'll help."

We are asking, said the triad then. And Adam knew it was all three asking.

"That's all you had to do," Shane replied.

37

THEY SAT and drank coffee, and then they dressed and took a long walk and had lunch and sat on the back deck and even called Shane's mother.

They wrote and wrote and wrote in Shane's book.

They shared all they could remember… and then they remembered more.

Adam called Ms. Minden, who was stunned at what he told her.

"A book," she said. "You'll help? I'll need your help."

Adam laughed. Help her write a book. Tell his story? His and Shane's story?

Was the world ready to find out that homosexuality was the norm in the universe?

He laughed all the more.

Did he care?

Yes, Shane thought. "We care. It will change the world. Gay people knowing what we have to say."

"No one will believe us," Adam said. "If we help her—if we tell our stories—no one will believe. We'll be laughed at. Ridiculed. The debunkers will attack our every word. Just like Travis Walton or Betty and Barney Hill. How many people will believe?"

"Does it matter?" Shane asked.

Did it?

"Can we think about it?" Adam replied.

Shane rolled his eyes. "Sure."

And that's what Adam told her.

"In the meantime, what about us?"

"What about us?" Adam answered.

"We've got a lot to figure out if we're going to make this work."

Adam nodded. "We'll figure it out," he said. "We're worth it."

Shane kissed him.

And they began to figure it out.

38

"ALIENS," DAPHNE said flatly.

Adam nodded.

She looked at him. Then at Shane.

Shane nodded.

And then she gave a single nod in response. No emotion.

No. Wait. Something. He saw something. She had cop face. But she'd been his sister for thirty-two years. She couldn't hide from him. There was something. But he just didn't have any idea what it was.

Daphne sipped her Buena Vista honey process, La Palma y El Tucán, direct trade from Colombia. They were all at The Shepherd's Bean. Daphne, who hadn't been bugging him too much for answers. Who had simply been thrilled that he and Shane were together.

It had taken him two weeks to tell her what had happened. And now he was trying not to piss his pants.

"You believe me? *Really*? But it's so crazy...."

She looked up. "I was the one who told you not to close *your* mind, wasn't I?"

"I...." He closed his mouth.

Then: "Stranger things." She gave him another single nod. "Stranger things under heaven and earth that you can dream of."

"My God," he said. "You really do believe me."

"I said it before. You won't believe the things *I've* seen."

"You gonna tell me?"

She took another drink of her coffee. Looked at him.

Adam thought she was never going to answer.

Adam had just given up when she said, "Do you remember the Voodoo Killer last year?"

"Voodoo?" he asked.

"People getting their hearts cut out...?"

Then he remembered. "Oh yeah." God yeah.... "But didn't it turn out to be some kind of Christian fanatic?"

"That doesn't mean it wasn't real," she replied.

"What do you mean real?" Shane asked.

"Voodoo spirits. *Vodou* spirits...."

Adam looked at his sister in surprise. "*Spirits*?" What the hell...?

Shane put a hand on his arm.

Listen to her.

Inside Adam's head.

Sometimes he could still hear his Shane's thoughts. Sometimes Shane could hear his. Especially when he'd been drinking a bit. When doubts and reason could be cast aside—because even after all he'd been through, there was still that part of him that wanted to shout, "This isn't real!"

I love you.

He looked at Shane and felt a delightful tingle.

I love you, he thought back.

Shane smiled.

Adam turned back to his sister. Yeah, okay.... "Stranger things?"

She lifted one of those perfect eyebrows.

"It all started when I met this reporter named Taylor Dunton and Myles, a vodou houngan...."

Stranger things....

39

HIGH ABOVE them, the aliens waited.
And watched.
And learned.

A NOTE FROM THE AUTHOR

SPECIAL THANKS to a number of people.

To Jamie Fessenden for getting me involved in the first place. And to Eli and Kim for welcoming me in. It has been a dream.

To Lynn West for letting me turn this in so late. I *really* wanted to write this story. And helping me with the "Un."

To Andi Byassee for the major fix she did!

To Scottie, Paul, Cammie, and Jamie for baseball stuff.

To Chrissy and Noah for research… geez, do you guys ever get tired?

To Paulle for urging, rooting, and cheerleading me on… and never stopping. Sometimes I think I couldn't do it without you.

To Mary Minden—you were invaluable.

And to my husband, Raymond—of course—who puts up with so much so I can do what I love, what I was meant to do.

And to anyone else I've forgotten on this late night.

You all are my family.

Oh! And to Betty, Barney, Kathleen, Whitley, Travis, Charles, Casey, Mark, Vickie, Colby, and Allen and so many more. You lived it. I really think it's very possible you did.

B.G. THOMAS lives in Kansas City with his husband of more than a decade and their fabulous little dog. He is lucky enough to have a lovely daughter as well as many extraordinary friends. He has a great passion for life.

B.G. loves romance, comedies, fantasy, science fiction, and even horror—as far as he is concerned, as long as the stories are character driven and entertaining, it doesn't matter the genre. He has gone to literature conventions his entire adult life where he's been lucky enough to meet many of his favorite writers. He has made up stories since he was a child; it is where he finds his joy.

In the nineties, he wrote for gay magazines but stopped because the editors wanted all sex without plot. "The sex is never as important as the characters," he says. "Who cares what they are doing if we don't care about them?" Excited about the growing male/male romance market, he began writing again. Gay men are what he knows best, after all—since he grew out of being a "practicing" homosexual long ago. He submitted a story and was thrilled when it was accepted in four days. Since then the stories have poured out of him. "It's like I'm somehow making up for a lifetime's worth of stories!"

"Leap, and the net will appear" is his personal philosophy and his message to all. "It is never too late," he states. "Pursue your dreams. They will come true!"

Website/blog: bthomaswriter.wordpress.com

By B.G. Thomas

All Alone in a Sea of Romance
All Snug
Anything Could Happen
The Beary Best Holiday Party Ever
Bianca's Plan
The Boy Who Came In From the Cold
Christmas Cole
Christmas Wish
Derek
Desert Crossing
Grumble Monkey and the Department Store Elf
Hound Dog and Bean
How Could Love Be Wrong?
It Had to Be You
Just Guys
Men of Steel (Dreamspinner Anthology)
A More Perfect Union (Multiple Author Anthology)
Red
Riding Double (Dreamspinner Anthology)
A Secret Valentine
Soul of the Mummy
Editor: A Taste of Honey (Dreamspinner Anthology)
Two Tickets to Paradise (Dreamspinner Anthology)
Until I Found You

GOTHIKA
(Multiple Author Anthologies)
Bones
Spirit
Contact

SEASONS OF LOVE
Spring Affair
Summer Lover
Autumn Changes
Winter Heart

Published by Dreamspinner Press
www.dreamspinnerpress.com

Don't miss the rest of

Gothika

stitch

gothika #1

sue brown
eli easton
jamie fessenden
kim fielding

Gothika: Volume One

When a certain kind of man is needed, why not make him to order? Such things can be done, but take care: Much can go wrong—but then, sometimes it can go wonderfully right. Imagine...

In *The Golem of Mala Lubovnya*, a seventeenth century rabbi creates a man of clay to protect the Jews, and the golem lives a life his maker never imagined, gaining a name—Emet—and the love of a good man, Jakob Abramov. But their love may not survive when Emet must fulfill his violent purpose.

In *Watchworks*, Luke Prescott lives as a gentleman in a London that never was. His unique needs bring him to famed watchmaker Harland Wallace. Romance might blossom for them if Harland can come to terms with loving a man and keeping him safe.

In *Made for Aaron*, a young man in an asylum for being gay met the love of his life, Damon Fox. Twenty years later, Aaron thinks his life is over when Damon dies and then disappears from the hospital. Aaron is determined to find the truth, but secrets hide the unthinkable.

Reparations unfolds on the harsh planet of Kalan, where weakness cannot be tolerated. When Edward needs help, his life becomes entwined with exceptional cyborg slave, Knox. But when Knox remembers things he shouldn't know, the two may pay a blood price for their taboo alliance.

www.dreamspinnerpress.com

bones
gothika #2

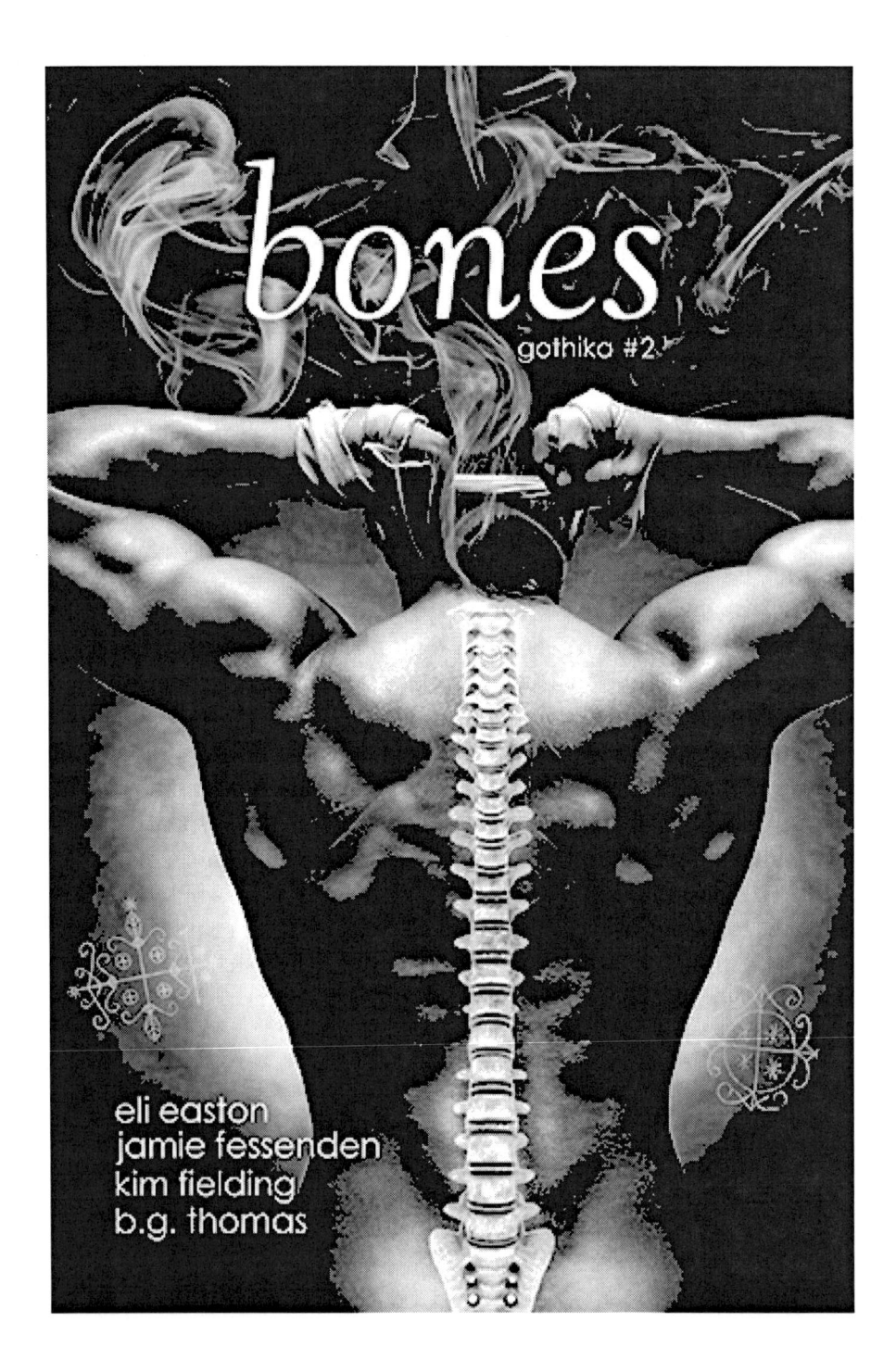

eli easton
jamie fessenden
kim fielding
b.g. thomas

Gothika: Volume Two

Vodou. Obeah. Santeria. These religions seem mysterious and dark to the uninitiated, but the truth is often very different. Still, while they hold the potential for great power, they can be dangerous to those who don't take appropriate precautions. Interfering with the spirits is best left to those who know what they're doing, for when the proper respect isn't shown, trouble can follow. In these four novellas, steamy nights of possession and exotic ritual will trigger forbidden passion and love. You cannot hide your desires from the loa, or from the maddening spell of the drums. Four acclaimed m/m authors imagine homoerotic love under the spell of Voodoo.

The Dance by Kim Fielding
The Bird by Eli Easton
The Book of St. Cyprian by Jamie Fessenden
Uninvited by B.G. Thomas

www.dreamspinnerpress.com

claw
gothika #3

eli easton
jamie fessenden
kim fielding

Gothika: Volume Three

Beasts lurk in the shadows of wild and forgotten places and in the hearts and souls of men. They are the stuff of dreams and nightmares, but are they feral and savage, or just misunderstood? Creatures of myth and legend stalk these tales of dark desire and animal passions. Three men come face-to-face with such creatures and find they are much more than they seem. While there is danger, there might be unexpected benefits as well, if they can accept the impossible and dare to venture into the primordial regions where nature and the beasts still reign. Three acclaimed authors of gay romance explore the boundaries between man and beast and the place where their worlds overlap.

Isolation by Jamie Fessenden
Transformation by Kim Fielding
The Black Dog by Eli Easton

www.dreamspinnerpress.com

spirit

gothika #4

eli easton
jamie fessenden
kim fielding
b.g. thomas

Gothika: Volume Four

Seeing dead people. Haunting and being haunted. Ghosts and those trying to deal with them add a supernatural flair to these four tales of romance.

In *Among the Dead*, Neil Gaven sees dead people. A gentle ghost guides him to Trist, who needs his help. But Trist is tormented by spirits, so maybe together they can find a way to live among the dead.

Dei Ex Machina is the story of Sabbio, a Roman slave who was killed 1700 years ago. He's been alone until he meets landscaper Mason. But because they're separated by centuries, it will take a miracle to make love work.

The Mill brings a supernatural challenge to Frank Carter and his team of paranormal investigators. The owner's personal psychic, Toby Reese, is supposed to help. Frank doesn't have much respect for psychics, but when the dangers of the old mill threaten his team, he realizes he and Toby will have to work together to survive.

Mike Ellsworth finds himself suddenly deceased. Now he's a ghost with lots left undone in *Unfinished Business*. He's never been able to be honest with his wife. He's never been able to tell the man he loves how he feels. He's barely been able to admit he's gay. If only there were a way he could make up for all he's failed to do....

www.dreamspinnerpress.com

Also from Dreamspinner Press

ONE PULSE

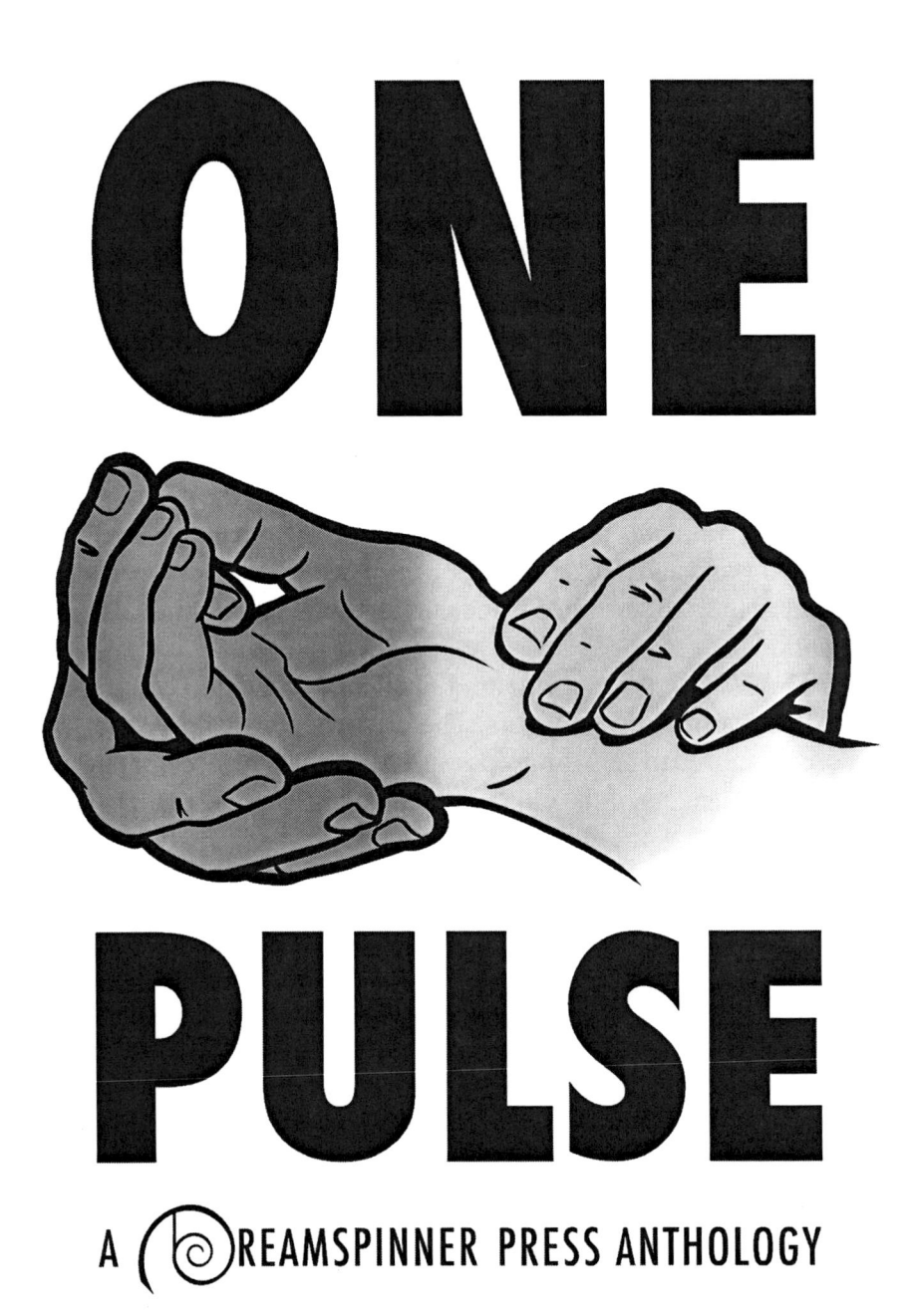

A **Dreamspinner Press** ANTHOLOGY

www.dreamspinnerpress.com

Also from Dreamspinner Press

STARSTRUCK

A DREAMSPINNER PRESS ANTHOLOGY

www.dreamspinnerpress.com

FOR
MORE
OF THE
BEST
GAY
ROMANCE

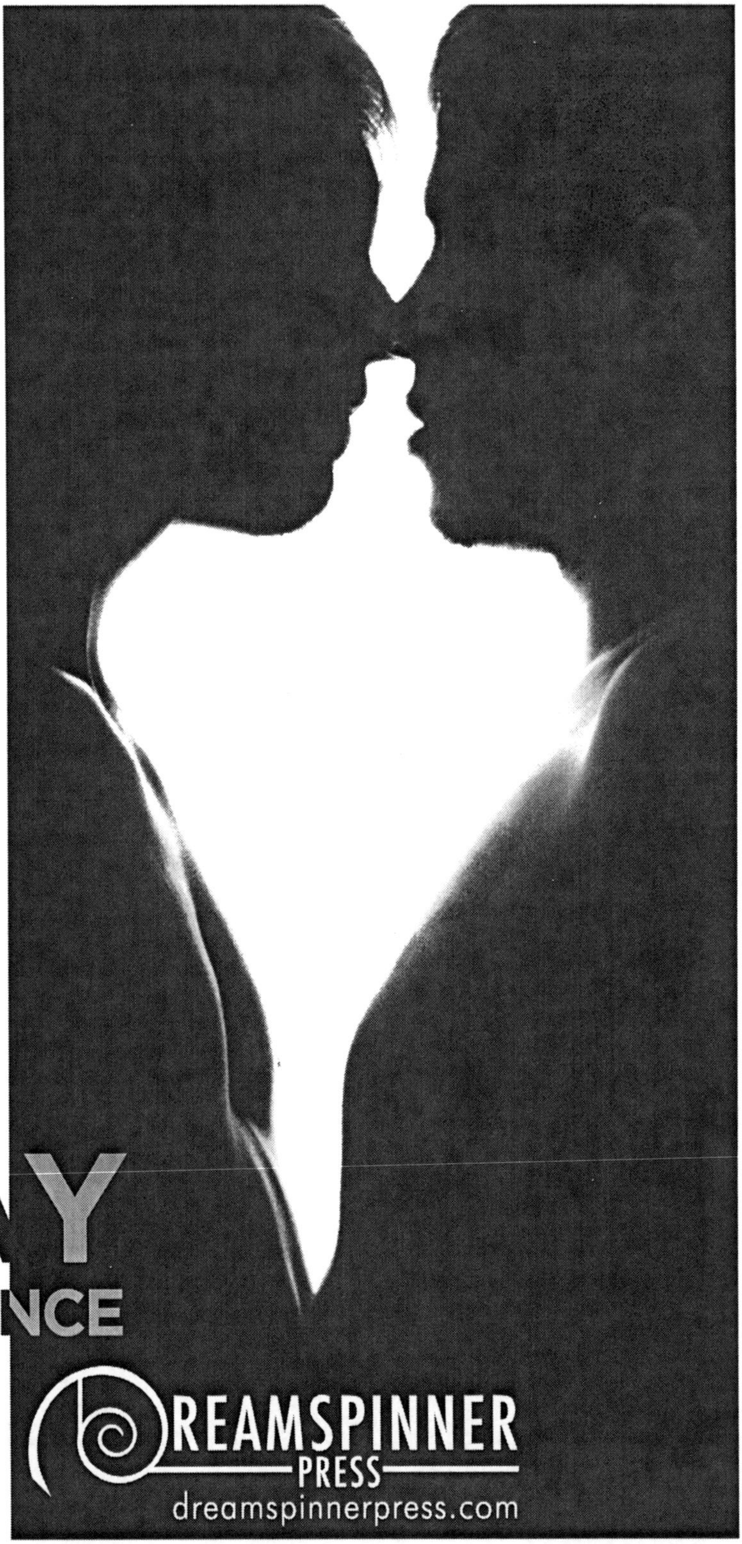